DOAN AND CARSTAIRS:
THEIR COMPLETE CASES

OTHER BOOKS IN THE ARGOSY LIBRARY:

Blood Ritual:
The Adventures of Scarlet and Bradshaw, Volume 1
BY THEODORE ROSCOE

Champion of Lost Causes
BY MAX BRAND

The City of Stolen Lives: The Adventures
of Peter the Brazen, Volume 1
BY LORING BRENT

The Complete Cabalistic Cases of Semi Dual,
the Occult Detector, Volume 2: 1912–13
BY J.U. GIESY AND JUNIUS B. SMITH

The King Who Came Back
BY FRED MacISAAC

The Radio Gun-Runners
BY RALPH MILNE FARLEY

The Scarlet Blade: The Rakehelly Adventures
of Cleve and d'Entreville, Volume 1
BY MURRAY R. MONTGOMERY

Sabotage
BY CLEVE F. ADAMS

South of Fifty-Three
BY JACK BECHDOLT

DOAN AND CARSTAIRS

THEIR COMPLETE CASES

NORBERT DAVIS

INTRODUCTION BY

EVAN LEWIS

ALTUS PRESS

2016

© 2016 Steeger Properties, LLC, under license to Altus Press • First Edition—2016

EDITED AND DESIGNED BY
Matthew Moring

PUBLISHING HISTORY
"Introduction" appears here for the first time. Copyright © 2016 Evan Lewis. All
    rights reserved.
"Holocaust House" originally appeared in the November 16 & 23, 1940 issues of
    Argosy magazine (Vol. 303, Nos. 4 & 5). Copyright © 1940 by The Frank A.
    Munsey Company. Copyrights renewed © 1967 & 1968 and assigned to Steeger
    Properties, LLC. All rights reserved.
The Mouse in the Mountain was originally published by William Morrow & Co. in
    1943.
Sally's in the Alley was originally published by William Morrow & Co. in 1943.
"Cry Murder!" originally appeared in the July 1944 issue of *Flynn's Detective Fiction*
    magazine (Vol. 154, No. 4). Copyright © 1944 by Popular Publications, Inc.
    Copyright renewed © 1971 and assigned to Steeger Properties, LLC. All rights
    reserved.
Oh, Murderer Mine was originally published by Handi-Book Mystery in 1946.

THANKS TO
Chad Calkins & Evan Lewis

ISBN
978-1-61827-228-7

Visit *altuspress.com* for more books like this.
Printed in the United States of America.

TABLE OF CONTENTS

EVAN LEWIS

I BLAME RON GOULART. If not for his 1965 anthology *The Hardboiled Dicks*, I might have led a relatively normal life. After scarfing up all the Hammett and Chandler I could find, I likely would have moved on to other interests. But Mr. Goulart's book was a peek behind the curtain—evidence that Hammett and Chandler, great as they were, were merely two tips of a hardboiled iceberg. As a result, I went barreling into the world of detective pulps, and have yet to escape.

The Hardboiled Dicks presented stories by eight authors, most of whom were unknown to me, and a suggested reading list including the works of eight more, instantly elevating those sixteen writers to a sort of hardboiled royalty.

The first story in that book was "Don't Give Your Right Name," a Max Latin adventure by Norbert Davis. The wit, humor and cock-eyed attitude of that tale aptly set the stage for what followed: kick-ass stories by John K. Butler, Frederick Nebel, Raoul Whitfield, Frank Gruber, Richard Sale, Lester Dent and Erle Stanley Gardner, with suggested books by W.T. Ballard, Charles G. Booth, Paul Cain, Raymond Chandler, George Harmon Coxe, Carroll John Daly, Dashiell Hammett and Robert Reeves.

I immediately wanted more. More Davis, more Nebel, more Sale, more of everybody. Trouble was, pitifully few of their pulp stories had been reprinted. In Davis's case, there were only one—"Red Goose" in *The Hardboiled Omnibus*, a book that had been out of print for twenty years, and "Kansas City Flash" in *Murder: Plain and Fanciful*, and even older anthology book I had never (and *still* haven't) seen.

The only Davis works on Goulart's list were his two hardcover novels, *The Mouse in the Mountain* and *Sally's in the Alley*.

At the time, those books were not too hard to come by, and, as I had

Norbert Davis

friends in the world of vintage paperbacks, I also snagged a copy of *Oh, Murderer Mine*. Before long, I was immersed the slap-happy world of Doan and Carstairs, and the three books blew me away. My sense of humor had always been a bit bent. My favorite book in those days was Vonnegut's *Breakfast of Champions*—a work that thumbed its nose at everything and everybody—and my favorite movie stars were the Marx Brothers. Doan and Carstairs slid right in between. In Norbert Davis, I saw a kindred spirit, a guy who appreciated the absurdity of life and reveled in expressing it.

But the truth was, my impression of Davis as a truly wacky humorist was based solely on those three books, plus a single Max Latin story, written around the same time and in much the same vein. And as I would later discover, that impression was shared by other hardboiled enthusiasts, who were reading the same limited sample of his work. It was only after my mania progressed to the next stage—that of collecting detective pulps—that I discovered there was much more to Mr. Davis.

These days, Davis is hailed as a comic writer, with emphasis on his ability to blend comedy and violence. His humor is treated as both as a hallmark and a handicap. While it distinguished him from the rest of the hardboiled field, the narrative goes, it also held him back, particularly in the eyes of *Black Mask* editor Joe Shaw.

But Davis was more complicated than that.

John L. Apostolou has astutely observed that Davis has an exalted reputation as a hardboiled pulp writer, but this reputation is based on very little evidence. That's still very true. Over the course of a 17-year career, Davis turned out over 125 stories and at least six novel-length works. Even today, with four fine collections of Davis's work in print (*The Complete Cases of Max Latin*, *The Complete Cases of Bail-Bond Dodd, Vol. 1* and the current volume from Altus Press and *Dead Man's Brand* from Black Dog Books), almost everything on display supports his reputation as a very funny guy. But while the Doan & Carstairs books have to rank as three of the funniest mysteries every published, the vast majority of his work—which remains un-reprinted—displayed no more humor (and often less) than that of his contemporaries.

In short, Davis was a writer first, and a humorist second.

Most writers of the era employed humor in some form, whether in snappy dialogue, narration, or simply attitude. This is certainly true of Hammett's Continental Op and Nick Charles. Frederick Nebel used humor to great effect in his long-running MacBride & Kennedy series, as did Carroll John Daly with Race Williams, and Erle Stanley Gardner with his array of pulp heroes.

Frank Gruber's Oliver Quade series—and the Johnny Fletcher books that sprang from it—are equal parts comedy and mystery. Cleve F. Adams is best remembered for the per-ceived (or misperceived) political incorrectness of his heroes. But the truth is that humor rang from every page he ever penned. As a narrator, Adams's tongue never left his cheek, and his stories are consistently amusing. Richard Sale wrote in many veins, but when he wanted to turn on the humor, as he did with the long-running adventures of Daffy Dill, there was nobody better. Jonathan Latimer (the pulp writer who never was) took hardboiled humor to new heights. And Raymond Chandler, whose amusement is always evident, rode his own sense of humor to critical acclaim.

Davis's prose was sharp, concise, and consistently engaging. He could produce a mood or rip the page with violence with the best of them. But in the majority of his work, he relied less on humor than most of the guys mentioned above. It was the amazingly hilarious adventures of Doan and Carstairs that formed and early and powerful impression of Davis, coloring our expectations of his work in general.

In Davis's earlier stories, his detectives are tough talking, wisecracking, clever guys, but rarely oddballs. Some supporting characters are quirky, but most are not. Most of the stories, and their protagonists, are deadly serious or grim. At most, the stories feature an occasional offbeat minor character.

Funny as Davis eventually proved to be, he used humor sparingly for most of his career. It didn't become obvious in his pulp work until 1940—the year Doan and Carstairs were born in "Holocaust House," and Max Latin and Bail-Bond Dodd debuted in *Dime Detective*.

Much of what we know about the life of Norbert Davis is due to the fine detective work of Ron Goulart, John L. Apostolou, Bill Pronzini, and Tom and Enid Schantz. I refer you to them for details, but the bare facts are these: After growing up in rural Illinois, he studied law at Stanford, where he began writing, and eventually settled in L.A., where he was befriended by W.T. Ballard, Cleve F. Adams and other members of the writing/drinking group, the Fictioneers. In 1949, he moved to Connecticut with his second wife, slick magazine writer Nancy Kirkwood Crane, and a few months later he was dead, at age 40, an apparent suicide.

When Davis made his first pulp sales in 1932, Joseph Shaw's vision of tough tales with grim humor dominated the detective field. After Shaw left *Black Mask* in 1936, things gradually loosened up, in that magazine and others. By 1939, *Detective Fiction Weekly* was headlining Richard Sale's Daffy Dill and other offbeat heroes, and *Dime* wasn't far behind.

Examining several Davis stories published between 1932

and 1935, we find heroes who are typical tough talking and tough acting hardboiled types. The first, from the April 1932 *Detective Tales*, is a relentlessly grim prison escapee. In *Black Mask* (March '33, Feb. '34 and Apr. '35) and *Dime Detective* (Jan. 15 '35) he introduced Mark Hull, Ben Shaley, Jake Tait and Max Clark, four hard and fast private detectives employing swift violence and no more than the standard amount of wisecracks.

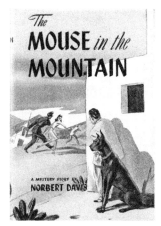

1936 and '37 were busy years, as Davis really got rolling in *Detective Fiction Weekly* and *Detective Tales*, with stops in *Argosy* and at least five more detective mags. These are lean years for reprints, but based on the eight stories in my collection, Davis' use of humor was extremely limited. Simeon Saxon, in two tales in *DFW* (Jan. 18 and Mar. 14 '36) is a public relations counsel with a serious do-gooder complex. After nobly (and willingly) serving prison time for a crime he did not commit, he devotes himself to protecting the poor and weak. And Michael Bartlett from *Detective Tales* (March, 1937) is only slightly less noble. A gambling house owner who doesn't like his clientele, he goes out of his way to help good people out of trouble. These guys

are a far cry from future heroes Max Latin and Doan, who profess (in a good-natured way) to be crooked and greedy.

Mark Stevens and John Dale, heroes of two other *Detective Tales* yarns (Nov. '36 and Sept. '37), were also falsely convicted. One is paroled with nothing but revenge on his mind, and the other crushes out with some serious criminals. In the November 21, 1936 *Argosy* story "Black Bandana," mining engineer Carson is getting shot at because folks believe he's carrying a fortune in diamonds at the behest of their bloody Central American dictator. If there's humor in that situation, Carson fails to see it. And in the March 13, 1937 *Argosy* adventure "Blue Bullets," Secret Service Agent Latimer has a couple of brief conversations with a whimsical, hard-drinking pal, but is too busy ducking a murder frame and a vengeful Central American Minister of War to exhibit any humor of his own. In the "Their Guardian from Hell," from *Star Western* (March, 1937), a mob plans to tar and feather the schoolmarm—a situation rife with comedic possibilities—but Davis plays it straight.

The stories I've examined from 1938 and '39 are no funnier.

"String Him Up!" from the February 1938 *Double Detective* (the story W.T. Ballard later expanded into *Murder Picks the Jury* by Harrison Hunt), is billed as a 50,000 word mystery novel, featuring ex-D.A. Randolph Lee, who combines, according the editors, "the deduction of Sherlock Holmes, the suavity of Nick Charles, the tenacity of Bulldog Drummond and the courtroom brilliance of Perry Mason." Don't know as I'd go that far, but it's a good yarn. Still, it's noticeably lacking in the humor department.

Les Free in "Never Say Die" (*DFW,* Nov. 11, '39) is a hotel owner who acts like a house dick, making him a successor to Michael Bartlett, the do-gooding gambling house owner, and a forerunner to Max Latin, the private detective who owns a restaurant. As in many later Davis stories, much of the humor is derived from minor characters with accents (you'll see a lot of that in *The Mouse in the Mountain*), which would probably be non-PC today. This was a pretty common practice at the time, and Frederick Nebel, in particular, got a lot of mileage out of it.

John Gaul of "A Vote for Murder" (*DFW,* July 15, '39), is another inveterate do-gooder. He functions here as deputy coroner, helping out the man who raised him, and he doesn't stand for nonsense.

Beginning with "Mad Money," in the June 25, 1938 *Argosy,* Davis churned out three novel-length serials featuring attorney Jim Daniels. Daniels appears to be a stand-in for Davis himself (who studied law before turning to writing) and looks much like photos of the author: "He was a tall young man (Davis was 6'5"), looking a little too thin and finely drawn. His features were clean-cut and even, and there was a bitter hard-driven expression around his eyes. His mouth was a straight, determined line unless it was relaxed, as it was now, smiling. He looked older than he should have and more tired." And in the 1939 sequel "Sand in the Snow, "He was thin with high, square-set shoulders, and even in repose he gave a greyhoundish effect of restless, hard-driving energy, of unquenchable and impatient ambition." The third serial "Hang Him High!" followed in 1941. This series offered a fine opportunity for Davis to dish out the humor, but once again, he didn't. Though we meet a quirky character or two—in particular Daniels' assistant Plunk, a wannabe orchestra leader—the plots themselves, the cases, and the main characters, including Daniels himself, are pretty straightforward.

The first story I've seen that drops a hint of things to come is "Drop of Doom," from the December 1939 *Dime Detective.* This, you'll note is only eleven months before the arrival of Doan and Carstairs themselves. The main character, another Davis stand-in named Dale, is studying for his final law exams, and more annoyed by than attracted to a pretty young woman who just happens to have a dog (though one likened to a dust-mop rather than a horse). Dale is a forerunner to one of the young, clueless romantic leads of the Doan and Carstairs novels.

Each D&C novel, you'll discover, has a romantic subplot, but since Doan (who likes women and enjoys fooling around) is not at all romantically inclined, the role of romantic lead always falls to another player. These fellows are themselves hopelessly unromantic, being conceited, clueless or just plain disinterested, but are somehow snared in the end by eccentric and clueless females. Dale and the female lead in "Drop of Doom" seem to auditioning for roles in a future D&C novel, and Lemuel the dust-mop dog is evidence that Davis was beginning to recognize the humorous potential of a canine character.

1940 brought the introduction of *Dime Detective* heroes Bail-Bond Dodd (Feb.) and Max Latin (July). With Dodd, stories become a bit quirkier, and Latin, with his *I-am-crooked* attitude set the stage for Doan. Like Dodd, Doan looks relatively harmless, but can be dangerous, and like Latin, he tells anyone who'll listen that he's corrupt.

In both series, Davis seemed to be letting go, having fun, and experimenting with his sense of humor. So when Doan and Carstairs made their debut in the November 16, 1940 issue of *Argosy*, he was prepared to get even funnier. (This is not to say that all post-1940 stories were humorous. Three *Black Mask* stories from May & November 1942 and May 1943, featuring piano-playing Army Intelligence sergeant John Collins are strictly unfunny, and WWII tales from the March and May 1943 issues of *Argosy* are straight adventure. Davis reserved most of his late-career humor for slick mags like *The Saturday Evening Post*.)

The surprising thing about "Holocaust" is that Doan and Carstairs come instantly full-blown and alive. Both characters are fully realized, and we're chummy with them within the first few pages. And that's a good thing, because a few pages is all Carstairs gets. For some reason, after introducing this great duo, Davis chooses to leave Carstairs offstage, sending Doan to solve the case on his own.

The story still works, and Doan, the innocent and harmless-looking barrel of dynamite, is still a joy to behold. In fact, while

Carstairs gets most of the attention (and even top billing from Rue Morgue Press), I find Doan to be the much more intriguing character.

Doan could carry a series on his own, and while it would have garnered far less attention, it would have made fine reading. But, of course, Doan doesn't have to carry on alone, because beginning with *The Mouse in the Mountain*, Carstairs becomes a near-constant sidekick. He sulks, protests and disapproves of Doan on numerous levels, but he obeys and understands him, and often exhibits loyalty and a protective nature.

I'm not going to rattle on about Doan and Carstairs. Part of the joy of this series is discovering them on your own. But I've been talking here about Davis and his sense of humor, and how it has shown itself (or not) in his pulp stories, so I do want to make a few observations about the humor of this series.

In some scenes, Carstairs functions as a straight man while Doan provides the comic relief, while in others Carstairs providing the yuks. But while the humor of the two pulp stories revolves around that duo, the humor of the novels goes way beyond. The effect is so different that the stories and the novels seem to take place in different worlds.

The pulp world of "Holocaust House" and "Cry Murder!" is the same one inhabited by Max Latin and Bail-Bond Dodd. No matter how wacky Doan and Carstairs behave, their supporting cast is relatively sane, and the universe is relatively real. The humor comes from the lead characters themselves, the way they interact, and the way the normal world responds to them.

With the novels, all bets are off. All characters are eccentric, if not insane, and all behavior is over the top. Everyone is dumber, sneakier, greedier, more cowardly or more murderous than pulp readers would find believable. If there are any normal characters in these novels, it's only because their roles are too brief for us to see how nutty they are. That's a big difference. But Davis didn't stop there. Just to make sure we're in no doubt that this is crazy time, Davis stepped on stage as narrator to introduce new settings, making it abundantly clear that modern society ad life itself is not only wacky but absurd.

I count myself as one of the series' most rabid fans, but at times, this worldview is a bit much even for me. And while I enjoy a good farce as much as anyone, there are a couple of characters in *Oh, Murderer Mine* I find so precious that they make me cringe. (I refer to the Aldrich twins. You'll see what I mean when you meet them.)

So that's it. I've said my piece. If this is your first encounter with Doan and Carstairs, I envy you. You have a lot of fun coming.

Evan Lewis received the 2011 Robert L. Fish Award from the Mystery Writers of America for his *EQMM* story, "Skyler Hobbs and the Rabbit Man." The adventures of Hobbs, who believes himself the reincarnation of Sherlock Holmes, continue in *Ellery Queen*, while an *Alfred Hitchcock* series features a modern-day descendant of Davy Crockett, a man bedeviled by the spirit of his famous ancestor. His *AHMM* story "The Continental Opposite" (the first of a new series) was selected for *The Best American Mystery Stories 2016*.

HOLOCAUST HOUSE

Introducing Mr. Doan, probably the most cheerfully cherubic of private detectives—certainly the most dangerous. He's going up to Desolation Lake, where all the year around is raging winter— and homicide is the favorite winter sport.

CHAPTER I

WHERE WAS I?

WHEN DOAN WOKE up he was lying flat on his back on top of a bed with his hat pulled down over his eyes. He lay quite still for some time, listening cautiously, and then he tipped the hat up and looked around. He found to his relief that he was in his own apartment and that it was his bed he was lying on.

He sat up. He was fully dressed except for the fact that he only wore one shoe. The other one was placed carefully and precisely in the center of his bureau top.

"It would seem," said Doan to himself, "that I was inebriated last evening when I came home."

He felt no ill effects at all. He never did. It was an amazing thing and contrary to the laws of science and nature, but he had never had a hangover in his life.

He was a short, round man with a round pinkly innocent face and impossibly bland blue eyes. He had corn-yellow hair and dimples in his cheeks. At first glance—and at the second and third for that matter—he looked like the epitome of all the suckers that had ever come down the pike. He looked so harmless it was pitiful. It wasn't until you considered him for some time that you began to see that there was something wrong with the picture. He looked just a little *too* innocent.

"Carstairs!" he called now. "Oh, Carstairs!"

Carstairs came in through the bedroom door and stared at him with a sort of wearily resigned disgust. Carstairs was a dog—a fawn-colored Great Dane as big as a yearling calf.

"Carstairs," said Doan. "I apologize for my regrettable condition last evening."

Carstairs' expression didn't change in the slightest. Carstairs was a champion, and he had a long and imposing list of very high-class ancestors. He was fond of Doan in a wellbred way, but he had never been able to reconcile himself to having such a low person for a master. Whenever they went out for a stroll together, Carstairs always walked either far behind or ahead, so no one would suspect his relationship with Doan.

He grunted now and turned and lumbered out of the bedroom in silent dignity. His disapproval didn't bother Doan any. He was used to it. He got up off the bed and began to go through the pockets of his suit.

He found, as he knew he would, that he had no change at all and that his wallet was empty. He found also in his coat pocket one thing that he had never seen before to his knowledge. It was a metal case—about the length and width of a large cigarette case, but much thicker. It looked like a cigar case, but Doan didn't smoke. It was apparently made out of stainless steel.

Doan turned it over thoughtfully in his hands, squinting at it in puzzled wonder. He hadn't the slightest idea where it could have come from. It had a little button catch at one side, and he put his thumb over that, meaning to open the case, but he didn't.

He stood there looking down at the case while a cold little chill traveled up his spine and raised pin-point prickles at the back of his neck. The metal case seemed to grow colder and heavier in his hand. It caught the light and reflected it in bright and dangerous glitters.

"Well," said Doan in a whisper.

Doan trusted his instinct just as thoroughly and completely as most people trust their eyesight. His instinct was telling him that the metal case was about the most deadly thing he had ever had in his hands.

He put the case carefully and gently down in the middle of

The dogs yelped. The dead man pointed a
stiff finger in the lantern glow.

his bed and stepped back to look at it again. It was more than instinct that was warning him now. It was jumbled, hazy memory somewhere. He *knew* the case was dangerous without knowing how he knew.

The telephone rang in the front room, and Doan went in to answer it. Carstairs was sitting in front of the outside door waiting patiently.

"In a minute," Doan told him, picking up the telephone. He got no chance to say anything more. As soon as he unhooked the receiver a voice started bellowing at him.

"Doan! Listen to me now, you drunken bum! Don't hang up until I get through talking, do you hear? This is J.S. Toggery, and in case you're too dizzy to remember, I'm your employer! Doan, you tramp! Are you listening to me?"

Doan instantly assumed a high, squeaky Oriental voice. "Mr. Doan not here, please. Mr. Doan go far, far away—maybe Timbuktu, maybe Siam."

"Doan, you rat! I know it's you talking! You haven't got any servants! Now you listen to me! I've got to see you right away. *Doan!*"

"Mr. Doan not here," said Doan. "So sorry, please."

He hung up the receiver and put the telephone back on its stand. It began to ring again instantly, but he paid no further attention to it. Whistling cheerfully, he went back into the bedroom.

He washed up, found a clean shirt and another tie and put them on. The telephone kept on ringing with a sort of apoplectic indignation. Doan tried unsuccessfully to shake the wrinkles out of his coat, gave up and put it on the way it was. He rummaged around under the socks in the top drawer of his bureau until he located his .38 Police Positive revolver. He shoved it into his waistband and buttoned his coat and vest to hide it.

Going over to the bed, he picked up the metal case and put it gently in his coat pocket and then went into the front room again.

"Okay," he said to Carstairs. "I'm ready to go now."

It was a sodden, uncomfortable morning with the clouds massed in darkly somber and menacing rolls in a sky that was a threatening gray from horizon to horizon. The wind came in strong and steady, carrying the fresh tang of winter from the mountains to the west, where the snow caps were beginning to push inquiring white fingers down toward the valleys.

Doan stood on the wide steps of his apartment house breathing deeply, staring down the long sweep of the hill ahead of him. Carstairs rooted through the bushes at the side of the building.

A taxi made a sudden spot of color coming over the crest of the hill and skimming fleetly down the slope past Doan. He put his thumb and forefinger in his mouth and whistled. The taxi's brakes groaned, and then it made a half-circle in the middle of the block and came chugging laboriously back up toward him and stopped at the curb.

Doan grabbed Carstairs by his studded collar and hauled him out of the bushes.

"Hey!" the driver said, startled. "What's that?"

"A dog," said Doan.

"You ain't thinkin' of riding *that* in this cab, are you?"

"Certainly I am." Doan opened the rear door and shoved Carstairs expertly into the back compartment and climbed in after him. Carstairs sat down on the floor, and his pricked ears just brushed the cab's roof.

The driver turned around to stare with a sort of helpless indignation. "Now listen here. I ain't got no license to haul livestock through the streets. What you want is a freight car. Get that thing out of my cab."

"You do it," Doan advised.

Carstairs leered complacently at the driver, revealing glistening fangs about two inches long.

The driver shuddered. "All right. All right. I sure have plenty of luck—all bad. Where do you want to go?"

"Out to the end of Third Avenue."

The driver turned around again. "Listen, there ain't anything at the end of Third Avenue but three abandoned warehouses and a lot of gullies and weeds."

"Third Avenue," said Doan. "The very end."

CHAPTER II

EXPLODING CIGAR

THE THREE WAREHOUSES—LIKE three blocked points of a triangle—looked as desolate as the buildings in a war-deserted city. They stared with blank, empty eyes that were broken windows out over the green, waist-high weeds that surrounded them. The city had been designed to grow in this direction, but it hadn't. It had withdrawn instead, leaving only these three battered and deserted reminders of things that might have been.

"Well," said the taxi driver, "are you satisfied now?"

Doan got out and slammed the door before Carstairs could follow him. "Just wait here," he instructed.

"Hey!" the driver said, alarmed. "You mean you're gonna leave this—this giraffe...."

"I'll only be gone a minute."

"Oh no, you don't! You come back and take this—"

Doan walked away. He went around in back of the nearest warehouse and slid down a steep gravel-scarred bank into a gully that snaked its way down toward the flat from the higher ground to the north. He followed along the bottom of the gully, around one sharply angling turn and then another.

The gully ended here in a deep gash against the side of a weed-matted hill. Doan stopped, looking around and listening. There was no one in sight, and he could hear nothing.

He cupped his hands over his mouth and shouted: "Hey! Hey! Is there anyone around here?"

His voice made a flat flutter of echoes, and there was no answer. After waiting a moment he nodded to himself in a satisfied way and took the metal case out of his pocket. Going to the very end of the gully, he placed the case carefully in the center of a deep gash.

Turning around then, he stepped off about fifty paces back down the gully. He drew the Police Positive from his waistband, cocked it and dropped down on one knee. He aimed carefully, using his left forearm for a rest.

The metal case made a bright, glistening spot over the sights, and Doan's forefinger took up the slack in the trigger carefully and expertly. The gun jumped a little against the palm of his hand, but he never heard the report.

It was lost completely in the round, hollow *whoom* of sound that seemed to travel like a solid ball down the gully and hit his eardrums with a ringing impact. Bits of dirt spattered around his feet, and where the case had been there was a deep round hole gouged in the hillside, with the earth showing yellow and raw around it.

"Well," said Doan. His voice sounded whispery thin in his own ears. He took out his handkerchief and dabbed at the perspiration that was coldly moist on his forehead. He still stared, fascinated, at the raw hole in the hillside where the case had rested.

After a moment he drew a deep, relieved breath. He put the Police Positive back in his waistband, turned around and walked back along the gully to the back of the warehouse. He climbed up the steep bank and plowed through the waist-high weeds to the street and the waiting taxi.

The driver stared with round, scared eyes. "Say, did—did you hear a—a noise a minute ago?"

"Noise?" said Doan, getting in the back of the cab and shoving Carstairs over to give himself room to sit down. "Noise? Oh, yes. A small one. It might have been an exploding cigar."

"Cigar," the driver echoed incredulously. "Cigar. Well, maybe *I'm* crazy. Where do you want to go now?"

"To a dining car on Turk Street called the *Glasgow Limited*. Know where it is?"

"I can find it," the driver said gloomily. "That'll be as far as you're ridin' with me, ain't it—I hope?"

The *Glasgow Limited* was battered and dilapidated, and it sagged forlornly in the middle. Even the tin stack-vent from its cooking range was tilted drunkenly forward. It was fitted in tightly slantwise on the very corner of a lot, and as if to emphasize its down-at-the-heels appearance an enormous, shining office building towered austere and dignified beside it, putting the *Glasgow Limited* always in the shadow of its imposing presence.

The taxi stopped at the curb in front of it. This was the city's financial district, and on Sunday it was deserted. A lone street car, clanging its way emptily along looked like a visitor from some other age. The meter on the taxi showed a dollar and fifty cents, and Doan asked the driver:

"Can you trip that meter up to show two dollars?"

"No," said the driver. "You think the company's crazy?"

"You've got some change-over slips, haven't you?"

"Say!" said the driver indignantly. "Are you accusing me of gypping—"

"No," said Doan. "But you aren't going to get a tip, so you might as well pull it off a charge slip. Have you got one that shows two dollars?"

The driver scowled at him for a moment. He tripped the meter and pocketed the slip. Then he took a pad of the same kind of slips from his vest pocket and thumbed through them. He handed Doan one that showed a charge of a dollar and ninety cents.

"Now blow your horn," Doan instructed. "Lots of times."

The driver tooted his horn repeatedly. After he had done it about ten times, the door of the *Glasgow Limited* opened and a man came out and glared at them.

"Come, come, MacTavish," said Doan. "Bail me out."

MacTavish came down the steps and across the sidewalk. He was a tall gaunt man with bony stooped shoulders. He was bald, and he had a long draggling red mustache and eyes that were a tired, blood-shot blue. He wore a white jacket that had sleeves too short for him and a stained white apron.

Doan handed him the meter charge slip. "There's my ransom, MacTavish. Pay the man and put it on my account."

MacTavish looked sourly at the slip. "I have no doubt that there's collusion and fraud hidden somewhere hereabouts. No doubt at all."

"Why, no," said Doan. "You can see the charge printed right

on the slip. This driver is an honest and upright citizen, and he's been very considerate. I think you ought to give him a big tip."

"That I will not!" said MacTavish emphatically. "He'll get his fee and no more—not a penny!" He put a ragged dollar bill in the driver's hand and carefully counted out nine dimes on top of it. "There! And it's bare-faced robbery!"

He glared at the driver, but the driver looked blandly innocent. Doan got out and dragged Carstairs after him.

"And that ugly beastie!" said MacTavish. "I'll feed him no more, you hear? Account or no account, I'll not have him gobbling my good meat down his ugly gullet!"

Doan dragged Carstairs across the sidewalk and pushed him up the stairs and into the dining car. MacTavish came in after them, went behind the counter and slammed the flap down emphatically.

Doan sat down on a stool and said cheerfully: "Good morning, MacTavish, my friend. It's a fine bonny morning full of the smell of heather and mountain dew, isn't it? Fix up a pound of round for Carstairs, and be sure it's none of that watery gruel you feed your unsuspecting customers. Carstairs is particular, and he has a delicate stomach. I'll take ham and eggs and toast and coffee—a double order."

MacTavish leaned on the counter. "And what'll you pay for it with, may I ask?"

"Well, it's true that I find myself temporarily short on ready cash, but I have a fine Swiss watch—"

"No, you haven't," said MacTavish, "because I've got it in the cash register right now."

"Good," said Doan. "That watch is worth at least fifty—"

"You lie in your teeth," said MacTavish. "You paid five dollars for it in a pawn shop. I'll have no more to do with such a loafer and a no-good. I've no doubt that if you had your just deserts you'd be in prison this moment. I'll feed you this morning, but this is the last time. The very last time, you hear?"

"I'm desolated," said Doan. "Hurry up with the ham and

eggs, will you, MacTavish? And don't forget Carstairs' ground round."

MacTavish went to the gas range, grumbling under his breath balefully, and the meat made a pleasantly sizzling spatter. Carstairs put his head over the counter and drooled in eager anticipation.

"MacTavish," said Doan, raising his voice to speak over the sizzle of the meat, "am I correct in assuming I visited your establishment last night?"

"You are."

"Was I—ah—slightly intoxicated?"

"You were blind, stinking, pig-drunk."

"You have such a pleasant way of putting things," Doan observed. "I was alone, no doubt, bearing up bravely in solitary sadness?"

"You were not. You had one of your drunken, bawdy, criminal companions with you."

MacTavish set a platter of meat on the counter, and Doan put it on top of one of the stools so that Carstairs could get at it more handily. Carstairs gobbled politely, making little grunting sounds of appreciation.

Doan said casually: "This—ah—friend I had with me. Did you know him?"

"I never saw him before, and if my luck lasts I'll never see him again. I liked his looks even less than I do yours."

"You're in rare form this morning, MacTavish. Did you hear me mention my friend's name?"

"It was Smith," said MacTavish, coming up with a platter of ham and eggs and a cup of coffee.

"Smith," said Doan, chewing reflectively. "Well, it's a nice name. Don't happen to know where I picked him up, do you?"

"I know where you said you picked him up. You said he was a stray soul lost in the wilderness of this great metropolis and that you had rescued him. You said you'd found him in front of your apartment building wasting away in the last stages of starvation, so I knew you were blind drunk, because the man had a belly like a balloon."

"In front of my apartment," Doan repeated thoughtfully. "This is all news to me. Could you give me a short and colorful description of this gentleman by the name of Smith?"

"He was tall and pot-bellied, and he had black eyebrows that looked like caterpillars and a mustache the rats had been nesting in, and he wore dark glasses and kept his hat on and his overcoat collar turned up. I mind particularly the mustache, because you kept asking him if you could tweak it."

"Ah," said Doan quietly. He knew now where he had gotten the instinctive warning about the metal case. Drunk as Doan had been, he had retained enough powers of observation to realize that the mysterious Smith's mustache had been false—that the man was disguised.

Doan nodded to himself. That disposed of some of the mystery of the metal case, but there still remained the puzzle of Smith's identity and what his grudge against Doan was.

CHAPTER III

THE TEMPESTUOUS TOGGERY

AT THAT MOMENT the front door slammed violently open, and J.S. Toggery came in with his head down and his arms swinging belligerently. He was short and stocky and bandy-legged. He had an apoplectically red face and fiercely glistening false teeth.

"A fine thing," he said savagely. "A fine thing, I say! Doan, you bum! Where have you been for the last three days?"

Doan pushed his empty coffee cup toward MacTavish. "Another cup, my friend. I wish you'd tell the more ill-bred of your customers to keep their voices down. It disturbs my digestion. How are you, Mr. Toggery? I have a serious question to ask you."

"What?" Toggery asked suspiciously.

"Do you know a man whose name isn't Smith and who doesn't wear dark glasses and doesn't have black eyebrows or a black mustache or a pot-belly and who isn't a friend of mine?"

Toggery sat down weakly on one of the stools. "Doan, now be reasonable. Haven't you any regard for my health and well-being? Do you want to turn me into a nervous wreck? I have a very important job for you, and I've been hunting you high and low for three days, and when I find you I'm greeted with inso-lence, evasion and double-talk. Do you know how to ski?"

"Pardon me," said Doan. "I thought you asked me if I knew how to ski."

"I did. Can you use skis or snow-shoes or ice skates?"

"No," said Doan.

"Then you have a half-hour to learn. Here's your railroad ticket. Your train leaves from the Union Station at two-thirty. Get your heavy underwear and your woolen socks and be on it."

"Why?" Doan asked.

"Because I told you to, you fool!" Toggery roared. "And I'm the man who's crazy enough to be paying you a salary! Now, will you listen to me without interposing those crack-pot com-ments of yours?"

"I'll try," Doan promised.

Toggery drew a deep breath. "All right. A girl by the name of Shiela Alden is spending the first of the mountain winter season at a place in the Desolation Lake country. You're going up there to see that nothing happens to her for the next three or four weeks."

"Why?" Doan said.

"Because she hired the agency to do it! Or rather, the bank that is her guardian did. Now listen carefully. Shiela Alden's mother died when she was born. Her father died five years ago, and he left a trust fund for her that amounts to almost fifty million dollars. She turns twenty-one in two days, and she gets the whole works when she does.

"There's been a lot of comment in the papers about a young girl getting handed all that money, and she's gotten a lot of threats from crack-pots of all varieties. That Desolation Lake country is as deserted as a tomb this time of year. The season don't start up there for another month. The bank wants her to have some protection until the publicity incident to her receiving that enormous amount of money dies down."

Doan nodded. "Fair enough. Where did her old man get all this dough to leave her?"

"He invented things."

"What kind of things?"

"Powder and explosives."

"Oh," said Doan, thinking of the deep yellow gouge the metal case had left in the hillside. "What kind of explosives?"

"All kinds. He specialized in the highly concentrated variety like they use in hand grenades and bombs. That's why the trust he left increased so rapidly. It's all in munitions stock of one kind and another."

"*Ummm,*" said Doan. "Did you tell anyone you were planning on sending me up to look after her?"

"Of course. Everybody I could find who would listen to me. Have you forgotten that I've been looking high and low for you for three days, you numb-wit?"

"I see," said Doan vaguely. "What's the girl doing up there in the mountains?"

"She's a shy kid, and she's been bedeviled persistently by cranks and fortune hunters and every other kind of chiseler." J.S. Toggery sighed and looked dreamily sentimental. "It's a shame when you think of it. That poor lonely kid—she hasn't a relative in the world—all alone up there in that damned barren mountain country. Hurt and bewildered because of the unthinking attitude of the public. No one to love her and protect her and sympathize with her. If I weren't so busy I'd go up there with you. She needs someone older—some steadying influence."

"And fifty million dollars ain't hay," said Doan.

J.S. Toggery nodded, still dreamy. "No, and if I could just get hold of—" He snapped out of it. "Damn you, Doan, must you reduce every higher human emotion to a basis of crass commercialism?"

"Yes, as long as I work for you."

"Huh! Well, anyway she's hiding up there to get away from it all. Her companion-secretary is with her. They're staying at a lodge her old man owned. Brill, the attorney who handles the income from the trust, is staying with them until you get there. There's a caretaker at the lodge too."

"I see," said Doan, nodding. "It sounds interesting. It's too bad I can't go."

Toggery said numbly: "Too bad you…. What! *What!* Are you crazy? Why can't you go?"

Doan pointed to the floor. "Carstairs. He disapproves of mountains."

Toggery choked. "You mean that damned dog—"

Doan snapped his fingers. "I've got it. I'll leave him in your care."

"That splay-footed monstrosity! I—I'll—"

Doan reached down and tapped Carstairs on the top of his head. "Carstairs, my friend. Pay attention. You are going to visit Mr. Toggery for a few days. Treat him with consideration because he means well."

Carstairs blinked balefully at Toggery, and Toggery shivered.

"And now," said Doan cheerfully. "The money."

"Money!" Toggery shouted. "What did you do with the hundred I advanced you on your next month's salary?"

"I don't remember exactly, but another hundred will do nicely."

Toggery moaned. He counted out bills on the counter with

trembling hands. Doan wadded them up and thrust them carelessly into his coat pocket.

"Aren't you forgetting something, Mr. Doan?" MacTavish asked.

"Oh, yes," said Doan. "Toggery, pay MacTavish what I owe him on account. Cheerio, all. Good-by, Carstairs. I'll give you a ring soon." He went out the door whistling.

Toggery collapsed limply against the counter, shaking his head. "I think I'm going mad now," he said. "My brain is simmering like a teakettle."

"He gets me that way too," said MacTavish. "Why do you put up with him?"

"Hah!" said Toggery. "Listen! If he wasn't the best—the very best—private detective west of the Mississippi, and if this branch of the agency didn't depend entirely on him for its good record, I would personally murder him!"

"I doubt if you could," said MacTavish.

"I know it," Toggery admitted glumly. "He could take on you and me together with Carstairs thrown in and massacre all three of us without mussing his hair. He's the most dangerous little devil I've ever seen, and he's all the worse because of that half-witted manner of his. You never suspect what he's up to until it's too late."

CHAPTER IV

WELCOME TO DESOLATION

DOAN ROLLED HIS head back and forth on the hard plush cushion, opened his eyes and blinked politely. "You were saying something?"

The conductor's face was red with exertion. "Yes, I was sayin' something! I been sayin' something for the last ten minutes steady! I thought you was in a trance! This here is where you get off!"

Doan yawned and straightened up. He had a crick in his neck, and he winced, poking his finger at the spot.

The roadbed was rough here, and the old-fashioned tubular brass lamps that hung from the arched car top jittered in short nervous arcs. The *whaff-whaff-whaff* of the engine exhaust sounded laboriously from ahead. The car was thick and murky with the smell of cinders. Aside from the conductor, Doan was the only occupant.

Doan asked: "Do you stop while I get off, or am I supposed to hop off like a hobo?"

"We'll stop," said the conductor.

He might have been in telepathic communication with the engineer, because that's just what they did right then. The engine brakes screeched, and the car hopped up against the bumpers and dropped back again with a breath-taking jar, groaning in every joint.

"Is he mad at somebody?" Doan asked, referring to the engineer.

"Listen, you," said the conductor indignantly. "This here grade is so steep that a fly couldn't walk up it without his feet were dipped in molasses first."

Doan took a look at the empty seats. "You didn't make this trip especially on my account, did you?"

"No!" The conductor was even more indignant at the injustice of it. "We got to run a train from Palos Junction through here and back every twenty-four hours in the off season to keep our franchise. Otherwise you'd have walked up. Come on! We ain't got all night to sit around here."

Doan hauled his grip from the rack, pausing to peer out the steamed window. "Is it still raining?"

The conductor snorted. "Raining! It's rainin' down on the coast maybe, but not here. You're eight thousand feet up in the Rocky Mountains, son, and it's snowin' like somebody dumped it out of a chute."

Doan was no outdoorsman, and he hadn't taken what J.S. Toggery had said about skis and snow-shoes at all seriously.

"Snowing?" he said incredulously. "Why, it's still summer!"

"Not up here," said the conductor. "She'll make three feet on the level, and it's driftin'. Get goin'."

Still incredulous, Doan hauled his bag down the aisle and through the end door of the car. This was the last car, the only passenger coach, and when he stepped out on the darkness of the platform the snow and the wind slapped across his face like a giant icy hand. Doan sputtered indignantly and went staggering off balance down the iron steps and plumped into powdery wet coldness that congealed above the level of his thighs.

The engine whistle gave a triumphant, echoing scream.

The conductor was a dim, huddled form with one gaunt arm stretched out like a semaphore. His voice drifted thinly with the wind.

"That way! Through snow-sheds… along spur…."

The engine screamed again, impatiently, and bucked the train ahead.

Doan had dropped his bag, and he scrambled around in the snow trying to find it. "Wait! Wait! I've changed my mind."

The red and green lights on the back of the car blinked mockingly at him, and the conductor's howl came blurred and faint through the white swirling darkness.

"Station… quarter-mile… snow-sheds…."

The engine wailed like a banshee, and the snow and the darkness swallowed the sound of it up in one gulp.

"Well, hell," said Doan.

He spat snow out of his mouth and wiped the cold wetness of it off his face. He located his bag and hauled it out into the middle of the tracks. He had a topcoat strapped on the side of the grip, and he unfastened it now and struggled into it. He was thinking darkly bitter thoughts about J.S. Toggery.

With the collar pulled up tight around his throat and his hat pulled down as far it would go over his ears, he stood huddled in the middle of the tracks and looked slowly and unbelievingly around him. He had a range of vision of about ten feet in any given direction; beyond that there was nothing but snow and blackness. There was no sign of any other human, and, aside from the railroad tracks, no sign that there ever had been one here.

"Hey!" Doan shouted.

His voice traveled away and came back after a while in a low, thoughtful echo.

"This is very nice, Doan," said Doan. "You're a detective. Make a brilliant deduction."

He couldn't think of an appropriate one, so he shrugged his shoulders casually, picked up his bag and started walking along the track in the direction the conductor had pointed. The wind slapped and tugged at him angrily, hauling him first one way and then the other, and the frozen gravel of the roadbed ground under his shoes.

He kept his head down and continued walking until he tripped over a switch rail. He looked up and stared into what seemed to be the mouth of an immense square cave. He headed for it, kicking through the drifts in front, and then suddenly he was inside and out of the reach of the wind and the persistent, swirling snow.

It began to make sense now. This high square cave was a wooden snow-shed built to keep the drifts off the spur track on which he was standing. If the rest of the conductor's shouted information could be relied on, the station was a quarter mile further along the spur track.

Doan nodded once to himself, satisfied, took a new grip on the handles of his bag and started trudging along the track. It had been dark outside, but the darkness inside the shed was black swimming ink with no slightest glimmer to relieve it. It was a darkness that enclosed Doan like an envelope and seemed to travel along ahead of him, piling up thicker and thicker with each step he took.

He lost his sense of direction, tripped over the rails and banged against the side of the shed, starting up echoes that clattered deafeningly.

Swearing to himself in a whisper, Doan put his bag down on the ground and fumbled around in his pockets until he found a match. He snapped it alight on his thumbnail and held it up in front of him, cupping his hands protectively around the wavering yellow of the flame.

There was a man standing not a yard away from him—standing stiff and rigid against the rough boards of the shed wall, one arm out-thrust awkwardly as though he were mutely offering to shake hands. His eyes reflected the match flame glassily.

"Uh!" said Doan, startled.

The man didn't say anything, didn't move. He was a short, thick man, and his face looked roughened and bluish in the dim light.

"Well… hello," Doan said uncertainly. He felt a queer chill horror.

The man stayed there, unmoving, his right hand outthrust. Very slowly Doan reached out and touched the hand. It was ice-cold, and the fingers were as rigid as steel hooks.

Doan went backward one stumbling step and then another while the shadows jiggled weirdly around him. Then the match burned his fingers and he dropped it, and the darkness slapped down like a giant soft hand. It was then that he heard a noise behind him—a stealthy skitter in the gravel, faint through the swish of the snow against the shed walls.

Doan turned his head a little at a time until he could see over his shoulder. He stood there rigid while the darkness seemed to pulsate with the beat of his heart.

There were eyes watching him. Luminous and yellow and

close to the ground, slanted obliquely at their corners. There were three pairs of them.

Doan stood there until the breath ached in his throat. The paired eyes didn't move. Doan exhaled very slowly and softly. He slid his hand inside the bulk of his topcoat, under his suit coat, and closed his fingers on the butt of the Police Positive.

Just as slowly he drew the revolver from under his coat. The hammer made a small cold click. Doan fired straight up in the air.

The report raised a deafening thunder of echoes. The eyes blinked and were gone, and a voice bellowed hollowly at Doan out of the blackness:

"Don't you shoot them dogs! Damn you, don't you shoot them dogs!"

The voice came from somewhere in back of where the yellow eyes had been. Doan dropped on one knee, leveling the revolver in that direction.

"Show a light," he ordered. "Right now."

Light splayed out from an electric lantern and revealed long legs in baggy blue denim pants and high snow-smeared boots with bulging rawhide laces. The yellow eyes were back of the legs, just out of the throw of light from the lantern, staring in savage watchfulness.

"Higher," said Doan. "Higher with the lantern."

The light went up by jerks like a sticky curtain on a stage, showing in turn a clumsy-looking sheepskin coat, a red hatchet-like face with fiercely glaring eyes, and a stained duck-hunter's cap with the ear flaps pulled down. The man stood as tall and stiff as some weird statue with his shadow stretched jagged and menacing beside him.

"I'm the station master. This here's company property. What you doin' on it?"

"Trying to get off it," said Doan.

"Where'd you come from?"

"The train, stupid. You think I'm a parachute trooper?"

"Oh," said the tall man. "Oh. Was you a passenger?"

"Well, certainly."

"Oh. I thought you were a bum or something. Nobody ever comes up here this time of year."

"I'll remember that. Come closer with the light. Keep the dogs back."

The tall man came slowly closer. Doan saw now that he had only one arm—the left—the one that was holding the lantern. His right sleeve was empty.

"Who's our friend here?" Doan asked, indicating the stiff frozen figure against the wall.

The tall man said casually: "Him? Oh, that's Boley, the regular station master. I'm his relief."

"He looks a little on the dead side to me."

The tall man had a lean gash of a mouth, and the thin lips moved now to show jagged yellow teeth. "Dead as a smoked herring."

"What happened to him?"

"Got drunk and lay out in the snow all night and froze stiff as a board."

"Planning on just leaving him here permanently?"

"I can't move him alone, mister." The tall man indicated his empty right sleeve with a jerk of his head. "I told 'em to stop and pick him up tonight, but they musta forgot to do it. I'll call 'em again. It ain't gonna hurt him to stay here. He won't spoil in this weather."

"That's a comforting thought."

"Dead ones don't hurt nobody, mister. I've piled 'em on trench parapets and shot over 'em. They're as good as sandbags for stoppin' bullets."

"That's a nice thought too. Where's this station you're master of?"

"Right ahead a piece."

"Start heading for it. Keep the dogs away. I don't like the way they look at me."

The light lowered. The tall man sidled past Doan, and his thin legs moved shadowy and stick-like in the lantern gleam, going away.

Doan followed cautiously, carrying the grip in one hand and the cocked revolver in the other. He looked back every third step, but the yellow eyes were gone now.

The shed ended abruptly, and the station was around the curve from it, a yellow box-like structure squashed in against the bare rock of the canyon face with light coming very dimly through small, snow-smeared windows.

The tall man opened the door, and Doan followed him into a small square room lighted with one unshaded bulb hanging behind the shining grillwork of the oval ticket window. Yellow varnished benches ran along two walls, and a stove gleamed dully red in the corner between them.

Doan kicked the door shut behind him and dropped his grip on the floor. He still held his revolver casually in his right hand.

"What's your name?" he asked.

"Jannen," said the tall man. He had taken off his duck-hunter's cap. He was bald, and his head was long and queerly narrow. He stood still, watching Doan, his eyes gleaming with slyly malevolent humor. "You come up here for somethin' special? There ain't no place to stay. There's a couple of hotels down-canyon, but they ain't open except for the snow sports."

Doan jerked his head to indicate the storm outside. "Isn't that snow?"

"This here is just an early storm. It'll melt off mostly on the flats. In the winter season she gets eight-ten feet deep here on the level, and they bring excursion trains up—sometimes four-five hundred people to once—and park 'em on the sidings over weekends."

There was a whine and then a scratching sound on the door behind Doan.

The tall man jerked his head. "Can I let my dogs inside, mister?"

Doan moved over and sat down on the bench. "Go ahead."

Jannen opened the door, and three shadowy gray forms slunk through it. They were enormous beasts, thick-furred, with blunt wedge-shaped heads. They circled the room and sat down in a silent motionless row against the far wall, watching Doan unblinkingly with eyes that were like yellow, cruel jewels.

"Nice friendly pets," Doan observed.

"Them's sled dogs, mister."

"What dogs?" Doan asked.

"Sled dogs—huskies. See, sometimes them tourists that come up here, they get tired of skiin' and snow-shoein' and then I pick me up a little side money haulin' 'em around on a dog sled with the dogs. Lot of 'em ain't never rid behind dogs before, and they get a big kick out of it. Them are good dogs, mister."

"You can have them. Do you know where the Alden lodge is from here?"

Jannen's lips moved back from the jagged teeth. "You a friend of that girl's?" His voice was low and tight.

"Not yet. Are you?"

Jannen's eyes were gleaming, reddish slits. "Oh, yeah. Oh, sure I am. I got a good reason to be." With his left hand he reached over and tapped his empty right sleeve. "That's a present from her old man."

Doan was watching him speculatively. "So? How did it happen?"

"Grenade. I was fightin' over in China. It blew up in my hand. Tore my arm off. Old man Alden's factory sold the Chinks that grenade. It had a defective fuse."

"That's not the girl's fault."

Jannen's lips curled. "Oh, sure not. Nobody's fault. An accident. Didn't amount to nothin'—just a man's right arm tore off, that's all. Just made me a cripple and stuck me up in this hell-hole at this lousy job. Yeah. I love that Alden girl. Every time I hear that name I laugh fit to bust with joy."

His voice cracked, and his face twisted into a fiendish grimace. The dogs stirred against the wall uneasily, and one of them whimpered a little.

"Yeah," Jannen said hoarsely. "Sure. I like her. Her old man skimped on that grenade job, and skimped on it so he could leave that girl another million. You'd like her too, mister, if an Alden grenade blew your right arm off, wouldn't you? You'd like her every time you fumbled around one-handed like a crippled bug, wouldn't you?

"You'd like her every time the pain started to bite in that arm stump so you couldn't sleep at night, wouldn't you? You'd feel real kind toward her while you was sleepin' in flop houses and she was spendin' the blood money her old man left her, wouldn't you, mister?"

The man was not sane. He stood there swaying, and then he laughed a little in a choking rasp that shook his thin body.

"You want me to show you the way to the lodge? Sure, mister. Glad to. Glad to do a favor for an Alden any old time."

Doan stood up. "Let's start," he said soberly.

CHAPTER V

MISS MILLION-BUCKS

DOAN SMELLED THE smoke first, coming thin and pungent down-wind, and then Jannen stopped short in front of him and said:

"There it is."

The wind whipped the snow away for a second, and Doan saw the house at the mouth of a ravine that widened out into a flat below them. The walls were black against the white drifts, and the windows stared with dull yellow eyes.

"Thanks," said Doan. "I can make it from here. If I could offer some slight compensation for your time and trouble…."

Jannen was hunched up against the wind like some gaunt beast of prey, staring down at the house, wrapped up in darkly bitter thoughts of his own. His voice came thickly.

"I don't want none of your money."

"So long," said Doan.

"Eh?" said Jannen, looking around.

Doan pointed back the way they had come. "Good-by, now."

Jannen turned clumsily. "Oh, I'm goin'. But I ain't forgettin' nothin', mister." His mittened left hand touched his empty right sleeve. "Nothin' at all. You tell her that for me."

"I'll try to remember," said Doan.

He stood with his head tilted against the wind, watching Jannen until he disappeared back along the trail, his three huskies slinking along like stunted shadows at his heels. Then he shrugged uneasily and went down the steep slant of the ridge to the flat below. The wind had blown the snow clear of the ground in places, and he followed the faint marks of a path across the stretch of frozen rocky ground.

Close to it, the house looked larger—dark and ugly with the smoke from the chimney drifting in a jaunty plume across the white-plastered roof. The path ended at a small half-enclosed porch, and Doan climbed the log steps up to it and banged hard with his fist against the heavy door.

He waited, shivering. The cold had gotten through his light clothes. His feet tingled numbly, and the skin on his face felt drawn and stiff.

The door swung open, and a man stared out at him unbelievingly. "What—who're you? Where'd you come from?"

"Doan—Severn Agency."

"The detective! But man alive! Come in, come in!"

Doan stepped into a narrow shadowed hall, and the warmth swept over him like a soft grateful wave.

"Good Lord!" said the other man. "I didn't expect you'd come tonight—in this storm!"

"That's Severn service," Doan told him. "When duty calls, we answer. And besides, I'm overdrawn on my salary."

"But you're not dressed for— Why, you must be frozen stiff!"

He was a tall man, very thin, with a sharp dramatically haggard face. His hair was jet-black with a peculiarly distinctive swathe of pure white running back slantwise from his high forehead. He talked in nervous spurts, and he had a way of making quick little half-gestures that had no meaning, as though he were impatiently jittery.

"A trifle rigid in spots," Doan admitted. "Have you got some concentrated heat around the premises?"

"Yes! Yes, surely! Come in here! My name is Brill, by the way. I'm in charge of Miss Alden's account with the National Trust. Taking care of the legal end. But of course you know all about that. In here."

It was a long living room with a high ceiling that matched the peak of the roof. At the far end there was an immense natural stone fireplace with the flame hooking eager little blue fingers around the log that almost filled it.

"But you should have telephoned from the station," Brill was saying. "No need to come out tonight in this."

"Have you a telephone here?" Doan asked.

"Certainly, certainly. Telephone, electricity, central heating, all that…. Miss Alden, this is Mr. Doan, the detective from the Severn Agency. You know, I told you—"

"Yes, of course," said Shiela Alden. She was sitting on the long, low divan in front of the fire. She was a small, thin girl with prim features, and she looked disapprovingly at Doan and then down at the snow he had tracked across the floor. She had lusterless stringly brown hair and teeth that protruded a little bit, and she wore thick horn-rimmed glasses.

"Hello," said Doan. He didn't think he was going to like her very well.

"This seems all very melodramatic and very unnecessary," said Shiela Alden. "A detective to guard me! It's so absurd."

"Now, not at all, not at all," said Brill in a harassed tone. "It's the thing to do—the only thing. I'm responsible, you know. The National people hold me directly responsible for your well-being. We must take every reasonable precaution. We really must. I'm doing the best I know how."

"I know," said Shiela Alden, faintly contemptuous. "Pull up that chair, Mr. Doan, and get close to the fire. By the way, this is Mr. Crowley."

"Hello, there," said Crowley cheerfully. "You're hardly dressed for the weather, old chap. If you plan to stay around here I'll have to lend you some of my togs."

"Mr. Crowley," said Brill, "has a place over at the other side of Flint Flat."

"A little hide-out, you know," said Crowley. "Just a little shack where a man can hole in and soak up some solitude now and then."

He had a very British-British accent and a hairline black mustache and a smile full of white teeth. He was every bit as handsome as those incredible young men who are always driving the latest sport motor cars in magazine advertisements. He knew it. He had brown eyes with a personality twinkle in them and wavy black hair and an expensive tan.

"Mr. Crowley," said Brill, "got lost in the storm this afternoon and just happened—just happened to stumble in here this afternoon."

"Right-o," said Crowley. "Lucky for me, eh?"

"Very," said Brill sourly.

Crowley was sitting on the divan beside Shiela Alden, and he turned around and gave her the full benefit of his smile. "Yes, indeed! My lucky day!"

Shiela Alden simpered. There was no other word for it. She wiggled on the cushions and poked at her stringy hair and blinked shyly at Crowley through the thick glasses.

"You must stay the night here, Mr. Crowley."

"Must he?" Brill inquired, still more sourly.

Shiela Alden looked up, instantly antagonistic. "Of course! He can't possibly get home tonight, and we have plenty of room, and I've invited him!"

"A little blow like this," said Crowley. "Nothing. Nothing at all. You should see it scream up in the Himalayas. That's something!" He leaned closer to Shiela. "But of course there's no chance to stumble on to such delightful company when you're in the Himalayas, is there? I'll be delighted to stay overnight, Miss Alden, if it won't inconvenience you too much. It's so kind of you to ask me."

"Not at all," said Shiela Alden.

Doan was standing in front of the fire with his arms outspread, gradually thawing out, and now someone tugged uncertainly at his sleeve.

"You're—the detective?"

Doan turned to look at another girl. She was small too, smaller even than Shiela Alden, and she had a soft round face and full lips that pouted a little. She had blond hair, and her eyes were very wide and very blue and they didn't quite focus.

"This is Miss Alden's secretary," Brill said stiffly. "Miss Joan Greg."

"You're cute," Joan Greg said, swaying just slightly. "You're a cute little detective."

"Cute as a bug's ear," Doan agreed.

"Joan!" Shiela Alden said sharply. "Please behave yourself!"

Joan Greg turned slowly, still keeping her hold on Doan's arm. "Talking—to me?"

"You're drunk!" Shiela Alden said.

Joan Greg made the words carefully with her soft lips. "Shall I tell you just what you are—you and that thing sitting beside you?"

The tension in the room was like a wire stretched to a breaking point, with them all standing and staring at Joan incredulously. She was swaying, and her lips were twisting to form new words, while her eyes stared at Shiela Alden with glassy, unblinking hate.

"I'll—kill—her," said Joan Greg distinctly.

CHAPTER VI

DANGEROUS LADY

"MISS GREG!" BRILL gasped, horrified. But he did not make a move. He just stood, gaping.

"Wait until I get warm first, will you?" Doan asked casually.

Joan Greg forgot all about Shiela Alden for the moment. She swayed against Doan and said: "You're just the cutest little fella I've ever seen. Lemme help you out of your coat."

Brill stepped forward. "I'll do—"

"No! No! Lemme!"

Fumblingly, she helped Doan take off his topcoat and staggered back several steps holding it in front of her.

"Gonna—hang it up. Gonna hang the nice cute little detective's coat up for him."

She went at a diagonal across the room, missed the door by ten feet, carefully walked backward until she got a new line on it, and made it through. They could hear her in the hall, stumbling a little.

"I could use some of that," Doan said.

Brill stared at him. "Eh?"

Doan made a motion as though he were lifting a glass.

"Oh!" Brill said. "A drink! Yes, yes. Of course. Kokomo! Kokomo!"

A swinging door squeaked, and light showed through the archway opposite the entrance to the hall. Feet scraped lumber-

"Stop!" Doan shouted. But the madman was swinging back his axe.

ingly on the floor, and a man came in through the archway and said in a surly voice:

"Well, what?"

He had shoulders as wide as a door and long thick arms that were corded with muscle. He was wearing a white apron over blue denim trousers and a checked shirt, and he had a tall chefs hat perched jauntily over the bulging shapeless lump that had once been his left ear. He carried a toothpick in one corner of his pulpy lips, and his eyes were dully expressionless under thick, scarred eyebrows.

"Ah, yes," Brill said nervously. "Bring the whiskey, Kokomo, and—and a siphon of soda."

"You want ice?"

"I've had mine tonight already," Doan said.

"No," Brill said. "No ice."

Kokomo lumbered back through the archway and appeared

immediately again carrying a decanter and a siphon on a tray with a stacked pile of glasses.

Brill took the tray. "Mr. Doan, this is Kokomo—the cook and caretaker. This is the detective, Kokomo."

"This little squirt?" said Kokomo. "A detective? Hah!"

Brill said: "Kokomo! That's all!"

"Hah!" said Kokomo, staring down at Doan. He moved his big shoulders in a casual shrug and padded back through the archway. The swinging door squeaked shut behind him.

"Really, Mr. Brill," Shiela Alden said severely. "It seems to me that I have grounds for complaint about your choice of employees."

Brill threw his hands wide helplessly. "Miss Alden, I've told you again and again that our Mr. Dibben had been handling all your affairs and that he was injured when an auto ran over him and that his duties were suddenly delegated to me without the slightest warning and that he hadn't made any note of the fact that you intended to come up here.

"When you called me I had to find a man at once who would act as caretaker and cook and open this place up for you. This man Kokomo had excellent references—a great deal of experience—all that. You must admit, Miss Alden, that in spite of his uncouth appearance, he is a very good cook, and it's very difficult to get servants to come clear up here...."

Shiela Alden wasn't through. "And I don't think much of your choice of a secretary, either."

Brill lifted his hands. "Miss Greg had the very finest references. There was nothing in them whatsoever that indicated she was—ah—inclined to drink too much."

"Lonely country," Crowley said. "Brings it on. Seen it happen to a lot of chaps in Upper Burma. Probably be all right as soon as she gets back to civilization, eh? By the way, Mr. Doan, how on earth did you find this place? I mean, I got jolly well lost myself, and I can't see how a stranger could find his way here."

Doan had filled a glass half with whiskey and half with soda

and was sipping at it appreciatively. "The station master brought
me around—not because he wanted to. He seemed a bit sour
on the Alden name."

"And that's another thing!" Brill said worriedly. "The man's
a crank—dangerous. He shouldn't be allowed at large. He holds
some insane grudge against Miss Alden, and he might—
might… I mean, I'm responsible. I tried to talk to him, but all
he did was threaten me. And those damned dogs. Mr. Doan,
you had better investigate him thoroughly."

"Oh, sure," said Doan.

Brill ran thin nervous fingers through his hair, mussing up
the blazed streak of white that centered it. "I don't like you
coming up here in this wilderness, Miss Alden. It's a great
responsibility to put on my shoulders." He fumbled in his coat
pocket and brought out a shiny metal case.

Doan stiffened, his glass half-raised to his lips. "What's that
you've got there?"

"This?" said Brill. "A cigar case."

The case was an exact duplicate of the one Doan had found
in his pocket—his deadly present from the mysterious Mr.
Smith.

Brill snapped the catch with his thumb, and the case opened
on his palm, revealing the six cigars fitted into it snugly.

Doan released his breath in a long sigh. "Where," he said,
clearing his throat. "Where did you get it?"

Brill was admiring the case. "Nice, isn't it? Just the right size.
Eh? Oh, it was a present from a client."

"What was his name?"

"Smith," said Brill. "As a matter of fact, that's a strange thing.
We have several clients whose name is Smith, and I don't know
which one of them gave me this. Whoever it was just left it on
my secretary's desk with a little note saying in appreciation of
services rendered and all that and signed, *Smith.*"

"What was in it?" Doan asked.

Brill looked surprise. "Why, cigars."

"Did you smoke them?"

"Well, no. You see, I smoke a specially mild brand on account of my throat. I gave the ones in the case to the janitor, poor chap."

"Poor chap?" Doan repeated.

"Yes. He was killed that very night. He had a shack on the outskirts of the city, and he was running a still of some sort there—at least that's what the police think—and the thing blew up and blasted him to bits. Terrific explosion."

"Oh," said Doan. He watched thoughtfully while Brill selected a cigar and put the case back in his coat pocket.

"Well," said Brill, making an effort to be more sociable. "Let's think of something pleasant…." His voice trailed off into a startled gulp.

Joan Greg had come quietly in from the hall. She was holding Doan's revolver carefully in her right hand. She was walking straighter now, and she came directly across the floor to the front of the divan. She stopped there and pointed the revolver at Shiela Alden.

"Here!" Crowley shouted in alarm.

Doan flipped the contents of his glass into Joan Greg's face. Her head jerked back when the stinging liquid hit her. She took one uncertain step backward, and then Doan vaulted over the couch and expertly kicked her feet from under her.

She fell on her back, coming down so hard that her blond head bounced forward loosely with the impact. Doan stepped on her right wrist and twisted the revolver from her lax fingers.

Joan Greg turned over on her stomach and hid her face in her arms. She began to cry in racked, gasping sobs. The others stared at her, and at Doan with a sort of frozen, dazed horror.

"More fun," said Doan, slipping the revolver into his waistband. "Does she do things like this very often?"

"Gah!" Brill gasped. "She—she would have…. Why—why, she's crazy! Crazy drunk! Where—where'd she get that gun?"

"It was in my topcoat pocket," Doan said. "Careless of me,

but I didn't think there were any homicidal maniacs wandering around the house."

Shiela Alden's face was paper white. "Get her out of here! She's fired! Take her away!"

"Yes, yes," said Brill. "At once. Terrible. Terrible thing, really. And I'll be blamed—"

"Take her away!" Shiela Alden screamed at him.

Doan leaned over and picked Joan Greg up. She had stopped crying and she was utterly relaxed. Her arms flopped laxly. Her eyes were closed, and the tears had made wet jagged streaks down her soft cheeks.

"She's passed out, I think," Doan said. "I'll take her up and lock her in her bedroom."

"Yes, yes," Brill said. "Only thing. This way."

Crowley was bending anxiously over Shiela Alden. "Now, now. It's all over. Gives a person a nasty feeling, I know. Saw a chap run amok in Malay once. Ghastly thing. But you're a brave girl. Just a little sip of this."

Brill led the way across the living room and down the hall to a steep stairway with a rustic natural-wood railing. Brill went on up it and stopped at the first door in the upper hallway. He was still shaky, and he edged away from the limp form of Joan Greg as a man would avoid contact with something poisonous.

"Here," he said, pushing the door open and reaching around to snap on the light. "This—this is awful. Miss Alden is sure to complain to the office. What do you suppose ailed her?"

Doan put Joan Greg down on the narrow bed under the windows. The room was stiflingly hot. He looked at the windows and then down at Joan Greg's flushed face and decided against opening one. While he was looking down at her, she opened her eyes and stared up at him. All the life had drained out of her round face and left it empty and bitter and disillusioned.

"What's the trouble?" Doan asked. "Want to tell me about it?"

She turned her head slowly away from him and closed her eyes again. Doan waited a moment and then said:

"Better get undressed and into bed and sleep it off."

He turned off the light and went out of the room, transferring the key from the inside of the lock to the outside and turning it carefully. He tried the door to make sure and then put the key in his pocket.

Brill was wringing his hands in a distracted way. "I—I can hardly bear to face Miss Alden. She will blame me. *Everybody* blames me! I didn't want this responsibility…. I've got to go down and out-wait that scoundrel Crowley."

"Why?" Doan asked.

Brill came closer. "He's a fortune hunter! He didn't get lost today! He came over here on purpose because he's heard that Miss Alden was here! She's an impressionable girl, and I can't let him stay alone with her down there. The office would hold me accountable if he—if she…."

"I get it," Doan said.

"I don't know what to do," said Brill. "I mean, I know Miss Alden will be sure to resent—But I can't let him—"

"That's your problem," said Doan. "But I'm not supposed to protect her from people who want to make love to her—only the ones that don't. So I'm not out-waiting our friend Crowley. I'm tired. Which is my bedroom?"

"Right there. You'll leave your door open, Mr. Doan, in case—in case…."

"In case," Doan agreed. "Just whistle, and I'll pop up like any jack-in-the-box."

"I'm so worried," said Brill. "But I must go down and see that the scoundrel doesn't…."

He went trotting down the steep stairs. Doan went along the hall back to the bedroom Brill had indicated. It was small and as neatly arranged as a model room in a display window, furnished with imitation rustic bed, chairs and bureau.

It, too, was stiflingly hot. Doan spotted the radiator bulking in the corner. He went over and touched it experimentally and jerked his fingers away with a whispered curse. It was so hot the water in it was burbling. Doan looked for the valve to turn it off, but there was none.

He stood looking at the radiator for some time, frowning in a puzzled way. There was something wrong about the whole setup at the lodge. It was like a picture slightly out of focus, and yet he couldn't put his finger on any one thing that was wrong. It bothered Doan, and he didn't like to be bothered. But it was still there. An air of intangible menace.

He discovered now that he had left his grip downstairs. He didn't feel like going and getting it at the moment. He wanted to think about the people in the house, and he had always been able to think better lying down. He shrugged and headed for the bed. Fully dressed, he lay down on top of it and went to sleep.

THE DOOR at the end of the hall was hers, and Brill pounded on the panels with both fists. "Miss Alden!" His voice was raw with panic now, and he tried the knob. The door opened immediately.

"Miss—Miss Alden," Brill said uncertainly.

"The light," said Doan, behind him.

Brill reached inside the door and snapped the switch. There was no sound for a long time, and then Brill moaned a little.

Doan said: "Come here, Crowley. I want you where I can watch you."

Crowley spoke in a jerky voice. "Well, Joan—I mean, Miss Greg. You can't leave her lying—"

"Come here."

Crowley edged inside Shiela Alden's bedroom and backed against the wall in response to a guiding flick of Doan's revolver barrel. Brill was standing in the center of the room with his hands up over his face.

"This will ruin me," he said in a sick mumble. "I was going

to get a partnership in the firm. They gave me full responsibility for watching out for her. Account was worth tens of thousands a year. They'll hound me out of the state—can never practice again." His voice trailed off into indistinguishable syllables.

This bedroom was as stiflingly hot as Doan's had been. Shiela Alden had only a sheet over her. She was stiffly rigid on her back in the bed. Her throat had been cut from ear to ear, and the pillows under her head were soaked and sticky with blood. Her bony face looked pinched and small and empty, with her nearsighted eyes staring glassily up at the light.

Doan pointed the gun at Crowley. "You talk."

Crowley made an effort to get back his air of British lightheartedness. "But, old chap, you can't imagine I—"

"Yes, I can," said Doan.

Crowley's mouth opened and shut soundlessly.

"It comes a little clearer," said Doan. "You were so scared you got a little rattled for a moment. Just how well do you know Joan Greg?"

Crowley's smile was an agonized grimace. "Well, my dear chap, hardly at all. I just met the young lady today."

"We can't use that one." Doan said. "You know her very well. That was what was the trouble with her. She was jealous. You've been living off her, haven't you?"

"That's not a nice thing to accuse a chap—"

"Murder's not nice, either. You've been living off Joan Greg. You haven't any more got a place on Flint Flat than I have. Have you?"

"Well…."

"No, you haven't. Joan Greg told you that she had gotten a job as secretary to Shiela Alden and was coming up here. You knew who Shiela Alden was, and you thought that was a swell chance for you to chisel in and charm the young lady with your entrancing personality.

"You must have let Joan Greg in on it—told her you'd make

a killing and split with her probably. But when it came right down to seeing you make passes at Shiela Alden, Joan Greg couldn't take it."

"Fantastic," Crowley said in a stiff unnatural voice. "Utter— rot."

"You!" said Brill, and the blood made a thick red flush in his shallow cheeks. "You rat! I'll see you hung! I'll—I'll—Doan! Hold him until I get my gun!" He blundered wildly out of the room, and his feet made a wild pattering rush down the hall.

Crowley had recovered his poise now. His eyes were cold and alert and hard, watching Doan. Brill's bedroom door slammed, and then his voice shrilled out fiercely.

"Get up! Get up, damn you! I know you're faking! I saw your eyes open!"

There was a scuffling sound from the hall, and Joan Greg cried out breathlessly. Crowley moved against the wall.

"No," said Doan.

Confused footsteps came closer, and Brill pushed Joan Greg roughly into the bedroom.

"There!" Brill raged. "Look at her! Look at your handiwork, damn you, you shameless little tramp!"

Joan Greg gave a stifled cry of terror. She held her shaking, blood-smeared hands out in front of her helplessly, and then she turned and ran to Crowley and hid her face against his chest.

"There they are!" Brill shouted. He was holding a .45 Colt automatic in his hand and he waved it wildly in the air. "Look at them! A fine pair of crooks and murderers! But they'll pay! You hear me, do you? You'll pay!"

Doan was looking at the radiator in the corner. He was frowning a little bit and whistling softly and soundlessly to himself.

"Why is it so hot?" he asked.

"Eh?" Brill said. "What?"

"Why is it so hot in the bedrooms?"

"The windows have storm shutters on them," Brill said impatiently. "They can't be opened in a wind like this."

"But why are the radiators so hot? The water in that one is boiling. You can hear it."

"What damned nonsense!" Brill yelled. "Are you going to stand there and ask silly questions about radiators when Shiela Alden has been murdered and these two stand here caught in the very act—"

"No," said Doan. "I'm going to find out about the matter of the temperature around here. You watch these two."

"Doan, you fool!" Brill shouted. "Come back here! You're in my employ and I demand—"

"Watch them," said Doan. "I'll be back in a minute or so."

CHAPTER VIII

HI, KOKOMO

HE WENT DOWN the hall, down the steep stairs, and across the living room. The log fireplace was dull, glowing red embers now. The wind had blown some of the smoke back down the chimney, and it made a thick murky blue haze. Doan went on across the room through the archway on the other side.

Ahead of him light showed dimly around the edge of the swinging door that led into the kitchen. The hinges squeaked as Doan pushed it back.

Kokomo was sitting in the corner beside the gleaming white and chromium of an electric range. He was still wearing his big apron, and the tall chefs hat was tilted down rakishly over his left eye. He had what looked like the same toothpick in one corner of his mouth, and it moved up and down jerkily as he said:

"What can I do for you, sonny?"

"Don't you ever go to bed at night?" Doan asked.

"Naw. I'm an owl."

"It's awfully hot upstairs," said Doan.

"Too bad."

"I notice you have a central hot water heating system here. What does the furnace burn—coal or oil?"

"Coal."

"Who takes care of it?"

"Me."

"Where is it?"

Kokomo jerked a thick thumb at a door in the back wall of the kitchen. "Down cellar."

"I think I'll take a look at it."

Kokomo took the toothpick out of his mouth and snapped it into the far corner of the room. "Run along and roll your hoop, sonny, before I lose my patience and lay you out like a rug. This here end of the premises is my bailiwick and I don't go for any mush-faced snoopers prowlin' around in it. I told the rest that. Now I'm tellin' it to you."

"On the other hand," said Doan cheerfully, "I think I'll have a look at the furnace."

Kokomo got up out of his chair. "Sonny, you're gettin' me irritated. Put that popgun away before I shove it down you throat."

Doan dropped the gun in his coat pocket, smiling. "Aw, you wouldn't do a mean thing like that, would you?"

Kokomo came for him with quick little shuffling steps, his head lowered and tucked between the hunched bulk of his thick shoulders.

Doan was still smiling. He made a fork out of the first two fingers of his left hand and poked them at Kokomo's eyes. Kokomo knew that trick and, instead of ducking, he merely tilted his head back and let Doan's stiffened fingers slide off his low forehead. But when he put his head back, he exposed his thickly muscular throat.

Doan hit him squarely on the Adam's apple with a short right jab. It was a wickedly effective blow, and Kokomo made a queer strangling noise and grasped his throat with both hands, rolling his head back and forth in agony. His mouth was wide open, and his eyes bulged horribly.

Doan hit him again, a full roundhouse swing with all his compact weight behind it. His fist smacked on the hinge of Kokomo's jaw. Kokomo went back one step and then another, shaking his head helplessly, still trying to draw a breath.

"I should break my hands on you, cement-head," Doan said casually. He took the revolver out of his coat pocket and slammed Kokomo on the top of the head with the butt of it.

The blow smashed the tall chefs hat into a weirdly lopsided pancake. Kokomo dropped to his knees, sagging loosely. With coldblooded efficiency Doan hit him again in the same place. Kokomo flopped forward on his face and lay there on the shiny linoleum without moving.

It had happened very fast, and Doan was standing there now, looking down at Kokomo, still smiling in his casually amused way. He wasn't even breathing hard.

"These tough guys," he said, shrugging.

He dropped the revolver in his coat pocket again and stepped over Kokomo. The cellar door was fastened with a patent bolt. Doan unlatched it and peered down a flight of steep wooden stairs that were lighted dimly from the kitchen behind him. He felt around the door and found a light switch and clicked it. Nothing happened. The light down in the cellar, if there was one, didn't work.

Doan went down the steps, feeling his way cautiously as he got beyond the path of the light from the kitchen door. The cellar was a warm, dark cavern thick with the smell of coal dust. Feeling overhead, Doan located the warmth of a fat asbestos-wrapped pipe and judged from the direction it ran that the furnace was over in the far corner.

He started that way, sliding his feet cautiously along the cement floor. He was somewhere in the middle of it, out of reach of either wall, when something made a quick silent breath going past in front of his face.

He stopped with a jerk, reaching for his revolver. The thing that had gone past his face hit the wall behind him with a dull ominous thud and dropped to the floor. Doan stayed rigidly still, his revolver poised. He was afraid to move for fear of stumbling over something. He listened tensely, his head tilted.

A voice whispered out of the darkness ahead of him. "Don't—don't you dare come any closer. I've got a shovel here. I'll—hit you with it."

Doan was a hard man to surprise, but he was as startled now as he ever had been in his life. He stared in the direction of the voice, his mouth open.

The voice said shakily: "You get out."

"Whoa," Doan said. "Wait a minute. I'm not coming any closer. Just listen to me before you heave any more of that coal."

"Who—who are you?"

"Name's Doan."

"The detective! Oh!"

"That's what I say. And who're you?"

"Shiela Alden."

"Ah," said Doan blankly. He drew a deep breath. "Well, I know I'm not drunk, so this must be happening. If you're Shiela Alden down here in the cellar, who's the Shiela Alden up in the bedroom?"

"That's my secretary, Leila Adams. She's been impersonating me."

"Oh. Sort of a game, huh?"

"No!"

"Well, I was just asking. What's the matter with the light down here?"

"I screwed the bulb out of the socket."

"Well, where is it? I'll screw it back in again. I need some light on the subject."

"Oh, no! No! Don't!"

"Why not?"

"I—I haven't any clothes on."

"You haven't any clothes on," Doan repeated. He shook his head violently. "Maybe I'm a little sleepy or something. I don't seem to be getting this. Suppose you just start and tell me all about it."

"Well, Leila and I came up here alone. Kokomo had come ahead to open up the place. Kokomo and Leila are in this together. When we got here they held me up and locked me in the cellar—in the back room beyond this one. Leila told me she was going to pretend she was me."

"Is Brill crazy? Didn't he know Leila Adams wasn't you?"

"No. Mr. Dibben in the law firm always handled all my business. I don't know Mr. Brill. He's never seen me."

"Well, well," said Doan. "Then what?"

"They just locked me in that cellar room. There's one window, and they didn't want to put bars over it, so they took all my clothes away from me. They knew I wouldn't get out the window then. If I did I'd freeze.

"It's two miles to the station and I didn't know which way. And Kokomo said if I screamed he'd…." Her voice trailed off into a little gasping sob. "He told me what he'd do."

"Yeah," said Doan. "I can imagine."

"Where is he now?"

"Kokomo? He's slightly indisposed at the moment. Go on. Tell me the rest."

"I broke a little piece of metal off the window, and I picked the lock on the door and got out here. I know how the heating system works. The valves are down here. I turned off the ones that controlled the downstairs radiators and opened the ones that control the upstairs radiators wide.

"Then I kept putting coal in the furnace with the drafts wide open. I thought if I made it hot enough in the upstairs bedrooms someone besides Kokomo would come down and look."

"Sure," said Doan. "Smart stuff. If I'd had any brains I'd have been down here hours ago. You stay right here and I'll bring you something to wear. Don't be afraid any more."

"I haven't been afraid—not very much. Only—only of Kokomo coming down here and—"

"He won't be coming down. Stay right here. I'll be right back." Doan ran back up the steps. All his cheerful casual air was gone now. His lips were thinned across his teeth, and he moved with a cat-like, lithe efficiency.

Kokomo was still lying flat on his face in the center of the kitchen floor. Doan, moving with the same quiet quickness, opened the cupboard door and located an aluminum kettle.

He filled it with water at the sink. Carrying it carefully, he walked over to Kokomo and, using the toe of one shoe, expertly flipped the big man over on his back.

He dumped the kettle of water in Kokomo's blankly upturned face. For a second there was no reaction, then Kokomo's pulpy lips moved, and he sputtered wetly. His eyes opened and he saw Doan looking thoughtfully down at him.

"Hi, Kokomo," Doan said softly. "Hi, baby."

Kokomo made noises in his throat and heaved himself up on his elbows. Doan took one short step forward and kicked him under the jaw so hard that Kokomo's whole lolling body lifted clear of the floor and rolled half under the stove. He didn't move any more.

"I'll have another present for you later," Doan said.

CHAPTER IX

BLACK SNOW

HE WENT IN through the living room to the front hall. He had opened the door of the closet and located his snow-damp topcoat when he heard a little shuffling noise at the top of the stairs. He turned around to look.

It was Brill. The light behind him made him look grotesquely thin, sagging in the middle like a broken pencil.

"Doan!" he gasped.

He got hold of the railing with both hands, and then he came down the stairs in a crazily shuffling dance, his skinny legs wavering and twisting weirdly. He tripped and fell headlong down the last ten steps before Doan could catch him.

The skin on his face was yellowish, the cheekbones bulging out in ugly lumps. Blood was streaked in a long smear across his forehead. Doan straightened him out on the steps.

"Doan!" he said desperately. "That damned scoundrel, Crowley. Tricked me. Hit me—hit me—chair." He heaved himself up on his elbows, eyes glaring. "Doan! I'll hold you responsible! Got away! Your fault!"

"They didn't hit *me* with a chair," Doan pointed out.

"You!" Brill gasped. "Leaving me with them. While you wander off…. They'll get away! They'll get to the station! Jannen will help them! Flat-car there—go down the grade…."

"We'll telephone ahead and stop them."

Brill rolled his head back and forth helplessly. "No telephone. Tried it upstairs. Line cut. You've got to go after them! They've got only a few minutes start! You can catch them! That girl—she can't go fast."

Doan said: "You mean you want me to go out in that storm again?"

"Oh, damn you!" Brill swore. "Don't you understand that my whole career is at stake? I hired your agency, and you failed me! I'll have you black-listed. I'll sue!"

"All right, all right," Doan said. "I'll go bring them back. Take another coat and give it to the girl you find down cellar."

He went to the front door and opened it. The wind whooped in triumphantly, driving a fine mist of snow ahead of it.

"Light," said Brill weakly. "They've got an electric lantern. You can see—"

Doan slammed the door shut. The wind came whipping down out of the black mouth of the ravine with a fierce howling intensity. Doan was struggling to get into his topcoat, and the wind billowed the coat out like a clumsy sail and blew Doan with it down the steps and across the black, rock-strewn ground.

He stumbled into a drift waist-deep before he caught himself. He stood still for a moment, one arm crooked up to shield his eyes from the cutting whip of the snow. The wind blasted at him, and then he caught the flicker of a light on the path that led up out of the flat.

Doan began to run. He was half-blinded with the snow, and the wind pulled and tugged at him, pushed him in staggering crazy spurts. He stumbled and half-fell, and then the gravel on the steep path grated under his shoes.

The light was high above him, much closer now, and as he watched, it flicked over the edge of the ravine and disappeared.

Doan fumbled under his coat and found the revolver. He went up the path at a lurching run. His breath burned icily in his throat. The air was thin and fine, with no weight to it, and his heart began to drum in a sickening cadence.

He was breathing in sobbing gasps when he hit the top of the ravine, sweat crawling in cold rivulets under his clothes. He paused there swaying, looking for the light, and found it off to his left.

He turned and plowed stubbornly in that direction, and there was no path here, nothing but thick drifts of snow piled against stunted brush that tore at his clothes with myriad clutching fingers.

The light tossed up high ahead of him, very close now, and showed stunted trees lined up in a ghostly gallery, leaning forward in the push of the wind as they watched.

Doan tripped over a snow-hidden log and went down flat on his face in powdery whiteness. He heaved himself stubbornly up on hands and knees, dabbed at his smeared face with his coatsleeve—and he stayed that way, half kneeling, rigid, staring into savagely cruel greenish yellow eyes on a level with his own and not a yard away.

"Hah!" Doan said, grunting with the exhalation of his breath.

The eyes came for him with the sudden slashing gleam of teeth under them. Doan poked the revolver straight out and fired, wondering as he pulled the trigger whether his fall had packed snow in the barrel and whether the gun would blow back at him.

The shot made a bright orange flare, and the eyes were gone. A heavy body kicked and squirmed in the snow. Doan struggled up to his feet, and another dark low form slipped sideways in the whirling darkness, circling him.

Doan leveled the revolver and fired instantly. A shrill *ki-yiing yip* echoed the smash of the shot, and the second dark form went tumbling over and over in the snow, contorting itself into desperate struggling knots.

The third one came in a black streak out of the darkness, up out of the snow in a long lunge, straight at Doan's throat. He fired going over backward. The flat-nosed .38 hit the animal in the chest and turned it clear over in the air. It fell back rigid and still beside the first.

Doan struggled in the snow, heaving himself up, and then Jannen loomed above him, yelling something the wind garbled into an unintelligible, frenzied scream. He had an ax in his hand, and he swung it back up over his shoulder and down at

Doan in a full sweep that made its head glitter in a bright, deadly line.

Doan whirled himself sideways, rolling.

"Jannen!" he yelled frantically. "Don't! Don't! I'll shoot—"

The ax-head hissed past his ear, and Jannen caught it on the upswing and chopped back down again with it.

Doan couldn't dodge this time. He didn't try. He shot Jannen just above the grassy gleam of the buckle on the wide web belt around his coat.

Jannen made a queer, choked sound. The ax stopped in midair. Jannen took one step back and then another, trying to get the ax up over his shoulder again.

"Drop it," said Doan.

The ax was going up inch by desperate inch. Jannen's breath made a high whistling sound. He made a clumsy step forward.

"All right, baby," said Doan.

He pulled the trigger of the revolver again. There was a dull, small click—nothing else. Before Doan even had time to grasp what that meant, Jannen reeled queerly sideways and went down full length on his face, as rigid as a log.

"Good God," said Doan in a whisper.

He got up slowly. The thing had happened in split-seconds, and the echoes of the gunfire were still rolling lustily ahead of the wind.

Doan stared at his gun. It was bright and deadly in his hand, with the snow moisture gleaming on its thick cylinder, and he remembered now that he hadn't reloaded it. He had fired once at the metal case and once in the snow-shed. There had been four cartridges left in the gun. He had used them all. If he had missed just one of those four shots….

The wind whistled shrilly through bare branches, chuckling in its high, cruel glee.

Doan stumbled forward, leaned down over Jannen. The man

was dead, and the snow already was laying a white cold blanket thinly across his distorted face.

Doan plowed back through the drifts and brush, found the hard surface of the path. He felt weak and numb with cold that was more than cold. His legs were stiff, unwieldy sticks under him as he went back down the steep path, across the flat toward the warmly welcoming glow of the windows that watched for him through the whirl of snow.

CHAPTER X

TOO MANY GUNS

DOAN WENT BLUNDERING across the porch with his head down and ran into the front door. He found the knob, fumbled it with numb fingers, finally turned it. The wind swept the door out of his grasp, banged it back thunderously against the wall.

Doan stamped through into the soft luxurious warmth of the hall, fought the door shut again behind him. Sighing in relief, he wiped snow moisture off his face with the palm of his left hand.

"Drop your gun on the floor."

Doan jerked to attention. Brill was standing in the doorway of the living room. He was wearing a blue dressing gown now over his pajamas. He lounged there, quite at ease, with the big .45 automatic bulking huge and black in his right hand.

"Drop your gun on the floor," he repeated in the same confident, quiet voice.

He looked very theatrical, with the white blaze showing up in his smoothly brushed hair, with his eyes narrowed. He was smiling in a dramatically sinister way.

Doan loosened the stiff fingers of his right hand and the .38 thudded on the carpet.

"It wasn't loaded anyway," he observed.

"Come in here," said Brill.

He backed out of the door, and Doan followed him into the living room. Someone had thrown kindling on the fire, and red flames crackled greedily in it.

"You know Miss Alden, I think," Brill said.

She was sitting on the divan. She was wearing a man's overcoat so big that it almost wrapped around her twice. She had brown hair cut in a long bob, mussed a little now, and the fire found warm glints in it. Her brown eyes were wide and scared, and her soft lower lip trembled. There was a smear of coal dust on the end of her short straight nose.

"Hello, again," said Doan.

She didn't answer, and Brill said:

"You're becoming a nuisance, Doan. What happened to Jannen? I heard you shooting."

"I was just target practicing," Doan said, "but Jannen, that dope, stepped right in front of my gun just when I happened to be pulling the trigger. I expect he's sort of dead."

Kokomo came in from the kitchen. There was a lopsided swollen lump on one side of his jaw, and his eyes glittered malevolently at Doan.

"You tricky little devil! When I get my hands on you—"

"I can hardly wait," Doan told him.

"Later, Kokomo," Brill said. He was watching Doan with gravely speculative eyes. "I suppose you are beginning to understand this now, aren't you?"

"Oh, sure," said Doan. "I figured it out quite a while ago."

"Did you, now?" said Brill sarcastically.

Doan nodded. "Yes. You were next in line for the management of Shiela Alden's trust fund after this gent Dibben. You had all the time in the world to figure things out and get ready for this little play. You saw that an accident happened to Dibben at the right time. You knew Shiela Alden was coming up here—

probably suggested the idea yourself—and you made all your arrangements beforehand.

"First you got Leila Adams, Shiela's secretary, to throw in with you by promising to split part of what you got from Shiela with her. Then you got Kokomo to do the muscle-work, promising him a split too. When you were prowling around up here beforehand you found out that Jannen was a crackpot with a grudge against the Aldens.

"Now, there was an ideal fall-guy for you all ready-made. Anything that happened you could always blame on him. But Jannen talks too much, and this poor guy, Boley, the regular station master, got suspicious of what you were cooking up with him, and either you or Kokomo or Jannen—or all three of you—got Boley drunk and probably doped him and left him out in the storm to freeze.

"Leila Adams wasn't going to impersonate Shiela Alden unless it was necessary on account of someone like me coming around. You definitely didn't want anyone around—not with the real Shiela Alden locked in the cellar.

"And so—" Doan paused, ran a hand over his cheek.

"Jannen knew a lot about explosives, and so you got him to fix up that little cigar case present for me. You knew I was going to be on the job because the trust company hired the agency, and Toggery told you he was going to send me up. So you dressed up in a fancy costume and laid for me with your cigar case bomb."

"How did you know I was the one who gave you that case?"

Doan grinned. "I couldn't miss. You spent so much time trying to cover yourself up that you stuck out like a sore thumb. You wanted to be sure that if anything went wrong no one could prove that you had anything to do with the whole business.

"That was the reason for your little fairy tale about the janitor and the cigar case and why you *put* on that elaborate, nervous and worried act and why you wanted to make sure that I knew you'd just been assigned to handle Shiela Alden's business. You wanted me to think that you were a jittery sort of a dope who couldn't possibly know the score. As a matter of fact, you *are* a dope."

Brill's lip lifted. "So? And I suppose you can tell me what happened tonight, too?"

"Easy," Doan agreed. "When you found out you hadn't put me away and that I was coming up here, you had to get a girl to act as secretary to the phoney Shiela Alden because you knew I'd expect to find a secretary.

"You hired the first girl you could find—Joan Greg. She wasn't in on the impersonation business. She thought Leila Adams was actually Shiela Alden—and, more important, so did her boy friend, Crowley.

"Crowley just messed the whole works up for you. He started impressing his personality on Leila Adams. He's a slick worker. She fell for him. She was a scrawny, homely dame, and she'd never had anybody like Crowley tell her how beautiful, breath-taking, marvelous and generally all-around wonderful she was before.

"She liked it fine. She liked it so well she began to get out of hand, and you knew that if Crowley worked much more of his sex appeal, she'd spill something to him. You killed her.

"Joan Greg was crazy jealous of Crowley, and she gave you the idea by trying it herself. You knew, then, that you could put Leila Adams away and blame it on Joan Greg.

"You had a master key. You could get into her bedroom. You cut Leila Adams' throat and then went in and planted the knife on Joan Greg and bloodied up her hands. When she woke up she actually didn't know whether or not she had killed the phoney Shiela Alden. As soon as I left you alone with her and Crowley, you told them to beat it. You planned to lay all the blame on them, knowing they'd keep under cover.

"Jannen was prowling around the place, and you tipped him off and then sent me out, thinking Jannen and his damned wolves would take care of me. You tipped your hand twice then.

First by that phoney entrance coming downstairs. Nobody who actually got banged with a chair ever acted so screwy as you did. And then you weren't even interested when I told you there was a girl down cellar. As an actor, you stink. What crackpot notion have you got up your sleeve now?"

Brill said smoothly: "I've had to alter my plans slightly, Doan, but I don't think it will really matter—certainly not to you. You see, at first all I wanted to do was to force Shiela to give me her power of attorney for a week or so after she got control of the trust fund. If I could have done that, as I planned, I would have made a fortune."

"Sure. By selling her a few million shares of phoney stock."

Brill looked contemptuous. "Nothing so crude. Merely by forcing the market up and down by alternately selling and buying the huge blocks of stock she owns in several corporations and being on the right side of the market myself each time.

"There would have been nothing criminal in that, and no way for her to prove afterward that she hadn't given the power of attorney voluntarily, because it would have been her word against myself, Kokomo and Leila Adams. But due to the way things have happened, I've been forced—not very reluctantly, I must admit—to ask Miss Alden to do me the honor of becoming my wife."

Shiela Alden spoke for the first time. "No," she said in a small, clear voice.

Brill paid no attention to her. "You see, Doan? Even if my original plan did go on the rocks, I can still pull things together. I'll have control over Miss Alden's money if she's my wife—you can be sure of that. And more important, she can't testify against me."

Shiela Alden said: "I am not going to marry you—now or any other time."

"I think you will," Brill said. "It's really quite essential. Kokomo, will you take Miss Alden into the other room and see if you can—ah—reason with her?"

CHAPTER XI

GOOD-BY NOW

SHIELA ALDEN DREW in her breath with a little gasp. Kokomo was grinning at her meaningly out of the side of his mouth that wasn't swollen. He came nearer the divan.

"It's warm in there," Brill said. "She won't need that coat."

Shiela Alden wrapped the coat tighter around her, clutching the lapels with fingers that were white with strain.

"No! You can't—"

"Brill," said Doan.

He hadn't made any noticeable move, but now he was holding a flat metal case on the palm of his right hand, looking down at it thoughtfully.

"That's mine!" Brill exclaimed.

"No," said Doan. "No, Brill. Not yours. It's the one you gave me."

Silence stretched over the room like a thin black veil, with the crackle of the flames in the hearth coming through it faint and distant.

"Foolish," Doan said, still staring at the case thoughtfully. "Foolish trying to alibi yourself by carrying one like it and pretending some mysterious Mr. Smith gave it to you and that the cigars in it subsequently blew the janitor to smithereens. There aren't any cigars—explosive or otherwise—in this case. It's packed with explosive."

"Brill said stiffly: "How—how—"

"You're a dope," Doan told him. "Don't you know that the bomb squad on any city police force has equipment—black light, X-ray, fluoroscope—so they can look into suspicious packages without opening them? I took this case down to a pal of mine on the Bay City bomb squad. He squinted into it and told me it was a very neat little hand-grenade, so I kept it for a souvenir. Here. Catch it."

He tossed the case in a spinning, glittering arc. Brill yelled in a choked, horrified voice. He dropped the automatic and grabbed frantically with both hands at the case.

Doan dived for him in a lunging expert tackle. He smashed against Brill's pipe-stem legs. The case was knocked whirling up in the air, and Brill spun around and fell headlong. His head cracked sickeningly against the edge of the hearth, and he stiffened, his whole body quivering, and then was still.

Doan rolled over and sat up and looked down the thick black barrel of the automatic at Kokomo's scared, sagging face.

"Hi, Kokomo," Doan said softly.

Kokomo held both big hands in front of him, fingers spread wide, as though he were trying to push back the expected bullet.

"Don't," he whispered. "Don't shoot."

"Oh, I think I will," Doan said.

Kokomo believed him. He had already had a demonstration of what Doan could and would do. His thick lips opened and shut soundlessly, little sticky threads of saliva glinting at their corners.

Doan got up. "Turn around, Kokomo."

Kokomo turned slowly and stiffly, like a mechanical doll that had almost run down. Doan stepped close to him and slammed him on the head with the barrel of the automatic.

"I'll bet even your cement knob will ache tomorrow after that," Doan said amiably. He winked at Shiela Alden, who was staring with wide unbelieving brown eyes.

"Weren't scared, were you? They never had a chance. They're amateurs. I'm a professional. That case was really Brill's—not the one he gave me. I picked it out of his pocket last night. Wanted to look at it more closely."

She continued to stare.

He went over to the door into the hall and picked up the

telephone. It was a French type handset with a long cord attached to it. Stringing out the cord behind him, Doan brought
the phone back to the divan and sat down on it beside Shiela
Alden. He held the receiver against his ear.

"The dopes," he said to Shiela. "They didn't even cut the line."

She turned her head stiffly, little by little, and looked from
Brill to Kokomo. "Are they—are they—"

"Dead?" Doan finished. "Oh, no." He was still listening at
the receiver, and now he said:

"Hello. Hello, operator? Get me the J.S. Toggery residence
in Bay City. I don't know the number. I'll hold the line."

He waited, smiling at Shiela Alden in a speculative way. She
had begun to breathe more evenly now, and there was a little
color in her cheeks.

"But—but you did it so easily—so quickly. I mean, it all
happened before I knew what—"

"The hand is quicker than the eye," said Doan. "At least mine
was quicker than theirs."

"I—I've never met anyone like you before."

"There's only one of us," Doan said.

The receiver crackled against his ear, and then J.S. Toggery's
voice said:

"What? What? Who's this?"

"Doan—the forgotten man. How are you, Mr. Toggery? How
is Carstairs?"

"You! That damned ghoulish giraffe! He pulled all my wife's
new drapes down! He broke a vase that cost me a hundred and
fifty dollars! He crawled under the dinner table and then stood
up and dumped the dinner on the floor! I've got him chained
in the garage, and let me tell you, Doan, if he pulls just one
more trick, I'll get an elephant gun and so help me I'll pulver-
ize him! You hear me?"

"He's young and exuberant. He probably misses me. You'll
have to excuse him. Good-by now."

"Wait! Wait, you fool! Are you up at the Alden lodge where you're supposed to be? Is everything all right up there?"

"Oh, yes. Now it is. There was a kidnapping and a couple of murders and some attempted thefts and a few assaults with intent to kill and such, but I straightened it all out. Get off the line, Toggery. I've got to call the sheriff."

"Doan!" Toggery screamed. *"Doan!* What? What did you say? Murders—kidnapping. Doan! Is Miss Alden all right?"

Doan looked at her. "Yes," he said. "Yes, Toggery. Miss Alden is—quite all right."

He hung up the receiver on Toggery's violent voice and nodded at Shiela Alden.

"You know," he said, "you're so very nice that I think I could like you an awful lot even if you didn't have fifty million dollars."

Shiela Alden's soft lips made a round, pink O of surprise and then moved a little into a faint tremulous smile.

II

THE MOUSE IN THE MOUNTAIN

CHAPTER I

WHEN DOAN AND Carstairs came down the wide stairway and walked across the pink-tiled floor that was the pride and joy of the Hotel Azteca, the guests in the lobby stopped whatever they were doing to pass the time away and stared openmouthed. Doan was not such-a-much, but Carstairs usually had this effect on people, and he left a whispering, wondering wake behind him as he stalked across to the glassed side doors and waited with haughty dignity while Doan opened one of the doors. He ambled through it ahead of Doan into the incredibly bright sunlight on the terrace.

Doan halted and drew in a deep breath of air that felt clean and dry and thinly exhilarating. He stared all around him with frank appreciation. He was short and a little on the plump side, and he had a chubby, pink face and a smile as innocent and appealing as a baby's. He looked like a very nice, pleasant sort of person, and on rare occasions he was.

He was wearing a white suit and a wide-brimmed Panama hat and white crepe-soled shoes.

"Breathe some of this air, Carstairs," he ordered. "It's wonderful. This is ideal Mexican weather."

Carstairs yawned in an elaborately bored way. Carstairs was a fawn-colored Great Dane. Standing on four legs, his back came up to Doan's chest. He never did tricks. He considered them beneath him. But had he ever done one that involved standing on his hind feet, his head would have hit a level far above Doan's. Carstairs was so big he could hardly be called a dog. He was a sort of new species.

A girl came very quickly out of the door behind Doan and said *Un!* in a startled gasp when she saw Carstairs looming in front of her.

Carstairs didn't move out of her way. He turned lazily to stare at her. So did Doan.

She was a small girl, and she looked slightly underfed. She had very wide, very clear blue eyes. They were nice eyes. Nothing startling, but adequate. Her hair was brown and smooth under a white turban, and she wore a white sports dress and a white jacket and white openwork sandals. She had a clear, smooth skin, and she blushed easily. She was doing it now.

"I'm sorry," she said breathlessly. "He—he frightened me."

"He frightens me, too, sometimes," said Doan.

"What's your name?"

The girl looked at him uncertainly. "My name? It's Janet Martin."

"Mine's Doan," said Doan. "I'm a detective."

"A—a detective?" Janet Martin repeated, fumbling a little over the word. "You don't look like one."

"Of course not," Doan told her. "I'm in disguise. I'm pretending I'm a tourist."

"Oh," said Janet, still uncertain. "But—do you go around telling everybody about it?"

"Certainly," said Doan. "My disguise is so perfect no one would know I was a detective if I didn't tell them, so naturally I do."

"Oh," said Janet. "I see." She looked at Carstairs. "He's beautiful. I mean, not beautiful but—but magnificent. Does he bite?"

"Quite often," Doan admitted.

"May I pet him?"

Doan looked at Carstairs inquiringly. "May she?"

Carstairs studied Janet for a moment and then came one

step closer to her and lowered his head regally. Janet patted his broad brow.

"Don't scratch his ears," Doan warned. "He detests that."

A long brown bus pulled around the curve of the drive and stopped in front of the terrace steps. A little man in a spic-and-span brown uniform popped out, clicked his heels snappily, and said, "The tour of sight-seeing presents itself to those who wish to view the magnificence with educated comments."

"Oh, you're the one I was looking for," Janet said. "I'm going on the tour to Los Altos. This is the bus that takes me there, isn't it?"

The little man bowed. "With comfort and speed and also comments."

"I was afraid I was late. What time do you start?"

"On schedule," said the little man. "Always on the schedule we start when it says. I am Bartolome—accent on the last syllable, if you please—chauffeur licensed and guide most qualified, with English guaranteed by the advanced correspondence school, conversational and classic. Do me the honor of presenting me your ticket."

Janet gave it to him, and he examined it with suspicious care, even turning it over and reading the fine print on the back.

"In order most perfect," he admitted. "Do me the graciousness of entering and sitting. We will start instantly or when I locate the other passengers."

"Here's two more," said Doan, handing him two tickets.

"Ah, yes," said Bartolome, and examined them as carefully as he had Janet's. "Is most fine. But there are the two tickets and of you only one. Where is the other?"

"There," said Doan, pointing.

Bartolome looked at Carstairs, turned his head away quickly, and then looked again. "It has a resemblance to a dog," he said slowly and cautiously.

"Some," said Doan.

"It is a dog!" Bartolome exclaimed. "A dog of the most incredible monstrousness! A veritable nightmare of a dog!"

"Be careful," Doan warned. "He insults easily."

Bartolome looked at the tickets and then at Carstairs. "One of this is for him?"

"Yes."

"No," said Bartolome.

"Yes," said Doan.

"Of a positively not, senor."

Carstairs sprawled himself out on the warm tiles and closed his eyes sleepily. Arguments offended his sense of the fitness of things, so he ignored them.

Bartolome stared narrowly at Doan. "The ticket of the sightseeing magnificence is not sold for dogs."

"This one was."

"Dogs do not ride in the luxury of the bus that precedes itself to Los Altos."

"This one does."

"No!" Bartolome shouted suddenly. "Not, not, not! It is the outrage most emphatic! Wait!" He darted through the glassed door into the lobby.

"I'm sorry," Janet told Doan.

"Why?" he asked, surprised.

"Because you can't take your dog to Los Altos"

"I can," said Doan. "And I'm going to. We always have little difficulties like this when we go places. It's a routine we go through."

A fat man wearing a magnificently tailored white suit and a painful smile came out on the terrace ahead of Bartolome. Bartolome pointed at Carstairs and said dramatically, "There is that which is not to go! Never!"

The fat man said: "I am so sorry. It is not permitted for dogs to ride on the bus."

Doan held up the two tickets and pointed eloquently first to himself and then to Carstairs.

The fat man shook his head. "I'm so sorry, sir, but that ticket does not cover a dog."

"It's made out in his name," said Doan.

The fat man shrugged. "But, you see, when your reservations at the hotel and your tickets for this trip were ordered we did not know that one was for a dog. The dog can stay at the hotel—yes. But he cannot ride on the bus."

Doan nodded casually. "All right. He stays here, then. But you'd better chain him up. He's going to get mad if I go away and leave him."

"Mad?" the fat man repeated doubtfully, looking at Carstairs.

Carstairs didn't open his eyes, but he lifted his upper lip and revealed glistening fangs that were as long as a man's little finger. He growled in a low, deep rumble.

The fat man backed up a step. "Is he dangerous?"

"Definitely," said Doan. "But delicate, too. He will attack anyone who tries to feed him, except me. And if he doesn't eat, he'll die. If he dies, I'll sue you for an enormous sum of money."

The fat man closed his eyes and sighed. "He rides in the bus," he said wearily to Bartolome.

"What?" Bartolome shouted, outraged.

"He rides!" the fat man snarled. "Do you hear me, or shall I repeat myself with a slap in the face?"

"I hear," said Bartolome glumly. He waited until the fat man had strutted back through the door into the lobby and then added: "You obese offspring of incredibly corrupt parents." He turned to Doan and made shooing motions. "Kindly persuade yourselves inside."

A woman opened the glass door and put her head out and shouted deafeningly: "Mortimer!" Instantly she pulled her head in again and slammed the door.

The echoes of her shout hung quivering in the still air, and

Carstairs raised his head and waggled his pricked ears uncomfortably.

The door opened and a man put his head out and yelled: "Mortimer!" He waited while the echoes died, eyeing the people on the terrace accusingly. "You seen him?"

"I don't recall it," Doan told him.

The man said: "I'll kill that little devil one of these days. Mortimer! Come here, damn you!" He got no results, and he sighed drearily and came out on the terrace. He was squat and solid-looking, and he had a red, heavy-jowled face. His clothes were new, and his shoes squeaked. "My name is Henshaw—Wilbur M. Henshaw."

"Mine's Doan. This is Miss Janet Martin."

"Pleased," said Henshaw. "You sure you haven't seen Mortimer? He's my kid. He looks something like Charlie McCarthy."

"How will that do?" Doan asked, pointing at a feather duster that was poked up over the balcony railing.

"Mortimer, you little stinker!" Henshaw shouted. "Come out from behind that chicken!"

The feather duster waggled coyly, and a wizened, freckled, incredibly evil face slid up into sight and peered at them gimlet-eyed through a tangle of bright red hair.

"What's the beef, punchy?" Mortimer said to his father.

"Now, damn it, I'm going to wring your neck if you don't stick around," Henshaw promised grimly. "I mean it. We're going on a sightseeing trip to Los Altos, and I'm not going to spend the whole day chasing you."

"Go chase yourself, glue-brain," Mortimer advised, "and forget to come back." He swarmed up over the railing like a pint-sized pirate boarding a ship. He was wearing the feather duster for a hat, and he had on khaki scout shorts and a khaki blouse. "A dog!" he exclaimed gleefully. "Watch me give him the hotfoot!"

He took a kitchen match from his pocket and began to stalk

the sleeping Carstairs like a big game hunter. Janet started to protest, but Joan winked at her and shook his head.

When Mortimer was still about a yard away, Carstairs sat up and looked at him. Sitting, Carstairs' face was on a level with Mortimer's. Slowly Carstairs opened his mouth until it was wide enough to take in Mortimer's whole head with room to spare. Mortimer stood paralyzed with shock, staring into the yawning red cavern.

Carstairs leaned forward and closed his jaws with a viciously grinding snap just an inch in front of Mortimer's nose.

"Yeow!" Mortimer shrieked. "Yeow! Maw! *Maw!*" He blew across the terrace and through the door into the lobby in a blurred, rust-tipped streak.

"Mister," said Henshaw enthusiastically, "I'll buy that dog! How much?"

"I couldn't sell him," Doan said. "He wouldn't allow it, and besides he supports me in my off-seasons."

"He does?" Janet asked. "How? Does he work?"

"Well," said Doan. "Yes and no. It's a rather delicate subject. You see, there are certain lady Great Danes who clamor for his attentions…."

Janet blushed again. "Oh!"

"Well, would you rent him to me by the day?" Henshaw requested. "I'll be awfully nice to him."

Doan shook his head. "I'm afraid not. I'll have him scare Mortimer for you whenever you want, though, if we're around."

"Friend," said Henshaw, "you do that, and you've got a life-long pal, and I mean it. I'm in the plumbing business—'Better Bathrooms for a Better America.' What's your line?"

"Crime," Doan told him.

"You mean you're a public enemy?" Henshaw asked, interested.

"There have been rumors to that effect," Doan said. "But I claim I'm a private detective."

"Oh," said Henshaw indifferently. "One of them, huh? Well, I always say a man's got to make a living some way."

The woman who had previously shouted for Mortimer appeared. Mortimer was close behind her, peering around her, first on one side and then the other, as she advanced.

"Now, Mortimer," she said firmly, "you show me that dog that attacked you and I'll—Oh! Oh! Wilbur, save me!"

"From what?" Henshaw asked sourly.

The woman pointed a plump, quivering finger at Carstairs. "From that—that horrible thing!" She was wearing a peasant smock and a varicolored full skirt, and she would really have looked like a peasant except that she affected pince-nez glasses with thin gold rims. "It's a savage beast!"

"You bet," Henshaw agreed. "Savage and smart. I've promised him Mortimer for dinner."

"Yeow!" said Mortimer. "Maw!"

The woman said severely: "Wilbur, you stop saying things like that! You know you'll give Mortimer nightmares!"

"Why not?" Henshaw said. "He gives me plenty. This is my wife, folks. Miss Janet Martin and Mr. Doan. When do we start this trip to Los Altos, anyway?"

"On schedule," said Bartolome. "Just as it exactly prints. Be so kind as to entering and sitting on the luxurious seats with legroom."

Doan flicked Carstairs' ear with his forefinger and said: "Up-si-daisy."

Carstairs got up and sauntered over to the bus.

"He's not going with us!" Mrs. Henshaw said shrilly. "Not that awful animal!"

"With my permission, positively not," Bartolome told her. "I refer you to the bloated brigand who proprietors this foul establishment and also the trips of sight-seeing magnificence."

"I won't go!" said Mrs. Henshaw. "And neither will Mortimer!"

"Good," said Henshaw. "See you later."

Mrs. Henshaw turned her head slowly and ominously and peered through the pince-nez at Janet Martin. She looked Janet over detail by detail once, and then repeated the survey, nodding her head knowingly.

"So," she said. "We're going."

"Maw!" said Mortimer. "That dog—"

"Shut up," said Mrs. Henshaw. "I know your father and his lascivious instincts—to my sorrow!"

Doan opened the door of the bus and helped Carstairs in by giving him a heave from the rear. Carstairs paused to look the bus' interior over in a leisurely way and then padded along the aisle to the back. He sat down on the floor and sighed and stared gloomily out the window. Doan elbowed him out of the way and sat down in the seat beside him.

Janet said shyly: "May I please sit here with you?"

"Certainly," said Doan. He put his hand on the side of Carstairs' head and shoved. "Move over, you oaf."

Carstairs grunted and shifted his position. When Janet sat down, he stared at her calculatingly, tilting his head first on one side and then the other. Finally he slid his forefeet out a little, lowering himself, and put his head in her lap.

Doan watched, amazed. "Why, he likes you!"

Janet patted Carstairs' head. "Doesn't he usually like people?"

"No. He hates them. He despises me."

"Despises you!" Janet exclaimed. "But why?"

"Well, I won him in a crap game. He resents that. And then my name's not in the social register, and his is."

"What is it? His name?"

"Carstairs. Dougal's Laird Carstairs to be exact."

"Does he have a pedigree?"

Doan nodded. "Ten miles long."

"Do you ever show him? I mean, enter him in dog shows?"

"Sure. It's just a bore, though. He always wins."

"He must be worth a lot of money."

"I was offered seven thousand dollars for him once," Doan said, sighing. "In cash, too. I turned it down. I wish I knew why."

"I think that's wonderful!" Janet said. "I mean that you didn't sell him."

"I wish he thought so. I hoped it would make him appreciate me, but he just sneered. Do you want to see him sneer? He does it beautifully. Watch." Doan leaned close to Carstairs and said in a stickily coy voice: "Who is Doansie-woansie's cutesy-wutesey 'itty puppy doggy?"

Carstairs looked up slowly and ominously. He raised one side of his upper lip. His eyes glowed golden-yellow and savage.

"I was only fooling," Doan said quickly.

Carstairs watched him warningly for a moment and then slowly lowered his head to Janet's lap again.

"He *can* sneer!" she said. "Horribly!"

"That was one of his milder ones," Doan told her.

"Do you ever punish him?"

"I tried it once," Doan said.

"What happened?"

"He knocked me down and sat on me for three hours. He weighs about a ton. I didn't enjoy myself at all, so I gave up the idea. Anyway, he has better manners than I have."

The Henshaws had seated themselves at the front of the bus, and Henshaw turned around wearily now and called:

"Say, when did that bird with the double-talk tell us we were going to start? Or is this trip just a rumor?"

"Here he comes," said Janet.

Bartolome trotted down the terrace steps and leaned in the door. "Starting instantly in a few moments. Have the kindness of patience in waiting for the more important passengers."

"Who are they?" Henshaw demanded, interested.

"The lady of incredible richness with the name of Patricia Van Osdel and her parasites."

"No fooling!" Henshaw exclaimed. "You hear that, Doan? Patricia Van Osdel. She's the flypaper queen. Her old man invented stickum that flies like the taste of, and he made fifty billion dollars out of it"

"Is she married?" Mrs. Henshaw asked suspiciously.

"That is a vulgarness to which she would not stoop," said Bartolome. "She has a gigolo. They come! Prepare yourselves!"

A short, elderly lady as thin as a pencil, dressed all in black that wrinkled and rustled and glistened in the sun, came out on the terrace and down the steps. She had a long, sallow face with a black wart on one cheek and teeth that popped out of ambush when she opened her mouth.

Henshaw had his hands cupped against the window, peering eagerly. "She sure has aged a lot, or else her pictures flatter her."

The elderly lady poked Bartolome in the chest with a stiff, bony forefinger. "One side!" She swished through the door into the bus, sniffed twice calculatingly, and then took a perfume atomizer from somewhere in her capacious skirt and squirted it in all directions vigorously. She selected a seat and dusted it with quick, irritated flicks of a silk dustcloth.

"Hey," said Henshaw. "Are you Patricia Van Osdel?"

"I am not," said the elderly lady. "I am Maria, her personal maid. Kindly turn around and mind your own business."

"Okay," said Henshaw amiably. He cupped his hands and peered through the window. "Hey! Here she comes! Get a load of this, Doan. Whee!"

The manager appeared, bowing and nodding and waving his hands gracefully in front of a girl who was as fair and fragile looking as a Dresden china doll. She was wearing a long white cloak, and her hair floated like spun gold above it. Her mouth was pink and petulant, but instead of being blue her eyes were a deep, calculating green. Her bearing and her manner and her features were all rigidly aristocratic.

A young man lounged along sullenly a step behind her. He was as magnificently dark as she was fair. He had black curly hair and an incredibly regular profile. He wore white slacks and a white pullover sweater with a blue silk scarf at his throat. He had a pencil-line mustache and long, slanted sideburns.

He stopped on the steps and pointed a forefinger at the bus. "Are we going in that thing?"

"Yes, Greg," said Patricia Van Osdel gently.

"I won't like it," Greg warned. "You know that, don't you?"

"Now, Greg," Patricia Van Osdel chided. "This is the democratic way, you see. This is the way we do things in America. We don't have any rigid class distinctions."

"It stinks," said Greg. "I mean the bus and Mexico and the United States and your democracy. I tell you that quite frankly because it's true."

"Get in the bus, Greg," said Patricia Van Osdel. "Don't be difficult."

"I don't approve of this," Greg said, getting in. "I'm warning you."

The manager and Bartolome handed Patricia Van Osdel gently through the door.

"You will enjoy yourself most exquisitely," the manager promised. "Bartolome, you cretin, point all the most beautiful views and do not hit any bumps. Not one bump, do you understand?"

Greg had seated himself and was glowering out a window. Maria ushered Patricia Van Osdel carefully to the seat she had selected and dusted.

The stir of movement floated some of the perfume to the back of the bus, and Carstairs sneezed and then sneezed again, more emphatically.

Maria jumped and glared. "That!" she said imperiously. "Out!"

"It is only a dog," the manager said quickly.

"A dog of the most intelligent marvelousness," Bartolome added.

"Please!" said Maria.

"Oh, no!" the manager denied, horrified.

"Emphatically never!" Bartolome seconded. "It is a dog of the most delicate and refined nature."

"It's quite all right," Patricia Van Osdel told her. She smiled at Doan and Janet. "I like dogs. They have so much character. Don't they, Greg?"

"No," said Greg.

Henshaw cleared his throat. "My name is Henshaw—"

"Who cares?" Greg inquired coldly.

"Greg," said Patricia Van Osdel, "now please be pleasant. Mr. Henshaw, I'm very glad to know you. And this is your wife and little boy? What a nice family group you make! I'm sure you all know who I am. This lady is my maid, Maria. And this is my refugee friend, Gregor Dvanisnos." She turned graciously toward the back of the bus. "And your names?"

"Doan," said Doan. "And this is Miss Janet Martin. On the floor, here, is Carstairs."

"Carstairs!" Patricia Van Osdel repeated, smiling. "What an amusing name for a dog!"

Carstairs opened one eye and looked at her and mumbled malignantly under his breath.

"Now!" said Patricia Van Osdel brightly. "We all know each other, don't we? We can all be friends having a pleasant day's excursion together, and that's the way it should be. That's the American tradition of equality. Although, in a way you are really all my guests."

"In what way?" Doan asked.

Patricia Van Osdel moved her shoulders gracefully. "It's really nothing. There was some silly hitch, some petty regulation— The hotel was going to cancel this trip to Los Altos until I persuaded them not to."

"How did you persuade them?" Doan inquired.

"Well, Mr. Doan, to be frank I bribed them. Money is a bore, but it's useful sometimes, isn't it?"

"So they tell me," said Doan. "Why did you bribe them?"

"Because I was determined to see Los Altos, of course. You've surely read about it, or you wouldn't be going there. A peaceful, picturesque village of stalwart peasants isolated deep in the mountains—happy in their primitive and peaceful way—unspoiled by the brutalizing forces of civilization. Why, until just recently, since the new military highroad was opened, there was no way to get there except by mule back. The village is famous for its peaceful, archaic atmosphere."

"Is that the only reason you bribed them to put on the trip?" Doan asked. "Just because you wanted to see the peaceful, peaceful peasants at play?"

"You're awfully curious, Mr. Doan, aren't you?"

"He's a detective," said Henshaw. "All them guys do is make trouble and ask questions."

Patricia Van Osdel's voice was sharp suddenly. "A detective? Are you a customs spy?"

"No," said Doan. "Why? Are you going to smuggle some jewelry into the United States?"

Patricia Van Osdel was still smiling, but her eyes narrowed just slightly. "Mr. Doan, I know you're joking, but you shouldn't suggest such a thing even in fun. You know that the very existence of our great country depends on all of us—rich and poor, wellborn and humble—obeying the exact letter of every law. Naturally I wouldn't dream of defrauding the government by not declaring any small jewels I may purchase."

"Oh," said Doan. "Well, I just asked."

"Yeah," said Henshaw. "And I'm just asking when we start this grand tour, if ever?"

"On schedule with preciseness," said Bartolome. "Instantly as printed. As soon as I consult with the tires, oil and gasoline."

"Species of a mumbling moron!" the manager snarled. "In! Start! Now!"

CHAPTER II

IN LOS ALTOS, there had been a rumor going the rounds that some rich tourists from the United States who were staying at the Hotel Azteca outside Mazalar were going to make the bus trip up to Los Altos. It was obvious, of course, that this rumor wasn't entirely to be trusted. Anyone with any brains or a radio knew that the people from the United States were too busy raising hell up and down the world to have any time to look at scenery except through a bombsight.

But tourists of any brand had been so remarkably scarce of late that the mere hint of their impending arrival was enough to touch off a sort of impromptu fiesta. The inhabitants of Los Altos shook the mothballs out of their scrapes, mantillas, rebozas and similar bric-a-brac and prepared to look colorful at the drop of a sombrero. They gathered in the marketplace with their pigs and chickens and burros and dogs and children, and slept, argued, bellowed, squealed, cackled or urinated on the age-old pavement according to their various natural urges.

All this was very boring to a man who, for the time being, was named Garcia. He sat and drank beer the general color and consistency of warm vinegar, and glowered. He had a thin, yellowish face and a straggling black mustache, and he was cross-eyed. He should really have been more interested in the tourists coming from the Hotel Azteca, because in a short time one of them was going to shoot him dead. However, he didn't know that, and had you told him he would have laughed or spat in your eye or perhaps both. He was a bad man.

He was sitting now in the Dos Hermanos, which was according to its brotherly proprietors, a cafe very high class. It was one door off the marketplace on the street running north. Since it was early and no one yet had any money to get drunk on and Garcia looked mean, he was the only customer. One of the proprietors was sleeping with his head on the bar while flies explored gingerly in the dark and gusty cavern of his mouth.

Garcia could look out the open front of the cafe and see kitty-corner across the marketplace, but it was hard for anyone outside to see him.

Private Serez of the Mexican Army had found that out some time ago. He was in the abandoned building directly across the street from the cafe. He was lying on his stomach on some very rough boards peering out and down through a high, glassless window. His rifle, bayonet attached, lay beside him. He was very tired, and his eyes ached, and his elbows were sore. He wanted a cigarette, a beer, and a siesta in that order, but he didn't really think he was going to get any of them for a long time to come.

The reason for this pessimism was a sergeant by the name of Obrian, also of the Mexican Army. Sergeant Obrian had inherited a red mustache and a violent temper from his Irish grandfather, and he was very sticky about having his commands obeyed literally. He had ordered Private Serez to lie right where he was and keep out of sight and watch Garcia with all due vigilance. Private Serez knew he had better do just that and keep on doing it until he got some further orders.

Even as he was thinking drearily about the prospect, he heard a board creak in the hall outside the closed door of his watch-room. That would be Sergeant Obrian with his bad disposition and worse vocabulary coming around to check up. Private Serez wiggled himself higher on his sore elbows and looked out the window in as soldierly and alert a manner as possible.

The heavy, wrought-iron door hinges creaked just slightly, and then something hit the floorboards beside Private Serez with a heavy thud. He looked back over his shoulder. The door was closing again very gently, but Private Serez didn't even notice it.

He was staring in paralyzed horror at what had made the thud. That was a diamondback rattlesnake five feet long and thicker around the middle than a man's doubled biceps.

The snake had had its rattles clipped off and had been submitted to other indignities that hadn't improved its temper. It whipped back into a coil—all lithely sinister muscle—and struck. It missed Private Serez's leg by half an inch.

He yelled—loudly. He could no more have helped that than he could have helped breathing. He scrambled frantically on the floor, grabbing for his rifle, trying to get back out of range of the next strike. There was no furniture in the room. The snake was between Private Serez and the door. He jumped for the only other place that promised temporary refuge. He climbed right up into the window.

Garcia heard the yell. He looked up, and he saw Private Serez in the window. His yellowish face showed neither shock nor fear, but his lips peeled back thinly from his teeth, and he drew a thick, nickel-plated revolver from his coat pocket. He got up from his table, watching the proprietor. The proprietor mumbled and rolled his head on the bar, faintly disturbed by the yell, but luckily for him he didn't wake up. Garcia went quietly to the back of the room, opened the door there and went down a short passageway past a kitchen that smelled abominably. At the end of the passageway he opened another door and stepped out into a small, high-walled patio paved with garbage and less mentionable refuse.

He was halfway across the patio, heading for the side door, when a soldier stood up behind the back wall. Garcia and the soldier stared at each other, rigid with surprise, for the space of two heartbeats, and then Garcia whipped up his revolver and fired.

The report was a flat, ragged crash, and the bullet hit the soldier just under his chin. He clapped both hands to his throat and flopped backwards out of sight. Garcia opened the side door and looked at the butcher who owned the shop next to the cafe.

The butcher had been interrupted in the process of carving up a skinny cow with the aid of three cats and one million flies. He opened his mouth to yell, but he didn't, because Garcia hit him on top of the head with the revolver and knocked him flat. The cats went in three directions, and the flies droned up in an angry swarm and then settled back on the beef and the butcher indiscriminately.

Garcia didn't hurry. He went cautiously along the alley in the direction of the marketplace, sliding along one wall with the revolver thrust out ahead of him. He reached the alley-mouth and peered out. The people in the marketplace were beginning to stir and wonder uneasily.

Sergeant Obrian stood up on the roof of a building two doors away and leaned over the parapet, peering down to see what was happening. Garcia raised his revolver and aimed carefully at him. He was shooting up at an angle and against the sun. He missed by six inches. The bullet slapped a silvery blob of lead against the adobe. Instantly Sergeant Obrian dropped back out of sight behind the parapet.

In the same split second, Private Serez managed to spear the rattlesnake with his bayonet. He didn't know exactly what to do with it now that he had it, so he pitched it out the window into the marketplace. The snake, still writhing, fell across the nose of a burro below. The burro kicked out backward with both heels and hit its master squarely in the stomach. He fell down and screamed and flailed the ground with his arms.

The burro stamped on the snake and then ran away, and the butcher woke up and yelled, and the whole marketplace went off like a time bomb. All the people decided they would go somewhere else right away and, if possible, take their various dependents, human and animal, along with them. The confusion was something terrific, and Garcia stepped right into the middle of it and disappeared.

CHAPTER III

THE ROLLED GRAVEL road was like a clean white ribbon laid in graceful loops along the side of the mountain that towered red and enormous up into the thin, clear blue of the sky. Heat waves shimmered and wiggled above bare rock, and the dust from the bus' passage drifted back in a lazy plume. The engine burbled and muttered to itself in quiet protest over the steepness of the grade.

"This is a pretty sizeable rock pile," Henshaw volunteered, trying to look out the window and up toward the summit.

"Kindly do not waste the astonishment," Bartolome ordered. "This is not yet the magnificence. This is called 'La Cabeza,' the head, because that is its name. The scenery here is only ordinarily wonderful." Janet Martin's eyes were shining. "It's the beginning of the middle range," she said in a low voice to Doan. "One of Cortez's lieutenants discovered it. He thought the whole length of the range looked like a sleeping woman. He saw it first from the other side of Azela Valley—a hundred and ten miles from here."

"What was the guy's name?" Doan asked.

"Lieutenant Emile Perona. He was a soldier of fortune—an adventurer. He was the younger son of a very noble Spanish family, and he was one of the first men to come to America. He loved this country—its beauty and its ruggedness. It just suited his own nature."

"Was he handsome?" Doan asked, watching her.

"Oh, yes," said Janet softly. "Very. He was tall and hawk-faced and dark, with piercing eyes and a smile that seemed like a light in a darkened room. He was ruthless and cruel, too, as all brave men could be cruel in those old days, but he had integrity and honesty—" Her voice trailed away dreamily.

"You seem to know him pretty well," Doan observed, "seeing he's been dead for four hundred years or so."

"I read about him," Janet said.

"I can read, too," said Doan, "and often *do.* But I never ran across Lieutenant Perona. Where'd you find him?"

"He was mentioned in Cortez's reports."

"Did Cortez say he was handsome?"

"No," Janet said stiffly.

"Tell me some more," Doan invited.

Janet shook her head. "No. You're laughing at me."

"I'm not," Doan denied. "Neither is Carstairs. We like you."

"Do you—do you think I look sexy?"

"What?" Doan said, startled.

Janet was blushing furiously. "You don't! You weren't think-ing of anything like that!"

"I was, too," Doan contradicted. "I was just working up to it in a roundabout way."

"Now you are laughing at me!" Janet bit down hard on her lower lip. "I don't care! It's not true, and it's wicked to make girls think it is!"

"What's not true?" Doan inquired.

"What they say in novels and movies about how you can go to beauty parlors and fix yourself all over and men will be—will be attracted to you."

"In a nice way, of course," Doan added.

"No!" said Janet angrily. "I don't want them to be attracted in a nice way!"

"I can work up a pretty fair leer if you give me time," Doan offered. "Will that help?"

"You stop making fun of me!"

Greg turned around in his seat and looked back at them. "Miss Martin, is that detective fellow annoying you?"

"What?" Janet said blankly.

"He looks like that sort," Greg said. "Wouldn't you like to sit up here with me?"

"Greg," said Patricia Van Osdel. "If you want someone to sit with you, Maria will."

Greg ignored her. He was smiling, and his teeth were white and glistening under the pencil-line mustache. He had quite a personality when he wanted to exert it. It hung around him like an aura.

Maria got up, and Greg turned to look at her with the slow,

dangerous movement of a snake picking out the place it is going to bite.

"Stay where you are, you hag," Greg said evenly. Maria sat down again quickly.

"I'll sit next to you, then, Greg," Patricia Van Osdel said sweetly.

"When I ask you to—not before," Greg told her. "Won't you join me, Miss Martin?"

"Thank you," Janet said uncertainly. "But—I'm quite comfortable here."

"Later, then," Greg said, and he made the two words a promise and an insinuation.

Janet sat still, her face stiff and surprised looking. Patricia Van Osdel watched her with greenish, calculating eyes.

Henshaw cleared his throat.

"The scenery we came to see," said Mrs. Henshaw, "is outside the bus."

"Yeah," Henshaw agreed absently. "Pretty, huh?"

"How do you know?" Mrs. Henshaw asked.

"Huh?" said Henshaw. "Oh." He peered industriously out through the window.

"Feel better now?" Doan murmured to Janet.

"Oh!" said Janet. "Why, then, it must be true about beauty parlors!"

"Undoubtedly," Doan agreed.

"I know it makes me sound awfully stupid," said Janet, "but you see I did spend seventy-five dollars in them before I started, and I was beginning to be very disappointed in the results. No men seemed to—to look at me. I mean—"

"I know what you mean," Doan told her.

Janet stretched out her legs. Carstairs grunted in sleepy protest as his headrest was shifted, but he didn't open his eyes. Janet looked at her legs thoughtfully.

"Are they the kind of legs men like?" she asked.

Doan studied them judicially. "Yes."

"I'm not wearing any stockings."

"I noticed."

"My toenails are tinted."

"Very prettily, too," Doan commented.

Janet relaxed again and sighed contentedly. "I can't believe I'm here and that this is really happening. It's much more wonderful even than I'd dreamed it would be. I've just got to talk to somebody. Can I tell you about it?"

"On one condition," said Doan. "And that is that you don't confess any crimes. Just because I'm a detective people are always taking advantage of me and confessing. You can't imagine how boring that is."

Janet looked at him. "Why, I should think you'd want people to confess to you. It would save so much time."

"That's the point," Doan told her. "I don't want to save time. I get paid by the week. The longer a job takes, the more I make. I always try to stretch them out, but it's pretty hard to do. Take the last one I was on, for instance. A clerk embezzled fifty grand or so from a loan company. No sooner did I walk in the joint and ask him his name than he started to confess."

"What did you do, then?" Janet asked, fascinated.

"Shut him up, of course, and went around making like I was looking for clues. But the guy wouldn't drop it. He haunted me. Every time I sat down to rest my feet, he started confessing all over again. It got so obvious I had to arrest him."

"Well, is that—ethical? I mean to—to stall around like you did?"

"Is it what?" Doan said.

"Ethical."

"I'm a detective," said Doan. "A private detective."

"Don't private detectives have ethics?"

"I don't know," Doan answered, frowning. "I never thought

about it. I'll have to look the matter up sometime. But what was it you were going to tell me?"

"You won't laugh or make fun?"

"I promise."

"I'm a schoolteacher," Janet whispered.

Doan looked shocked. "No!"

"You promised!"

"I'm sober as a judge," Doan said.

Janet said: "I'm a schoolteacher in the Wisteria Young Ladies' Seminary."

"Now, after all," said Doan.

"It's true! There is such a place, and I teach in it. I'm on a leave of absence to visit my sick aunt. I haven't any aunt, of course. I haven't any relatives at all. I was raised in an orphanage—until I was eighteen. It was horrible there. We had to wear *uniforms!* With cotton stockings that were all prickly and lumpy."

"That's bad," Doan agreed.

"The orphanage got me a job at the seminary. I'm really very clever at studies and books. But little girls are horrible people, specially rich ones—and I was just a frump and—and a drab. I never saw any men, and if I did they didn't see me. And the seminary is in a small town and terribly strict and conservative, and I was just turning right into an old maid!"

"Until you discovered Mexico and Cortez—and Lieutenant Perona."

"Yes. I was studying Spanish because the seminary is going to give courses in it. They never did before, because it wasn't refined enough. But now, with all the horrible things that are happening in Europe—"

"Lots of people are rediscovering America," Doan commented. "Including our flypaper queen up ahead. She never got closer to the United States than the south of France or Bali until Hitler and Hirohito started on the prowl. Now she's suddenly discovered she's wild about democracy. But go on—you were studying Spanish."

"It's such a beautiful language! And then I got interested in the countries where it is spoken, and their histories. I read just thousands of books. Even dusty old manuscripts that had never been printed. The seminary has a marvelous historical library that no one ever uses. I read all about Cortez and his men, and then I came across the diary of a man called Gil De Lico. He was a scribe—a sort of a secretary and historian for Cortez. He kept all the official records, and he wrote this diary just for his family back in Spain. He traveled around with Lieutenant Perona, and he wrote lots about him. They were good friends. I—I feel as though I knew them both—personally, I mean."

"I understand," said Doan.

"And then I started reading about modern Mexico—the way the country they traveled through looks and is now. It—it's perfectly fascinating!"

"I know," said Doan.

Janet's eyes were shining. "I had to come and see it! I *had* to! I've never had a real vacation in all my life, and I saved and saved, and I came. I'm here! I'm really and truly here in Mexico!"

"That's right," Doan told her.

"Oh, you don't know how I've dreamed about it. All the glamour, and color and—and romance! I ached for it until I could hardly stand it, and there I was teaching horrid, stupid, rich girls how to parse French verbs!"

"Hunting for romance is much more fun," Doan said.

Janet nodded seriously. "It is, and that's just what I'm doing. I know it's foolish and crazy, but I've done sensible things all my life. I was getting—getting moldy! A girl has a *right to* romance and glamour and—and other things, hasn't she? There's nothing wrong with that, is there?"

"Not a thing," Doan said. "I hope you find romance by the carload. If I see any, I'll run it down and hogtie it for you."

Janet sighed again. "I feel better now that I've told somebody." She said suddenly and seriously, "What are you looking for?"

"A cop."

"A policeman?" Janet inquired blankly.

"Yeah. From the United States."

"Well, what's he doing in Mexico?"

"Hiding."

"Why? Did he commit some crime?"

"Oh, I suppose so," Doan said indifferently.

"Well, are you going to find him and bring him back to justice?"

"What?" said Doan, startled. "Me? No! I'm going to persuade him to keep on hiding."

"But why?"

"Because I'm hired to," Doan answered patiently.

"I don't understand," said Janet. "Why were you hired to persuade him to keep hiding?"

"He's not like you. He doesn't like Mexico. He can't speak Spanish, and the food gives him indigestion, and he doesn't think the people are friendly. He says he would rather be in the United States—even if he's in jail—than to have to stay here any longer."

"You mean he wants to come back and give himself up and answer for his crimes?"

"Yeah."

"And you're going to try to persuade him not to?"

"Not try," Doan corrected. "I am going to persuade him."

"But that's wrong! That's against the law!"

"It probably will be before I'm through," Doan admitted casually.

Janet stared at him. "Well then, you shouldn't do it, Mr. Doan. Why don't you let this man surrender like he wants to?"

Doan sighed. "The guy—Eldridge is his name—was a police captain in Bay City. They had a big graft scandal and a grand jury investigation there. Everybody in the city administration was involved. So the rest of them persuaded Eldridge to beat it to Mexico. Then they said he was to blame for everything that had happened since the city was founded. If he came back, he would pop off about some of his old pals. They're still holding their jobs, and they want to keep them. They won't if Eldridge starts telling secrets."

Janet studied over it for a moment. "It doesn't sound quite—quite *honest* to me, some way. Are you sure you have your facts right, Mr. Doan?"

"Reasonably sure," said Doan.

"Oh," said Janet, still studying. "Well, perhaps these other city officials are afraid Eldridge would tell *lies* about them if he came back?"

"He'd certainly do that," Doan agreed. "He couldn't tell the truth if he tried."

"That's it, then!" said Janet triumphantly. "I understand it all now."

"That's good," said Doan.

"Of course, I knew all the time that you wouldn't do anything that was *really* dishonest."

"Oh, no," said Doan. "Not me."

The road dipped into a little swale and slid through the deep shadow between two needle-like rock pinnacles. A black and white striped board, like a railroad crossing guard, swung out slowly and blocked the way. Bartolome yelped angrily and hit the brake so hard that everything movable in the bus slid forward six inches.

The bus stopped with its radiator a foot from the board. Bartolome leaned out the window and screeched fiercely, "Do not delay this bus under extreme penalties. It contains tourists of the most vital!"

There were two soldiers standing beside the braced white pivot from which the warning gate swung. They were small men with dark and impassive faces. They stared gravely at the bus. Neither of them said anything.

"What's all this?" Henshaw demanded.

"Is a military outpost," Bartolome explained, "full of soldiers of the most incredible stupidity. Kindly ignore the unforgivable insolence of this delay." He yelled out at the soldiers again: "Donkeys! Elevate the gate instantly!"

The soldiers stared, unmoving and unmoved. There was a little white building, so small it reminded Doan of the cupola of an old-fashioned roof, pushed in against the steep rock face. A man came out of it now.

"You!" Bartolome shouted belligerently. "There will be punishments of unbelievable severity—" He caught a glimpse of the man's face. His mouth stayed open, but he didn't say anything more.

The man walked up to the bus. He was wearing a field uniform, and there were no rank markings on it. He was short and thickset, and there was a broad white scar on his right cheek. His eyes were as cold as greenish glass. He spoke English in a flat, toneless voice without any accent.

"Yes?" he said, looking up at Bartolome. "You wanted something?"

Bartolome swallowed. "This is the bus of sight-seeing from the Hotel Azteca," he said meekly. "Is of the utmost harmlessness and innocence."

The thickset man said: "You were asked not to schedule this trip to Los Altos."

"Not I!" Bartolome protested. "I am only a humble employee of that flesh-laden criminal who owns the Hotel Azteca."

Patricia Van Osdel opened the window beside her. "What is it, please? Why can't we go to Los Altos?"

"It is not advisable."

"Why not?"

"There is trouble in Los Altos."

"What trouble?" Patricia Van Osdel demanded

"It is a military matter and not a concern of civilians."

"Nonsense!" said Patricia Van Osdel. "I've paid a great deal to take this trip, and I intend to finish it."

"Why?" the thickset man asked casually.

"What? Well—well, to see the scenery and buy some native handicrafts—"

"The scenery," said the thickset man, "and the handicrafts will be there after the trouble is gone. I would wait, if I were you."

"Are you proposing to stop us by force?" Patricia Van Osdel demanded.

"Not I, senorita. I never stand between fools and their follies. I have warned you. That is the end of my responsibility. Now you may do as you please."

"We will!" Patricia Van Osdel snapped. "Bartolome, drive on! Drive on!"

The soldiers swung the warning board aside, and the bus rumbled slowly past it and picked up speed. Patricia Van Osdel's thin face was flushed, and she was breathing rapidly.

Henshaw cleared his throat. "Say, who was that tough-looking monkey?"

"Major Nacio," Bartolome answered soberly. "A very great bandit chaser. A supremely superb fighter."

"Well, that don't give him any right to try to scare us. Where does he get that trouble talk? He's just tryin' to show off his authority, that's all."

"Soldiers are always fools," said Greg.

"What army do you belong to?" Doan asked.

"Greg is going to join the United States Army just as soon as we return from this trip!" Patricia Van Osdel snapped. "Aren't you, Greg?"

"No," said Greg.

"And besides," said Patricia Van Osdel, ignoring the answer, "just why aren't you in service, Mr. Doan?"

"Aw, they wouldn't let him in the army," Henshaw said. "They got rules against admitting detectives and immoral characters like that."

"It's not true!" Janet protested.

"It certainly is," Mrs. Henshaw informed her. "They wouldn't let our boys be submitted to any influences like that."

Janet poked Doan in the ribs. "Why don't you answer them?"

"I wouldn't lower myself," said Doan disdainfully. "Anyway, Carstairs is in the army."

"What?" Janet said, amazed.

"Yes, he is," Doan assured her. "He trains dogs to help defend airfields and things. He's on furlough now."

"How does he train them?" Janet asked curiously.

"I'm his assistant and interpreter and orderly. I tell him what the other dogs are supposed to do, and he does it a few times while they watch. Then I tell them to do it, and if they don't, Carstairs reasons with them."

"How?" Janet inquired.

"Show her," Doan ordered.

Carstairs mumbled sleepily.

"We didn't like that," Doan told him. "Again."

Carstairs didn't open his eyes, but he made a noise like a buzz saw hitting a nail in a log. Janet jumped and jerked her hands away from his head.

"That was better," Doan said. "Go to sleep again, but no snoring." Carstairs yawned stickily and wiggled his head into a more comfortable position on Janet's lap.

CHAPTER IV

IT WAS JUST after noon now, and the sun was a hot, brassy disc in the thin blue bowl of the sky. The bus rumbled labori-

ously around a hairpin turn at the summit of a straight, mile-
long climb and paused there, puffing.

"Now," said Bartolome. "This is the scenery nearly supreme.
Have the goodness to admire it."

Azela Valley spread out below them—an incredibly enormous raw-red gash with nothing green in it to hide the jagged
rock formations, with nothing alive anywhere, nothing moving
except the tireless heat waves. It stretched endlessly down, down
and away from them, like the landscape of a new world that
was as yet only half-formed. As their eyes traveled over it, trying
to comprehend its immensity, the red shaded slowly into bluish
rust and then into dull, flat brown in the distance. On beyond,
still further away, mountains rose steep and serrated and savage
against the horizon.

"Wow!" said Henshaw softly.

Doan said to Janet: "Your lieutenant—Perona—came across
that?"

She nodded, her eyes wide. "Yes. He walked most of the way.
His horse was lame."

"Was he wearing armor, too?"

"Yes."

"What a man," said Doan.

"It looks like a city dump," said Henshaw. "Multiplied by
seven hundred million. What lives there, Barty?"

"Rattlesnakes," said Bartolome.

"They can have it," said Henshaw.

"It is one hundred and fifty miles with no road and no water,"
said Bartolome, "to Santa Lucia on the other side of those
mountains."

"I don't want to go there," Henshaw told him. "Where's Los
Altos?"

"It approaches," said Bartolome, releasing the brake. The road
wove in and out along the mountain top, and the valley followed
it, unending and unchanging, stalking them with sinister pa-

tience, until suddenly they turned inward between narrow, massive rock walls. Shadows folded down over them darkly.

The road straightened and tilted down like a long, smooth chute. Bartolome kept dabbing at the foot brake, but the bus gathered speed until the wind whistled breathlessly past the windows and Doan could hear a queer, light singing in his ears. "Hey, Barty!" Henshaw said, alarmed.

"Quiet, please," said Bartolome.

The moan of the tires grew higher and higher, and then abruptly the cut opened away from them, bringing the sun in a bright flood, and the road stretched as straight and clean as a tight-wire with nothing on either side of it.

"Yeow!" Mortimer yelled suddenly.

The brakes groaned dismally, and the thick, hot smell of the linings came up into the bus. The tires caught and slid, screaming like souls in torment, and the bus rocked and slewed and suddenly stopped.

"Now observe," said Bartolome.

There was a choked silence for a long time.

Henshaw coughed finally. "What's holdin' this road up here where it is?"

"Is not a road," said Bartolome. "Is a bridge. Kindly get out and exclaim in appreciation."

They got out slowly and stiffly, reluctant to leave the island of comparative safety that was the bus. Carstairs sat down and looked bored and put upon. Mortimer went crawling to the edge of the road and peered over.

"Hey!" he said in a strangled voice. "There ain't nothin' under us but air!"

"That's just what I was afraid of," said Henshaw. "Let's get the hell out of here."

"Observe," Bartolome repeated. "One long span unsupported except at either end."

They could see it more in perspective now, and it was still

like a tight-wire strung across space that was a canyon so deep that the sunlight could not penetrate it and the shadows grew darker and darker in its depths until they blended into a thick, formless haze that had no bottom. The steel supports underneath the anchoring pillars were intertwined like spiderwebs and looked as delicately fragile. The wind was a hot, smooth rush in their faces.

"The Canyon of Black Shadow," said Bartolome proudly. "By the bridge, two minutes across. Before the bridge, by mule trail, three days to get down, one day to rest, three days to get up the other side—total one week."

"Did Perona cross this, too?" Doan asked.

Janet nodded, staring down into the shadows. "Yes. The first time he saw it he didn't believe his guides when they said it could be crossed, and he didn't want to risk his men; so he went down and up the other side alone and then came back to get the others."

"I'd like to have met him," said Doan.

He found a big white rock that someone had left as a marker and heaved it over the side. It glistened in the sunlight and slid down smoothly into the shadow and was gone. Everyone waited, listening.

There was no sound.

"That stone," said Bartolome severely, "was a possession of the government."

"I'll go right down and bring it back," Doan promised. "Lend me your parachute."

"I wanna go home!" Mortimer wailed.

"Where's Los Altos, Barty?" Henshaw demanded.

"There," said Bartolome.

They could see it high above them on the other side of the canyon, red roofs and white walls, neat and dainty in the clear air, clinging to what looked like the barren side of a cliff.

"Let's go," said Henshaw.

They climbed back into the bus, and it rumbled on across the threadlike span and commenced to climb on a road that was much narrower and more twisting than the new highway. Bartolome blew his horn at each curve.

"Burros," he explained. "They are often walking in the road and violating the traffic."

The road slanted up a rock ledge, followed its crooked, steeple-like summit for a while, dipped down and turned again, and they were in Los Altos.

The street was narrow and paved raggedly with dark rock. It was like one tread of a steep stairway, with houses going on above it and on down below. The walls of the houses were not quite so white and neat, seen more closely. They were blank, aged faces with cracks like jagged wrinkles in them and narrow, iron-barred windows for eyes and iron-studded doors for mouths.

There was no one in sight. The bus rolled along, rumbling vacantly, to the point where the street widened into the market square. It was empty.

"Is this a ghost town?" Henshaw asked.

Bartolome's mouth was open. He stopped the bus at the curb and got out and looked around. He put his hands over his eyes, took them away, and looked again. The marketplace was still empty. He got in the car and blew the horn loudly and repeatedly. It made noise, but nothing else happened. He got out of the bus again.

"There is no one here," he said in a small, unbelieving voice. "It is unreasonable."

The passengers climbed out of the bus one by one and stood in the street close together, staring uneasily.

"What do you suppose it is?" Janet whispered to Doan.

"I don't know," Doan said. "But I've got a feeling it's something we won't like."

There was a ragged, blunt report that echoed dully. Instantly afterwards a man spun out of a narrow alleyway across the square. It was Garcia approaching his destination. He still had his shiny revolver in his hand, but he wasn't so well in control of the situation any more. He was breathing in great, sobbing gasps, and he stopped and tried to steady himself and fired twice back into the alleyway.

"Revolution!" Henshaw said shakily.

"Revolutions are forbidden," Bartolome said in a numb, incredulous voice.

Garcia turned and ran toward them. His mouth was wide open with the agony of breathing, and his eyes were glazed blearily. He didn't see the bus or its passengers until he was no more than thirty paces from them.

He half tripped, then, and staggered sideways, but the shiny revolver flipped up in his hand and roared again. The bullet popped metallically against the side of the bus. There was a sudden chorus of yells and a thin, bubbling scream from Mrs. Henshaw.

Doan put his left hand against Janet's shoulder and pushed hard. With his right hand he drew a short, stubby-barreled revolver from under his coat. He produced it as casually as a man would take out a cigarette lighter. He kneed Carstairs out of the way and walked steadily toward Garcia.

"Drop that gun," he said conversationally. "Now."

Garcia fired at him. The bullet went over Doan's head and hit a wall somewhere and bounced off in a whooping ricochet. Doan shot at him, and Garcia sat down suddenly on the pavement, looking blandly incredulous. He stared at Doan, his teeth white and jagged under his stringy mustache, and then he raised his right hand slowly.

Doan's second bullet hit him in the mouth. Garcia fell backwards, and his head made a wet, thick sound as it hit the ground. He didn't move again. Carstairs growled softly from behind Doan.

"I know," Doan said. He was leaning forward tensely, watching the alley from which Garcia had appeared.

A second man jumped out into sight and dropped instantly on one knee. He was carrying a Luger automatic with a long, thin barrel.

"Alto ahi!" he called sharply. *"Manos arriba!"*

"Same to you," said Doan.

They stared at each other for long dragging seconds. The kneeling man turned his head a little at last, taking in the huddled passengers, the parked bus. He smiled suddenly and nodded once. He spoke in smooth, unaccented English

"You may put away your gun now."

"So may you," said Doan.

The man laughed and slid the Luger inside his coat. He was dressed in a tan gabardine suit that was rumpled and smeared with dust. He was young and very tall, and he had a quick, sure way of moving. His features were thin and even, and his eyes were a deep blue-gray with a hard little twinkle of amusement in them. He got up and walked over to Garcia and prodded him casually with the toe of one brown oxford. Garcia's head rolled loosely. Blood spilled slickly from the corner of his mouth.

"Dead," said the tall man. "That is unfortunate."

"For him," Doan agreed.

The tall man studied Doan thoughtfully. "Ah, yes. A little, mild, fat man with an enormous dog. We were expecting you, but not quite so soon. What is the name? I have it! Doan! The detective who looks so harmlessly stupid."

"I know how you look, too," said Doan. "But what's your name?"

"I am Captain Emile Perona."

"Oh!" Janet exclaimed.

Perona looked at her. "Yes, senorita?"

"Oh," said Janet, staring with eyes that were enormously dilated.

"What is it, senorita?" Captain Perona asked politely. "Are you ill?"

"No," said Doan. "She's a little surprised, and so am I. You've been promoted since the last time we heard of you, although I suppose anyone could work up from lieutenant to captain in four hundred years."

"What?" said Captain Perona.

"How is Cortez getting along these days?"

Captain Perona frowned. "Perhaps I do not understand your language as well as I thought. The only Cortez I know of is the great explorer and conqueror of this country."

"That's the boy. Didn't you serve under him?"

"Please do not be ridiculous. It is quite useless for you to try to disarm my suspicions with silly remarks. My ancestor—the first Emile Perona—was one of Cortez's lieutenants, but that is none of your business and has nothing whatsoever to do with your presence here—which, I may add, we consider not only unfortunate but undesirable."

"Well, thanks," said Doan.

Captain Perona pointed to Garcia. "We were warned that things like this happen when you are in the vicinity."

"Somebody's been kidding you," said Doan.

"You shot this man."

"Well, certainly," said Doan. "But he shot at me first. Ask anybody. He shot at me twice, in fact, and was all set to go again. What was I supposed to do—stand here and make noises like a target?"

"He saved our lives!" Janet said indignantly.

Captain Perona looked at her, and his eyes sharpened suddenly. "Why were you so startled when you heard my name?"

"B-because we were just talking about the other Emile Perona on the way here."

"Why?"

"I'd read about him—"

"Where?"

"In—in Cortez's reports—"

"In that diary, too," Doan reminded.

"Diary!" Captain Perona snapped. "What diary?"

Janet said uncertainly: "Well.... Well...."

Captain Perona came a long, pouncing step closer to her. "What diary?"

Janet swallowed. "Gil De Lico's diary."

"Hah!" said Captain Perona, expelling his breath triumphantly. "I thought so!"

A soldier trotted wearily out of the alley across the square. He came to a sudden halt, half raising his rifle, when he saw the bus and passengers. He stood there peering uncertainly for a moment and then turned and yelled back into the alley

"Aqui! Aqui esta el capitan!"

He trudged toward them, bayonet glittering dangerously. Three other soldiers came out of the alley and trailed along behind him.

"Hey, pop," said Mortimer. "This fella ain't got no back to his head, and his mouth is all full of pieces of teeth and blood and stuff."

"Mortimer!" Mrs. Henshaw warned. "You come right here! Don't you look!"

"Why not?" Mortimer asked reasonably. "He ain't near as sliced up as them two guys I saw in that auto wreck last summer."

"Police!" Mrs. Henshaw screamed. "Police!"

Captain Perona looked at her impatiently. "Senora, please be quiet. I am the police."

"What police?" Doan asked.

"The Military Secret Police."

It seemed that this was true enough because the first soldier—Sergeant Obrian of the red mustache and the evil temper—came up and saluted Perona and stood waiting for orders.

Captain Perona pointed absently to Garcia. "Take that away somewhere."

"Yes, sir," said Sergeant Obrian.

"What army is this, anyway?" Doan inquired.

"The Mexican Army, dumbness," said Sergeant Obrian. "I can speak your lingo on account I used to be a waiter in double New York."

"Where?" Doan said.

"New York, New York. It ain't New York City—didn't you know that? It's New York. Just like Mexico City is Mexico."

"Take that body away," said Captain Perona.

"Si, Capitan!" said Sergeant Obrian.

He snarled at his three soldiers. One of them—Private Serez—had a black eye and a limp. They slung their rifles and picked Garcia up and carried him down the street. One of his skinny legs swung loose, and his heel dragged on the pavement with a sly, grating sound.

Captain Perona hadn't taken his eyes from Janet. "Where is that diary, senorita?"

"What?"

"You have it, eh? Give it to me."

"Why, I—I don't—"

"I think you lie."

"I bet this is that old-time Mexican courtesy," Doan observed.

Captain Perona said shortly, "Be quiet. This is important to me. That diary belongs to my family. It is a very precious heirloom. I want it."

"Inquire at the Wisteria Young Ladies' Seminary," Doan advised.

"At what?" Captain Perona asked blankly.

"I didn't believe there could be such a joint, either, but there is, and she teaches in it. That's where she read the diary. It belongs to the school."

"It does not. It belongs to me. Is it true that you found the diary at the school, senorita?"

Janet nodded. "Yes."

"Where is the school?"

"Valley View, Ohio."

"I will go there at once," said Captain Perona.

"Wait a minute," Doan said. "Before you go, suppose you sort of explain this and that."

"Eh?" said Captain Perona.

Doan made a wide gesture. "The shooting and the soldiers and the dead man and where all the people are hiding—"

There was no longer any need to ask about the people. They appeared as suddenly and as thickly as a mob on the stage. Every door and most windows on the street disgorged a few, and they scurried around breathlessly, slamming up wood shutters, hauling counters of goods out on the pavement. Someone clanged a gong, and a little girl shrieked shrilly.

"Is American speaken in this store very nice! Is prices guaranteed cheapest on anything! Here, here, here! Beautiful, beautiful! Cheap, cheap!"

"Feelthy pictures?" a sly little man whispered in Doan's ear. He saw Captain Perona looking his way and disappeared in the crowd like a puff of smoke.

A fat, thick-shouldered woman tackled Mrs. Henshaw. "Serape! See? Hand wove most pretty! Cheap!"

Three mongrel dogs came up and barked at Carstairs. Carstairs closed his eyes and looked bored. Doan rapped him sharply on top of the head with his knuckles and said:

"None of that, now."

"What did he do?" Janet demanded.

"Nothing, yet. He hates mongrels—especially ones that bark at him. He was just getting ready to tear a leg off the nearest one. Carstairs. Relax."

Carstairs opened his eyes and leered malignantly at the three mongrels. They went away quickly.

"Come this way, please," said Captain Perona. He took Janet's arm and led her through the crowd, fending off storekeepers and souvenir salesmen by merely scowling at them. Doan trailed right behind.

Clear of the crowd, Captain Perona said to Janet: "Please pardon the way I spoke to you. I am very anxious to recover that diary. For many years we have been trying to trace it."

"I hate to interrupt," said Doan, "but how about that bird I killed?"

Captain Perona shrugged. "You should not have done that, really. It is annoying."

"No doubt," said Doan. "But who was he?"

Captain Perona shrugged again. "He called himself Garcia most of the time, I believe. He was of no importance in himself. He was allowed to escape from the Islas Tres Marias."

"The what?" Doan asked.

"You heard me,"

Janet said: "It's a Mexican prison. It's on an island like Alcatraz. It's for the most dangerous confirmed criminals."

Captain Perona nodded. "Correct."

"You say he was allowed to escape?" Doan inquired.

"Yes. At my orders. I wanted to follow him in order to find a confederate of his. I followed him here successfully, but then his confederate threw a rattlesnake at one of my men and frightened him so badly that he shouted and thus let Garcia know that he was being watched."

"A rattlesnake?" Doan repeated. "Threw it?"

"Yes."

"That confederate must be sort of a tough bimbo," Doan observed. "No wonder you wanted to find him. Did you?"

"Did we find him? No. But now we are positive he is here somewhere in Los Altos, so we will soon. I had hoped that if we kept chasing Garcia back and forth through the town long enough his confederate would try to help him, but of course you spoiled that possibility."

"Who is this confederate, anyway?"

"It is a military matter," Captain Perona said, politely but definitely.

"Oh," said Doan. "Well, what should I do now? Go and lock myself in jail?"

"No. I will make the proper reports to the authorities. This is a military district. You may go and see the Senor Eldridge. He lives on the Avenida Revolucion—three streets up and south one block. I will talk to the senorita."

"Okay with you?" Doan asked Janet.

She nodded, a little uncertain. "I wanted to look at a little church"

"I know the one you mean," Captain Perona said. "It is no longer a church, but it is kept as a museum. I will take you there."

"So long, then," said Doan.

Captain Perona said: "One moment, please. As I told you, we have been expecting you. You may go and see Senor Eldridge, but you are not to strike him or beat him or torture him in any other manner to persuade him not to return to the United States as he wishes to do. If you harm him, you will be held very strictly to account."

"Me?" said Doan. "Torture him?"

"We have heard of your methods of detection," said Captain Perona stiffly. "They are not allowed in Mexico. You are warned."

"I am warned," Doan admitted. "Come on, Carstairs."

CHAPTER V

THE AVENIDA REVOLUCION was narrow and straggling and dusty, built on a slope so steep that even the road itself had a tilt to it. The houses were older and more decrepit than those on the main street, with tiles on their roofs missing and plaster crumbling at the corners of the walls.

The people here evidently weren't sure the shooting was over. Faces peered through barred windows at Doan and Carstairs, but there was no one on the street. Several dogs came out of hiding to investigate Carstairs, and he began to dawdle along pretending to snip at the walls while he watched them out of the corners of his eyes.

Doan bunted him in the rear with his knee. "Go on. Keep moving."

Carstairs swung his head toward the sightseers and lifted his upper lip. The dogs went away yipping in incredulous terror. Carstairs ambled arrogantly on ahead of Doan. He stopped at the corner and looked around it, ears pricked inquiringly, and Doan stopped beside him to look, too.

There was nothing in the little jog in the street except an easel, looking like a foreshortened skeleton of an Indian tepee, with a big canvas fastened on it. There was no sign of the artist.

Doan walked up to the easel and examined the canvas. It was a half-finished painting, and he turned his head first one way and then the other, trying to figure out what it was meant to represent.

"Hey, you!"

Doan turned and after a moment spotted the source of the voice. It was coming out of the barred porthole of the front door of a house across the street.

"Yes?" he said.

"Have they nailed that gun-crazy screwball?"

"Yes," said Doan.

"You're sure?"

"Sort of," said Doan.

The door opened and a woman came out. She was short and squat and broad without being a bit fat. She had an upstanding mane of gray hair that frizzed wildly around a face as lined and weather-beaten as an old boot. She wore an orange painter's smock and a floppy pair of moccasins.

"A hell of a note," she said. "Shooting in the streets. How can you paint with stuff like that going on? What's your name, and where'd you come from?"

"Doan. United States."

"I'm Amanda Tracy. Ever heard of me? Don't lie."

"No," said Doan.

"Good. Know anything about art?"

"No."

"Fine. What do you think of that picture?"

Doan studied it again. "Well—"

"It's lousy, isn't it? It looks like a cold fried egg in a pan of congealed grease, doesn't it?"

"Yes," Doan admitted.

Amanda Tracy whacked him on the back so hard his neck snapped. "That's the old pepper, fatso! Now I know it'll sell! If they stink, they sell. Always. Remember that when you start painting pictures."

"Okay," said Doan, feeling the back of his neck tenderly.

Amanda Tracy pointed at Carstairs. "Where'd you get that stilt-legged abortion?"

"I won him in a crap game," said Doan. "And he's not an abortion. He's a very fine dog."

"The only good dog is a dead dog, Doan. No one but morons and perverts keep pets. Are you a pervert?"

"No," said Doan. "Just a moron."

"Good," said Amanda Tracy. "I like morons. Did you come on the bus with that burbling little twerp of a Bartolome?"

"Yes."

"Any more morons come with you?"

"A couple," Doan admitted.

"Any dough in the crowd?"

"Plenty."

Amanda Tracy picked up the easel, painting and all. "Then I'll go down and paint in the marketplace and act artistic as all hell and probably I can take some sucker for a dime or two. See you later."

"Wait a minute," Doan requested. "Do you know which of these houses Eldridge lives in?"

"Don't tell me you're a friend of that mealy-mouthed rum-dumb."

"No friend," said Doan. "But which house?"

"Second one around the jog. See you later, fatso. Keep your nose clean."

"All right," said Doan.

He watched her stride solidly around the corner and out of sight down the slope, easel trailing behind her.

"That's quite a character," he said absently to Carstairs. "Let's go."

They went on around the jog. The second house was set a little apart from its neighbors. The bars on the front windows were newer and thicker and not so ornamental, and it was walled up high with no windows at all on either side.

There was a knocker in the shape of a stirrup on the wide, arched front door, and Doan hammered it loudly. He could hear the echoes inside the house, sodden and dull, but there was no answer.

Doan waited awhile and banged the knocker again, even more emphatically. There was still no answer, and he tried the long, wrought-iron latch. It clicked, and the big door swung silently and slowly inward. Carstairs growled in a low rumble.

"Shut up," said Doan.

He stepped into a narrow hallway. The air felt still and moist and cool against his face. He blinked his eyes, trying to ac-custom them to the deep shadow. The hall was floored with stone, and its walls were dimly white.

Doan jerked his head at Carstairs. "Come in, lame-brain."

Carstairs' growl raised a little in tone. He stood with his feet braced in the doorway, head lowered. His eyes glistened dully. Doan caught him by his spiked collar and hauled him inside. "Don't get temperamental with me."

Carstairs' claws scraped on the floor, and then a voice—a little sad and a little thick—said, "I guess he smells the blood."

The man who had spoken was standing in the shadow of a draped doorway back a little along the hall. His face was invisible, but he was short and thick-bodied, and he was holding a revolver in his right hand.

Doan let go of Carstairs and straightened up slowly. "Eldridge?" he asked.

"Yes."

"Are you planning on using that gun in the near future, or are you just carrying it around to scare small children?"

"Oh," said Eldridge. "This? Well, I guess I'm kinda scared, to tell the truth. You're Doan, huh? I mean, I know you on account of the dog. I'm glad you got here so quick. You wanna drink?"

"Sure."

Eldridge led the way along the hall and out into the bright-walled enclosure of a tiled patio. There were palms and ferns, green and lacy, around the borders, and a fountain burbled softly in the center.

Carstairs strolled over and lapped at the water and then turned his head to watch Doan, drops drooling from his broad muzzle. When Doan glanced at him, he ambled over to a green trash box half hidden behind a fern against the back wall. He snorted once at it and then came back and sat down beside the fountain and began to pant comfortably.

"What's in the box?" Doan asked.

"That was what he smelled, all right," Eldridge said. "Go look."

Doan walked over and lifted the hinged lid. The box was half filled with empty cans and bottles. A small dog that looked like a dusty, black mop lay on top of them. The dog's eyes were rolled back, and its tongue protruded purple-red between its teeth. Its throat had been cut.

"Nice," said Doan, dropping the lid. "Are you saving it for supper?"

"That there was a nice dog," said Eldridge. "It wasn't no fancy number like you got, but it was a friendly little guy, and I think it maybe liked me."

"So you killed it."

"Now, Doan," said Eldridge. "You know I wouldn't do a dirty thing like that."

"Who did, then?"

"A fella," said Eldridge vaguely. "A fella that don't like me, I guess." He had very light blue eyes shot with reddened veins, and even when he was relaxed, as he was now, his hands shook slightly. His thick body had a weakened, self-pitying sag. "Sit down, Doan."

Doan sat down in one of the rawhide easy chairs. Eldridge walked slowly over to another one that was pushed flush against the back wall of the house. He lowered himself into it laboriously, breathing hard.

"Want a drink, Doan?"

"I haven't changed my mind," Doan answered.

"Concha!" Eldridge called. "Whiskey!"

A girl came through the rear door of the patio. She was carrying a bottle and two glasses on a tray. She was young and slim and lithe, and her hair gleamed blue-black in the sunlight. Her eyes were lowered modestly, and the front of her dress was just lowered.

"Pour him one," Eldridge said. "It's Johnny Walker Black, Doan. You want a chaser or a mix?"

"No," said Doan, watching Concha. "Where'd you find this little gadget?"

Concha presented the tray to Eldridge, and he poured himself an eight-fingered dollop.

"This here is that fella Doan I told you about, Concha," he said. "Concha's my wife, Doan."

"Another?" Doan asked. "What did you do with the one you left in the States?"

"Oh, I divorced her."

"Does she know it?"

"I guess not," Eldridge admitted. "I just never did get around to telling her about it."

Doan raised his glass to take a sip and looked at Concha over the top of it. Her eyes weren't lowered now. They were staring at Doan with such pure venom in them that he could feel it plainly at a distance of ten feet. He lowered his glass very carefully.

"Come here, honey," he said softly. "You take a sip of this before I drink it."

Concha stepped closer and jerked the glass out of his fingers. She didn't drink out of it. She threw it at the patio wall. It made a crunch and an ugly little splatter against the clean white plaster.

"Now Concha, lovey," said Eldridge mildly.

Concha went back through the rear door and slammed it violently behind her.

"She's shy with strangers," said Eldridge.

"I never would have guessed it," Doan told him.

"But don't think she'd poison your drink. Why, she don't know any more about poison than I do."

"That's what I was afraid of."

"Well, have a drink out of the bottle, then."

"I'll sit this one out," Doan said. "You go ahead and get drunk for both of us."

"Okay." Eldridge took a big gulp of whiskey and sighed contentedly. "Well, Doan, how much are they offering?"

"How much is who offering of what?" Doan asked.

"Dough. How much are the boys willing to pay?"

"Oh, that. They said the best they could do was dollar sign decimal zero zero."

"Dollar sign decimal—" Eldridge sat up straight with a jerk. "What? You mean, nothing?"

"Correct," said Doan.

"Why, they can't do this to me! I'm gonna go right back to the States and raise hell!"

"Oh, no."

"Why ain't I?"

"Look real closely," Doan invited.

"At you?" Eldridge said. "You mean you think you could stop me?"

"Yes," said Doan.

"Hah!" said Eldridge, taking another drink. "Well, you couldn't. And even if you could—for a little while—there's nothing to prevent me from going back as soon as you leave."

"I know one thing that would."

"What?" Eldridge asked skeptically.

"A funeral," Doan said. "Yours."

"Well, of course, if I was dead I couldn't—Hey! Just what do you mean by that?"

"Just what you think I mean."

Eldridge had laid his revolver down in his lap. He picked the gun up now and looked warily from it to Doan. Doan didn't move a muscle. Eldridge put the revolver down again and took another drink.

"You wouldn't dare pull anything like that in Mexico," he said defensively. "You ain't got no drag down here, and I have."

Doan shrugged. "Do you remember the guy who was district attorney when you pulled out of Bay City?"

"You mean Bumpy? Sure, I remember that oily little rat."

"He's going to be elected governor any minute now."

"Bumpy?" Eldridge said incredulously. "Governor?"

"Yes. If somebody got in trouble down here, Bumpy could fix it for the guy to be charged with treason or murder or something and then request the Mexican government to extradite him. As soon as the guy got out of Mexico, Bumpy could kill the charge against him."

Eldridge stared. "Bumpy never thought that one up—he's too dumb!"

"I thought it up," said Doan. "Before I came down here."

"What a twister you are!" said Eldridge admiringly. He sat still for a moment, thinking. "How much are you making out of this, Doan?"

"Just my salary—a hundred and fifty a week. I figured the job would take four weeks, and if it does I can jump my expense account for another four hundred."

"A thousand bucks," Eldridge said. "Not bad—not good. How would you like to make another thousand in a hurry?"

"Just dandy."

"Ummm," said Eldridge. "Bumpy.... Governor.... That sort of throws a new light on the situation. Now I wasn't kidding the boys, Doan, about not being so fond of this dump. The people ain't friendly. They don't seem to like me."

"I can't imagine why not," Doan observed.

"Neither can I. It bothers me. It ain't as if I wasn't legitimate. If I was a crook on the lam or something, it'd be different. But just because there was a little misunderstanding about some presents I took— Why, all cops take honest graft! You know that yourself, Doan."

"Oh, sure," said Doan.

"But, of course, I was kiddin' about wantin' to go to jail. Nobody with good sense wants to go to jail. I was just tryin' to shake the boys up a little bit."

"Sure," Doan repeated. "I thought I heard you say something about a thousand dollars."

"I'm coming to that. I wouldn't go to jail if Bumpy was governor. I know enough about him to hang him six times. He wouldn't dare even sneeze at me. Why, I could damned near own that state, Doan! Now listen. Supposing you missed fire on this job—supposing I turned up in the States right away—would you lose your job with the agency you're working for?"

"No," said Doan. "They don't dare fire me. I know too much about the outfit."

Eldridge nodded. "I figured you would. All right, Doan. I'll give you a thousand bucks the day I step over the border into the United States. No use tryin' to pump the price up any higher than that, because I ain't got any more."

"It's a deal," said Doan.

"No!" Concha shrieked. She came out of the rear door like a small whirlwind and stood in front of Eldridge's chair and stamped her foot. "No! You big drunker! You big cheat! You do not take the college money! No!"

"What's this?" Doan asked. "Are you going to college, Eldridge?"

"No," Eldridge said. "Concha is. Acting college. In Hollywood. She's going to be a movie star."

"Think of that," Doan remarked.

"Big liar!" Concha said to Eldridge. "You promise to send me! Thief!"

"Now, lovey."

Concha pointed at Doan. "Why do you give him my money? Why, why, why? He is nothing! He is not even a policeman!"

"He's a private detective."

"Pah! Not here! Not in my country! Here he is nothing but what he looks like! Nothing but a little man with too much fats and a big, lazy dog."

"That's right," Doan admitted, looking down at Carstairs, who was sleeping peacefully.

Concha stamped both feet, one after the other. "You do not give him my money! No, no, no!"

"Now, lovey," said Eldridge. "Why don't you be reasonable. A thousand dollars! Chicken-feed! Peanuts! When I get back, Bumpy is gonna give me the key to the state treasury, and I can run in and fill my pockets any old time. I'll buy you a movie studio—just for you!"

"Pah! Big-mouth!"

"Now, now. Be nice, lovey."

"You give me the ditch! You try for run away with this fats and leave me!"

"Aw, Concha," said Eldridge. "Now you know I wouldn't do that. I love you."

"Pah! Pooey! I spit!" She did.

"Lovey," said Eldridge persuasively. "I'm gonna make you famous. You'll be the best actress in the world. I'll give you fur coats and dresses and rings and a house with an inside toilet. I mean it!"

Concha leaned close over him. "Coward!"

"I'm not, neither!"

"Bautiste Bonofile!" Concha hissed at him.

Eldridge cringed slightly and took a quick drink.

"See?" Concha sneered. "You are with the shakes like the jello! You think to give the fats my money to keep away Bautiste Bonofile. Pah! Bautiste Bonofile takes the fats in one bite. Crunch, crunch, crunch! Then he takes the big, dumb dog in another bite. Crunch, crunch, crunch!"

"You've got it all wrong, Concha," said Eldridge. "This is just a business deal. We're gonna make a big profit, and we'll be rich."

"You—don't—give—the—fats—my—money!"

"Yes," said Eldridge.

"No! No, no, no! I'm telling Colonel Callao! He fixes you and the fats, too! He shoots you both! Bang, bang, bang! Pah!"

She whirled and ran across the patio and through the door into the hallway. The front door of the house boomed behind her like a sullen gun. Eldridge smiled painfully at Doan and shrugged his shoulders.

"So far," said Doan, "I'm due to be eaten—crunch, crunch, crunch—and then shot for dessert."

"Concha exaggerates," Eldridge told him.

"Yes. But how much? Who is Colonel Callao?"

"This is a military district, and he's supposed to be in charge of it. He's a dope."

"Is he a friend of Concha's?"

"Yeah. Anyway, he was. I sort of acquired her from him."

"How?" Doan asked curiously.

"I married her—or so they tell me. I don't remember much about it. I was drunk at the time."

"How about the other party she mentioned?"

"Him?" Eldridge said vaguely. "Oh, I was gonna mention him to you. It might be that he'd start a little something or other if I was to leave here, and then maybe you'd have to calm him down. He's the gent who cut my dog's throat."

"What's his name?"

"Bautiste Bonofile. At least, that was his name. I don't know what he calls himself now."

"All right," said Doan. "I'll go have a chat with him. Where is he?"

"I don't know."

"Well, what does he look like?"

"I don't know that, either."

"Maybe it would help if you explained a bit," Doan suggested.

Eldridge sighed. "There were two of them at first—brothers. Bautiste and Louis Bonofile. They were Canadian breeds—half some kind of Indian. They were always tough guys. They served a few terms in Canadian jails, and then they sneaked across into the United States. They were arrested in a dozen states for everything in the book, but they only served a couple of short terms. The rest was probation, parole, bailskips, indictment quashed, insufficient evidence—"

"The payoff," Doan finished.

"Yeah. Bautiste was the one who could put in the fixes. He was sharper than a razor, but he finally got caught short on a federal charge and had to beat it. He came to Mexico. Louis stayed in the United States. He was a dumb one. Just a killer. I nailed him for shooting a clerk in a cigar store during a ten dollar holdup."

"And he couldn't fix you?"

"Not for ten dollars. And he didn't have any other dough, so naturally he got hung. I mean, I had to turn somebody up once in awhile, or how could I have kept my job?"

"Sure," said Doan. "So Bautiste blames me for gettin' Louis hung. He claims I framed Louis."

"Did you?"

"Well, yes. He was guilty, though—I think. Bautiste wrote me some dirty letters at the time, but I didn't worry because I knew he didn't dare come back to the United States, and I figured he'd forget it or get killed pretty quick, but he didn't. He's here in Los Altos and he's still mad. He's been writin' me notes about what he's gonna do to me when he gets to it, and throwin' rocks and knives in the windows and cutting my dog's throat and dirty stuff like that. He's mean. He says he wants to make me suffer before he finishes me off. He wants to scare me."

"Of course he hasn't succeeded."

Eldridge reached for the whiskey. "Naw, I just laugh it off." The neck of the bottle rattled a little against the edge of his glass. "The hell of it is, I don't know who he is now. I've never seen him when he was pullin' his tricks. He might be anybody in the damned town. He's had years to get himself a new name and a new identity, and he did a honey of a job. Even Perona hasn't been able to dig him out."

"Perona?" Doan repeated. "Captain Perona? What's he got to do with it? I thought he was in the Intelligence or something."

"He is. That's why he's looking for Bautiste Bonofile. Did you ever hear of Zapata?"

"No."

"Well, Pancho Villa was to Zapata what Mussolini is to Hitler. I mean, Zapata was big stuff. He controlled all of middle Mexico at one time—even took over Mexico City. He was a revolutionary raider, not a bandit or a holdup man. He was an Indian, and he didn't like white men. Bautiste Bonofile got in with him because Bautiste was part Indian. He was one of Zapata's lieutenants for a long time. That was a long time ago. Bautiste is no spring chicken. He's older than I am a lot."

"Tell me more," Doan invited.

"Zapata was killed finally, and his army was broken up. Bautiste took over his own particular company and started playing bandit. The government ran him down and killed most of his men and put Bautiste away on the Islas Tres Marias."

"I've heard of it," said Doan.

"Yeah. After a few years Bautiste crushed out. They've never had hold of him since, and that was ten-fifteen years ago. He could be anybody by this time."

"Why does the government want him so badly? They seem to be taking quite a lot of trouble."

"Well, in the old days in Mexico the government was very corrupt at times. An officer of the army would have the right to purchase supplies for his men. Some of them who commanded twenty or thirty soldiers would order supplies—and rifles and ammunition—to equip five hundred. If no one protested the orders, the seller kicked back a percentage on the deal."

"I wondered how so many of those old-time Mexican generals got to be millionaires."

"They had a soft racket," Eldridge said regretfully. "Anyway, all the stuff they couldn't use, they just stored. Zapata, when he raided military outposts and forts and such, picked up thousands of rifles and millions of rounds of ammunition. What he couldn't use, he hid. Bautiste knows where he did the hiding. This is a bad time to have thousands of rifles lying around loose. They're old now, but they're Mausers, and they could be used."

"Yes," said Doan thoughtfully. "Hitler's army uses Mausers. I can see why the government might be a little worried about the matter. Why doesn't Bautiste cough up and make a deal?"

"Naw," said Eldridge. "Not him. He's mean. Anyway, the government wouldn't deal with him. He's a murderer about ninety times over."

"That's nice to know," Doan observed. "So Concha was right. You were going to pay me a thousand dollars to stand in front of you when Bautiste started shooting."

Eldridge dropped his glass, and it made a little tinkling sound. "Doan! You ain't gonna back out! We made a deal! You promised! You got to keep Bautiste off my back until I can get out of here!"

"What's the good of that? He'll just follow you."

"Naw! He couldn't do that—not with Perona after him. Perona is smart, and with the country at war like it is, he's got all kinds of power and the whole army to hunt with. Bautiste will have to stay under cover right where he is now—which is here in Los Altos. Once I get away from here, I'll be free as the air."

"After," Doan said warningly, "you pay me a thousand dollars."

"Sure. That's what I meant."

"If I got you to the border in one piece," Doan said, "and you didn't have the thousand dollars, I wouldn't think it was a bit funny. And you wouldn't, either."

"I've got it. I'll pay you. Why, I wouldn't double-cross you, Doan!"

"Not twice," Doan agreed. "What about Concha?"

"Oh, her. She stays here, of course."

"After all that song and dance about Hollywood and a house with an inside toilet?"

Eldridge shrugged. "You know how a guy talks to a dame. I was only fooling. What would I want with a little stupe like her? Once I contact Bumpy I'll get something really fancy. Colonel Callao can have Concha back."

"I have an idea," Doan said, "that when Colonel Callao finds out he's going to get Concha back, we're going to have more trouble with him than we do with Bautiste Bonofile."

"Callao's a dope, like I said. And besides that, he's ignorant."

"I hope so," said Doan. He stood up. "Well, I'm going to find Perona now and tell him you and I have come to an agreement, and after that we can arrange—"

The tiles moved slightly under his feet. It was just a slight shudder back and forth that made his knees feel queerly stiff and numb. Carstairs got up very quickly.

"That's just an earth tremor," said Eldridge. "We have them all the time here. There's a fault through this range. We never have a serious one—not what you'd call an earthquake or anything like that."

The tiles moved in a quick little jerk. Carstairs barked angrily at Doan.

"Shut up, you fool," Doan told him. "I'm not responsible for this."

The tiles rippled. There was no other word for it. It was as though someone had stirred their hard surface with a spoon, and they cracked and crumbled and split. Doan went staggering, and dust came up hot and acrid into his nostrils. Carstairs sneezed indignantly.

There was a long, ominous rumble that was like thunder but more terrible and spine-chilling, and the earth began to move back and forth slowly and relentlessly. Doan went headlong. Carstairs scrambled desperately for his balance, slipped and fell hard on tiles that were slick from the water that had been in the fountain.

The dust was a thick veil, and through it things clumped and banged and groaned weirdly. The patio mall moved and hovered over Doan, and before he could get up it moved back again reluctantly, back and back at an impossible angle, and then it crumbled away and hit the ground, and dust rose from it in a yellow, rolling puff like a smoke signal. The noise of its fall was lost in the greater jarring rumble that came from everywhere.

The seconds dragged like hollow centuries. Doan got up, and the ground moved out from under him, and he went down again. Carstairs clawed frantically, breathing in short, hard snarls, trying to get his feet under him. The ground stopped jerking, and quivered like jelly and then quieted.

Doan sat up and looked across the patio. Eldridge was still sitting in his chair against the house wall. His eyes were bulged wide, and he moved his lips stiffly. Everything was suddenly deathly still.

Very slowly, as if it were tired now, the earth moved up and then dropped back again. In the house, timbers screamed like agonized things, and then the roof sagged a little and started to slide.

Doan's throat was tight. "Eldridge! Look out!"

Eldridge tried to move, tried to fight out of his chair, and then a solid waterfall of plaster and tile and broken adobe poured down over him.

Doan got up and scrambled toward the pile of debris. It had knocked Eldridge forward and down. Doan heaved at a broken timber, threw it sideways, pulled out another. He clawed tile and thick chunks of adobe right and left behind him, and then he saw Eldridge's head and shoulders, queerly flattened and deflated, gray with plaster dust.

Doan dug his hands under Eldridge's armpits and hauled back. A tile fell off the roof and tucked into the ground beside him, and the top of the house wall crumbled slightly. Doan heaved again, and then Eldridge was free. Doan dragged him toward the empty space at the side of the patio where the wall had fallen outward.

Eldridge was limp and unmoving, but he was breathing in

short, choked gasps. His legs and lower body were twisted grotesquely askew.

Doan took his handkerchief from his coat pocket and dampened it in the water that was left in the fountain. He wiped the layer of plaster dust from Eldridge's face and saw that there was a thin trickle of bright, arterial blood coming out of the corner of Eldridge's mouth.

Eldridge opened his eyes. "Why, Doan," he said in a faint, surprised voice.

"Take it easy," said Doan.

"Why, what're you looking at me that way for, Doan? I ain't hurt. I can't feel—Doan!"

"Take it easy," said Doan. "Don't try to move."

"Doan! My legs won't— Doan! Something's wrong with me! Don't stand there! Get a doctor!"

"A doctor won't do you any good."

"Doan! I'm not—I'm not—"

"Yes," said Doan.

Eldridge's face was purple-red, and his throat bulged with his straining effort to hold up his head.

"No! I won't—I can't— Bumpy... governor whole state.... No! Doan! You're lying, damn you!"

"Your back's broken," said Doan. "And you're all scrambled up inside."

Eldridge's breath bubbled and sputtered in his throat. His lips pulled back and showed the blood on his teeth, and he said thickly but very clearly:

"God damn you to hell."

His head rolled limply to one side. Doan stood up lowly. He looked at the wadded, damp handkerchief in his hand and then dropped it with a little distasteful grimace.

From behind him a voice said: "You will stand still, if you please."

Doan didn't move, but he looked at Carstairs murderously.

Carstairs was involved in a complicated exercise that would enable him to lick one hind paw. His legs were sprawled out eccentrically in all directions, and he stared back at Doan with an expression of sheepish apology.

"You brainless, incompetent giraffe," said Doan.

"Do not blame your dog for not warning you," said the voice behind him. "I was downwind, and I can move so very quietly sometimes. Please do stand still."

Doan didn't move his arms or legs or body or head, but he flicked his eyes to the left, then looked at Carstairs, and then flicked them to the left again. Carstairs got up instantly and began to sidle to his own right.

"No," said the voice. "I would not like to kill your dog. Stop him."

Doan nodded once. Carstairs sat down, watching him.

"No," said the voice.

Doan nodded again. Carstairs slid his forelegs out slowly and sprawled on the broken tiles.

"That is so much better," said the voice. "Your dog is beautifully trained. It would be a shame if he were hurt. I think you have a gun. Do not try to use it. Keep your hands away from your body and turn around slowly."

Doan turned around. The voice belonged to a thin, elderly man who looked very neat and well-tailored in a gray tweed suit. He had a long nose and a shapeless, bulging mustache, and he wore thick glasses that distorted his watery blue eyes. He had no gun, but he was holding a rolled green umbrella under his right arm, and Doan was not so foolish as to think it was actually only an umbrella.

"What is your name?"

"Doan," said Doan. "What's yours?"

"I am Lepicik. Were you robbing that man?"

"I hadn't gotten around to it yet."

"Did you kill him?"

"No," said Doan. "The earthquake did. We just had one, or didn't you notice?"

"Yes," said Lepicik pleasantly. "It was quite violent, wasn't it? From where did you come here?"

"From the Hotel Azteca in Mazalar."

"You have been staying there?"

"For a couple of days."

"How did you come here to Los Altos? By what means of travel?"

"On a sight-seeing bus."

"Who came with you?"

"Why?" Doan asked.

Lepicik moved the umbrella slightly. "You would really be so much wiser to answer my questions."

"Okay," said Doan. "An heiress by the name of Patricia Van Osdel and her maid, name of Maria, and her gigolo, name of Greg. A man named Henshaw and his wife and kid. A school-teacher by the name of Janet Martin."

"Thank you," said Lepicik. "Thank you so very much. Good day."

"Good day," said Doan.

Lepicik walked backwards away from him. He didn't hesitate or feel his way. He walked as confidently as though he had eyes in the back of his head. He disappeared around the edge of the broken patio wall.

Doan leaned over and picked up a chunk of adobe and hurled it at Carstairs. Carstairs jumped up nimbly and let the adobe skid harmlessly under him.

"What do you think I drag you around for?" Doan demanded angrily. "Keep your eyes open after this."

Carstairs looked even more apologetic than he had at first. He moved back and forth in tight, uneasy steps, lowering his head.

"All right," said Doan. "Come on, and we'll see if there's anyone else left alive in this town."

CHAPTER VI

WHEN DOAN LEFT them at the corner, Janet and Captain Perona stood still for a moment watching him trudge up the slope toward the Avenida Revolucion with Carstairs wandering along ahead of him.

"Why did you say that to him?" Janet demanded.

"I beg pardon?" said Captain Perona.

"Why did you warn him about torturing and beating Eldridge? That's perfect nonsense."

"I think not," Captain Perona denied.

"Mr. Doan is a very mild, polite, pleasant person. He would no more torture anyone than I would."

"Oh, yes," said Captain Perona. "We have his record, you see. He is what you call a private detective. Very successful. His record is full of violence. He does not care at all what he does to solve a case. But he never quite gets caught breaking the law. He is very clever and very lucky."

"Clever!" Janet echoed incredulously. "Mr. Doan? Why—why, he's the most talkative, open, naive, boyish—"

"Oh, no," said Captain Perona positively. "That is also in his record. He fools people with his innocent manner, but he is not innocent in the slightest. Assuredly not."

"I think you're just making this up."

"Senorita," said Captain Perona, "I do not make things up, if you please."

"Well, you're mistaken, then."

"And I do not make mistakes."

"Not ever?" Janet asked in an awed tone.

"No. I am—" Captain Perona stopped short, staring narrowly at her. "So you are mocking me!"

"Yes," said Janet.

Captain Perona breathed hard. "I will forgive you—this time, senorita. Mocking people and ridiculing them is, I understand, a custom in your detestable country."

"My what?" Janet said, stung.

"The United States. I have heard that its people are very ignorant and uncouth."

"They are not!"

"Especially the women. They have loud, shrill voices, and they shout in public."

"They do not!" Janet cried.

Captain Perano smiled at her blandly. Several passersby turned to look curiously at her. She began to blush, and she put her hand up to her lips. "You see?" asked Captain Perona. "Even you do it. Shouting in public is considered very unmannerly in Mexico."

Janet said in a choked whisper: "You said those things just to make me mad so I'd raise my voice and—and make myself look foolish!"

"That is correct," said Captain Perona. "And you did. Very foolish."

"Please go away and leave me alone."

"No," said Captain Perona.

Janet turned around and started blindly across the marketplace. After three steps she staggered just a little, groping for her balance, and then Captain Perona's hand was under her arm, supporting her.

"You are ill, senorita?" he asked. There was no mockery in his voice now.

Janet said: "If—if I could just sit down...."

"Here, senorita! This way. The bench. One step and now another...."

Janet sank down on the cool stone of the bench in a shaded niche in the thick wall. The wavery black haze in front of her eyes cleared away, and she could see Captain Perona's thin, worried face.

"It's nothing," she said breathlessly. "I'm all right now, really. It—it was just that man. The dead man. I'd never seen a man killed before, and—and I tried to act—to act nonchalant. But the blood and the way his face looked and his leg dragging when they carried him away...."

Captain Perona sat down beside her. "It is understandable, of course. Do not think about him any more. He is not worth it, and besides he killed one of my soldiers when he first discovered we were watching him. I was going to kill him sooner or later, myself."

"Talk about something else, please," Janet begged.

"Surely," said Captain Perona. "We will talk about Gil De Lico's diary, because I wish to know much more about it. What is the name of this place where you found it, again?"

"The Wisteria Young Ladies' Seminary."

"How peculiar," said Captain Perona. "It seems odd to me to name a school such a thing. Who owns it—the state?"

"Oh, no. It's a private school."

"I see. What is the name of the owner?"

"Why—why, I think it's a corporation. I mean, it isn't *owned* by anyone. Different people contributed money to found it."

"Do you know who these people were?"

"Some of them."

"Would one be called Ruggles?"

"Oh, yes! Ebenezer Ruggles. He was the main founder. He was a very old-fashioned, strict, conservative sort of man, and he thought colleges were teaching girls too much they shouldn't know. Nobody would pay any attention to his ideas, so he started a school of his own. He's been dead for several years now."

"Good," said Captain Perona. "He was a thief."

"Ebenezer Ruggles?"

"Yes."

"Are you sure?"

"Yes. My mother told me so."

"What?" Janet said blankly.

"My mother told me so. My family did not realize they had been robbed by this Ruggles criminal until she told them. But she knows. She knows everything about people from the United States because she came from there herself."

"You mean, your mother is an American?"

Captain Perona looked at her. "That is a very disgusting habit your countrymen have. Calling themselves Americans as though they were the only ones. I will have you know that Mexicans are Americans. We are more Americans than people from the United States are, because we came to America before they did."

"I'm sorry," Janet said meekly.

"You should be. Kindly be more careful of your language in the future. My ancestor, Emile Perona, was one of the first men to come to this continent. That is why we wish Gil De Lico's diary. It was presented to our family by the family of Gil De Lico three hundred-odd years ago. I can show you the presentation letter if you wish to see it, although you could not read it, of course."

"Yes, I could."

"No," said Captain Perona patronizingly. "It is in old-fashioned Spanish and written in script."

"I could still read it. How do you think I read Gil De Lico's diary?"

Captain Perona stared at her. "You *read* the diary? Really read it? All of it?"

"Why, yes."

"It is incredible," said Captain Perona, respectfully though. "No one in our family ever read it. It was so very difficult. Only professors can read such old-fashioned script."

"I'm a professor."

"Oh, no. You are a woman."

"I'm—a—professor!"

"How strange. Well, if you are a professor and really did read the diary, then you must know what it says about the first Emile Perona—where he went and all the things he saw and did."

"Yes, I do."

"Then tell me, please."

"But there's so much of it!" Janet protested. "Why, it would take days and days!"

"Good," said Captain Perona.

"But I haven't time! I'm leaving on the bus!"

"I am, too," said Captain Perona.

"There still wouldn't be enough time. I'm only going to stay at the Hotel Azteca another two days, and then I'm going to Mazatlan."

"I am too," said Captain Perona.

"Why?"

"It is a military matter."

"It is not! You're just going to follow me!"

"Please, senorita," said Captain Perona severely. "Are you accusing me of being a—a— What is that fascinating word? I have it! Masher! Are you accusing me of being a masher?"

"Yes."

"I will have you know, senorita, that I am a gentleman and an officer of the Mexican Army. I have many important and confidential duties. Do you think I would waste my time following a mere woman around—even a very pretty one?"

"What?" said Janet, surprised.

"Oh, yes," said Captain Perona. "You are very pretty, indeed. Has not anyone told you that before? What is the matter with the men in the United States?"

"Why, I—I don't—"

"You blush, too," said Captain Perona. "That is very attractive, I think."

Janet swallowed hard. "Well…. Please tell me some more about Ebenezer Ruggles being a thief. That's very hard for me to believe."

"A long time ago he was traveling in Mexico. He was invited to the home of my grandfather and grandmother. He was their guest, you understand? He collected books at that time—old books."

Janet nodded. "I knew he did. He left his collection to the school. It's enormous."

"No doubt. My grandfather and grandmother showed him the heirlooms of my family. We have a great many. They are very precious to us. This Ruggles villain saw the diary of Gil De Lico. He was fascinated. He could not take his hands off it, although he could not read it, of course. He wanted it for his own. He hinted and hinted, and finally he asked my grandfather for the diary."

"Well?" Janet inquired.

"So my grandfather said he could have it. And he took it, the thief!"

"But why?" Janet asked, puzzled. "If your grandfather gave him the diary, how does that make him a thief?"

"Ah!" said Captain Perona. "That is the whole trick! We did not understand until my mother explained. She was very angry when she heard about it. You see, when you are a guest in Mexico everything in the house is yours. That is the custom here. When you enter, the host says: 'This house is yours.' He means it."

"That's a very beautiful custom," Janet said.

"Certainly. Unless dishonest foreigners take advantage of it. Like that thief, Ruggles. He knew he could not buy the book, but he also knew—since he was a guest—that if he asked for it my grandfather could not think of refusing him because that would be a violation of hospitality. My grandfather was very sad, but he thought he could do nothing else but present the diary to Ruggles. He thought Ruggles would do the same thing in the same circumstances. My mother says he would not have."

"She's right," said Janet.

"So that makes Ruggles a thief," said Captain Perona. "A swindler. A trickster. He takes advantage of a custom in which he does not join or believe. He abuses his privilege as a guest to rob my family. But I will fix things. I will go to this school and swindle the book back. I will offer to buy it and then pay in counterfeit money or with a bad check."

Janet stared at him. "You can't do that!"

"Oh, yes. I am very clever at swindling, and I understand the people in the United States are exceedingly stupid about such things."

"You'll be arrested!"

"All right," said Captain Perona. "I have heard there is no justice in the United States, but I will get the diary back for my family, so I will be contented in prison."

Janet cleared her throat. "The—the diary isn't at the school now."

Captain Perona sat up straight. "What? Have you been lying to me?"

"No! I said I found it there and read it there. Mr. Doan was the one who told you it was there now. I didn't."

"Where is it?"

"In my suitcase at the hotel Azteca."

"Good!" Captain Perona chortled triumphantly. "You can give it to me!"

"No, I can't. The school doesn't know I have it. If I didn't bring it back, they'd say I stole it and put me in jail."

Captain Perona shook his head. "I cannot understand this at all. It seems very weird that they put people in prison in the United States for taking things from thieves. A thief does not own what he steals. It should be perfectly all right to take such things away from him and return them to their real owners. It must be that there are so many thieves in the United States that they have gotten laws passed to protect themselves from honest people."

"The school didn't steal your book!" Janet protested.

"If it is Ebenezer Ruggles' school—and you said it was—then it certainly did. He stole it for the school. It is all the same thing."

Janet moved her hands helplessly, giving it up.

Captain Perona said: "And what are you doing with our diary, if you please? Why did you steal it from the school?"

"I didn't steal it!"

Captain Perona shrugged. "All right. But what are you doing with it?"

"I was interested. I wanted to go to the places that were mentioned in it and see what they looked like now. I wanted the diary for reference."

"What places?" Captain Perona asked suspiciously.

"The places that Lieutenant Perona went."

"Why?"

"To see them!"

"Why?"

"Stop saying that! It's none of your business!"

"It is," Captain Perona corrected politely. "It is my ancestor, hence it is my business. Why, please?"

"I won't tell you!"

"Hmmm," said Captain Perona. He sat for a moment watching Janet in thoughtful silence, and then he said: "Did you know that Lieutenant Perona, my ancestor, was a very immoral man? That he forced his attentions on hundreds of poor, innocent, helpless Indian maidens?"

"That's a lie!" Janet snapped indignantly.

"Ha!" said Captain Perona. "I thought so! You are not interested in where my ancestor went. You are interested in him personally."

Janet got up and started to walk away from him. She walked determinedly, holding her head high, clicking her heels hard. After she had gone about fifty yards, Captain Perona said from behind her:

"Senorita."

"Go away. Leave me alone."

"Senorita, it is said that I resemble my ancestor very closely."

"That's a lie, too. He was a gentleman. You stop following me! Go away!"

"Senorita, unless you give me my diary it will be my sad duty to arrest you."

Janet stopped short. "What?"

"Yes," said Captain Perona.

"You wouldn't dare! Why would you arrest me?"

"I do not know," Captain Perona admitted. "But I will think of some reason."

Janet stuttered with fury. "Why, you—you—"

"Want me to poke him one for you, dearie?"

Janet whirled around, startled. The woman who had spoken was watching them, looking grimly amused. She had gray, frizzy hair that floated around her weather-beaten face like a lop-sided halo, and she was wearing an orange smock. She had a bundle of sticks that Janet identified as a collapsed easel tucked under one arm.

"So it is you, again," said Captain Perona sourly.

"Yeah, baby. And I'm going to tell Colonel Callao that you're annoying tourists."

"That greasy pig!" said Captain Perona.

"I'll tell him you called him that, too. And mind your manners. Introduce me to the little lady."

Captain Perona said awkwardly: "Senorita, may I present to you Amanda Tracy?"

"Hah!" said Amanda Tracy. "I thought so! You don't even know her name! What is it, dearie?"

"Janet Martin."

"Howdy, Janet," said Amanda Tracy. "Want to come along with me? I'm looking for a sucker to sell one of my smears to. Don't let Perona worry you. If he tries to arrest you, I'll push him in the puss with this easel."

"You are flouting military authority," Captain Perona warned her. "Besides, I am escorting the senorita on a sight-seeing tour."

"Is he?" Amanda Tracy asked Janet.

"Well, he started to."

"I will continue it," said Captain Perona stiffly.

"To the jail?" Janet asked.

Captain Perona cleared his throat. "Not at the moment. To the museum. It is very beautiful, senorita. Full of many ancient treasures."

"I'd like to go," said Janet, "but not if you're going to threaten me and—and accuse me—of things."

"If he does," said Amanda Tracy, "just come and tell me. I'll run him clear out of town."

"Bah!" said Captain Perona. "Good day." He took Janet's arm firmly and started to lead her away.

"Hey, Perona," said Amanda Tracy. "There's another tourist wandering around you'd better keep an eye on. A little fat number called Doan. He's a crook if ever I saw one."

"Mr. Doan's a detective," Janet told her.

Amanda Tracy shrugged husky shoulders. "Maybe so. That wouldn't mean he wasn't a crook. Better watch him, Perona. He's a tough cookie, and that dog of his is a bad dream."

"I am watching him," said Captain Perona. "Kindly attend to your painting and leave my business to me."

"From me to you—phooey," said Amanda Tracy. "So long, dearie. See you later." She walked on into the market square, easel trailing behind her.

"She is an artist," Captain Perona told Janet. "She lives here and paints and paints, and everything she paints is most horrible, but tourists buy it and pay good sums for it. I think tourists are crazy, myself."

"I'm one," Janet reminded.

"Senorita, you are trying to trick me into insulting you, as I understand is the custom of women from the United States. They trick a man into insulting them, and then they threaten to have the man arrested unless he marries them. They are so unattractive they cannot get a husband in any other way. But it is useless for you to try that method on me. I refuse flatly to marry you."

"Why, you—you arrogant, ignorant—"

"Never mind," Captain Perona comforted. "Perhaps you can find someone more stupid and marry him. Shall we proceed?"

Janet was speechless. She tried to drag back, scuffling her heels, but Captain Perona pulled her along with no effort at all. They turned a corner and followed a straggling street down the steep slope of the mountain.

"This is the older part of the town," Captain Perona explained. "Some has been rebuilt, of course. But some is very ancient, indeed."

The buildings here looked lower and thicker, and their windows were mere slits. Their walls were not white, either, but faded to a mottled gray by age and weather.

"There is the museum," Captain Perona said.

It was a long one-story building nudged in sideways against the slope. The front had once been built up high, like the false front of a western store, but it had crumbled away in jagged, cracked crevices. The immense black door was slightly ajar.

It was old, this building. But the word old was not enough to express the aged, tired look of it. There was an air of decay—of ancient-ness beyond expression. It was a thing of another age—something that had been left behind in the march of the centuries and was now forlorn and deserted and alone.

Janet breathed in deeply, staring at it with a sort of awed

fascination, forgetting all about her quarrel with Captain Perona.

"It was a church once, as you know," he said softly. "The very first church in this whole state. It was built by a priest, who came with Lieutenant Emile Perona and Gil De Lico, with the help of my ancestor's soldiers and converted Indians. Services were held here for many, many years, and then a hundred and fifty years ago there was an earthquake that shook it badly. You can see the front—how it is broken away. After that it wasn't thought to be safe, and another and larger church was built in the center of town."

Janet didn't answer. Captain Perona was watching her with a sympathetic little smile.

"It takes one's breath away if one imagines all it has seen and endured. The people, when they left it, thought there would be other earthquakes, but there have been no serious ones. Of course, if we ever have another bad one the old church will surely be destroyed. It will collapse. Shall we go inside, senorita?"

"Yes," said Janet.

They went up the steps, and the great iron hinges squealed as Captain Perona pushed the heavy door open wider. The air in the tiny vestibule was thin and dry, and dust motes danced in the narrow shaft of sunlight that filtered through a side window. The shadows were as old and patient as time.

"Yes?" said a soft voice. "Yes? May I help you?"

He was standing in the doorway ahead of them—tall and dressed in black that rustled slightly when he moved. His face had the delicately soft pallor of old ivory, and his eyes were long and slanted a little at the corners, luminously black.

"This is Tio Riquez," Captain Perona said to Janet. "He has been the keeper of this museum for many years. The senorita is a North American, Tio, but not ignorant like most of them. She knows much of our history and is very interested in it."

"You shall see my treasures, senorita," said Tio Riquez, smiling. "They are very beautiful. Come."

Janet followed him through the doorway into a long, narrow room with age-blackened beams across its ceiling. The floor was stone, and through the centuries shuffling feet had worn smooth little pathways in it.

"Oh!" said Janet breathlessly.

The windows were narrow niches, with the sun bright and piercing back of them. Its yellow shafts were like spotlights focused on the displays along the walls. They were not moldering relics, these ancient things. They had been cleaned and restored with infinite care.

"You like this?" asked Tio Riquez.

Janet nodded wordlessly.

The sunlight reflected from burnished conquistador armor, from gold hammered Damascus steel, from the linked plates that had protected the chest of a horse when there were only sixteen horses in all of America. A bell-mouthed harquebus slanted over the red leather of a high-backed saddle, and two pistols as long as a man's arm crossed their clumsy barrels above a thinly wicked lance.

There were native weapons, too, jag-toothed and ugly. And handwoven cloths with the colors in them still brightly defiant. And on beyond the weapons were household goods—drinking cups and plates and even a lopsided spoon beaten out of copper ore. There was the frail shadow of a wooden water canteen and vases made with delicate, sure grace. And then, also, the clumsy tools that had chipped and scraped the rock of Los Altos four hundred-odd years ago.

Janet wandered like a child lost in a candy store, gasping as she saw and comprehended each new wonder. She made the circuit of the room once and then again and then came back and sat down beside Captain Perona on a hand-carved wooden bench.

"They're wonderful," she said, sighing. "Are they all *yours,* Mr. Riquez?"

"No," said Tio Riquez, chuckling. "They belong to the state, senorita. I speak of them as mine because I have been here with them so long. It gives me pleasure to see you admire them, too. Many people nowadays are bored with the old and beautiful."

"They're just wonderful," Janet repeated. "I'd like to look and look…. May I see the cellar, too?"

The sound of her voice echoed a little and fell in the stillness.

"Pardon?" said Tio Riquez. "The what?"

"The cellar," Janet said. "Underneath here"

"There is no cellar," said Tio Riquez.

"But there is," said Janet. She turned to Captain Perona. "It tells all about building this church in Gil De Lico's diary. They dug a cellar in solid rock because they wanted a storage place for supplies and seed they were leaving for the priest in charge."

"It was filled up long ago," said Tio Riquez.

"Why?" Janet asked. "Why would they fill it up? It was very difficult to dig, and they put a concealed door on it—a balanced and pivoted stone."

"The church was built over many times," said Tio Riquez. "They cemented up the doorway."

"Why, no," said Janet. "That's it, there. That oblong stone. You just push at the top. Let me show—"

"Senorita," said Tio Riquez, "it is forbidden to tamper with the property of the museum."

"Of course it is," Captain Perona said. "Naturally. Come along now, senorita. We are not interested in imaginary cellars, and it is boring and close in here." He jerked at her arm urgently.

Janet pulled back. "I'm not going! I want to sit here and look and look and look. Why, I saved for years and came thousands of miles—" She stared at Captain Perona. "What? What is it?"

Captain Perona's face was white. He didn't answer.

Tio Riquez said mockingly. "Captain Perona is surprised.

He has been looking for me so industriously, you see, and now he has suddenly found me where I was all the time—right under his nose. Stand still, Captain."

Tio Riquez had a revolver in his hand. It was a big revolver with a pearl handle and a long, elaborately silvered barrel.

Captain Perona had his right hand inside the loose front of his coat.

"No," warned Tio Riquez. "Don't. It is too late for that now, Captain. You didn't think fast enough or act quickly enough. You were too interested in the senorita."

"What—what's the matter?" Janet demanded.

"She knows nothing about this—or you," Captain Perona said. "She is just a harmless tourist."

"No," Tio Riquez denied. "Not harmless any more. The cellar is there, senorita. You will see it now. You and Captain Perona. Push the stone as you suggested. It works very easily."

Janet swallowed. "What's the matter with the cellar? What—what's down there?"

Tio Riquez smiled at her. "Guns, senorita. Rifles. A great many of them. A trifle obsolete, but not as much as you'd think. Many of the troops in your up-to-date country are armed with Springfield rifles of a similar model. Captain Perona has been hunting them and some others I know about. Hunting me, too. Releasing old companions of mine and following them, hoping they knew where to find me. They didn't know, as a matter of fact, Captain. They knew ways they could make themselves known, so I could contact them if I wished. They didn't know my identity or where I was hiding. I contacted Garcia and had him come here. I could have used him in a little project I have in mind."

Janet said: "The rattlesnake! You're the one—"

"Yes," said Tio Riquez. "I thought that was rather clever of me, didn't you? I didn't know just what would happen when I threw the snake in with the soldier, but I imagined the results would have been violent enough to warn Garcia, and in that way I didn't have to risk revealing myself to him or to anyone else."

"Who are you?" Janet asked.

"Hasn't Captain Perona told you? I am Bautiste Bonofile, and I've been convicted of murder, armed rebellion, train robbery, kidnapping and a few other things I can't recall at the moment. Do you know what that means—to you?"

Janet shook her head wordlessly.

"I can't let you go now, senorita. I'm sorry, but it took me many years and much effort to build up this identity, and I like it. Open the cellar door. And you, Captain Perona. Don't move at all. You are going to die anyway, as you know, but it would take you much longer to do it if I shot you in the stomach."

Janet backed slowly and woodenly away from the two of them, back and back, until the stone wall felt cool through her thin dress. She put out one arm and pushed at the pivot stone. The stone moved reluctantly, and as if in protest the earth growled and grumbled deep within itself.

"Don't move," Tio Riquez warned sharply. "It is just an earth tremor. We have many of them here. It is nothing."

The earth rose to make a roaring denial of that. The floor rocked sickeningly, and Janet saw a crack widen and run down the crumbling wall like a quick black snake. Dust swirled in a blinding cloud that thrust stinging fingers into her eyes.

A shot plopped out dully, dwarfed by the greater uproar, and then Captain Perona's voice shouted:

"Janet! Run! Run outside!"

There were more shots, like a string of small firecrackers in the distance, and the stone floor heaved and moaned in its agony. Janet staggered away from the wall, and a rafter swung down slowly in front of her and shattered into ancient shards. She had lost all sense of direction, and she cried out weakly and breathlessly.

Captain Perona's arm whipped around her waist and dragged

her forward. She could hear his short, sharp gasps for breath. He was swearing in Spanish.

The floor stretched like the loose hide of an animal. Janet fell and tripped Captain Perona. Dust smothered them, and a piece of armor rolled and clanged brightly past.

Captain Perona was up again, staggering drunkenly. His fingers dug into Janet's arms. He thrust and pulled and bunted her with his shoulder, and then they were in the tiny vestibule.

The dust was thinner, and Janet stared with burning eyes at the side wall. It was bulging inward slowly and awfully, as though a giant fist was pushing it from the outside. The big front door was closed now, and Captain Perona gripped the collarlike latch in both hands and heaved back.

Janet wondered dully why he didn't just open the door and get them out of here. It was dangerous. The wall was behaving in a way no wall should or could. It was coming inexorably closer. And so were the other walls now.

The cords stood out on the back of Captain Perona's neck, and the shoulder seam of his coat split suddenly. The door moved and threw him backward, and then he had Janet's arm again, and they were outside running down the steps that slid under them like an escalator.

Janet looked back. The old church was wavering, crumbling, slumping slowly down. And then the earth gave one sharp final heave. The church groaned under that death blow, and then it fell majestically in on itself and was no longer a building but merely a heap of rubble with dust rising over it like a pall.

As suddenly as the noise had come, it was gone. The silence was so intense it was a pressure against the eardrums. Sensation returned to Janet like a stinging slap in the face, and she was suddenly more frightened than she had ever been in her life.

Captain Perona seized her by both shoulders and shook her until her teeth rattled. His face was dust-smeared and pallid, staring tensely into hers.

"Are you hurt?" he yelled. "Answer me? Are you hurt?"

"N-no," Janet whimpered, and then she caught her breath and her self-possession and was instantly angry. "You stop that! Let go of me!"

"*Gracias a Dios!*" said Captain Perona reverently. "I was afraid for you. You would not speak. You would only look without seeing anything."

"Was that an earthquake?" Janet asked.

Captain Perona stared at her out of bleary, reddened eyes. "Was that—was that...." He drew a deep breath. "Yes, senorita. That was an earthquake."

"Well, don't be so superior! I've never been in one before!" Janet turned to look at the pile of rubble that had been the church, and then she was suddenly frightened all over again. "Oh! If we hadn't gotten out...." She remembered, then, and looked at the split shoulder-seam of Captain Perona's coat. "If you hadn't gotten us out.... Your hand is hurt!"

Captain Perona sucked ruefully at his torn fingers. "I pulled too hard at the door. It was stuck, and I was really in a great hurry."

"You—you saved my life."

"Yes," Captain Perona admitted. "I did. And you are a fool."

"What?" Janet cried. "What?"

"I said you were a fool. Why did you not inform me about the location of that cellar?"

"How did I know you didn't know it was there? It was your ancestor who built the church!"

"So it was," Captain Perona agreed. There was dust even on his eyelashes. "But you should have told me anyway. Then I would have caught that devil."

"Oh," said Janet, remembering more. "That Tio—that Bautiste person! He had a gun!"

"Yes," said Captain Perona. "When the floor moved it threw him off balance, and I hit him with my fist." He looked at the fist distastefully. "We Mexicans do not believe in brawling and mauling at people with our fists as you people do, but I did not have time to draw my gun and shoot him."

"Somebody shot," Janet said.

"Yes. He did. But the dust blinded him."

Janet looked at the church. "Where…."

"I hope he's under that," Captain Perona answered grimly. "But I am afraid he is not. He is too smart and too quick. He probably has a dozen secret exits. If we could get out, so could he. If you had only told me about that cellar…."

"Why did that give everything away?" Janet demanded.

"We have spent a long time narrowing down possibilities. We suspected Bautiste Bonofile was hidden somewhere near here, and we knew that if he was, there was also a cache near here because he has been selling loot. Not rifles—but other things he had stolen and hidden long ago. When Garcia came here, we were sure we were right. As soon as you mentioned that cellar, I thought that must be the cache. I tried not to show it, but he knew. He had no intention of letting me get away after that."

"But you'd have been missed at once."

"Yes. You, also. But he would have had time to remove some of the most valuable loot and to disappear himself if he thought he would be suspected. I do not think he would have been. He has had his position as Tio Riquez for over ten years. He is a fixture in Los Altos."

Faintly, all around them, like some weird off-scene chorus, cries and shouts began to rise. A woman wept in wailing shrieks. The dust clouds had heightened and thinned, and the sun showed ghastly yellow-red through it.

Captain Perona straightened up. "I forget myself! I must go at once, senorita! There must be a guard put here by this build-ing, and there will be injured people to care for and property to protect. I must find my men. Will you go to the main square and wait? You will be perfectly safe now, I think."

"Yes," said Janet. "Go ahead. Hurry. I'll be all right."

Captain Perona trotted up the steep street toward the marketplace. Janet watched him until he disappeared, and then turned to stare at her surroundings.

She felt a sort of awed disbelief. There was no real change. The squat houses were still there, just as they had been before. There were fresh cracks in the walls, and roofs sagged, and tile lay broken in the street, but there was no vast waste of desolation such as she had expected.

And the people were there, too. Scurrying in and out of their houses like ants on a griddle—afraid to stay where they were, and afraid to go anywhere else. Janet saw a woman in her black, rustling Sunday dress kneeling quite alone in the middle of the street, praying. A man came out of the house across the way carrying a wicker bird cage with a parakeet inside. He stopped and stared cautiously in all directions and then yelled crazily and pelted up the street with the bird cage flopping and the parakeet screeching.

"*Senorita! Senorita Americana!*"

Janet turned around. A ragged little girl with a smear of dirt around her mouth was staring up at her with eyes that were as bright and gleaming as black jewels. She wasn't scared. She was panting with delicious excitement.

"*Senorita, venga usted! La otra senorita—la turista rica! Venga!*"

She seized Janet's hand and pulled at her, and Janet followed. The little girl danced beside her, gesturing with impatience. She turned the first corner into a narrow lane.

"*Aqui! Mira!*"

There was a little group of people, both men and women, standing there in the lane, and they turned at the little girl's cry, separating.

Janet saw the blond, loose swirl of hair first, like spun gold against the dust. Her breath caught in her throat, and she ran forward and stopped suddenly. Patricia Van Osdel was lying crumpled on her side. Her profile was white and austere and aristocratic. Her eyes were closed, and a trickle of blood made a bright, jagged streak across her cheek.

A little man wearing a faded serape knelt beside her. He looked up at Janet with sad, regretful eyes.

"She is—died," he said in careful English. He made a shy, quick gesture with his hands. "All died."

CHAPTER VII

DOAN CAME OUT on the Avenida Revolucion, and it seemed to him now that the street was appropriately named. It looked as though it had just gone through a revolution or one had gone through it. Broken tile lay in windows, and a stovepipe, canted over a wall, leered like a warped cannon. A house across the way had lost its front wall, and its owners capered around inside like zany actors in a movie set. They were making enough noise for a massacre, but none of them seemed to be injured.

Right in front of Doan a little boy sat in the center of the street with his eyes shut and his fists clenched and his mouth wide open. He was howling mightily, and no one paid him the slightest attention.

Doan walked over to him. "Hey, shorty. Where are you hurt?"

The little boy turned off his howl and opened his eyes cautiously. He looked Doan over and then saw Carstairs. His mouth made a round O of admiration. He looked back at Doan and smiled winningly. He had three front teeth missing.

"Gimme dime."

Doan gave him a dime. The little boy tested it with a couple of his remaining teeth.

"Denk goo," he said.

He put the dime carefully in the pocket of his ragged shirt, shut his eyes and opened his mouth. He started to yell exactly where he had left off.

Doan walked on down the street. The houses, and apparently their inmates, were mostly intact. Roofs sagged, and broken glass glittered dangerously, and open doors leaned like weary drunks. Women hopped and ran and screamed, and children squalled. Men worked feverishly carrying things out of their houses into the street and then back into their houses again.

Doan went down the steep slope to the market square. There was more noise and even less sense here. The quake had jarred the display counters and rolled their goods out into the gutters in jumbled piles. Owners—and evidently some non-owners—fought and scrambled over the piles like carrion crows.

Doan found Bartolome sitting on top of a ten-foot heap of debris. Bartolome was slumped forward, holding his head in his hands.

"Are you hurt?" Doan asked.

"I am dying," said Bartolome.

"You don't look it," Doan told him. "Where'd you park the bus?"

"Under," said Bartolome, pointing down.

Doan stared at the heap of debris. "You mean the bus is underneath all that?"

"Yes," said Bartolome, dignified in his grief. "It is catastrophe beyond reason."

"Where are the passengers?"

"I do not know," said Bartolome. "And I do not care. Of passengers there are a great number too many—of the bus only one too less. It is unendurable."

A thin harassed young man in a smeared khaki uniform hurried across the plaza toward them. He said to Doan

"Dispenseme, senor, pero donde esta—"

"I can't speak Spanish," Doan interrupted.

"English?" said the young man. "Good. I am Lieutenant Ortega, the medical officer in charge of this district. Did you come with the party in this bus?"

"Yes," Doan answered. "Was there anyone in it when the quake dumped all this on top of it?"

"No. I was just across the square. All the party had left the bus before that. Will you please find them if you can? Tell them to report here and they will be taken care of. If any are injured, bring them to that white building there, and I will attend them. If they cannot be moved, send for me. Will you do this at once?"

"Sure," said Doan.

"You will pardon me…. There are injured…."

He trotted back across the square, pausing to bark angry orders at a pair of soldiers who were standing and gaping around them with the casual air of sightseers at a fair. The soldiers jumped to attention and then followed him at a snappy run.

"Which way did the others go?" Doan asked Bartolome.

"I am in a state of nervous collapse," Bartolome informed him. "I have many things on my mind. The one with the loud mouth and the stupid wife and the hellish child went in that direction. The others I did not notice."

Doan crossed the square, and Carstairs followed, picking his way distastefully through the debris and the yowling throng that was growing in numbers and volume every second. Doan took the first side street and found Mr. and Mrs. Henshaw in the middle of it fifty yards further along.

Mrs. Henshaw was sitting down on the pavement with her peasant skirt draped in a swirl over her chubby legs. One of the lenses in her pince-nez had cracked, and she glared narrow-eyed through the whole one.

"I can't get up," she informed Doan. "I'm paralyzed. Call an ambulance."

"There ain't no ambulance," said Henshaw wearily. "And anyway you ain't paralyzed. You ran out of that store like a rabbit with its pants on fire."

"It's shock," said Mrs. Henshaw. "My nerve centers are shattered. I can feel them."

"Baloney," said Henshaw.

"It's your fault," Mrs. Henshaw accused bitterly.

"What?" Henshaw yelped. "My fault? Did I think up this earthquake?"

"You brought me here."

"Now damn it, I didn't. It was you that brought me. You're the one that heard about Mouser Puddledip at the Ladies' Aid and insisted on seeing this anthill because he once lived here and it was full of artistic history."

"Monsieur."

Mrs. Henshaw corrected. *"Monsieur Predilip.* This town and its beautiful primitive surroundings were his inspiration."

"They're a pain in the neck to me. Did you feel that earthquake we had, Doan?"

"Faintly," said Doan. "Where's Mortimer?"

"Hi-yo, Silver!" Mortimer screeched. He came sailing across the street carrying a pair of silvered spurs in one fist and a sombrero so big he could have used it for a tent in the other. "Look, Pop! Look what I snitched! Here. Hold 'em while I go back for another load. Boy, I wish the gang was here!"

Henshaw took the spurs and sombrero helplessly. "Now look, you little rat! These belong to somebody!"

"Hi-yo, Silver!" Mortimer yelled. "A-waay!" He pelted back across the street and dived into the broken doorway of a store.

Mrs. Henshaw got up instantly. "Mortimer! You come right out of there! Don't you touch anything! Don't you dare! *Mortimer!"*

"The hell with it," said Henshaw wearily. "I think I'll get paralyzed myself."

Doan said: "When you get around to it, report back in the square where the bus was parked."

"Was?" Henshaw repeated. "What do you mean—*was?"*

"A building fell on it."

"No foolin'," said Henshaw. "Well, how do we get back to the Hotel Azteca? Ride a mule?"

"I won't ride one of those nasty little beasts," Mrs. Henshaw snapped. "They're dirty. Don't you argue with me, either! I won't do it, that's all."

"Have you seen any of the other passengers?" Doan asked.

"That bird, Greg, was ahead of us. I haven't seen him since the big shake."

Doan and Carstairs walked on, and behind them Mrs. Henshaw shrieked:

"Mortimer! Put that down! Don't you dare eat that horrible candy! It's got *germs!*"

Doan and Carstairs detoured around a group of people busily burrowing into what had evidently been a bakery, and then a voice called:

"Doan."

Greg was leaning against a cracked building wall. His handsome face was drawn now, and his lips were pale with agony. He had his scarf wrapped around his right arm above the elbow. He was holding his right forearm cradled across his chest with his left hand.

"Do you know where I can find a doctor?" he asked.

"Back in the square. The big white building on the west side. Want me to help you?"

"No. It's just my arm. It's broken. I fell over that damned horse trough there when the quake came."

"Where is Miss Van Osdel?" Doan asked.

"Who wants to know?"

"I do," said Doan.

"Try and find out," Greg told him, and walked back up the street, leaning over sideways to ease his arm.

"Hey, fatso!"

Amanda Tracy came up at a lumbering run, dragging the easel behind her. Her hair was frizzed more wildly than ever, and her eyes gleamed bright and excited in the leathery toughness of her face.

"Some shimmy, huh? Listen, fat, I'm gonna make my fortune out of it!"

"How?" Doan asked.

Amanda Tracy pulled the canvas out of the easel clamps and thrust it in front of his face. "See that? That's a picture of some buildings, believe it or not. See how squeegeed and cockeyed they look?"

"Yes," Doan admitted.

"Well, they weren't ruins when I painted them, but they are now. Get it? The ruins of Los Altos. I got a lot more pictures just as lousy as this one. I'll sell them for souvenirs of the disaster!"

"If you live in that house where you were when I first saw you—and your pictures are there—you'd better run up and take them in out of the weather."

"Hah?" Amanda Tracy barked.

"You haven't got a roof any more."

"Wow!" said Amanda Tracy. She ran up the street, whacking at anyone who was unfortunate enough to get in her way with the legs of the easel. "Gangway! Gangway!"

Somebody poked Doan in the stomach. He looked down into the face of a little girl who had a smear of dirt around her mouth. Her eyes were black beads that goggled at him excitedly.

"*Senor! La senorita rica y la otra senorita turista son....*"

Doan was shaking his head.

The little girl shook her head, too.

"*No habla Mexicano?*"

"I guess not," said Doan.

The little girl dug at her ear with one finger, and then her face lighted up. "*Mira!*" She struck herself in the head with her fist. "Bong!" She staggered dramatically and fell down in the street.

Doan got it. "Where? Who? Which way?"

The little girl jumped up. *"Venga usted!"*

They went down a steep side street and through a lane where chickens squawked and scurried frantically to get out of Carstairs' way. They turned to the right and to the left and scattered a family group who were trying to haul a sewing machine out through a shattered window.

"Mil," the little girl shrilled, *"Ahiston las senoritas!"*

The little group was still there in the lane, and they drew back now, murmuring among themselves. Doan saw Janet Martin and the little man in the faded serape kneeling down in the dust beside the limp form of Patricia Van Osdel.

"What is it?" Doan asked breathlessly. "Is she hurt?"

The little man shook his head sadly.

Janet said in a stifled voice: "She's dead, Mr. Doan. Her head…. I think she died instantly."

"Let me see." Doan knelt down. The golden hair was as soft as mist in his fingers, and then he saw the deep-sunken wound in the back of the small head. "Yes."

He stood up and looked around slowly—at the ground, at the walls of the buildings on either side of the lane.

"Was she moved?" he asked. "Did someone carry her in here?"

"No," said the little man. "No. Was lie here."

"Why?" Janet inquired blankly. "What difference does that make?"

"None right now," said Doan. "You go on up to the main drag and find Captain Perona. He ought to know about this right away. If you can't find him, there's a lieutenant by the name of Ortega in the big white building across from where the bus parked. Tell him. I'll wait here."

"All right," said Janet obediently. She turned and ran out of the lane.

Doan squatted down on his heels.

The little man nodded at him shyly and said, *"Es lastima."*

"Probably it is," Doan agreed.

A voice, far away, shouted an indistinguishable string of words. Other voices, closer, took up the cry. Excitement gathered like an electric charge in the air, and the little man's eyes were wide and shocked staring into Doan's.

"What's the matter?" Doan asked.

The little man struggled for words. *"Puente!"* He braced his forefingers together end-to-end and stared at Doan over the top of them. *"Puente!"*

"Arch," Doan guessed. "Roof." Then he jumped. "Bridge!"

"Si! Si, si! Bridge! Is away!"

"What?"

"Gone. No longer."

"You mean the earthquake shook the bridge down?" Doan demanded.

The little man nodded. "Si. Shook down. Bust."

"That makes everything just dandy," Doan commented.

The small girl with the dirty face burst through the onlookers blubbering words in a stuttering stream. She planted herself in front of Doan and waved both arms at him.

"What's the beef, sister?" Doan inquired.

The girl pointed down at Patricia Van Osdel and then held up one finger.

"One," said Doan, nodding.

The girl pointed back the way she had come and held up two fingers.

"Two," said Doan, and then he leaped to his feet. "What? Another? Who? Where?"

"Venga usted!"

They went down the lane—the girl in front and Doan and Carstairs right behind her, and the little man running along behind with his serape flipping in the breeze of their passage. They went around the corner and up the street and across into another lane.

A muttering, peering crowd of people was huddled close

around a fat woman kneeling on the ground. Doan looked over the fat woman's shoulder and saw the long, bony form of Maria, the personal maid, flattened on the dusty ground. Maria's face was pallidly white and empty, and the mole was like a black spider crouched on her cheek.

Doan dropped down beside her and touched one skinny, outstretched arm. "She's not dead! She's—"

The fat woman shoved him angrily. *"No! Cuidado!"*

"What's your trouble?" Doan asked.

"She feex," said the little man.

"Is she a nurse?" Doan demanded.

"Nurse?" said the little man, testing the word. "No." He pointed to the small girl and then held his hands about a foot apart. "Child," said Doan. "Dwarf. Midget. Baby!"

"Si. Baby."

"You mean the old doll is a baby nurse?"

"No. Middle momma."

"Baby," Doan said. "Middle. Momma. Midwife!"

"Si."

"Well, this is a little out of her regular line of business," Doan commented, "but she probably knows more about it than I do."

A pudgy little man with an enormous mustache bustled out of the house next door carrying a steaming kettle of water carefully in front of him. He had clean cloths folded over both his forearms. He put the kettle down on the ground beside the fat woman. She selected one of the cloths, moistened it in the water, and dabbed carefully at Maria's temple.

"Muy malo," she said.

"Hurts bad," the little man translated.

Doan nodded absently. "Yeah. I can see that."

The fat woman snapped her fingers, and the pudgy man instantly presented her with a pair of blunt surgical scissors. She snipped at Maria's lank hair.

"Sister," said the little man, pointing at the man who had brought the water.

"She's his sister?" Doan inquired.

"No. He."

"He's her sister?"

"Si."

"I don't get that," said Doan. "Sister, sister…. Assistant! He assists her!"

"Si. Sisted. Also hatband."

"Hatband," Doan repeated. "Husband?"

"Si, si!"

Doan nodded at Carstairs. "I'm catching on, kid. I'll be able to rattle off Spanish in no time at all."

Carstairs looked skeptical.

The small girl shrieked suddenly: *Soldados!*"

Sergeant Obrian was peering around the corner at them. He turned back now and called:

"Captain! I found him! Here he is!"

Captain Perona and Janet came into the lane. There were two soldiers behind them, one carrying a rolled army stretcher on his shoulder.

"Now what is this?" Captain Perona demanded.

"It's Maria!" Janet exclaimed. "She's Miss Van Osdel's maid! Is she—is she—"

"She's not dead," Doan said. "From the looks of her eyes, I think her skull is fractured. She got a smaller dose of the same thing Van Osdel did. You'd better run her up and let Ortega look her over."

Captain Perona nodded to the soldiers. They unrolled the stretcher and lifted Maria on it with the help of Sergeant Obrian and the fat midwife and her assistant.

"Stay here, Sergeant," Captain Perona said.

The two soldiers carried Maria carefully out of the lane.

Captain Perona was staring at Doan. "Just what did you have to do with this?"

"Not a thing," said Doan. "I was sitting over there by Van Osdel, waiting for you, when this little kid— Where'd she go? She was here a minute ago. Anyway, she came along and said there was another casualty down here. So I came to see if I could help. Ask Ignatz, here. He was with me all the time."

"Es verdad?"

Captain Perona inquired, looking at the little man.

"Si, Capitan."

"That rock over there is what hit Maria," said Doan, pointing to a jagged piece of stone slightly larger than a paving brick. "You'd better save it."

"Why?"

"Because I'm pretty sure it's the same one that hit Patricia Van Osdel."

"What?" said Captain Perona, startled.

Doan nodded. "Yeah. There was nothing near the Van Osdel that could have given her the kind of a bat she got. But that rock *is* just about the right shape. Of course, I could be wrong, but you'd better check up."

"State plainly what you mean!" Captain Perona ordered.

"I don't think either Maria or the Van Osdel was hit by accident. I think they were in that alley where Patricia was found, talking to some third party. When the earthquake let loose, the third party picked up that rock and slammed Patricia with it. Maria ran. The third party chased her and caught her here in this alley and bopped her with the same rock. During the earthquake everyone was yelling and running back and forth like crazy, so no one would pay much attention. Maybe you might find some witnesses, though, if you look."

"What made you think of all this?"

"Patricia Van Osdel was carrying a purse—a big red patent leather affair about the size of a brief case. It's gone."

Captain Perona looked at Janet, and she nodded.

"Miss Van Osdel *did* have a purse like that. I noticed it, and it wasn't in the lane where she was found."

Captain Perona looked back at Doan. "Have you got any more remarks to make at this time?"

"Well, there was one other thing."

"What?"

"About Eldridge. His roof fell on him"

Captain Perona breathed in deeply. "I do not suppose he was hurt? I do not suppose he was injured seriously, by any chance?"

"No," Doan admitted.

"I knew it! He is dead, of course!"

"Yes," said Doan.

"And what were you doing at the time? Something entirely innocent, I have no doubt!"

"I was just picking myself up from where the earthquake dumped me."

"How very convenient that earthquake was!" Captain Perona snarled. "You came here to prevent Eldridge from returning to the United States, and now you have succeeded!"

"Well," said Doan, "if you put it that way—yes."

"Consider yourself under arrest!"

"Hey, now," Doan protested mildly. "I didn't push Eldridge's roof over on him."

"Captain," said Janet, "I'm sure Mr. Doan is telling the truth! You're making a terrible mistake to—"

Captain Perona turned on her. "Do you wish to be arrested also?"

"No," said Janet.

"Then be quiet. Sergeant! Take this man to the barracks and keep him there until I investigate."

"You heard him, pudgy," said Sergeant Obrian. "On your way. And don't try any tricks. I don't carry this bayonet just because it shines so pretty."

"Can I take Carstairs?" Doan asked. "He usually goes to jail with me."

"Yes!"

Doan rapped Carstairs on the forehead with his knuckle. "Up-si-daisy, pal. Off to clink, we go."

"I'm so sorry, Mr. Doan," Janet told him.

"Think nothing of it," Doan said. "We'll get right out again. We always do."

"Do not be too confident," Captain Perona advised dangerously.

CHAPTER VIII

DOAN WAS SITTING on one end of a bench in a very small, very barren room with one narrow window and a rough board floor that was covered with dust which the quake had shaken from the walls and ceiling. Carstairs was sleeping on the rest of the bench. Sergeant Obrian stood just inside the door and watched them both grimly.

Captain Perona and Lieutenant Ortega came in the door.

"Tell us what you learned," Captain Perona ordered. "Speak in English so he may understand."

Lieutenant Ortega said: "I examined the body of Senor Eldridge. There was dust and plaster and bits of mortar in his clothes and in his hair. His spine was broken and severed below his waist, and his left arm was fractured, and he had five fractured ribs, one of which penetrated the lung cavity close to his heart. These wounds resulted in his death."

"Could Doan have given him those wounds?"

Lieutenant Ortega looked at Doan. "Oh, I think not."

"Look again," Captain Perona said. "His appearance is very deceptive."

Lieutenant Ortega shook his head. "There is no evidence of any human agency. I think Senor Eldridge was crushed by the fall of his roof."

"Sure he was," said Doan. "Why, I've even got a witness who saw me try trying to give Eldridge first aid."

"Who?" Captain Perona demanded.

"A fellow by the name of Lepicik."

"I do not know anyone by that name," said Captain Perona. "Was he a Mexican or a foreigner?"

"Foreigner, I guess."

Captain Perona looked at Sergeant Obrian inquiringly.

Sergeant Obrian shook his head. "No. There ain't nobody by that name in this burg—foreigner or otherwise. I checked 'em all."

"Well, I saw the guy," said Doan.

"No," Captain Perona contradicted flatly. "It is impossible for anyone to come into this district without us knowing him and identifying him. You are lying again."

"But, please," said a voice outside the door. "If you will pardon me, I must see the Captain. It is really quite important."

Sergeant Obrian jumped outside the door and came back in again immediately shoving Lepicik ahead of him. Lepicik smiled and nodded in a mildly apologetic way.

"I'm so sorry to bother you, but I was informed that I must report my presence in Los Altos to you."

"What is your name?" Captain Perona demanded.

"I am Leon Lepicik."

"Ahem," said Doan.

Captain Perona bowed ironically. "I apologize. You were not lying—again. Senor Lepicik, how did you come to Los Altos?"

"I came from Santa Lucia."

"He's screwy," said Sergeant Obrian. "That's a gutbuster of a hike. No old droop like this could make it."

"Nevertheless," said Lepicik, "you will observe that I am here."

"Who guided you?" asked Captain Perona.

"A man by the name of Adolfo Morales and a burro named

Carmencita. They—or at least Adolfo—are now in the process of getting drunk at the Dos Hermanos, if you wish to verify my story."

"We do wish to," said Captain Perona. "And we will. Are you a North American?"

"No, sir."

"Let me see your passport."

Lepicik produced a worn leather folder, and Captain Perona examined it carefully.

"Albanian, eh?" he said, looking up.

Lepicik nodded. "Yes. But you will note that the passport was issued before the Italian invasion and also bears the stamp of the Albanian government-in-exile."

"Hmmm," said Captain Perona, handing back the passport. "Have you ever seen this man?"

"Yes," said Lepicik. "Once."

"Where?"

"In the patio in back of a house on the Avenida Revolucion."

"What was he doing?"

"Attempting to help a man who was fatally injured in the earthquake."

Doan had been holding his breath, and he let it out now in a long, gentle sigh.

"How do you know the man was injured in the earthquake?" Captain Perona asked.

"I saw it happen. I saw the roof of his house fall on him."

"How could you see that? The patio is enclosed by a high wall."

"The earthquake demolished the wall, and besides I was up on the hill above and in back of the house."

"What were you doing up there?"

Lepicik smiled at him. "Exploring. I find that a very interesting and educational pastime."

"Why did you come to Los Altos?"

"To explore."

"I see," said Captain Perona coldly. "Doan, you are released—for the moment. Go to the Hacienda Nueva Inglesa and register—and stay there. Senor Lepicik, you accompany him and do the same."

"I have already registered," said Lepicik, "and met the other charming members of the tourist party."

"Doan," said Captain Perona, "before you leave I wish to tell you certain things we know about your recent actions. You are employed by an agency called the Severn International Detectives, which has headquarters in New York. The agency was employed by a certain group of politicians in a certain state to send you to Mexico to bribe Senor Eldridge to stay here and to stop bothering them. You were given ten thousand dollars for that purpose, but you did not bring the ten thousand dollars to Mexico."

"Didn't I?" Doan asked.

"No. Instead you deposited it in the Commercial Trust Bank in Chicago under the name of D.L. Carstairs."

"It's a fund for his college education," said Doan, indicating Carstairs.

"I find your humor nauseating," Captain Perona told him shortly. "You never had any intention of paying that money to Eldridge. You embezzled it."

"Shame on me," said Doan. "I guess these certain politicians will sue me or put me in jail or something, then, won't they?"

Captain Perona scowled at him in silence.

"What is it?" Lieutenant Ortega asked. "I do not understand."

Captain Perona said: "He knows the politicians do not dare prosecute him because then they would have to explain why they gave him the money which would result in just the scandal they are trying to avoid."

"Hey!" Sergeant Obrian exclaimed. "You mean that pudgy gets to keep the ten grand? And then they try to tell you that crime don't pay!"

"Did you speak?" Captain Perona inquired.

"No, sir," said Sergeant Obrian.

Captain Perona pointed to Carstairs, to Doan, and to Lepicik. "Get out. All of you."

Doan nudged Carstairs with his elbow. "Come on, chum. We beat the rap."

CHAPTER IX

THE HACIENDA NUEVA INGLESA was neither a ranch nor new, and English only by adoption, but it had adobe walls six feet thick that had survived the earthquake with only a few exterior cracks. It was a narrow, two-story building on the west side of the plaza. Doan and Carstairs and Lepicik went in through the side entrance into a low, dim, musty-smelling room optimistically labeled a restaurant-bar.

"Mr. Doan!" Janet greeted. She was sitting at one of the round wire-legged tables under a poster which luridly proclaimed the virtues of Guinness Stout. "You were released! Oh, I'm so glad!"

"I told you not to worry about him," said Mrs. Henshaw. She was seated at another of the tables, writing busily in a leather-mounted diary with a tiny gold pencil. "I knew he'd manage to bribe somebody."

"I saved my money this time," Doan said. "Lepicik got me out."

"It was nothing," said Lepicik politely. "If you will excuse me now, I think I will take a nap in my room. I am very weary."

He went up the steep stairway to the second floor.

"Miss Martin," said Mrs. Henshaw, "what was that queer dish we had for lunch?"

"Chiles rellenos," Janet told her.

"How do you spell it?"

Janet spelled it for her.

Greg was sitting by himself in the corner staring darkly at

the tall, round bottle of Plymouth gin on the table in front of him. Doan walked over to him.

"Can I have a drink of that?"

"I suppose so," Greg said. "If you pay for it. There are some glasses on the shelf back of the bar. If you want a mix, yell for Timpkins."

"I'll try it straight," Doan said. He found a glass and sat down at the table opposite Greg. "Let's get drunk, shall we?"

"Okay," said Greg.

Doan took off his hat and put it down on the table and unbuttoned his coat. He poured some gin into his glass and tasted it.

"It's good," he said. He finished the drink and poured himself another.

Carstairs walked up to the table and growled at him.

"As for you," said Doan. "You can go straight to hell."

Carstairs growled at him again.

"I'll get drunk if I feel like it," Doan told him. "It's my stomach. Lie down before somebody bops you with a bottle."

Carstairs lowered himself to the floor with a series of loose, bony thuds. He snorted once and then closed his eyes in a resigned way.

"Doesn't he like you to drink?" Janet asked.

"No " said Doan. "I got maudlin once when I was crocked and kissed him. He's never forgotten it. Every time he smells alcohol, he tarts acting like he just bit into a lemon. He's intolerant. It's a serious defect in his character."

"Mr. Doan," said Mrs. Henshaw severely, "don't annoy Mr. Greg. He is mourning Miss Van Osdel."

"Are you?" Doan asked him.

"No," said Greg. "I'm trying to think of the name of a girl I met in London last summer. Her father owns a glue factory. Do you know anyone in England who owns a glue factory?"

"Nope," said Doan. "Did Ortega fix your arm for you?"

"Yes. He said he set it. I think personally that he cut it off. It feels like hell."

"Have a drink," Doan invited.

"Okay."

Feet thundered along the hall above them, and then Henshaw shouted down the staircase:

"Hey! Have you seen this bathroom up here?"

"Now, Wilbur," Mrs. Henshaw said absently. "No business on this trip. You promised."

"Business, hell!" Henshaw said. "Why, the thing is a disgrace! I bet it's fifty years old! Where's the guy that owns this dive? Timpkins! *Timpkins!*"

A man came in through the door beyond the end of the bar. He was scrawny and small and bow-legged, and he was wearing a soiled flour sack for an apron. He looked as though being born had been such a disappointment to him that he had never recovered.

"Well, what?"

"Timpkins," said Henshaw, "that bathroom of yours is a terrible hole."

"It works, don't it?"

"After a fashion. But that isn't the point, Timpkins. It's obsolete. Why, it's an antique."

"If you don't like it, you don't have to use it."

"What would I do if I didn't?" Henshaw asked blankly.

"That's your question," said Timpkins. "You answer it."

"Hey, you," said Doan. "Captain Perona told me to stay here. Trot out your register, and I'll sign up."

Timpkins stared at him sourly. "You the chap that goes around killing people?"

"Now and then," Doan said.

"You ain't to kill nobody in my hotel, just remember that. I'm a British subject, and I know my rights. One murder, and out you go, Captain Perona or no Captain Perona."

"Okay," said Doan amiably.

"The register is under the bar. You sign yourself up—and by your right name, too. If there's a room upstairs that's empty, you can use it…. And just remember I marked the level on that gin bottle and one of you two is gonna pay for what's gone out of it. And I don't want none of you guests hollerin' at me and botherin' me any more because I'm busy."

Henshaw had come very quietly down the stairs. "Timpkins," he said softly. "Timpkins, look." He whipped a shiny, colored folder out of his pocket. "Look at Model 9-A illustrated here. Orchid tile, Timpkins!"

"Arr!" Timpkins snarled. He went back into the kitchen and slammed the door violently behind him.

"He's a tough prospect," Henshaw said in a pleased tone. "But that's the kind I like. I'll work up a little sales talk especially for him. Would you like to see Model 9-A, Doan?"

"No," said Doan.

"Where's Mortimer, Wilbur?" Mrs. Henshaw asked.

"He's takin' a nap. He said he was tired."

"The little sweet," said Mrs. Henshaw. "He's been so brave through it all."

"Brave, hell," said Henshaw. "He loved it. He's got no more sense than a sawhorse."

"Gangway! Gangway!" Amanda Tracy shouted hoarsely. She slapped the side door back against the wall and wiggled her way through, almost hidden under an immense stack of canvases. She dumped them carelessly on the floor and shouted over the racketing clatter:

"Hello, Janet, dearie. Hello, Doan. Hi, everybody else. Where's Timpkins? Timpkins, you dirty little thief! Come here! Front and center!"

Timpkins opened the kitchen door. "Well, what? Oh, it's you now, is it? What you want?"

"I want a room and a good one," said Amanda Tracy. "And no bedbugs, either."

"Ain't got one," said Timpkins.

"You'd better find one, chum," said Amanda Tracy. "Starting now. And I mean a room, not a bedbug."

"Why don't you stay home where you belong?"

"My house has got no roof. Scram, Timpkins! Scat!"

"Arr," said Timpkins sullenly, retiring back into the kitchen.

Amanda Tracy nodded cheerily at Doan. "I got to hand it to you, fatso. You must not be near so dumb as you look. That was very nifty the way you rubbed out Eldridge."

"Mr. Doan didn't do that," Janet protested. "The earthquake killed Mr. Eldridge."

"Ha-ha," said Amanda Tracy. "Don't you believe it, dearie. Doan did it. He's sneaky. He'd just as leave kill you as spit. Wouldn't you, Doan?"

"Sure," said Doan. "Massacres organized any hour of the day or night."

"Yeah," said Amanda Tracy. "And don't think I think you're fooling, either."

"Pardon me," said Captain Perona.

"Here's that man again," Greg observed gloomily.

Captain Perona was standing in the doorway. He was in uniform now, and he looked tall and leanly competent. He crossed the room and stopped beside Doan's table.

"And the stooge," said Greg.

Sergeant Obrian came in the room and said: "I heard you. Do I have to take cracks like that from a lousy tourist, Captain?"

"Yes," said Captain Perona. "Doan, I find that in my haste I neglected a certain formality. Stand up and raise your hands."

Doan sighed and got up.

"Search him," said Captain Perona.

Sergeant Obrian searched fast and expertly. "One .38 caliber Colt Police Positive revolver and—fifteen extra rounds for same. That's all the weapons."

"Look once more. He is reported to carry two."

"Nope," said Sergeant Obrian. "He's clean."

"Where did you hide your other weapon?" Captain Perona asked coldly.

"Nowhere," said Doan. "I didn't have one."

Captain Perona looked speculatively at Carstairs. "Tell your dog to stand up."

"Up-si-daisy," said Doan.

Carstairs lumbered reluctantly to his feet.

"Tell him to open his mouth."

"Say 'ah,'" Doan ordered.

Carstairs lolled out a thick red tongue at him.

"All right," said Captain Perona. "Tell him to lie down again."

"Boom," said Doan.

Carstairs dropped on the floor with a thud and a grunt.

Greg said: "That's a very nice hat you have, Doan. May I see it?" He reached out and picked it up with his good hand. There was a clasp knife lying on the table under the hat. "Oh, excuse me," Greg said.

Doan nodded at him. "Hi, pal."

Captain Perona pounced on the knife. It looked something like a scout knife, except that it was larger and longer. Captain Perona pressed a catch on the haft, and a thick, wide blade snapped suddenly into view.

"Very nice," he said. "Very efficient."

"It isn't mine," said Doan. "I never carry a knife. They give me the creepies."

"Then how did it get under your hat?"

"I'll give you one guess," said Doan, looking at Greg in a speculative way.

"Did you put this under his hat?" Captain Perona asked.

"No," said Greg.

"I'm afraid," said Lepicik, "that you are not telling the truth." He was standing on the stairs, just far enough down them so he could see under the ceiling. "You did put the knife under Mr. Doan's hat."

"You're a liar," said Greg.

"I'm so sorry," said Lepicik politely. "But I saw you do it."

"Well?" said Captain Perona.

Greg shrugged his left shoulder. "Okay. I did. I was afraid you and your stooges were going to search us all, and I didn't want it found on me. I just bought the thing today—for a souvenir."

Captain Perona balanced the knife on his palm. "You bought this in Los Altos?"

"Yes."

"Where?"

"From a street peddler."

"What did he look like?"

"Oh, he was a little guy with a funny face. What's the matter with you, anyway? You don't really think I'd carry a thing like that around with me all the time, do you?"

"Yes," said Captain Perona. "I really think you would—and do."

"Prove it," Greg invited.

"Perhaps I will," said Captain Perona, putting the knife and Doan's revolver in his pocket. "And some other things as well. Colonel Callao, the commandant of this district, is coming to interview you tourists soon. I have some important matters to tell you before he arrives. Are you all here now?"

"Mortimer's upstairs asleep," said Henshaw.

"Don't you dare wake my little darling!" Mrs. Henshaw warned.

"I would not think of it," said Captain Perona. "I would be very pleased if he continued to sleep permanently. Now attend to me, please. You all know that Patricia Van Osdel was killed during the earthquake. You know also, I think, that Doan suspected her death was not an accident. I ask you again, Doan:

Why were you so quick to suspect that on the meager evidence available?"

"I've got an evil mind," said Doan. "Can I sit down and rest it?"

"Yes."

"Can I have a drink?"

"Yes."

"Pour me one, too," Greg requested.

Doan looked at him.

"Oh, I'm sorry about the knife," Greg told him. "Forget it. It was just one of those things."

"Some day you're going to pull one too many of those things," Doan said, pouring gin.

"Are you quite comfortable?" Captain Perona asked. "Can you give me your attention now?"

"Go right ahead," Doan said.

"Thank you. As a result of investigation, we have found that your suspicions were justified. Patricia Van Osdel was not killed by accident. She was murdered by being struck on the head by a jagged piece of stone, which was subsequently found in a lane beside her maid, Maria, who was seriously injured by being struck with the same stone."

"How is Maria?" Janet asked.

"Doan was right in his diagnosis there, also. Her skull is fractured. She is not conscious and probably will not be so for several days. She is under guard at the military hospital, and I do not wish to hear of any of you attempting to visit her. As soon as she recovers she will be able to tell us who murdered Patricia Van Osdel and attacked her, but I do not propose to wait that long to find out."

"Why not?" Doan asked. "You've got lots of time."

"Patricia Van Osdel," said Captain Perona, "was an enormously rich and influential citizen of your country. Your country and mine are now allies in the war. We do not wish any incidents to occur which would disturb our relationship. If it were known that Patricia Van Osdel had been murdered here, it would inevitably arouse suspicions of our ability to protect visitors and tourists, and start demands for investigation of the circumstances surrounding her death and rumors of fifth column activity in military zones and such things. Do I make myself clear?"

"Not yet," said Doan.

"I will proceed. Patricia Van Osdel's death is to be known as an accident until such time as we can find and arrest her murderer and prove that the Mexican Army and Government were in no way responsible or negligent."

"Now I get it," said Doan. "Hush-hush."

"Yes. There is no way for any of you to communicate with anyone outside Los Altos. All exits and entrances are guarded by soldiers. All telephone and telegraph wires went down with the bridge."

"Some bridge," Henshaw remarked. "Couldn't even stand a little shaking up."

Captain Perona eyed him narrowly. "I recall that not so long ago a bridge in the United States—a new one—blew down in a high wind."

"Oh," said Henshaw, subdued. "Yeah, I remember that, now you mention it…. Well, what're we gonna do?"

"Stay here. The bridge supports at either end are intact. We will put cables across as soon as we receive the equipment. We are in touch with Major Nacio by military field wireless now."

"Who's he?" Henshaw asked.

"The man who warned you not to come here."

"Yeah," said Henshaw. "He did at that, didn't he? And was he right!"

"He was," Captain Perona agreed. "Your presence here is a needless complication. However, if you will give me the names of the people concerned, I will see that they are notified that you are safe. You may be forced to remain here for a few days, but there will be no shortage of food or supplies. Now I wish to ask you: Do any of you know why Patricia Van Osdel was so determined to come to Los Altos at this particular time?"

No one answered.

"You," said Captain Perona, pointing at Greg.

"I don't know," said Greg. "I didn't know anything about her business affairs. I was strictly a social acquaintance of hers."

Captain Perona pointed at Doan. "You."

"Now, look," Doan protested. "You're going to have to make a choice here. I can't have killed both Eldridge and the Van Osdel at the same time when they were a half mile apart."

Captain Perona counted on his fingers. "Garcia. Eldridge. Patricia Van Osdel. Maria. A death by shooting, a so-called accidental death, a murder, and a near-fatal attack. All since you came to Los Altos."

"Don't forget the earthquake," Doan suggested. "I had that hidden in my hat along with Greg's knife."

"Captain Perona," Janet said, "I think you're just being silly with your suspicions of Mr. Doan."

Captain Perona turned to look at her. "I asked you earlier this afternoon if you wished to be arrested. You said, no. Have you changed your mind?"

"No," said Janet.

"Then do not meddle in affairs that do not concern you."

"Slap his ugly face, dearie," Amanda Tracy urged. "Kick him in his shins."

"What are you doing here," Captain Perona inquired, "besides making a nuisance of yourself?"

"I'm staying here, fancy-pants, because the roof came off my house. Only Doan, thank God, wasn't around to shove me under it when it started to fall. You'd better pinch him, Perona, before he kills all the rest of us."

"Mind your own business."

"All right," said Amanda Tracy. "How about the earthquake, then? That's my business from now on."

"All rescue work has been organized completely by the military. Property is being guarded, people have been removed from dangerous buildings, and the injured—and others—have been taken care of. There is no disorder of any kind, and there will be none."

"Too bad," Amanda Tracy remarked. "How many people killed?"

"Nine, including Senorita Van Osdel and Senor Eldridge."

"How many hurt?"

"Seventeen severely injured, including Maria. They are in a temporary hospital in charge of Lieutenant Ortega and military nurses and attendants. There were thirty-four others who were injured, but not seriously enough to require more than first aid treatment. Only about five buildings collapsed completely. Many others were damaged badly. We have not had time for a complete survey as yet. The earthquake was sharply localized. Both Mazalar and Santa Lucia felt it only faintly. Is that sufficient information to satisfy you?"

"Yup," said Amanda Tracy.

Doan said casually: "How about witnesses? Did you find anybody who saw what happened to Maria and the Van Osdel?"

"Not yet. There was very great confusion at the time of the earthquake, as you know. People were too interested in their own affairs and their own safety to pay much attention to their surroundings or what other people were doing. We are still investigating."

"I don't get this," said Henshaw. "Why all the argument about Patricia Van Osdel's death and the attack on Maria? It's easy to see what happened. Some of these natives around here noticed how spiffy she was dressed, and one of them just batted her one and Maria, too—and ran off with her dough and stuff. This burg looks to me like it's practically full of thieves."

"Speaking of thieves," said Captain Perona, "it *is* my duty to inform you that unless you make immediate cash retribution for the articles you stole this afternoon, you will be arrested and tried by a military court."

"What?" Henshaw shouted indignantly. "Articles I stole?"

"You were seen and identified by six witnesses."

Henshaw slapped himself on the forehead. "That damned Mortimer! I told him not to lift that junk! Look, Captain. It was the kid took them, not me."

"You are responsible for him."

"Like hell! I'm no more responsible for Mortimer than you are for Hitler!"

"Will you pay, or will you go to jail?"

"Put Mortimer in jail," Henshaw invited.

"Wilbur!" Mrs. Henshaw shrieked.

"One hundred and fifty dollars, please," said Captain Perona evenly.

"What!" Henshaw moaned. "Oh, now wait a minute. It was only some old spurs and a hat. Look, I'll make Mortimer give 'em back!"

"The owner does not want them back. He wants the money to repair his store. And, in this case, he has the choice. I might mention that the jail is very crowded and uncomfortable at this time and that, under military law, the penalty for looting is death."

Henshaw stared. "You said—death?"

"Yes."

"Oh!" said Henshaw. "Oh—oh—oh!" He produced a book of travelers' checks and a fountain pen. "One hundred fifty.... Here! Take 'em! Oh, that Mortimer! Oh, just wait!"

"Wilbur," said Mrs. Henshaw, "you won't lay a hand on him—not even a finger. It's all your fault. You tempted him."

"I—I tempted... I never did! I did not! I'll tear him limb from limb! I'll wring his scrawny neck!"

"Enough," said Captain Perona, folding the travelers' checks carefully. "There is another very vital matter. The reason for the trouble with the man, Garcia, and for the presence of a company of soldiers here, and the reason you were warned not to come is that it was suspected that a criminal by the name of Bautiste Bonofile was hiding in disguise in Los Altos. He has now been identified as one Tio Riquez."

"Hey!" Amanda Tracy blurted in amazement. "You don't mean the old drip who had charge of the museum?"

"That old drip," Captain Perona confirmed bitterly. "He had held that position for years, and he had managed to fool everyone. As it was, he was uncovered by accident."

"Well, I like that," said Janet.

"A very attractive accident," Captain Perona corrected, bowing in her direction. "This man is still at large in Los Altos. He cannot—and neither can any of you—possibly escape from the town. We will find him in a short time, but in the meantime I warn you to stay close to this hotel. This man is desperate and very dangerous."

"A public enemy, I bet," said Henshaw. "I've never met one. Bring him around when you catch him."

"I do not think he will be taken alive."

"What was in the museum cellar?" Janet asked curiously.

"We have not been able to determine fully as yet. There were rifles, as he said, as well as a considerable amount of other loot."

"Where'd the old boob steal it?" Amanda Tracy asked.

"That is a military affair," said Captain Perona.

Doan yawned. "He picked it up when he was riding around with a gent named Zapata."

Captain Perona spun on his heel. "How did you know that?"

"Eldridge told me."

"What else did he tell you?"

"Nothing," Doan answered warily.

Captain Perona leaned over the table. "If you knew—if you even suspected—that Tio Riquez was Bautiste Bonofile and did not inform the military authorities, you are going to find yourself in some serious trouble. Very serious, indeed."

"Why don't I keep my big mouth shut?" Doan asked, sighing. "I didn't know. Eldridge didn't, either. Honest."

"Ah-lou," said a thick, wheezing voice, and an incredibly fat man in a rumpled uniform that was too loose for him everywhere except across his paunch and too tight there rolled himself through the door and peered at them glassily through eyes that were yellowish, bloodshot marbles pouched in bluish puffs of flesh.

Captain Perona saluted stiffly. "This is Colonel Callao. He is a filthy, stupid swine, as you can plainly see. He thinks he understands and speaks English, but he does not. Nevertheless, he will be insulted if you attempt to speak to him in Spanish. Speak English, and he will grin like the fool he is and pretend to understand you. Am I not correct, Colonel?"

"Yuzz," said Colonel Callao, grinning proudly. "Ah-lou. Goom-by."

"He is not," said Captain Perona, nodding politely to him, "representative of the Mexican Army. He is a holdover from the old days. He is slightly drunk now but not enough, I do not think, to collapse or vomit on the floor or to perform any of the other antics such pigs usually indulge in when they are intoxicated to a sufficient degree."

Concha burst through the door like an explosion, her short skirt swirling, her magnificent eyes shooting sparks.

"I heard you! I heard every words you say! And I tell him, too!"

"I would not advise you to," Captain Perona warned smoothly. "For your own—safety. This one, ladies and gentlemen, calls herself Senora Eldridge."

"I am!" Concha shrilled furiously. "I have the papers to prove!"

"Forged, no doubt," said Captain Perona.

"Sure! Forged absolutely genuine!" Concha jerked at Colonel

Callao's arm. "There! That one! The little fats with the big, dumb dog! He's killing my husband!"

"Goom-by," said Colonel Callao helpfully.

"He is! Give him the pinch! Puts him in jail! Shoot him!"

"Bang-bang," said Doan.

"Stop that screaming," Captain Perona said to Concha, "and tell us why you think Doan killed your husband."

"Think! I never think! I see him with these eyes. I see him say to my husband he is going to bury him in Mexico! Then comes the earthquake! Grrrrumble-boom-boom! Right away the fats jumps on my husband and beats him and kicks him and hits him on the head and chokes him and bites him with the big, dumb dog!"

"I'm so sorry," said Lepicik, "but you really didn't see any of that."

Concha glared at him. "You are a little, skinny, big liar!"

"No," said Lepicik, "because I saw you on the Avenida Revolucion going away from the house toward the market square just before the earthquake. I noticed you particularly because you are so beautiful."

"Hah?" said Concha, startled.

"Beautiful," Lepicik repeated. "Very. And photogenic, too."

"What's does that mean?" Concha demanded suspiciously.

"It means you would photograph well. Your features are superbly proportioned, and—if you will pardon me—you have a lovely figure. I trunk you would be an outstanding success in motion pictures."

"Why you think that?"

Lepicik smiled apologetically. "I'm a motion picture director."

"Hah! You? Where you work?"

"I'm temporarily at liberty, but I think I can arrange for you to have a screen test, if you wish."

Concha's eyes glistened. "I wish lots!"

"Senora Eldridge," said Captain Perona, "did you see Doan kill your husband?"

"Me?" Concha asked. "No. I am in the streets being beautiful where the skinny one sees me."

"You were lying, then."

"Sure," said Concha. "I don't like the fats. We got no troubles until he comes and kills my husband, I guess."

"Get out of here!" Captain Perona snarled. "And stay out!"

Concha put her thumbs in her ears and wiggled her fingers at him. "Pah! Pooey!" She stuck out her tongue and made a horrid face.

Captain Perona made a move toward her, and she whirled and ran gracefully out the door.

"Goom-by," said Colonel Callao placidly.

"You are right for once, you drooling donkey," said Captain Perona in his smoothest tones. "We are leaving. You tourists, remember what I have told you and govern yourselves accordingly. You will hear from me again soon."

"Not too soon, I hope," Greg told him.

Captain Perona ignored him. He and Sergeant Obrian escorted Colonel Callao politely out the door.

"I got to go get some more of my junk," Amanda Tracy stated. "See you later, kids."

"If you will pardon me," said Lepicik, "I think I will continue my nap."

He went back up the stairs, and Henshaw followed him quietly and purposefully.

"Wilbur," said Mrs. Henshaw. "Where are you going?"

Henshaw didn't answer.

"Wilbur!" Mrs. Henshaw shouted. "Don't you dare sneak in and strike Mortimer! Wilbur!" She got up and ran up the stairs after Henshaw.

"I think I'm drunk enough for the present," Greg said. "I'm a little short of cash. I'll let you pay for the gin."

"Well, thanks," said Doan. "You're too good to me." He waited until Greg had gone upstairs and then nodded to Janet. "Have you got your purse with you?"

"Yes," said Janet, picking it up from the chair beside her. "Here."

"Let me see it, will you? Just throw it over."

She tossed the purse to him. It was a large one made of composition leather, and Doan opened it and fumbled around in its interior while Janet stared at him in amazement. He finally came up with a .25 caliber automatic hardly larger than a package of cigarettes.

"You'd be a sucker for a pickpocket," he said.

"Did you—did you put that in there?" Janet asked.

Doan nodded. "Yeah. I was afraid I might be met by a welcoming committee here and searched like I was just now." He searched in the purse again and found an extra magazine for the automatic.

"Mr. Doan," said Janet, "you lied to Captain Perona. You did have another weapon, and you should have given it to him when he asked you to."

"He doesn't need it. He's got lots of guns." Doan put the automatic and the extra magazine in the breast pocket of his coat. It made no noticeable bulge. "Have a drink?"

"I don't drink."

"What a pity," said Doan, having one himself.

Carstairs growled at him.

"Mr. Doan," said Janet, "I think he's right. I don't think you should impair your faculties when everyone suspects you of— of everything."

"I don't have any faculties to impair," Doan answered. He leaned down and blew his breath at Carstairs.

Carstairs looked at him with a martyred air and then got up and walked over to Janet. He sat down beside her and put his head in her lap.

"Sissy," said Doan. He beat time in the air with his forefinger and sang hoarsely: " 'Oh, it's a great day for the Irish!' "

Carstairs mumbled to himself in disgust.

"I'd like to hear you do better," Doan told him. "Janet, did you ever hear of a painter named Predilip?"

"Yes," Janet said. "I don't know much about art, but I've read about him. I believe he's a sort of a modernist, on the order of Van Gogh."

"Is he dead?"

"Oh, yes. I think he died about 1911. He used to live here in Los Altos, you know. His pictures are one of the reasons why the town is famous."

"Yeah. Are his pictures worth much?"

"In money? Yes, they are. I read in a newspaper a little while ago that one had been sold at auction in New York for nine thousand dollars, and that wasn't a good one. His best ones were painted here just before he died."

"Oh," said Doan, taking another drink.

"Mr. Doan," Janet said, worried, "are you sure you feel all right?"

"Marvelous," Doan answered.

"Well, I've never had much experience with intoxicants. I've never seen anyone just sit down and—and get drunk."

"Stick around, kid," Doan told her. "Stick around."

CHAPTER X

JANET AWOKE AND found she was sitting bolt upright in bed with terror like a cold hand clutching at her throat. For what seemed like eons her faculties fought to free themselves of numbing layers of sleep and exhaustion.

She couldn't remember where she was, and the bare room looked enormous and shadowy with the windows like heavy-lidded eyes in their deep niches in the opposite wall and the high, ugly head of the bed looming over her in silent menace.

And then the yell came again. It was choked and half muffled, but the unadorned terror in it was like an electric shock. Janet threw the covers aside and thrust herself to the edge of the bed, ready to flee somewhere, anywhere.

The bedroom door thundered under a series of heavy blows, and Captain Perona's voice said sharply:

"Open this! Open it at once!"

The door thundered again, jumping against its hinges.

"Wait!" Janet cried. "I'm coming!"

She stumbled against a chair and then felt the twist of the iron latch under her groping hand. She turned the big key, and the lock creaked. Instantly the door slammed back against her, knocking her into the corner, and then Captain Perona gripped her arm with fingers like metal hooks.

"Is there anyone in here with you?" he demanded.

"Wha—what?" Janet said dazedly.

Two soldiers thrust past them. One carried a big flashlight, and its brilliant round eye flicked questioningly through the darkness. The second soldier had a carbine, and the steel of its bayonet flashed savagely as he prodded under the bed and into the cubbyhole closet.

"Let go of me!" Janet cried. "What do you mean—coming in this way.... Stop that!"

Captain Perona released her. "Senorita, is it your custom to greet visitors unclothed?"

Janet looked down at herself. "Oh! Oh, my!" She turned her back and then turned around again and crouched down protectively.

Captain Perona picked up her dress from a chair and dropped it on top of her as though it were something unclean. "Please put this on and stop offending my modesty."

Janet fought with the dress. "I can't.... It's caught.... Don't you touch me!"

Captain Perona yanked the dress down over her head. "Please, senorita! This is no time to be flirtatious!"

Janet's head emerged from the dress. "Oh! You—you— You know very well I had no nightclothes with me, and I had to wash out my underthings, and I didn't have anything—"

"No doubt," said Captain Perona.

He shoved her at the soldier with the carbine. The soldier took her arm and hustled her out into the hall. It was a flickering nightmare tunnel with flashlights reflecting from the cold blue of gun barrels, from gleaming brass buttons. There were more soldiers, crowded so close Janet had no chance to count them, their faces dark and tense, excitedly eager.

The one who had hold of her hurried her along, steered her down the stairs at a stumbling run. The big kerosene pressure lamp was lighted, swinging violently on its chain, and its shadows chased and jumped crazily over more soldiers. There were three of them at the door, peering in, and more at the window and the door into the kitchen. The one who was escorting Janet let go of her and ran upstairs again.

"Pardon me," said Doan, "while I put on my pants." He hopped industriously on one leg and then the other.

Carstairs sat on the floor looking rumpled and sleepily indignant. Lepicik was sitting at a table beside the staircase. He was fully dressed and as neat as ever. He was even carrying his green umbrella. He was not at all concerned by the uproar. His expression was one of vaguely polite interest.

"My dress!" Janet exclaimed, pulling at it frantically. "And—and I haven't got any shoes on!"

"Neither have I," said Doan cheerfully. He sat down and put his bare feet up on a chair. "The Captain seemed to be in a bit of a rush."

"What is it?" Janet demanded. "What's the matter?" She looked at the soldiers. "*Querasa?*"

One soldier shrugged. The others shook their heads at her.

"That clears everything up," Doan observed.

"Are you sober now?" Janet asked him suspiciously.

Doan nodded. "Just about."

"Well, do you feel—awfully bad?"

"No," said Doan.

"I thought people always felt bad after they got drunk."

"You have to have brains to get a hangover," Doan told her. "I'm never troubled."

"You *were* very drunk, you know. You sang questionable songs and beat on the table and told jokes that had no point and spilled three drinks."

"That's me," Doan agreed. "That's your old pal, Drunken Doan, when he gets curled."

"Carstairs was very angry with you."

"He's an evil-tempered brute," Doan said. "He's always mad at something."

The Henshaws, all three of them, came rumbling down the stairs like a group of frightened sheep with a soldier herding them along with judicious thrusts of his carbine butt.

"Say!" Henshaw said, struggling with his suspenders. "What gives here, anyway? Are we invaded?"

Mrs. Henshaw screamed: "I'll tell the President! I'll write him a letter! He'll send a battleship right down here and blow you all up!"

"Yeow!" Mortimer screeched. "Maw!"

Mrs. Henshaw enveloped him in a stranglehold. "Don't cry, baby! I won't let the beasts shoot you!"

Henshaw was tucking in his shirttail. "This is sure a fine way to treat tourists and allies. Just wait until I talk before the Rotary Club. I'll sure put the blister on these birds."

"What were you yelling about a minute ago?" Doan asked him.

Henshaw looked sheepish. "You hear me? Well, I was havin' a nightmare. A lulu, too. You know this mountain range is supposed to be a sleeping woman. I dreamed she was lying there all peaceful when a big mouse that looked like Carstairs came sneaking along, and she jumped up and let out a screech and shook her skirts, and the whole damned town fell into the canyon. And then six soldiers started to shake my bed to wake me up! I woke up, all right! Out loud!"

Heels made a quick, crisp clatter on the stairs, and Captain Perona came down and looked at them. His eyes were narrowed, gleaming slits.

"Quiet!" he barked. "Quiet, all of you! Where is the man, Greg?"

No one answered until Janet snapped suddenly: "Was that who you thought was in my room? Why, I'll—"

Captain Perona took a step toward her. "Will you be quiet?"

"Yes," said Janet, scared.

There was a sudden uproar of voices in the kitchen and the metallic clangor of a pan rolling on the floor. Timpkins was thrust headlong into the room. He was wearing a long white nightshirt, and his nutcracker face was contorted and red with rage above it.

"Here now! What's all this? I'm a British subject, I'll have you know! I'll protest—"

"Silence!" Captain Perona ordered. "Where is the man, Greg?"

"Arr?" said Timpkins blankly. "Greg? In his bed, I suppose."

"No! His bed has not been slept in!"

"Why all the sudden interest in Greg?" Doan asked.

Captain Perona watched him narrowly. "Tonight the maid of Patricia Van Osdel—the woman, Maria—was stabbed and killed in her hospital bed. The soldier guarding her was also killed. Three hand grenades were stolen from the armory."

"Don't blame me," said Doan. "I didn't have any grudge against Maria, and besides I was so drunk I wouldn't have known a hand grenade from a howitzer. Ask anybody. Those hand grenades sound like our old pal, Bautiste Bonofile, is out and about again."

"No," said Captain Perona. "He would not need to steal explosives. He has plenty of his own."

"That's nice to know, too," Doan commented. "Looks like, what with this and that, we're going to have a quiet weekend among the peaceful peasants."

"As I may have mentioned before," said Captain Perona, "I do not appreciate your humor. Kindly be quiet. I do not believe that the absence of the man, Greg, at the time of the murderous attack on Maria can be a coincidence."

"Pardon me," said Lepicik. "Please. But it might be."

"Why?" Captain Perona demanded.

"I'm so sorry, but I think perhaps I frightened him."

"How?"

"I believe he recognized me."

"Why would that frighten him?" Captain Perona asked skeptically.

Lepicik smiled. "He would know, of course, that I came here to kill him."

"So?" said Captain Perona. "You came here to kill him. Did you?"

Lepicik shook his head regretfully. "No. I haven't as yet had a good opportunity. Now I'm afraid he has eluded me again. He is so very clever. I had no idea that he knew what I looked like, and he gave no sign that he recognized me. But perhaps he had a description or a picture of me. I have, after all, been hunting him for quite some time."

"This is very interesting," said Captain Perona icily. "Tell me why you have been hunting him."

"Greg is not a refugee from anything except the law in a dozen countries and his own conscience, if he has one. He was a member of a Balkan terrorist group that specialized in political assassination for pay. My brother was a government official before the invasion. A minor official. He had a wife and a very beautiful daughter. One Sunday morning when they were all on their way to church, Greg or one of five other men—I was never able to narrow it down more closely than that—tossed a hand grenade into their small automobile."

There was a heavy little silence.

"And your relatives?" Captain Perona inquired softly.

"My brother and his wife were killed instantly. Both of my niece's legs were blown off. She was seventeen."

"Oh," said Janet, sickened.

"Fortunately," said Lepicik in his mild way, "she did not live. She died three weeks later. I sat beside her hospital bed all that time. She was in great pain."

"The other five men," said Captain Perona. "The ones, besides Greg, who were involved. What happened to them?"

"They died," said Lepicik. "Now, if you will excuse me, I will go find Adolfo Morales and his burro, Carmencita."

"And then what do you propose to do?" asked Captain Perona.

Lepicik looked faintly surprised. "Continue to hunt for Greg, of course."

"He cannot possibly have gotten out of Los Altos."

"I'm so sorry," Lepicik contradicted. "But I'm afraid he has. He is very clever."

"No," said Captain Perona. "He is here somewhere, no matter how clever he is." He hesitated. "I can understand how you feel, and I sympathize with you, but I cannot allow you to remain at large unless you give me your word you will not attempt to find Greg or to harm him."

Lepicik merely smiled.

Captain Perona shrugged. "Then I am forced to place you under technical arrest."

"It will be quite useless for you to do that," Lepicik told him. "I will find Greg sooner or later."

"But not in this district while I am in charge of his safety. You will be placed in my quarters under guard. You will be comfortable there."

"Thank you," said Lepicik.

Sergeant Obrian came part way down the stairs. "Captain, didn't that old artist doll say she was gonna flop here? She ain't around now."

"Amanda Tracy!" Captain Perona exploded. "Where is she?"

"Now how do I know?" Timpkins asked drearily. "I was sleepin' peaceful as a baby—"

"Somebody want me?" a hoarse, wheezing voice asked. "Well, here I am. What's left of me."

The soldiers shoved and squeezed in the doorway, and Amanda Tracy staggered past them. One side of her frizzed hair was matted into a crusted tangle, and blood lay like a red, glistening hand across her cheek. She braced herself on thickly muscular legs and swayed back and forth, staring blearily at Captain Perona.

"That fella Greg," she said. "You wait until I get my mitts...." She groped out vaguely with bloodstained hands. "Goes and socks a lady with a rock just because she says hello.... You wait—"

She fell forward as swiftly and suddenly as a tree toppling, and her head clunked solidly against the floor.

Mrs. Henshaw decided to scream and did so, frantically and senselessly, holding on to Mortimer so tightly that his eyes popped.

Captain Perona barked an order over his shoulder, and one of the soldiers in the doorway ducked away into the darkness. Captain Perona dropped to his knee beside Amanda Tracy and felt for the pulse in one of her thick, tanned wrists.

"She is alive," he said, breathing deeply in relief. Carefully he parted the matted, blood-soaked hair. "Ah! It is here! A blow like the one that killed Senorita Van Osdel, only this one glanced and cut instead of striking deep." He looked up. "Do any of you know anything of this?"

"Greg did it," said Henshaw. "Didn't you hear her? Greg

smacked down Patricia Van Osdel and Maria and this one, too. Just find him and everything is solved."

"How do you know?"

"I deduced it," said Henshaw.

"Keep your deductions to yourself after this."

"Okay," said Henshaw. "But don't come around and say I didn't tell you—"

"Be quiet!"

Timpkins cleared his throat. "I was kind of muzzy-like from sleep first off…. Seems like I remember—"

"What!" Captain Perona barked angrily.

"Here now," said Timpkins indignantly. "Not so rough, if you please. All I was gonna say was that she was complaining about the bedding I gave her—without no reason at all, you may be sure and she said something about goin' over to her place and diggin' some of her own out of the wreckage."

"Why didn't you stop her?"

"Arr?" said Timpkins. "Me? Stop her? Oh, no. I've had a brush or two with her before this."

"I warned you all to stay in the hotel!"

"Now, Captain," said Timpkins. "Naturally, she thought that just applied to these here tourists—not to old residents like me and her."

The soldier came back, panting heavily, with a rolled-up stretcher over his shoulder. He and an other soldier unfastened the straps, opened it out, and put it on the floor beside Amanda Tracy.

"*Cuidado!*" Captain Perona warned.

The soldiers lifted Amanda Tracy's thick body gently and put her down on the stretcher.

Captain Perona stood up. "You see now—from this—that it pays to give attention to my warnings. I do not talk to you merely for the pleasure it gives me. The rest of the night you will all stay in this hotel. I will leave soldiers to see that you do.

If the man, Greg, returns he will be arrested. If he does not return, we will find his hiding place and very soon, I will take Senorita Tracy to the hospital now. Senor Lepicik, you will come with me, please."

"Certainly," said Lepicik. "Mr. Doan, will you take care of my umbrella for me, please?"

"Sure, pal," said Doan.

"You will be careful of it?"

"Indeed, yes," said Doan.

Lepicik and Captain Perona followed the soldiers carrying the stretcher out the door. Sergeant Obrian came down the stairs ahead of more soldiers.

"Don't none of you birds try to fly this coop," he warned. "Some of us will be outside, and we're feelin' nasty." He counted the soldiers as they filed through the door, nodded once meaningly, and followed them.

"Now I don't care for this!" Timpkins snarled. "Not a little bit! Turning my hotel into a jail and a slaughterhouse. I'm tellin' you, and you all hear me say it, no more of this hanky-panky or out you go. Right into the street. Captain Perona or no Captain Perona, I know my rights. I'm a British subject, and I'll protest to the ambassador."

He marched out the back way, his bony bare feet slapping on the floor and his nightshirt fluttering indignantly behind him.

"I'm going to bed," said Henshaw. "I got to snag old Timpkins for a bathroom tomorrow, and I can't sell good unless I get my sleep."

He went upstairs, and Mrs. Henshaw, trailing Mortimer, followed him.

Doan was examining Lepicik's green umbrella cautiously. "I wonder how this works."

"Why, just like any umbrella," Janet told him. "Let me show you."

"Ah-ah," said Doan. "No. Get away. I've got it now."

There was a sudden loud pop.

"Reminds me of champagne," said Doan.

"Did the umbrella make that noise?" Janet asked curiously.

Doan nodded. "Yeah. It also made that." He pointed toward the bar.

There was a bright sliver of steel, about the size and half the length of a knitting needle, stuck deep in the hard wood.

Janet stared. "It—it shot that?"

"Yes. It's an air-gun. A dandy, too. I'd hate to have somebody pop one of those pins into my eye. I bet it wouldn't be very healthy. Let's see. It should pump up here somewhere…. Ah!"

The crooked handle turned and slid out six inches, revealing an inner sheathing of oiled metal.

"Sure," said Doan, working it experimentally. "Just like a bicycle pump. Throws air pressure into this cylinder and holds it until you release this catch and then blows it—and the steel pin—out through the length of the barrel. Very neat. I'll bet it's damned accurate at close range, too."

While Janet watched him he went over and started to work the steel needle loose from the bar.

"I thought air-guns were toys," Janet said.

"What do you think now?" Doan asked.

"Why—why, that's a murderous thing!"

"I'll bet it is, at that," said Doan. "This needle is stuck in here two inches. It's got a leather washer here on the reverse end to hold the air pressure…." He stopped working at the dart and looked over the bar. "I think it's about time Doan should have another drink."

Carstairs sat back on his haunches and yelled. There was no other word to express the sound. It was a cry of sheer animal frustration so loud that its reverberations rattled the lamp chain and set the shadows to dancing again.

"All right!" Doan said, when he could make himself heard.

"You spoil-sport! You blue-nose! If you feel that badly about it, we'll go to bed instead!"

CHAPTER XI

IT WAS MORNING, and the sun was gleaming and grinning generously, regardless of earthquakes, murders, or even Hitler. Janet sat on the parapet that circled the roof of the Hacienda Nueva Inglesa and kicked her heels against the rough plaster, relaxing luxuriously. There was just a slight breeze, and the air felt dry and gentle touching her face.

Los Altos spread away under her—crooked little streets jogging between red, scarred roofs—each detail clear and perfect in miniature. People were splotches of color—serapes and rebozos and white sombreros—moving busily about their affairs like jerky, self-satisfied bugs. Occasionally she could hear the faint overtones of their voices—the thin chittering of words in the mass.

Far on down below, beyond the borders of the town, the Canyon of Black Shadow was like a blue, crooked vein laid against the pink flesh of the earth. So clear was the air that Janet could see the toylike soldiers working around the jagged needle of the bridge support on the far side. A heliograph near them blinked a constant barrage of bright signals at other soldiers on the near side.

Janet breathed deeply, enjoying it all. She turned after a little to look the other way, up the slope of the mountain. The houses above frowned down on her like white, dull faces.

Off to her right, west of the town, the slope stretched upward in a brown, tangled sweep, and Janet looked across its waste absently until her eyes caught and came back to an upthrust of queerly shaped rock. She studied it casually until she could make out a blocky, rough-cut profile. It was as though some giant had taken an oversize ax and cut out nose and mouth and bulge of brows with three expert blows.

Janet turned to her left, still lazily indifferent, and looked up the east slope. They were there—three square, stone monuments in a line like the three bears, big and then medium and then small. Janet smiled a vague greeting at them and wondered how she knew they were where they were. She decided she would have to think about the matter some time when she was more industrous and less comfortable.

From somewhere far off there came a faint, humming buzz. It had no direction at first. It resounded in the whole limitless vault of the sky. Janet stared, shielding her eyes against the glare with a cupped hand.

The buzz deepened to a drone. It localized itself toward the north, faded away, and then swept down with redoubled strength, coming closer with incredible rapidity.

At last Janet's eyes found it—a blurred, black dot moving across the blue of the sky. The drone blended into deep, smooth thunder, and the dot picked up stubby little crossbars on either side.

Heels made a sudden racket on the rickety steps that led up to the roof's trapdoor, and Captain Perona popped breathlessly into sight.

"Pardon, senorita. But this is the best place…. Where is it—the plane?"

Janet pointed. "There."

The black dot heeled over and became a stubby cross as the plane swerved and dipped down toward the canyon. The heliograph flickered at it.

The engine roared in a sudden blast of power, and the plane climbed steeply and then came down over the town in a smooth, careful glide with the engine punctuating it in nervous blurps. Janet could see now that it was a short-winged, short-bodied military pursuit ship with an enormous barrel of an engine.

"Yes!" Captain Perona shouted triumphantly. "It is Enrique!"

"Who?" Janet asked.

"My brother. He is a lieutenant—a pilot. He is bringing

medicine—anti-tetanus vaccine for Lieutenant Ortega. Watch! Watch now!"

The plane dipped over the plaza, very low, like a swiftly dangerous bird of prey, and blurred little blobs fell out behind it—one, two, three. They jerked and skittered in the slipstream, and then suddenly blossomed out. They were small green parachutes, and they settled down toward the ground, swaying dignifiedly, while soldiers ran and shouted under them, trying to plot their course.

The plane bored upward into the air in tight spirals.

"Your scarf!" Captain Perona begged. "Give me your scarf, please!"

Janet pulled it from her neck. "But why?"

Captain Perona jumped up on the parapet and balanced there, waving the scarf in wild circles around his head.

"He can't see you," Janet said.

"But, yes! He knows I am here! He will be looking!"

The plane suddenly flattened out. The stubby wings waggled up and down, reflecting the sun in dazzling streaks.

Captain Perona waltzed precariously on the parapet. "You see? That Enrique! He has eyes like a hawk!"

Janet caught one booted leg. "Come down off that parapet! You'll fall!"

Captain Perona landed beside her breathlessly. "He saw me! Watch, now! Look!"

The plane rolled over with a sort of deadly precision and then dove straight down at them. The power was full on, and the sound deepened and bellowed until it was like a giant drum in Janet's head. The plane came down and down like an enormous bullet, and Janet could feel her knees trembling with the vibration, and then it flipped up and away, and its black shadow touched them and was gone.

Captain Perona laughed gleefully. "That Enrique! He tried to scare us!"

"He—he did?" Janet asked, swallowing.

Captain Perona grinned. "Enrique is the best pilot in Mexico. Watch him!"

The plane found altitude incredibly fast, and now it came slanting down again, sideslipping. It went past the roof so close that Janet thought she could have reached up and touched it. It was canted over at an impossible angle, and she caught one flashing glimpse of the opened, bonnet-like glassine that covered the cockpit. The pilot was leaning out, pointing with one stiff, black-clad arm.

"Yes!" Captain Perona shouted, making wildly affirmative gestures with his arms and head. "Stand up on the parapet, senorita!"

"Wh—what?" said Janet.

"Quick! So he can see you more plainly!"

Before Janet could move, he caught her around the waist with both hands and swung her up on the parapet. Janet opened her mouth to shout, and then the plane was back again, going much faster now, but closer and lower. She swayed dizzily in the tempest of its passage, and she had an eye-wink sight of the pilot's sinisterly helmeted head peering at her.

Captain Perona swung her down off the parapet again. "Now watch!"

The plane flipped over and roared at them, and as it went by Janet saw the pilot's arms sticking up straight out of the cockpit. He was shaking hands with himself like the victor in a prize-fight.

Captain Perona laughed. "That Enrique! He is congratulating me!"

"What for?" Janet asked dizzily.

"Because he agrees with what I said about you."

"What you said…. When did you tell him anything about me?"

"Over the military wireless—before he started on this trip."

The plane engine growled ominously.

Janet cringed. "Please tell him to go away!"

"He is going now. See?"

The plane came over the roof, much higher, and then scooted down over the soldiers on the far side of the canyon and waggled its wings at the heliograph. It climbed very rapidly and changed back into a black dot and disappeared over the mountain.

"He would have shown us more tricks," Captain Perona said, "only he is very busy now, and that is one of our newest pursuit ships, and he is not supposed to stunt needlessly with it. Here is your scarf, senorita. Thank you."

"What did you tell him about me?" Janet asked suspiciously, taking the scarf.

"I told him that you were very pretty and very silly."

"Silly!" Janet echoed.

"Oh, that is nothing personal, and besides he would know you were even if I had not told him."

"Well, why would he?"

"He knows all about young ladies from the United States, because he went to school there."

"Where?" Janet demanded. "What school?"

"A place called Harvard. It was very unfortunate, but we could do nothing about it,"

"Unfortunate?" Janet repeated. "Why?"

"He is the third son, you see, and we could not afford to give him a good education."

"Good…. Why, Harvard is one of the finest universities in the United States!"

"As you say—in the United States."

Janet glared at him. "Well, where did you go to school?"

"I was very lucky. My family could afford to give me the best education. I studied in Mexico and Spain and Peru at the finest universities in the world. I know a great deal about everything, which is why I found your pretensions to learning so ridiculous."

"Oh, you did, did you? I'll have you know that the school system in the United States is the best there is anywhere!"

"You are mistaken."

"I am not!"

"Then why are there so many stupid people in the United States?"

"Why are there so many stupid people here?"

"Where?" asked Captain Perona politely.

"Very—near—here!"

"You are referring to me, no doubt?" said Captain Perona.

"Yes!"

"You think I am stupid?"

"Yes!"

"You see? Now you are being silly. You do not have the capability to appreciate true learning. And it was silly of you to tell me that falsehood about your being a professor."

"Now you look here!" said Janet. "Now you just look here! I studied nights and weekends and summers and all the rest of the time, and I have an A.B. and a M.A., and I have qualified for an associate professorship in two different colleges!"

"In what field?" Captain Perona inquired.

"Romance languages!"

Captain Perona raised his eyebrows. "Romance?"

"And it's not what you think, either!"

"I trust not. Have you anything more to say to me at this time, senorita?"

"You just bet I have!"

"Then do you mind if I sit down, please, while I give you my full attention? I am very tired."

"Oh," said Janet. "Haven't you had any sleep?"

"None," Captain Perona admitted ruefully. "I was sitting up all the night waiting for Senorita Tracy to regain consciousness, and then at dawn I started the searching parties and laid out territories and areas for each of them to cover."

"How is Miss Tracy?" Janet asked.

"She is all right now. She can leave the hospital this evening. The blow was painful but not serious."

"And Mr. Lepicik?"

"When I last saw him, he was sleeping on my bed. He looked as though he were enjoying himself thoroughly."

"I feel so sorry for him," Janet said. "That terrible tragedy...."

"Save your sympathy for Greg," Captain Perona advised. "I think he will need it."

"Have you found him yet?"

"No."

"What did Miss Tracy tell you about him?"

"It was as Timpkins suggested. She did not think my warning applied to her, and besides she is very sure of her ability to take care of herself. She went to her house to get some bedding and some clothes after dark last night. On her way back she saw Greg near the back of the hospital, and she spoke to him in the bold way she has. He struck her with a stone he was carrying."

"But why?"

"He was waiting to sneak in the hospital, then, I think. So he could find and kill Maria before she could give evidence that he was the one who had murdered Patricia Van Osdel and attacked Maria."

"Have you found Bautiste Bonofile?"

"No!" said Captain Perona. He made an angrily frustrated gesture. "And it is a thing that is not possible! Look, senorita. One can see the whole of this small town from this roof. Every house in it. And there is no way that either Bautiste Bonofile or Greg could get out of town. All exits and trails are guarded. And my men can see the whole of the country for many miles around from a number of sentry posts near here. We have searched everywhere thoroughly, and now we are searching a second time. Greg and Bautiste Bonofile are not here, and yet they could not be anywhere else!"

Doan cleared his throat. He was standing on the stairway with his head and shoulders protruding up through the trap-door. He smiled at them benignly and said:

"Sorry to interrupt, but I wondered if I could send a wireless message through your soldier setup."

"You could not," said Captain Perona definitely. "I have already sent a message to your agency, telling them that you are safe—at the moment."

"Oh now, be reasonable," Doan requested. "I'm not trying to sneak out any information or anything you wouldn't want me to send. I just want to reassure my wife and kids."

Janet looked surprised. "I didn't know you were married."

"Sure. Didn't I tell you? I've got three kids. Little girls. Cute as bugs' ears. They'll be worried about me if they don't get a personal message, and so will my wife. See, I send the kids a telegram every couple of days when I'm away from home. It goes on my agency expense account, of course. But they'll know that if I don't send them a message after this earthquake it's because I'm not able to do it, and they'll imagine I'm at death's door or something. Please, Captain. The seven-year-old is sick with the measles, and the whole joint is quarantined, and they're pretty lonesome."

"Oh, let him!" Janet begged.

Captain Perona stared narrowly at Doan. "What kind of a message do you want to send?"

"Just dopey stuff that kids like. How Papa and Carstairs are okay and thinking of them and loving them. I mean, your man will see that it's addressed to the kids."

"Well…." said Captain Perona doubtfully. "All right."

Doan looked embarrassed. "Well, would it be okay if I sent it in pig-Latin?"

"What?" said Captain Perona. "Pigs?"

Janet said: "It's a sort of a schoolchild language. Switching the syllables of words around."

"For the kids," Doan explained. "They dote on that stuff. I

always send them telegrams that way. Anybody can read it, of course, but they think it's a code all for them, and they get a big kick out of it."

"You give me your word you will not give them any information about the murders here or about Bautiste Bonofile?"

"Absolutely," said Doan. "I promise."

Captain Perona took a notebook from his pocket, scribbled on a page, and tore it out. "Here. The transmitting set is at headquarters. Give this to the sergeant in charge. He will send your message—if it is addressed to your children."

"Thanks a lot," said Doan. He kicked backwards. "Get off the ladder, Carstairs. Go on. Back down, you big goop." His head disappeared through the trapdoor.

"I think he's nice," Janet said.

"I wish I thought so," Captain Perona stated gloomily. "I really think Eldridge's death was accidental, and I do not believe Doan could possibly be concerned in the murders of Patricia Van Osdel and Maria, and I am sure that I know more about this affair than he can know. But still he worries me. I wish he were anywhere but here. He is too quick and too clever and too experienced, and this whole thing can be very bad for me unless it is cleared up at once."

"Why?" Janet asked. "It isn't your fault."

Captain Perona spoke slowly: "It is like this. Major Nacio is in charge of the search for Bautiste Bonofile. I am his second-in-command. I am not under the authority of Colonel Callao, although I must defer to him to a certain extent because of his rank. He is merely the district officer here. Major Nacio and his troops are specialists in anti-espionage—in work against subversive elements and spies as well as bandits. I asked to serve with them. It is an honor."

"Of course," said Janet.

"When we trailed the man Doan shot—Garcia—to Los Altos, then we knew that Bautiste Bonofile must be here somewhere close, because we knew that Bautiste Bonofile had some contact with Garcia, although we did not—and do not now—know what it was. Then Major Nacio's plan was put into effect. Every exit and entrance was watched day and night. Lepicik got through as he did only because of the excitement caused by the pursuit of Garcia. He would have been reported very soon if he had not reported himself. We watched Garcia continuously—to see whom he spoke to, whom he met, whom he even looked at. But Bautiste Bonofile managed to warn him anyway. After that, we chased Garcia back and forth through the town, blocking him off each time he tried to get out, hoping that Bautiste Bonofile would attempt to help him. It was a very small chance, I admit. Bautiste Bonofile is too cold-blooded to risk betraying himself to help anyone. However, had your tourists tried to get back out of Los Altos, you would have had a great deal more difficulty than you did coming in."

Janet shivered. "No wonder!"

"So then," said Captain Perona, "Garcia was shot by Doan. Major Nacio had planned for even a contingency like that. The town had been separated into small area units and soldiers assigned to each area. They went to work instantly, searching, questioning each person. You see, I was not neglecting my duties when I took you to the museum. There was nothing for me to do, then. The men are experts. They knew just what to do and how to do it. I had only to wait and sift any evidence which they found. Then came the earthquake."

"Even Major Nacio couldn't foresee that," Janet observed.

"No. Not even he. But since I am isolated here for the moment, I must handle what happens quickly and efficiently. The murders of Patricia Van Osdel and Maria… they must be solved at once, or it will reflect on me and on Major Nacio, too. I must find Greg. I have uncovered Bautiste Bonofile, due to your help, and I must find him, also. It is directly my responsibility, and it is a very grave one."

"Perhaps I could help you," Janet suggested.

Captain Perona looked at her. "Senorita, do you think this

is some children's game? Do you realize the type and kind of men I am seeking? Do you realize that Greg and Bautiste Bonofile are murderers and would not hesitate for a second to strike again?"

"Of course I realize it."

"Then kindly occupy yourself with your ludicrous sight-seeing and leave serious matters to those who understand them. I must go now. Excuse me, please."

"Good-by!" Janet said definitely.

CHAPTER XII

JANET FELL IN with local custom and took a siesta, and it was early in the afternoon when she came sleepily down the stairs into the bar-restaurant of the Hacienda Nueva Inglesa. The room was warm and shadowy, and the odors of spilled wine and tobacco hung comfortingly close in the air.

"This one!" said Mrs. Henshaw enthusiastically. She was holding up one of Amanda Tracy's paintings. "This is the one I want. It'll look wonderful in the living room."

"Relax," Henshaw advised. He was sitting in front of the door into the kitchen like a cat waiting at a mousehole. "You ain't gonna buy any pictures."

"In the living room," Mrs. Henshaw repeated, staring at the picture raptly. "Right over the mantel."

"Over my dead body," Henshaw corrected.

Timpkins came in from the kitchen. "Dinner'll be served at six sharp, if you please. It ain't gonna be fancy, and them as don't like it don't need to eat it."

"Mr. Timpkins," Janet said. "Has my room been cleaned today?"

"No," Timpkins answered.

"Well—who cleans it?"

"You do," Timpkins informed her. "If it gets cleaned."

"Haven't you any help at the hotel?"

"No. I don't need none."

"Timpkins," said Henshaw.

Timpkins looked at him. "What, now?"

"Sit down," Henshaw invited, crooking his finger and smiling enticingly. "Right here in this nice chair. Rest yourself, Timpkins. You've been working too hard all day."

Timpkins sat down slowly and suspiciously.

"I've been spending a lot of time thinking about your business problems," Henshaw told him.

"I ain't got no business problems."

"That's just it," said Henshaw. "That's your trouble right there. Now you've got a swell setup here. You could make this hotel a gold mine."

"How?" Timpkins inquired skeptically.

"Think of your situation. Analyze it, Timpkins. That's the first step, always. Los Altos, with its scenery, with its quaintness, with its artistic history. It's a sure tourist-puller. And you're on the ground floor. I envy you, Timpkins. I see you as independently rich in the near future."

"Arr?" said Timpkins.

"Yes, indeed. Now consider the international situation. After this war, Europe is going to be a mess. Take my word for it, Timpkins. I know. People aren't going to want to go there any more. Besides that, they won't be able to afford it. They'll want to see new and different things closer to home. They'll want the atmosphere and adventure of foreign lands. Where will they go to get that, Timpkins?"

"Where?" said Timpkins.

"Here. In Los Altos. They'll come by the hundreds with money in their pockets. And when they come to Los Altos, they'll come here to this hotel—naturally. You'll coin dough. The place could be a mint for you. For instance, how much do you charge for rooms now?"

"Five dollars a day."

"You robber—I mean to say, that goes to prove what I'm telling you. You could charge much more—if you were progressive."

"Progressive?" Timpkins repeated.

"Yes. For instance, take the matter of a bathroom. Now I'm not trying to sell you a bathroom, Timpkins. Don't think that for a minute. I'm just using it for an illustration. Suppose tourists come in here after sight-seeing in the town—tired, dirty, discouraged—and they step into the hotel bathroom and they see something like this." Henshaw flipped out the shiny folder like a magician producing a rabbit. "4A, right here. A beautiful setup. Lavish and luxurious. Yellow and black tile with a guaranteed imitation marble trim and plastic streamlined fixtures."

"Naw!" said Timpkins.

"Wait, now. I'm not suggesting you should buy it. Maybe something else would be more suitable. But the tourists would be impressed, Timpkins. In the United States people judge you by your bathroom. It's the most important part of your house. These tourists, after they'd seen 4-A, would go away feeling impressed and refreshed. They'd advertise you by word-of-mouth to other tourists. Now just look through this folder. Pick out something to your own taste."

"Naw!" said Timpkins.

Doan was sitting in the corner near the end of the bar with his hat down over his eyes. Carstairs lay in front of him, snoring in pleasantly deep gurgles.

"Timpkins," said Doan, pushing his hat up. "What part of England do you come from?"

"I'm a British subject," said Timpkins.

"Also a Canadian, I'll bet."

"Arr," said Timpkins. "What's it to you?"

"Nothing. Ever been in England?"

"Yes!"

"For how long?"

"Two weeks," said Timpkins sullenly. He got up. "Now I don't want none of you botherin' me any more. I'm busy."

He went back into the kitchen and slammed the door.

"Thanks, Doan," Henshaw said. "That gives me a new lead. I don't know what kind of bathrooms they got in England, but I've been in Canada once. I went to Niagara Falls and walked across the bridge. I'll run in some references to that the next time I catch him. Always establish some common ground with a prospect. You notice how I sneaked up on him, then? I'm gonna sell him. You watch."

"Mr. Doan," said Janet, "did you get your message off all right?"

"Yes, thanks," Doan told her. "My little girls will get a great kick out of it."

"How old are they?"

"Five and seven and nine. Two brunettes and a blonde."

"What color is your wife's hair?"

"It changes. It's red now."

"Hi-yo, Silver!" Mortimer yelled. He came galloping in through the front door. He had strapped the spurs on over his tennis shoes, and he had to run both bowlegged and pigeon-toed to keep from tripping over them. He had stuffed paper in the band of the sombrero, and it waggled precariously on his head, the enormous brim extending far out beyond his puny shoulders.

"Whoa, Silver," he commanded belligerently, prancing and kicking out with the spurs. He had a braided leather quirt in his hand, and he slashed furiously at the air around him.

"Where'd you get that whip?" Henshaw demanded.

"Just picked it up," Mortimer answered.

"Well, you just pick it back again. Do you wanna get me shot or something, you little rummy?"

"Go dive for a pearl," Mortimer invited. He pranced over to Doan. "Hey, puffy, can I ride the flea-trap?"

"Carstairs?" Doan asked. "Oh, sure. Go right ahead, Mortimer."

Mortimer straddled the sleeping Carstairs. "Get up!" he yelled, punching Carstairs with the quirt.

Carstairs got up—and fast. Mortimer did a neat back-flip in the air and landed flat on his face on the floor. Carstairs sat down on him.

"I figured that would be it," said Doan.

Mortimer yelled in a choked, wheezing gasp. Mrs. Henshaw screamed and ran for him. One of Mortimer's arms stuck out from under Carstairs, and she grabbed that and tugged with all her might.

"Get off, Carstairs," Doan said. "You'll squash the little dope."

Carstairs looked interested but not cooperative. Doan sighed and got up. He took hold of Carstairs' spiked collar and heaved. Mrs. Henshaw pulled at Mortimer. Nothing happened.

"Quit it, Carstairs," Doan ordered. He spat on his hands, took a new grip on the collar, and heaved back with all his might.

Carstairs stood up. Doan sat down hard, and so did Mrs. Henshaw. Mortimer's face was blue, and his mouth was wide open, and his eyes were popped like grapes. He drew in his breath in a strangled gulp and promptly let it go again.

"Yeow! Maw!"

Mrs. Henshaw blubbered over him. "Mama's poor, poor baby! Don't you cry! We'll have the soldiers shoot the nasty, dirty, old dog!"

"The hell we will," said Henshaw. "We'll buy him a medal or a beefsteak or something."

Doan got up and brushed himself off tenderly. "Damn you," he said to Carstairs. "That floor has got slivers in it."

Carstairs yawned and walked to the door. He stood there looking back over his shoulder at Doan.

"Well, go on out," Doan said. "The soldiers are gone now. Nobody will stop you."

Carstairs mumbled deep in his throat.

"Listen," said Doan, "you're a big dog now. You can go out and attend to your private affairs without me supervising you or them."

Carstairs barked once and made the kerosene lamp jump and jingle on its chain.

"All right," Doan said. "All right!" He went to the door and bunted Carstairs in the rear with his knee. "Get going then, stupid."

Mortimer sat up and wiped his nose on his sleeve.

Mrs. Henshaw dabbed and cooed at him in her worried, futile way.

Timpkins opened the kitchen door. "What's all this noise, now? I ain't gonna have no riots in my hotel!"

"Timpkins," said Henshaw quickly, "I didn't know you were from Canada. That's a beautiful country, and I've always admired it. I went across from Niagara Falls, and that reminds me of our new waterfall flushing system. If you'll just sit down I'll explain—"

"Naw!" said Timpkins, and slammed the door.

"He's weakening," Henshaw said in a satisfied tone. "I'll get him."

Running footsteps made a crisply angry tattoo on the paving outside, and Captain Perona burst through the door.

"Where is he?" he demanded. "Where is that Doan?"

"He just stepped out a second ago to walk his dog," Janet answered. "What's the matter?"

Captain Perona had a slip of yellow paper in his hand, and he waved it in front of her face. "Look! Look at this!"

Janet caught at the paper. "It's a message addressed to Mr. Doan."

"Read it!" Captain Perona snarled.

The message was printed in block letters in pencil, evidently just as the military wireless operator had taken it down. It said in English:

WHY THE PIG LATIN IT TOOK ME AN HOUR TO FIGURE OUT YOU WERENT DRUNK AND DROOL-ING BUT YOU HIT THE JACKPOT ALL RIGHT I CALLED VAN OSDEL LAWYERS AND THEY HAD NO IDEA THAT PATRICIAS DEATH WAS MURDER AND HIRED US AT ONCE AT FLAT RATE WITH BONUS IF SOLVED AND OPTION ALL FUTURE FLY GOO BUSINESS CONGRATULATIONS AND HIT THIS ONE HARD WITH NO SHARP SHOOT-ING OR CHISELING.

The signature, written out in the same block letters, was:

A. TRUEGOLD
PRESIDENT
SEVERN INTERNATIONAL DETECTIVES.

Janet looked up. "But—but what—"

"Children!" Captain Perona exploded. "Pig's Latin! That criminal sent a message to his detective agency and got them hired to solve the murder of Patricia Van Osdel!"

"How could he have done that?"

"The names of his children are nothing but a code address—an accommodation address! As soon as the message was received there, it was sent to the agency!"

"But your operator—"

"He understands and reads English, but not well. And Doan deceived him. He gave the operator the message a word at a time, constantly correcting and changing it, until the operator was confused. Doan showed him how to transpose the words, or pretended to, but the operator could not do that in a strange language and send them with corrections all at once."

"Doesn't Doan have any children?"

"No! He is not even married!"

"Why, he—he told me—"

"Yes!" Captain Perona agreed fiercely. "He told you! And you told me! You, if you recall, begged me to let him reassure his family! You!"

"Well, I didn't know—"

Captain Perona leaned close to her. "Senorita, the number of things you do not know constantly amazes me!"

"Is that so?"

"Yes! After this kindly keep your ignorance to yourself and cease annoying me!"

Captain Perona whirled around and ran out the door.

"Acts like he was mad or something," Henshaw observed.

"He is," Janet agreed. "And I really don't blame him." She started for the door.

"Where you going?" Henshaw asked.

"I'm just tired of people!" Janet said. "I'm going to talk to a stone image!"

"There are sure a lot of whacks around this joint," Henshaw observed. "I hope it ain't catching."

CHAPTER XIII

DOAN AND CARSTAIRS were on a narrow little street high on the mountainside above the main part of the town. They had arrived there by easy stages, wandering back and forth aimlessly among the crooked lanes, and now Doan stopped and gazed curiously at a ten-foot wall with broken glass making a faint, sinister glimmer along its top. The wall ran for a good hundred yards along the street. There were some fresh cracks in it, mementos of the earthquake, but it still looked formidably solid.

"Hoo!" said a voice suddenly.

Doan looked around and saw a little boy about ten feet behind him.

"Beeg," said the little boy, pointing at Carstairs. He grinned at Doan. He had three front teeth missing.

"Big and dumb," Doan agreed. "Haven't I seen you before somewhere?"

"Gimme dime."

"I thought so." Doan took a dime out of his pocket and held it up. "But let's you earn it this time. Ever hear of a guy named Predilip?"

"Ah?"

"An artist named Predilip."

The little boy nodded triumphantly. "Boo yet."

"Boo yet," Doan repeated thoughtfully. "Boo yet…. You bet?"

The little boy nodded again. "Boo yet."

"Have it your way, then. Where did he live?"

The little boy made flapping motions with his arms and rolled his eyes piously skyward.

"Flying," said Doan. "Up. Angel in heaven?"

"Boo yet."

"I know he's dead," said Doan. "Where did he live before he got dead?"

"Live?"

"Home. House. Shack. Domicile."

"Los Altos."

Doan sighed. "I know he lived in Los Altos. But where?"

"Los Altos."

"Okay," said Doan. "Did you ever see any of his paintings?"

"Ah?"

"Paintings. Pictures."

The little boy looked around cautiously. "You wanna buy feelthy picture?"

"No!"

"My uncle, he sell. Very good. Very joocy. Oooh, my!"

"I don't want to buy any dirty pictures. I'm talking about an artist named Predilip."

"Gimme dime."

Doan gave him the dime.

"Denk goo," said the little boy, putting the dime carefully in his shirt pocket. He spun around like a top and ran headlong down the street.

"Hey, you!" Doan called. "Wait a minute! What's behind this wall here?"

The little boy shrilled over his shoulder. *"Casa del Coronel Cal-lao! Muy malo!"*

"I got part of that, anyway," Doan said to Carstairs. "It seems that our pal, Colonel Callao, lives back of this Maginot Line somewhere. Let's go have a chat with him."

CHAPTER XIV

THE WEST SLOPE above los altos was much steeper than it looked from the safe distance of the hotel roof, and Janet began to regret her impulse to climb it before she was halfway to the rock-face. The tough, stunted brush tore at her skirt with stubborn, clinging fingers, and there was no breeze to disturb the gleeful jiggle of the heat waves.

A loose pebble got into her shoe, and she had to stop and shake it out. She breathed deeply, and the air was so thin and hot in her lungs that it was not refreshing at all. She almost gave it up then, but she thought of Captain Perona and Doan and his three nonexistent children and man's deceit to woman in general and put her head down and plodded on.

She reached the stone face at last and leaned against it, puffing. The rock pedestal, too, was much larger than it had seemed from the hotel. She looked despairingly up at the overhang that marked its brows, and then she found a series of weatherworn niches on one side.

She climbed up laboriously, flattened against the rock, fingers clutching frantically at the warm, rough stone, until her face was even with the brow. Now all she had to do was to turn around and look in the direction the stone face was looking. That wasn't easy. It took her ten minutes and a broken fingernail, and her neck began to ache abominably.

Finally she got the angle. The stone face was looking at the east slope, and Janet did, too, sighting professionally with one eye squinted shut. Miraculously the three pillars lined up for her—the big one, the medium one, and the small one. Their tops made a neat, down-slanting diagonal.

Janet sighted and calculated and figured, trying to fix the point where the line of that diagonal would hit the slope on beyond the three pillars. She thought she had it finally, and she crawled down the pedestal again and started to work her way across the slope.

The heat seemed to have redoubled, and the warmth of the sun was a sharp-edged weight against the back of her neck. Her mouth felt like it was full of absorbent cotton.

She reached the three pedestals and went on grimly past them. A stubby bush tore a jagged rip in her skirt and left a red, angry mark on the calf of her leg. She stopped and stamped her foot and swore, but she kept her eyes pinned on the spot she had marked ahead.

And then, when she got there, she found she wasn't any place. The spot looked just like the rest of the slope even more so. There was brush, and there was rock, and that was all.

Janet kicked at the brush, and a scorpion scuttled away from her feet. Janet stood still, staring after it, afraid to move. It was an ugly little horror with shiny, jittering legs that clawed at the rock surface and a sting that arched up over its back. Janet swallowed hard and looked longingly down toward the cool shelter of Los Altos.

A voice came hollow and soft from just behind her: "Yes. This is the place."

Janet whirled around. A stunted bush that was like any other bush and the rock under it that was like any other rock had turned out to be something entirely different. The rock had tilted back and up on a pivot, and the shadowed, thin face and liquidly dark eyes of the man who was sometimes Tio Riquez and other times Bautiste Bonofile looked out of the black, square hole underneath it.

"Come here," he said softly.

Janet stood braced and rigid, and she moved one foot back a little.

The long, silvered barrel of Bautiste Bonofile's revolver glinted in the sun. "I won't hesitate to kill you. I have no prejudice against killing women. I've killed a good many at one time and another. Come here."

Janet took a step and then another. Her shoe sole scraped on rock, reluctantly. She drew a deep breath.

"Don't do that," said Bautiste Bonofile. "Don't scream. I'll shoot."

"You—you don't dare—"

"The noise?" said Bautiste Bonofile. "Is that what you're thinking of? That won't stop me. You couldn't find this place, even when you knew where it was and what to look for. No one who didn't know it was here would even suspect such an improbable thing. It would be thought that someone shot you and ran off. Come here."

Janet's feet moved her unwillingly to the black hole, and Bautiste Bonofile drew back and out of sight.

"I can see you," he said. "Very plainly. Come inside. There are steps."

Janet groped down with one foot and found a square, small step cut in the rock. She went down, found another and another. The air felt cool and damp and thick against her face, and she shivered.

There was a little grating noise and a solid thump as the rock door swung shut over her, and the blackness was like a thick cloth over her eyes. She made a little gasping sound.

There was a click, and the bright, round beam of a flashlight moved up and steadied on her face. The dazzling white circle was her whole world, and she could see nothing else and hear nothing until Bautiste Bonofile said in his soft, thoughtful voice:

"How did you know this place was here?"

"I—read about it."

Fingers moved out of the darkness and touched her throat silkily. "Don't lie, please."

Janet pressed her shoulders back hard against cool stone. "I'm not! I did read it—in that same old diary that described the cellar under the church. I remembered it after I noticed the stone face from the roof of the hotel this morning. The diary told how Lieutenant Perona—not the Perona in Los Altos now, but his ancestor—had built another, auxiliary cache above the church. It was a smaller one—for emergencies. It told how to locate it by lining up the rock face with the three pillars."

"I see," said Bautiste Bonofile. "I didn't know all that. I stumbled on the place quite by accident, and I saw that it had possibilities. I didn't know it had a history. Your research must be very interesting, but twice now it has proven to be dangerous for you. Why did you come here?"

"Why, I was just curious. I wanted to see if it was still here— the cache—and if there were any relics...."

"I see," Bautiste Bonofile repeated. "There were several things here when I first found it—some old tools and some boxes that had rotted away to dust. I spent a considerable amount of time improving the place."

The flashlight flicked away from Janet's face and swung around to show a narrow, dark doorway in the opposite wall.

"A—a tunnel?" Janet asked.

"Yes."

The flashlight came back to her face, and the silence grew and lengthened interminably.

Janet swallowed. "What—what are you going to do?"

"With you?" Bautiste Bonofile inquired. "You've caused me quite a lot of trouble."

"I didn't mean—"

"No. Of course not." Bautiste Bonofile chuckled gently. "It's amusing to think that Perona's ancestor is furnishing me a hiding place, isn't it? I would have appreciated it even more all this time if I'd known that. I'm glad you told me. Now as for you. I wonder—"

"Are you going to—to shoot me?"

"That's what I'm wondering," said Bautiste Bonofile.

It was weird and unbelievable, and it was chillingly real. He didn't grit his teeth or snarl or run through any gamut of emotions, but Janet knew with a queer, cold clarity that if he decided it was a good idea to shoot her he would do it right here and now without any further fuss. She waited, holding her breath, and a pulse began to pound in her throat.

"I wonder," said Bautiste Bonofile again, "I think perhaps I could use you. Captain Perona seemed very interested indeed."

Janet tried to keep her voice from quavering. "You know he wouldn't let you go even if—even if—"

"Even if he knew I was holding you for a hostage?" Bautiste Bonofile finished. "I think it very likely that he might. He knows me, you see. He knows that whatever I promised to do to you, I'd do. And even if he didn't care for you much personally, you are a citizen of the United States, and that might mean diplomatic difficulties for him if you should die in some particularly unpleasant manner in public, as it were…. Go through that door there. Walk straight ahead."

The flashlight moved away and outlined the narrow doorway. Janet moved stiffly toward it, and the rough sides brushed her shoulders. Her body blocked all but stray flickers of the lights, and she groped uncertainly.

"Watch your head," Bautiste Bonofile warned. He made no noise behind her. "Keep going."

The tunnel went on endlessly, and the air grew dust-choked

and stifling. Several times Janet bumped her head against projections of rock, and time and the tunnel stretched into nightmare proportions in her dazed mind.

"Slowly now," Bautiste Bonofile said.

And then suddenly there was a scratching, scraping sound right over her head. Janet stopped with a jerk. The barrel of the revolver made a round, dangerous period pressed against her back. Bautiste Bonofile's hand slid over her shoulder and touched her lips warningly.

"Quiet," he whispered.

The fast, irregular scraping stopped, and something snorted loudly. Then Doan's voice, sounding muffled but quite clear, said:

"Don't you think you're a bit too old and too big to dig for field mice?"

There was another snort and a mumbling growl. The scraping sound started again.

"Quit it, stupid," said Doan. "Get away from there and stop playing puppy."

Carstairs bayed angrily, and the sound of it was like a blow against Janet's eardrums.

"Well, what?" Doan demanded. "I don't see anything."

Carstairs bayed again, more loudly.

"Less noise, please," said Doan. "We're trespassers, you know. Do you want to get me an interview with some of Perona's soldiers?"

Bautiste Bonofile moved in the darkness and murmured in Janet's ear: "Reach up over your head. Push the rock."

The rock was counterweighted like the other, and it swung back and up in a solid square. Sunlight bit brilliantly into Janet's eyes.

She was staring up into Doan's surprised face. He made a quick, tentative motion with his right hand that stopped as soon as it started.

"That's right," said Bautiste Bonofile. "I will shoot her unless you do exactly as I say."

Doan smiled blandly. "Well, of course. I'm not hostile. I was just startled. You're Bautiste Bonofile, huh? I've been wanting to have a talk with you."

"Step down into the tunnel," said Bautiste Bonofile. His hand touched Janet's shoulder. "Back up."

She went back three shuffling steps. Doan swung agilely through the square opening and dropped into the tunnel. He kept his hands half raised.

Above them Carstairs barked angrily.

"Make him stop that noise!" Bautiste Bonofile ordered. "Make him come down here!"

Doan turned around and hauled himself half out of the opening. He grabbed Carstairs by the collar. He pulled. So did Carstairs—in the opposite direction.

"Get him in here quickly," Bautiste Bonofile said in a dangerous tone. "Don't play tricks."

"He's afraid of holes," Doan panted. "Come on, damn you! Get in here!"

Carstairs' claws skittered on the edge of the opening. Doan was hanging down from his collar, half suspended.

"He got stuck—in a culvert once," Doan gasped. "Scared—ever since. Come on, Carstairs. Hike!"

He let go and ducked. Carstairs sprang straight over his head with a raging snarl, fangs bared, eyes greenish and savage. His broad chest struck Janet with the weight of a pile driver and knocked her sideways and down, and as she fell she saw Doan spin around as lightly and gracefully as a dancer with the little .25 automatic in his hand. He shot and shot again instantly.

The powder flare burned Janet's face, and the echoing roar of the shots deafened her. The smoky tunnel tipped and swerved dizzily in front of her eyes.

Doan's hands were under her arms, lifting her. "Are you hurt?"

"N-no," Janet gasped. "I guess—"

Carstairs growled in the darkness.

"Let him alone," Doan said. "He's not going anywhere."

Janet swallowed hard, fighting against the numb sickness that was creeping over her. "Is he—hurt?"

"Not a bit," said Doan. "He's just dead. Here! Brace up!"

"I—I think—"

Doan scrambled out of the tunnel and leaned back through the opening. "Here! Grab my hands!"

Janet caught at them, and he swung her lightly upward into fresh, clean air and sunlight.

"Sit down. That's it."

Janet sat down and breathed deeply again and again.

"Feel better now?" Doan asked, watching her.

"Yes," said Janet firmly. "Did you really kill Bautiste Bonofile?"

Doan nodded. "I thought it was a good idea. He might have been carrying another rattlesnake in his pocket, and I'm allergic to them. Carstairs."

Carstairs put his head out of the square opening. Doan caught his collar and heaved. Carstairs grunted and scrambled and came up on to solid ground. He shook himself distastefully, looking at Doan.

"That was nice interference you ran for me," Doan told him. "I thank you very kindly."

Carstairs sat down and looked pleased with himself. He lolled out a tongue that had an ugly little smear of red on it and panted cheerfully at Janet. Doan walked over and kicked the tunnel entrance stone, and it swung on its pivot and thumped shut and became part of the smooth unbroken tile of the patio in which they were sitting.

"Neat," Doan commented.

Janet looked around. A high wall stretched on three sides of them, and the other side was taken up by the long sun veranda of a house. There were chrome easy chairs with gaily colored leather cushions on the veranda and a swing with a striped canopy and tables with glass tops.

"Quite a gaudy dive," said Doan. "The earthquake knocked a piece out of the wall over there." He pointed to a V-shaped notch with a pile of rubble lying below it. "Carstairs and I came in that way. I think that tunnel must have an air-hole or a ventilator in it. Carstairs trailed it clear across the patio. How did you get into it?"

"From the other end. I read about a cache that Lieutenant Perona had dug, and I was looking for it when—"

"That Perona," said Doan, "turned out to be quite a dangerous guy for you to know. And you'd better watch that descendant of his pretty closely, too."

"You lied to him," Janet accused, remembering.

"What about?" Doan asked.

"You're not married! You don't have any wife and three small girls!"

Doan watched her. "How'd you find that out?"

"From the answer to your message"

"Answer?" said Doan. "Answer! Did that damned, dumb Truegold send me a straight answer through the military wireless setup?"

"Yes, he did."

"What did it say?"

"It said that he had informed the Van Osdel interests about Patricia's murder and that your agency had been hired to solve the mystery."

"All right," said Doan. "But that Truegold is too dumb even for the president of a detective agency. Wait until I see him again."

"That's not the point, Mr. Doan. You appealed to Captain Perona's pity by telling him about your children being quarantined with the measles, and you gave your word that you wouldn't send out information about Patricia Van Osdel."

"I told him I wouldn't tell my kids," Doan corrected. "But that's just a weasel. Yes, I lied to him."

"Well, aren't you ashamed? You involved me, too."

"You shouldn't have believed me," Doan said. "And neither should Perona have."

"Why not?" Janet demanded indignantly.

"Because I'm a detective," Doan said. "I told you something in the same line before. Detectives never tell the truth if they can help it. They lie all the time. It's just business."

"Not all detectives!"

Doan nodded, seriously now. "Yes. Every detective ever born, and every one who ever will be. Honest. Perona should have known that. He lies himself whenever he thinks it's a good idea. I'm sorry, though, if he got mad at you on my account."

"You had no right…." Janet paused. "Oh dear! You just saved my life, and now I'm talking to you this way…. I'm sorry, Mr. Doan!"

Doan chuckled. "Forget it. So many people are mad at me for so many different reasons that one more or less—"

Carstairs growled, and Doan whirled around tensely. *"Aqui!"* a voice shouted.

A soldier was peering at them through the niche in the wall. He climbed over and dropped into the patio. Another soldier and another and another scrambled over after him. They advanced in a raggedly spaced line. Their bayonets glittered, and their brown faces were grimly set.

"Something tells me," said Doan, "that I'm going to have a heart-to-heart chat with Captain Perona in the very near future."

CHAPTER XV

IT WAS THE same small, square room in which Doan had been incarcerated before, but now Captain Perona and Colonel Callao and Lieutenant Ortega sat in a solemn, official row behind a table in the center of the floor. None of them spoke when the soldiers ushered Doan and Janet into the room. Carstairs was between Doan and Janet, and he sat down and looked at the three officers for a moment and then yawned in a pointed way. Captain Perona nodded at the soldiers, and they went out and closed the door.

"Senorita Martin," said Captain Perona formally, "I regret to see you in your present company."

"Mr. Doan and Carstairs are my friends!" Janet told him.

"That shows loyalty but also a lamentable lack of brains," said Captain Perona. "Now kindly keep silent until you are addressed. Doan, this is a military court of inquiry. We would have met sooner to consider some of your actions if it had not been for the confusion resulting from the earthquake."

"No need to apologize," Doan said amiably.

Captain Perona's lips tightened. "That was not my intention. By a very contemptible sort of trick, you deceived me and sent a message to the detective agency which employs you inform-ing them of Patricia Van Osdel's murder. As a result—which you intended—you have been hired to solve the mystery of her death, although there is no mystery."

"No?" said Doan.

"No. You will receive no fee from this case. I have solved the murder, and I have no intention of letting you steal the credit for it. We have learned through our own sources of inquiry that Patricia Van Osdel drew twenty-five thousand dollars in United States currency from her bank in Mexico City four days ago. She made no major purchases subsequent to that time, and it is reasonable to assume, since a search of her possessions at the

Hotel Azteca failed to reveal it, that she brought the money to Los Altos with her."

"In her purse," said Doan.

"That is immaterial. The money furnished the motive for her murder. Her companion, Greg, knew she had it. He was looking for an opportunity to steal it. The earthquake gave him an excellent chance. He struck down Patricia Van Osdel and the maid, Maria, and stole the money. But Maria was only wounded. She could identify Greg as the murderer when she recovered consciousness and would certainly do so. He came to the hospital and killed her last night to insure her silence. He was seen by Amanda Tracy, and he struck her down, again to keep from being identified."

"Greg got his arm broken in the earthquake," Doan observed.

"Yes. He fell while he was pursuing Maria. That is why he only wounded her then. He was in great pain and anxious to get away from the scene of his crime. We have not apprehended him as yet, but we will very soon. That ends the matter. Also, it absolves the Mexican government and the army of any responsibility. Patricia Van Osdel virtually caused her own death by her choice in friends and by secretly carrying such a sum of money with her without informing us of the fact so we could take extra precautions to protect her. Now have you anything to say?"

"Oh, a hell of a lot," Doan answered.

"Proceed," said Captain Perona.

"Well," said Doan. "First there's me. You were under a little misapprehension as to why I came to Los Altos. I wasn't hired by any crooked politicians to come down here and persuade Eldridge not to come back to the United States."

"No?" said Captain Perona.

"No. I was hired by a Committee of Good Government to bring him back so they could give the brush-off to the crooked outfit that is running the state. That outfit is slightly on the subversive side, and a lot of people would like to see them go away and not come back any more. If Eldridge testified to what he knew, it would have done the job up. But the Committee couldn't get him extradited because he had too much influence here and there."

"This is very interesting," said Captain Perona, "if true."

"It's true. Due to slander, libel, defamation of character, and unfounded rumors I have the reputation of being a little sharp in my business activities."

"Yes, indeed," Captain Perona agreed.

"So they hired me to pretend I was hired by Eldridge's crooked pals to scare him into staying here. That would naturally make him slightly resentful. Then he and I would cook up some sort of a supposed double-cross of his crooked pals, and he would return to the United States voluntarily so the Committee could lay hands on him and throw him in jail until he got talkative. Eldridge actually had no intention of returning, before we started to work on him. He was just talking in the hopes of shaking down his pals."

"You actually expect me to believe this?" Captain Perona asked politely.

"Sure."

Captain Perona watched him. "You forgot to mention the matter of the ten-thousand-dollar bribe."

"No, I didn't. There wasn't any bribe or any ten thousand dollars. That was just a rumor."

"What is in the safety deposit box in Chicago?"

"A well-gnawed steak bone," said Doan. "Carstairs is progressive. He doesn't bury his bones like other dogs. He deposits them in banks."

"Bah!" Captain Perona exploded.

"Honest," said Doan. "I'll sign a power of attorney, and you can have your consular agent go and look in the box."

Captain Perona breathed deeply. "If this fantastic nonsense has the faintest relation to the truth," he said with a certain amount of satisfaction, "you have failed in your mission."

"Oh, no," said Doan. "Eldridge dictated a dying statement to me—signed, sealed, and witnessed in triplicate."

Lieutenant Ortega looked up quickly. "That is impossible. Eldridge could not possibly have dictated a statement after receiving the injuries which caused his death."

"He did, though," Doan maintained.

Captain Perona frowned at him. "You intend to forge a statement."

"Me?" said Doan. "Oh, no. Why, if I did that all those crooked politicians would haul me into court and prove the charges in the statement were false."

Captain Perona opened his mouth and shut it again, helplessly. "Doan," he said at last, "the United States is an ally of this country's, and as such we wish to treat its nationals with all due consideration, but I warn you to get out of Mexico and stay out."

"Wait a minute," said Doan. "I want to set you straight on a couple of other matters first."

"What matters?" Captain Perona inquired icily.

"I want my dough. I want you to give me the official credit for solving the mystery of Patricia Van Osdel's death."

"And what possible reason could I have for doing that?"

"Because if you do, I'll tell you where to find Bautiste Bonofile."

There was a dead, ominous silence.

Captain Perona stirred a little in his chair. "I now retract what I said a moment ago. You are not going to leave Mexico. You are going to stay here for about twenty years, I think."

"It's nice of you to ask me," said Doan. "But no."

"Where—is—Bautiste—Bonofile?"

"Do I get credit on the Van Osdel deal?"

"No! If you do not tell me at once where Bautiste Bonofile is, you are going to regret it."

"Don't get tough," Doan warned, "or I'll dummy up on you,

and then you'll never find him. Come on, Perona. Let's make a deal. I get credit for Van Osdel. You get credit for Bautiste Bonofile. That's a nice offer."

Captain Perona rubbed his hand over his face and sighed deeply. "I dislike you, Doan. I dislike you very much, indeed. You are an unscrupulous, cold-blooded criminal, and I think— and hope most fervently—that you will come to a bad end one day soon."

"I can hardly wait," said Doan. "But let's make a deal first."

Captain Perona said: "I have failed to find Bautiste Bonofile, and that is a reflection on me and on Major Nacio's organiza- tion. The cables will be in place over the Canyon of Black Shadow by tonight. My failure will then be a matter of public knowledge. You have won, Doan. I must bargain with you because I have no choice. You will be given the credit for solving Patricia Van Osdel's death. Where is Bautiste Bonofile?"

"In a tunnel under Colonel Callao's patio."

"What?" said Captain Perona sharply.

Doan nodded. "Yeah. He is."

Captain Perona turned slowly to look at Colonel Callao. Colonel Callao's face was as loosely blank as ever, and he was smiling, but there was a sheen of perspiration on his forehead.

"Don't let him kid you," said Doan. "He understands English. Enough to get by, anyway. He's got a swell poker face, but he can't control his eyes. I think he's been dealing for and covering Bautiste Bonofile all along."

Colonel Callao stood up very slowly and leaned his weight against the table. His face was darkly leaden now. No one else in the room spoke or moved. Finally Colonel Callao pushed himself away from the table, swaying a little, and walked toward the door, pushing one foot ahead of the other.

Captain Perona looked at Lieutenant Ortega and nodded once. "I assume all responsibility here. I order you to follow Colonel Callao and place him under close arrest."

Lieutenant Ortega got up and saluted stiffly. He walked out of the room behind Colonel Callao. The door boomed shut.

Captain Perona looked at Doan. "I like you even less after this. Colonel Callao is a drunken pig, but he has done some very brave things in his day. I had some suspicion of him. I thought he understood English, and I have been trying to trick him into betraying himself by insulting him in that language, but he was too clever. Explain to me how you knew where to find Bautiste Bonofile."

"I didn't know, and I didn't find him. Janet did."

Captain Perona glared at her. "You! You knew! And you stood there silent and let me compromise my honor by bargaining with this criminal!"

"You told me to keep still until you addressed me," Janet said.

"So! You choose this particular time—the only time since I have met you—to obey my orders!"

"Stop shouting at me."

"I will shout at you if I please!" Captain Perona roared. "You do not have the brains of a two-year-old child! I think I will put you in jail and keep you there until I decide whether or not I want to marry you!"

"What?" Janet said dazedly. "What did you say? Until you decide whether or not you want—"

"Do not be coy," Captain Perona ordered. "I detest that in a woman. I have not made up my mind as yet whether you would be a suitable wife for me, and after this performance I have grave doubts. But I am a just man, and I will give you one final chance to prove you are worthy of the honor. How did you find Bautiste Bonofile?"

Janet stamped her foot. "If you dare to think I would even consider—"

"Answer my question!"

"I won't!"

Doan said mildly: "It was that diary again. There was another cache dug by your illustrious ancestor mentioned in it. Janet

was looking for it. Bautiste Bonofile had found it. I forgot to
tell you that he's dead."

"Dead!"

"Yes," said Doan. "And I'll save you the trouble of asking. It
was me again. I shot him."

"So!" said Captain Perona. "You lied about that also! You did
have another gun!"

"Don't you *dare* talk to him like that!" Janet shrilled. "Mr.
Doan saved my life! That Bautiste had a gun poked right against
my back, and Carstairs jumped at him, and Mr. Doan shot him,
and it was good enough for him! And if you weren't such an
arrogant dumb-head it never would have happened because
you would have found Bautiste months ago!"

"I am afraid that is correct," Captain Perona admitted ruefully. "So then, Doan, the matter becomes settled. Now all that
is needed is for us to find the man, Greg."

"Oh, I know where he is, too," said Doan.

"What?" said Captain Perona incredulously. "You know...
Well, where is he?"

"In his grave."

Captain Perona stared at him. "You said—grave?"

"Sure. I knew that right away when you couldn't find him.
Greg couldn't hide in Los Altos for five minutes without being
spotted if he was alive. A dead man—a buried one doesn't take
up much room. There are lots of fresh ruins around here."

"You are insane," said Captain Perona.

"Nope. Look at it this way. Patricia Van Osdel drew a lot of
money out of the bank and made a big point of coming here
at this particular time—even bribed the hotel to put on the bus
trip after they had canceled it. Why? Because she had an appointment with someone here yesterday. Greg might have
known about the money she was carrying, but there was one
other person who would be sure to."

"Who?" Captain Perona asked numbly.

"Why, the person she was going to pay it to."

The hinges on the door at the back of the room creaked just slightly, and then a voice said bitterly:

"You dirty little rat. You dirty, stinking crook."

"Hello, Amanda," said Doan. "I was just telling the Captain that if he really wanted to find Greg he could probably uncover what's left of him if he dug around under your house a bit."

Amanda Tracy was wearing a bandage like a lopsided turban over her frizzed hair. Under it the tanned skin of her face looked dry and yellowish.

"No," Janet breathed softly. "Oh, no."

"Yes," said Doan. "Amanda cooked up a deal to do Patricia out of some of her dough. Offhand I'd bet that she told Patricia that she had uncovered some of Predilip's paintings. The reason I say that is because Patricia was careful never to mention Predilip's name, although he's one of the best reasons to come to this town. Patricia was a bit of a chiseler in her refined way, and if she thought she could get an undercover bargain in some previously undiscovered paintings which now are very valuable, she'd come running, and she'd bring cash to overawe the person she was dealing with. How about it, Amanda?"

"You're so damned smart," said Amanda Tracy. "I'll tell you something you don't know. I didn't take anything from Patricia Van Osdel that wasn't mine. Do you know where her old man got his flykiller formula? From my mother. She made it up herself and used it around the farm. Old Van Osdel came along selling phony patent medicine one day, and he saw it work. He got my mother to tell him how she made it and got her to sign a release of all her rights in it for five dollars. Five dollars!"

"Patricia came by her chiseling honestly," Doan commented.

Amanda Tracy made a savage gesture with her clenched fist. "Just five dollars, and Van Osdel made millions out of it! And then later, when my father died and we lost our farm, I asked him to give us just a little to help us out—to keep my mother from dying in the county poor-house. He refused. I told him then that I'd get some of his dirty money whether he gave it to me or not—plenty of it. I waited for a long time before I got a chance. I painted up some damned good imitations of Predilip, and I contacted Patricia when she came back to America. I told her I'd found the pictures in an attic of a house Predilip had lived in. I made a good story of it. I intended to sell her the fakes and then tell everybody about it and laugh like hell when she tried to get her money back."

"Not a bad idea," said Doan. "Why didn't you do that instead of killing her?"

"You should ask, little man. Because of some others like you, and that's why I've always hated the whole breed. When I threatened old Van Osdel, he lured some private detectives to follow me around for awhile. I knew that, but I didn't know they had taken pictures of me—candid shots. I knew Patricia had never seen me, but she *had* seen those pictures. She recognized me right away. She knew then that the whole deal must be a gyp, and she just laughed at me. She didn't laugh long, though."

"*Dios mio,*" Captain Perona whispered.

Amanda Tracy laughed at him. "The earthquake was just what the doctor ordered. Patricia was walking away from me when it happened. I picked up a rock and slammed her and grabbed her purse. Maria started running and squawking, but so was everyone else right then. I chased her and hit her with the rock. I thought I'd finished her. No one noticed me before or afterward. They're used to me in this town."

"What about Greg?" Doan asked.

"He followed me from the hotel last night. He knew why Patricia had come here, and he guessed what had happened. He wanted the twenty-five thousand. All of it, if you can imagine the nerve of him. He was a nasty one, that boy. But I knew he didn't have his knife with him. I did have mine. He slammed me with a rock once. That was all he had time for."

Janet made a little gulping sound.

"Brace up, dearie," Amanda Tracy said. "I've got a surprise for the three of you." She held out her right hand. "Isn't it pretty?"

"Mother of God—a hand grenade!" Captain Perona exclaimed.

"One of yours," Amanda Tracy agreed. "You should really keep better track of them." She reached behind her with her left hand. "I'm going to leave this little iron egg with you. There'll be quite a dust-up when it lets go, and after it's all over I'll be in my little hospital bed looking very surprised and innocent, and I don't think any of you will tell stories about what I've just said."

"Wait!" Captain Perona shouted. "You can't"

"Good-by, now," said Amanda Tracy. Her left hand had found the latch, and she pulled the door open behind her.

Lepicik was standing in the doorway looking politely interested. He nodded casually to Doan and then hit Amanda Tracy in the back of the neck with the edge of his palm. Her head snapped forward, and Doan dove for her. He caught her right hand in both of his and held it rigid while her thick body twirled and slumped loosely down.

"Get it!" Doan gasped. "Get the grenade! Look out! She's got her finger through the firing pin ring!"

Captain Perona knelt down beside him, breathing hard. With infinite care he untwisted the thick fingers. He had the grenade then, and he shifted it from one hand to the other uneasily and then put it down on the desk.

Doan let go of Amanda Tracy and stood up and wiped his forehead thoughtfully.

"Mr. Doan," said Lepicik. "Excuse me, but I have a message here that came through the military wireless. It's a little confusing, and I thought perhaps you could explain it. It's from a man named Carpenhyer, who is a motion picture agent in Hollywood, California. Have you ever heard of the man?"

"Yes," said Doan. "He's one of the best. Are you really a director?"

"Certainly," said Lepicik. "I have directed many cinema productions—in London, Rome, Stockholm, Berlin, Paris, Vienna, Moscow. Before the war, of course. But this Carpenhyer says he can get me a job at—" Lepicik stopped to verify the figure "—one thousand seven hundred and fifty dollars a week. Could that be correct?"

Doan nodded, wincing. "I'm afraid so, if Carpenhyer says it is. Take it. But quick."

"You!" said Captain Perona, suddenly recovering himself. "How did you get out of my quarters? Where is the soldier who was guarding you?"

"He had a headache," Lepicik said. "So I gave him some opium."

"Opium!" Captain Perona repeated wildly.

Lepicik looked surprised. "Just a small pill. It is very good for headaches. But it put him to sleep."

Sergeant Obrian burst in the room through the front door. "Say, that old artist doll has scrammed out of the hospital, and I can't find—" His mouth stayed open.

"You," said Captain Perona dangerously, "have arrived, as usual, in the nick of time. There is the artist doll. She has just been frustrated in an attempt to massacre us all. Put her in jail and make sure before you do that she does not have any hand grenades or other deadly weapons concealed about her person."

Amanda Tracy stirred and moaned.

"Oh!" said Janet. "I can't stand to see…. I've got to get out of here!"

She dodged nimbly around Sergeant Obrian and ran headlong out the door and across a neat, graveled plot of parade ground toward the plaza. Behind her she could hear both Doan and Captain Perona shouting at her anxiously, but she couldn't stop. And then she saw something that did make her stop.

"Yes!" said Bartolome proudly. "Is it not a wonder of wonders most incredible?"

It was the bus. It had dents in it as big as footballs. It was lopsided and swaybacked, and both the rear tires were flat. But it was out from under the debris and up on its own wheels.

Carstairs and Doan and Captain Perona pulled up beside Janet and stared, too.

"The engine," said Bartolome, "has fallen out and broken itself lamentably, but that is only a matter of the most minor."

Henshaw came pacing gloomily up to them. His head was bowed, and his hands were folded behind him.

"Observe!" Bartolome commanded him. "The bus of scenic magnificence resumes itself!"

"It ain't gonna do me no good," Henshaw said.

"What's the matter?" Doan asked him. "Didn't you sell Timpkins the bathroom?"

"No," said Henshaw. "I didn't sell him the bathroom." His voice rose to a wail. "Timpkins sold me his damned old hotel!"

III

SALLY'S IN THE ALLEY

CHAPTER I

THIS WILL PROBABLY strike you as highly improbable if you know your Hollywood, but the lobby of the Orna Apartment Hotel, off Rossmore south of Melrose, is done in very nice taste. It is neat and narrow and dignified, with a conservative blue carpet on the floor and a small black reception desk on a line straight back from the unadorned plate glass door.

At this particular moment its only occupant was the desk clerk. He was small and very young-looking, and he had dark curly hair and a snub nose with freckles across the bridge. His blue eyes were staring with a look of fierce, crosshatched concentration at the pictured diagram of a radio hookup he had spread out on the desk.

The plate glass door opened, and a man came into the lobby with a quietly purposeful air. He was blond and a little better than medium height, and he was wearing an inconspicuous blue business suit. He looked so much like an attorney or an accountant or the better class of insurance broker that it was perfectly obvious what he really was.

He walked up to the desk and said, "Have you a party by the name of Pocus staying here?"

The desk clerk was following the whirligig line that indicated a coil on his diagram with the point of a well-chewed pencil. The pencil point hesitated for a split second and then moved on again.

"No," he said. He didn't have to bother about being courteous because he intended to quit the apartment hotel any minute now and get a job at a fabulous salary in a war plant installing radios in fighter planes.

The blond man took a leather folder from his pocket, opened it, and spread it out on the radio diagram. "Take a look at this."

The clerk studied the big gold badge for a second and then looked up slowly. "You're a G-man."

The blond man winced slightly. "I'm a special agent of the Department of Justice. Let's start over again. What's your name?"

"Edmund."

"All right, Edmund. Have you got a party by the name of Pocus staying here? H. Pocus or Hocus Pocus?"

"No," said Edmund. He cleared his throat. "Will you excuse me for a second? I've got to call and wake up one of our tenants. He works on the swing shift, and he has to get waked up and eat before—"

The blond man punched him suddenly and expertly in the chest with a stiffened forefinger. "Get away from the switchboard. You're not tipping anybody off." He whistled shrilly through his teeth.

Another man came in the front door. He was short and stocky, and he had sleepy brown eyes and a scar on his nose. A third man came in from the hall that led to the back door. He was very tall and thin, stooped a little. He wore a light topcoat, and he kept his hands in its pockets.

"They're here," said the blond man. "Come on, Edmund. Give. Which apartment are they in?"

Edmund stood mute.

The blond man watched him curiously. "Are you scared of them?"

"Yes," said Edmund.

"Listen, son," said the blond man. "This is the government you're talking to now. If either one of them even made a pass at you, we'd put them away in Alcatraz."

"How do I know they'd stay there?" Edmund asked.

"All right," said the blond man. "Come on out from behind that desk. Sit down in that chair and rest your feet. Look up the tenant index, Curtis."

The stocky man went behind the desk, found the file of register cards, and ran through them expertly.

"In two-two-nine," he said. He looked under the desk. "Here's the pass key." He flipped it to the blond man.

"Okay," said the blond man. "Stay here and watch the board, Curtis. If anybody comes down the elevator, they wait in the lobby. If anyone comes in the front, they wait, too."

"Sure," said Curtis.

"You come with me, Barstow," the blond man said. "We'll take the stairs. Go easy."

They went up to the second floor and along a hall that was carpeted in the same dark blue as the lobby, and stopped in front of the door numbered 229. The blond man fitted the passkey in the lock and turned it without making the slightest sound. He opened the door just as silently.

It was a single apartment, and the big combination living room-bedroom was bright and cheery with the sun coming in a warm, slatted flood through the Venetian blinds. There was no one in sight, but a door to the left was slightly open and through it came the pleasantly languid gurgle and splash of bathwater.

The blond man and his tall companion came into the apartment and shut the front door. The blond man nodded meaningly and then, with the tall man close behind him, walked over and opened the bathroom door.

It was a big bathroom and a beautiful one, tastefully decorated now with fat little coils of steam that clung cozily against the ceiling. It was equipped with an outsize sunken tub, and Doan was sitting in it with his back to the door. He was chubby and pink and glistening, and he looked even more innocent and harmless than he usually did. He held a big sponge up over his head and squeezed it and made happy sputtering noises through the resultant flood.

"Now that you're here," he said amiably, "would you mind telling me if I've gotten all the soap off my back?"

"Yes, you have," said the blond man. "How did you know we were here?"

"There's a draft when the front door opens," Doan answered. He turned around in the tub to peer up at them. "Well! The government, no less. I'm honored."

"Yes," said the blond man. "I'm Arne. Department of Justice. This is Barstow. Where's Carstairs?"

"Well," said Doan, "if there should be a fire and you should try to get out of here in a hurry, you'd probably run across him en route."

Barstow turned around with a jerk to look behind him. "Uh!" he said, startled.

Carstairs was standing in the doorway, watching him with narrowed, greenish eyes. Carstairs was a fawn-colored Great Dane about as big as a medium-sized Shetland pony, only Shetland ponies at least make a try at looking amiable most of the time and Carstairs never did. He looked mean. Probably because he was. He had many responsibilities and problems to shorten his temper. Carstairs was so big that the first sight of him was liable to be a considerable shock. It was as though something had suddenly gone wrong with your perspective.

"Relax, stupid," Doan ordered. "These are friends—I hope. At least, if they aren't we can't do much about it."

Carstairs watched him for a second and then turned and disappeared from the doorway.

"Wow!" said Barstow. "I'd heard he was a whopper, but I certainly didn't expect anything like that."

"People rarely do," Doan said. He reached over and turned the drain lever. "Hand me that towel, will you?"

Arne handed him the towel. "You were notified to come in and report to us. Why didn't you do it?"

"I was just getting around to it," Doan said. "Hand me that robe, please."

Arne looked in both pockets of the white robe and then gave it to him. "You didn't get around quick enough, so we did."

"It was nice of you," said Doan. "Let's go out and sit where it's comfortable."

They went out into the living room, and Doan lay down with a luxurious sigh on the blue chesterfield that was pushed in slantwise against the corner.

"Have a chair," he invited. "I'd offer you a drink only Carstairs doesn't approve of it, and he's mad enough at me as it is."

"Where is he?" Barstow asked.

"Behind the chesterfield in the corner where he was when you came in. He's sulking."

"What's he mad at?" Barstow inquired curiously.

"He had to sleep down cellar last night. That offends his dignity."

"Where does he usually sleep?"

"There are twin pull-down beds behind that door," Doan said. "He sleeps in one. I sleep in the other."

"Why didn't he sleep in it last night?"

"Well, it was like this," said Doan. "I had a friend calling on me. She's a very nice girl."

There was a rumbling mumble from behind the chesterfield.

"She is, too!" Doan said indignantly. "Just because she works in a dime store and chews gum is no reason for you to get so huffy about her, you snob. Anyway, we were sitting here doing this, that, and the other, and she said she positively was not going to do the other any more with Carstairs sneering at her while she did it. So I ran him down cellar. Hey, you. Come up for air."

Carstairs' head appeared slowly from behind the chesterfield. He rested his chin on the top of it and looked Doan in the eye without any signs of approval at all.

"Now, look," said Doan. "I've had enough temperament for today. I said I was sorry you had to sleep in the cellar. I apologized."

Carstairs sighed deeply and wearily.

"And I said I'd buy you a steak to make it up to you," Doan told him. "A steak. Get it? Slaver-slaver, mumble-mumble, crunch-crunch. Steak. Now come out from behind there and act civilized."

Carstairs jumped from a sitting position without any visible effort. It was a heart-stopping performance. He sailed clear over the chesterfield and Doan, landing hard enough to rattle the window panes. He licked his chops delicately and politely with a long, red tongue.

"Yes," said Doan. "I said, steak. But not right now. Wait until I finish my business with these gentlemen. In the meantime, lie down before somebody knocks you down."

Carstairs sprawled out on the floor and rolled over on his side with a resigned snort.

Doan nodded at Arne and Barstow. "Well, what can I do for you?"

"You're not a private detective any more," Arne told him.

"Oh, yes," said Doan.

"No. You don't work for the Severn International Detectives now."

"Yes, I do," said Doan. "They don't dare fire me. If I started to talk about that outfit, they'd be bankrupt in five minutes and on their way to jail in ten—if they weren't lynched first."

"Maybe. But anyway, they've loaned you to the government temporarily."

"No," said Doan.

Arne took a letter from his pocket and opened it. "Read this."

Doan read the letter. He came to the signature, and his eyes widened slowly. He read the letter again, and then he folded it up very carefully and handed it back to Arne.

"If you want to call Washington at your expense, you can verify the signature," Arne said.

Doan shook his head. "That won't be necessary. So I'm loaned to the government. All right. What does that make me?"

"A Japanese," Arne said.

"Oh, I don't think the Japs would go for that," Doan told him. "My eyes don't slant enough."

"Not a Japanese national," Arne explained. "A Jap agent."

"A spy!" Doan chortled, pleased. "Now that's something like it! I've always wanted to be a spy. Does it pay well?"

"To you, it pays nothing," Arne informed him. "You're donating your services."

"Oh," said Doan glumly. "What services?"

"You are to go to the Mojave Desert and find a man named Dust-Mouth Haggerty and buy from him the secret of the location of an ore deposit."

"What kind of ore?" Doan asked.

"You wouldn't know if I told you, and besides it's none of your business. Dust-Mouth will know what you're after. Don't pretend to be a mining expert. Tell him you're the forerunner of a Japanese invasion force, sent ahead to locate this deposit so they can take it over when they come and use what they get out of it to blow Washington off the map. Understand that?"

"Yes," said Doan. "But if you don't mind me saying so, it sounds a little on the screwy side from where I sit."

"That's how we want it to sound."

"Oh," said Doan. "I take it that this Dust-Mouth Haggerty doesn't like Washington?"

"Not even any at all," Arne confirmed.

"Why not? That is, providing you admit that you need a reason."

"Have you ever heard of Boulder Dam?"

"Sure."

"That's why. Dust-Mouth claims it was built as part of a conspiracy to defraud him."

"Was it?" Doan asked.

"You'd better practice up thinking so if you're going to negotiate with Dust-Mouth. He had a gold claim on the Colorado River. He was washing out about thirty cents in gold a day. After Boulder Dam was built the river backed up over his claim so that now he can't get at it. He says that was the real reason the dam was built, just to destroy his claim."

"It seems like the long way around," Doan commented.

"Not to Dust-Mouth. His claim was investigated, and he was offered compensation for it, but he wouldn't accept. He says the thirty cents a day was merely the forerunner. He says he was just about to uncover the greatest gold deposit the world has ever seen, such an immense quantity of gold that it would have made him financial emperor of the United States, disturbed the world's balance of trade, and resulted in international crises by the dozen. He says the politicians in Washington built the dam to prevent him from doing that."

"When did he get out?" Doan inquired.

"Of where?"

"Of the insane asylum."

"Six months ago. Don't get the idea that he's a complete whack. He's not. He's a monomaniac. He's hipped on this one point. Other than that, he's pretty shrewd and sometimes nasty. He's just got a mad on with Washington, and he really means it. We've come at him from every direction, but he can spot a government man for a mile, and all he does is froth at the mouth."

"Hmmm," said Doan. "This ore I'm on the hunt for doesn't have anything to do with his gold claim, does it?"

"No. Dust-Mouth is an old-time desert rat. He's been prowling around in the Mojave for forty years. He came across the ore deposit we want on one of his trips. He never filed a claim on it, because the stuff was worth nothing at that time. It is now. In relation to the war effort, it's worth just about any amount you want to name. You'll probably have to promise to pay him a billion dollars for the location."

"What happens if I do, and he shows me where the stuff is, and then I don't pay off?"

Arne shrugged. "That's your problem."

"Yeah," said Doan sourly. "How about giving me some counterfeit money to pay him off with? You've got plenty of that around, haven't you?"

"Yes," Arne said. "But we're not so foolish as to trust you with any of it. You just talk your way out. All we're interested in is the location of that ore deposit."

"Huh," said Doan. "How do I find this guy, Dust-Mouth? The Mojave is a big place."

"Start at a town called Heliotrope."

"Where's that?"

"Either in California or Nevada."

"You said either?" Doan asked.

"Yes. The State of California is now suing the State of Nevada in the Supreme Court to compel Nevada to annex it. Nevada has started a countersuit to compel California to annex it."

"What's the matter with the place?"

"Just everything. Offhand, I can't think of any crime that isn't committed there regularly. You'll feel right at home."

"People circulate more nasty rumors about me," Doan said mildly.

"We don't deal in rumors," Arne said. "Only facts."

"Oh," said Doan.

Arne nodded at him. "Don't cut any corners in front of us. We've got quite a file on you and this hound of yours. There's a car parked in front, downstairs. Use it. In the dash compartment you'll find strip maps with the route to Heliotrope marked on them and an emergency gas rationing book made out in your name."

"What kind of a car?" Doan asked. "Carstairs is particular what he rides in."

"It's a Cadillac."

"Whee!" said Doan. "A new one, I hope, shined up all pretty?"

"Yes. And don't try to mortgage it or sell it because it's government property. Also, don't stall around giving joyrides to people who work in dime stores. Get started for Heliotrope right away"

"Like a flash," said Doan. "How will I get hold of you if I locate the ore deposit?"

Arne stood up. "We'll get hold of you. We can do that very easily, any time. Remember it. Come on, Barstow."

Barstow paused in the doorway and nodded at Doan. "Good luck."

"Well, thanks," said Doan, pleased.

"You'll need it," said Barstow, closing the door softly.

Doan got up off the chesterfield and kicked Carstairs in the stomach. "Stop snoring, and act a little more alert. We are starting on a secret government mission of enormous and far-reaching importance." Carstairs raised his head and looked at Doan and licked his lips slowly and meaningly.

"Stop nagging!" Doan ordered. "I'm working on that steak right now. Give me time, will you?"

Carstairs let his head fall back on the rug with a disgusted thud.

CHAPTER II

DOAN PACKED IN ten minutes flat, and when he got through the apartment looked as though he had done just that, but he didn't. He looked neat and fresh and cool in a light gray suit and a lighter gray hat and gray suede oxfords. He parked his two big, battered suitcases at the door, and as a last move pulled the cushions off the chesterfield and unearthed a Colt Police Positive revolver.

He slid that inside the waistband of his trousers, hooking it in a cloth loop sewn there for that purpose, and then he went over and pulled up the rug in the corner behind the bridge lamp. He found a .25 caliber automatic hidden there. He put that in the breast pocket of his coat and pushed an ornamental dark blue handkerchief down on top of it to keep it in place.

He was all ready to go when he had another thought. He took out his wallet and counted the money in it. The sum did not impress him. He put the wallet away and picked up the telephone from its stand beside the chesterfield.

The line clicked, and then a voice said cautiously

"Yes?"

"Is this Edmund, you rat?" Doan snarled. "I'll have something to say to you in a minute, but right now you connect me with the manager! I've got a beef with him!"

"This—this is the manager, Mr. Pocus."

"Oh, it is, is it? Well, what do you mean by tipping me off to those government men? Do you want to get me hung or something? You squealer! You double-crosser! Do you think I'm going to recommend this joint to any of my pals as a hideout if that's the way you're going to act?"

"Wha-wha-what?"

"Don't try that innocent stuff! I'm going to come down there and tear you up in little pieces! Just listen!"

Doan kicked Carstairs again and then leaned down and held the telephone close to his face. "Give," he whispered.

Carstairs snarled into the receiver. He looked enormously bored while he was doing it, but over the telephone the sound must have been horrible, because Carstairs had a company snarl that began low and ended high and undulated blood-chilling-ly in the middle register.

"There!" said Doan into the telephone. "Did you hear that? That's just a sample of what you're going to get when…." He listened and then said in a milder inquiring tone, "Hello? Hello, Mr. Rogan? Are you there?"

There was no answer.

Doan put the telephone back on its stand, took hold of Carstairs' spiked collar and heaved. "Come on. Hurry up."

Carstairs got up one foot at a time and sauntered to the door. Doan opened it for him and picked up the suitcases and bunted Carstairs in the rear with one of them.

"Go on. Get moving."

They went down the hall and down the stairs into the lobby. There was not a soul in sight.

Doan put his bags down and hammered vigorously on the desk. "Service! Service here! Mr. Rogan! Edmund!"

No one answered. No one appeared.

"Now imagine that," Doan said to Carstairs. "Obviously I can't be expected to pay my bill if there isn't anyone to pay it to, can I? The answer is no. So I won't pay. That will be a lesson to them to give more attention to their business in the future."

He picked up the suitcases again and negotiated them and Carstairs through the plate glass door. There was a black sedan glittering with chrome and a beautifully high, lustrous polish parked at the curb.

"Ah-ha!" said Doan. He opened one of the rear doors and heaved the bags inside and then walked all around the car twice, rubbing his hands blissfully. "Take a squint at this, kid. We're coming up in the world…. Carstairs! Where are you?"

There was a slight typhoon taking place in the thick, neatly trimmed shrubbery that marched precisely along the front of the apartment building. Shrubs heaved back and forth wildly, and branches crackled.

"Carstairs!" Doan shouted. "Oh, you would pick a time like this! Rogan is going to get over being scared and call copper on us or something if we don't get out of here. Hurry up!"

Carstairs' head appeared out of the greenery. He did not look like he was hurrying or even intended to. He blinked at Doan in a fatuous and pleased way. Doan started for him. Carstairs sighed comfortably and came out of the bushes. Doan got him by the collar and dragged him across the walk to the open rear door of the Cadillac.

"Get in there!"

He heaved vigorously, and Carstairs allowed himself to be urged through the door. Doan slammed it with a thump and crawled into the front seat. He started the car and drove off down the street with a viciously triumphant clashing of gears.

He drove over to Rossmore and up Rossmore to where it turns into Vine, and up Vine to Sunset Boulevard. He swung around to the right on Sunset, narrowly missing twenty-five sailors, sixteen soldiers and two marines who were doing sentry duty on the corner in the hopes of seeing a movie star. He drove two blocks farther and pulled up in front of an open air market.

It was really quite a marvelous place. It covered an area half the size of a city block, and you could buy anything in it from lollipops to life insurance. Doan got out of the car and headed for the long and empty meat counter. There was only one butcher behind it, and he looked as though he wished he were somewhere else.

"I'd like a three-pound porterhouse steak," Doan told him.

"So would I," said the butcher.

"I know you've got one hidden out in the icebox," Doan said.

"How do you know?" the butcher asked.

"I'm a Japanese spy. We spies get around."

"Palooey," said the butcher in a disgusted tone. "Now it's jokes I have to put up with. In my financial condition. All right. So suppose I've got a steak in the icebox. So why should I give it to you?"

"That's my car out in front—the big, shiny one. Take a look at what's in the back seat."

The butcher said: "I wouldn't care if…." He paused for a long moment. "Just what is that?"

"A dog."

"It's got awful big teeth for a dog," the butcher said slowly. "And I don't know as I like the way he's lookin' at me."

"The teeth are bigger at closer range," Doan said. "Would you like a demonstration?"

"No," said the butcher quickly. "Now listen, chum. I don't want no trouble with you or that gargoyle, but I can't sell you that steak. It was ordered three weeks ago by an old customer of mine. She's a very, very special customer. She's Susan Sally, the movie gal."

"She doesn't need a steak. She's too fat now."

"Fat?" the butcher echoed, stunned. "Susan Sally? Say listen, she comes in here all the time in nothing but shorts and a bandanna. I mean, short shorts and a bandanna the size of a cocktail napkin. She ain't fat."

"She will be if she eats too many steaks. You wouldn't want that to happen, would you?"

"I should say not," said the butcher.

"Give me the steak and save the risk. Look at my car now."

"Hey!" said the butcher, alarmed. "He can't get through that window, can he?"

"He probably could if I called to him. Shall I? The only trouble is that I can't control him. He runs around snapping and gnashing, and he's awfully careless about what he gnashes on."

"You're threatening me," said the butcher. "That's what you're doing."

"I'm glad you finally found it out. Are you going to give me a steak out of the icebox or off of you?"

"It's a hell of a fine thing, that's all I got to say. A man can't even do business any more without being submitted to terrorism."

The butcher went stamping down the counter and opened the heavy icebox door and went inside. He came out again carrying a big, rich red steak reverently in front of him. He plopped it down on the scales, and the dial swung just short of the three-pound mark.

"Okay," said Doan. "Now put it through the grinder."

"Grinder!" the butcher repeated, horrified. "This steak? This steak here?"

"Yes."

"Oh-oh," the butcher mumbled. He ran the steak through the grinder, turning his head away to keep from witnessing its desecration. He wrapped up the results in oiled paper and slapped it on the counter. "There! Now I hope you're happy!"

"Sure," said Doan. "I see you've got your ceiling prices pasted up over there."

"Yeah. And we follow 'em, too."

"That's fine. I notice that the ceiling price on dog meat is twelve cents a pound. This wasn't quite three pounds, but I'll be generous about it. Here's thirty-six cents and a penny for tax, and you won't need my rationing book because dog meat and scraps don't come under the rules."

The butcher's face was very pale. "Chum," he whispered, "you can't do this to me."

"Thanks," said Doan. "Good-by." He headed for the car.

The butcher leaned over the counter and pointed a long, accusing arm. "Oh, you wait! If you ever meet up with Susan Sally…. And I'm gonna tell her you said she was fat! You're gonna be a sad man if she ever lays hold of you!"

Doan ignored him. He got in the car and let Carstairs sniff the meat and then drove down Sunset until he located an open-air, car-service restaurant. He drove the Cadillac in under the wooden, pagodalike awning and parked. Grunting and groaning with the effort, he leaned over the back of the seat and opened one of his bags and took out a square cardboard carton.

A very trim and trig little girl in red pants and a red jacket and a high bussar's hat with a red plume on it came up and slapped a card on the windshield and leaned in the window, all glistening teeth and lipstick and beaded eyelashes.

"Good afternoon, sir! And what will—"Her smile went away and left her face as blank as a freshly whitewashed wall. "What's that in the back seat?"

"Just a dog," Doan said. "A poor, harmless, little puppy that loves women and children."

"He looks awful—hungry."

"That's because he is. And speaking of that...."

Doan unwrapped the meat and held it up for her to see, rich and luscious in its nest of pink oiled paper.

"Gee!" said the waitress. "Meat!"

"Right," Doan agreed complacently. "Now I'll tell you what I want you to do with it. Take it into your kitchen and put it in a pan and put the pan in the oven. Warm the meat. Don't cook it or sear it. Just warm it. Then take it out and put it in a big bowl—a clean one. Follow me?"

The waitress nodded doubtfully. "Yes."

Doan held up the cardboard carton. "Know what these are?"

She nodded again. "Sure. Those are special-extra-fancy English tea biscuits. I've seen them in some of the real high-priced markets in Beverly Hills."

"Okay. After you get the meat warm, take the biscuits out of the box, crumple them carefully, and stir them into the meat. Mix them up nice and smoothly. Got it?"

The waitress had backed a step away from the window. "Yes," she said warily.

Doan took a small green bottle from his pocket. "When you get through mixing the biscuits, pour three drops of this in the bowl and mix that in, too. It's concentrated cod liver oil. Bring a door tray back when you come, Carstairs refuses to eat off the floor. He knows it makes him look like a giraffe taking a drink."

"Is this for the dog?" the waitress asked incredulously.

"Sure."

"Oh!" she gasped, relieved. "I thought it was for you!"

"I wish it was," said Doan, "But if I tried to eat it, you'd hear an awful lot of hell-raising around here. You haven't got anything in the meat line you could put in a sandwich for me, have you?"

"Oh, no."

"Okay. Bring me six melted cheese sandwiches with chopped nuts spread on them and a quart of beer and three glasses of water."

"A quart of beer and three glasses of water?" the waitress repeated.

"Yes."

She shrugged. "It's your plumbing, mister."

She sauntered back into the restaurant. Doan explored in the dashboard compartment and found the strip maps and the gas rationing book Arne had said would be there. He studied his route to Heliotrope, muttering to himself as he calculated mileages.

The waitress reappeared, loaded down with trays. Doan ran down one of the back windows, and she slid one tray inside and fastened it to the door. She clamped the other one over the steering wheel and then made another trip and returned with sandwiches, water, and beer on one arm and a shiny earthenware bowl under the other.

Carstairs mumbled happily at her as she put the bowl on his tray. She gave Doan the beer and the water and the sandwiches and stood watching for a moment, shaking her head slightly, and then went away.

Carstairs was too well-bred to slobber or slop things around, but he ate with a sort of deadly efficiency. Doan was only on his second sandwich when Carstairs began to snuffle commandingly behind his right ear.

Doan picked up the water glasses one after the other and, leaning over the seat-back, poured them into the earthenware bowl which was now as clean and glistening and empty as it had been when it came from the store.

Carstairs slapped his tongue happily in the water and then said: "Whumpf," in a moistly satisfied way. The car rocked back on its springs as he hurled himself full length on the rear seat. He began to snore instantly.

When he had finished his sandwiches, Doan beeped the horn softly, and the waitress came back. She looked at the empty beer bottle and the three empty water glasses and then said:

"It's right over there."

"Thanks," Doan said. "But not now."

"You'll be sorry," said the waitress. "Listen, did you know your back trunk compartment isn't locked? The handle is turned wrong. Somebody's liable to steal your spare if you don't watch out."

"I don't care," Doan told her.

She stared at him. "You don't care if somebody swipes your spare?"

"No. I can easily get another."

"Are you one of these ration bootleggers?"

"No," said Doan. "I'm a Japanese spy. Rationing doesn't apply to spies. Look it up if you don't believe me"

"Huh!" said the waitress. "I'm going to die laughing some day at the funny cracks I hear on this job."

"How would you like to go for a ride?" Doan asked. "Up around the hills, and look at the city and stuff."

"The stuff is what I wouldn't go for," she said.

"You'd like me if you knew me better," Doan told her.

"I doubt that, but we'll never find out, will we?"

"Are you married?" Doan inquired.

"Yes."

"Oh, that's a shame," Doan said. "But then we all make mistakes. Why don't you get a divorce? You can get one cheap in Nevada. I'm on my way up that way to do some spying. Come on along. I'll split the expenses with you."

"I can hardly resist, but I think I will. Here's your bottle of cod liver oil. Your bill is a dollar and fifty-three cents"

Doan counted out a dollar and sixty cents. "You gave us such nice service that I'm going to let you keep the change, all for yourself."

"You're too good to me," said the waitress. "Come back again—three weeks after never."

"It's a date," said Doan.

CHAPTER III

THE MOJAVE DESERT at sunset looks remarkably like a painting of a sunset on the Mojave Desert which, when you come to think of it, is really quite surprising. Except that the real article doesn't show such good color sense as the average painting does. Yellows and purples and reds and various other violent subunits of the spectrum are splashed all over the sky, in a monumental exhibition of bad taste. They keep moving and blurring and changing around, like the color movies they show in insane asylums to keep the idiots quiet.

After this gaudy display is over the shadows move in, swift and blue and silent, and then the place resembles a rundown graveyard slightly haunted by rattlesnakes and battered beer cans. It is quite uncanny.

The highway that Arne had marked in red on the maps swooped and curved and coiled casually through draws, canyons, barrancas and such other natural barriers as cluttered up the landscape, and Doan drove along it in sort of a mild coma. The sun had rippled the highway surface just enough to give the car a sleepy, rocking motion that was very pleasant. Doan was driving at exactly thirty-five miles an hour. Not entirely from choice. Someone had installed a governor on the Cadillac. It wouldn't go any faster.

Doan and Carstairs and the Cadillac were all alone and had been for the last two hours. There hadn't been any signs of civilization at all, not even an abandoned gas station. No other cars had passed him going in either direction. It was as though the highway had decided to run off somewhere at random on an errand of its own.

Doan saw the figure when it was almost a mile ahead of him, standing beside the road with the shadows pooling deep around its feet. It looked like a totem pole sawed off at top and bottom, and then as he rolled closer it moved and jiggled its arm, semaphore fashion, and became human.

Doan slowed up. The desert at dusk is not a one hundred percent safe place to pick up hitchhikers. Quite often they rap you on the head and throw you in a ditch where, after suitable curing, your skull makes a nice nesting place for scorpions. However, the prospect didn't bother Doan much. He knew from some spectacular experiences in that line that he was difficult to murder.

The figure, on closer inspection, turned out to be a female one complete in all its component parts and encased in a neat blue slack suit and possessing blond hair done up precisely in a blue snood. It was a young female figure and had an air of coordinated and trained determination.

Doan pulled up beside her. She opened the door opposite him before he had a chance to, and leaned in the car and looked at him. Her features were even and assembled with good taste, and she had earnest, deep blue eyes.

"Hello," said Doan mildly. "Would you like a ride?"

"What's your name?"

"Doan," said Doan.

"I'm Harriet Hathaway, and I'm on my way to Fort Des Moines to join the WAACs and serve my country."

"Happy to meet you," said Doan. "Would you like a ride?"

"Do you propose to make improper advances to me, Mr. Doan?"

"Well, I hadn't thought of it," Doan told her. "But if you really insist I can probably turn up something in that line."

"I don't insist! And if you have any such ideas I advise you to discard them."

"Plunk," said Doan. "Gurgle-gurgle. They're discarded. Would you like a ride?"

"Yes, I would. Don't bother to move, please. I can handle this." She picked up a small, dark blue bag and placed it precisely in the middle of the front seat. She got in and sat on the far side of it and closed the door efficiently. "I'm ready."

Doan started the car.

"If you'd use the clutch properly the gears wouldn't grate that way," Harriet Hathaway informed him.

"No doubt you're right," said Doan.

"Men are very nasty beasts."

"Aren't they, though?"

"I've just gone through a singularly unpleasant experience with one."

"A fate worse than death?" Doan asked.

"What? No! I'm quite capable of protecting myself from anything like that. I'm the woman's golf champion of Talamedas County."

"Oh," said Doan.

"I was also the runner-up in the finals of the Basin City National Tennis Tourney last year."

"Oh," said Doan.

"I'm also considered the best horsewoman in the Rio Hondo Riding Club."

"Oh," said Doan.

"This experience had nothing whatsoever to do with—with sex."

"It must have been rather dull," Doan observed.

"It was not! It was beastly! This person offered me a ride in Masterville. He was wearing dark glasses and I detest people with weak vision, but I accepted. I was willing to accept any means of transportation to get to my post of duty as rapidly as possible."

"Sure," said Doan. "Through rain and snow the postman always rings twice."

"What?" said Harriet Hathaway. She watched him narrowly for a moment. "Are you intoxicated?"

"Just slightly dizzy," Doan answered.

"It's probably because the sun has been so bright today. You should pull your windshield visor down when it glares. That's what it's for. But to go back to this horrible person who gave me the ride. He was a slacker. He admitted it!"

"How interesting," said Doan.

"Interesting! It's criminal! If I only knew his name I'd report him. I asked him what he was doing to serve his country in this emergency and he said, 'Nothing.' I asked him what he intended to do in the future and he said, 'Less.' Have you ever heard of anything like that?"

"Never in my life," said Doan. "Did you tell him you were going to join the WAACs?"

"Yes."

"What did he say to that?"

"He asked me if they knew it."

"Do they?"

"Well, no. I put in an application, but they haven't replied to it. Naturally they'll accept me."

"Naturally," Doan agreed.

"I told that to this horrible person. I told him that no matter how degrading and disgusting the work they assigned me might be, I would smile and serve."

"What did he say to that?"

"He just said, 'Oh, God,' in a very disgusted tone. I didn't mind the profanity, although I think it's bad taste. It was the sentiment behind it I disapproved of. I told him so, very emphatically. I explained to him the duties and responsibilities we owe our country for the glorious privilege of being one of its citizens."

"Then what?"

"He stopped the car and told me to get out. He said he wanted to vomit, and he always vomited in private if he could manage it. He literally pushed me out! Right on this deserted road in the middle of the desert! And then drove off and left me!"

"You said you didn't know his name," Doan remarked. "Haven't got any idea where he hangs out, have you?"

"No. Are you going to try to find him and teach him to respect patriotic American womanhood?"

"Well, not exactly," Doan said. "I think maybe I could use a slacker like he is in my business"

"What is it—your business?"

"It's rather confidential."

"Oh!" said Harriet Hathaway, thrilled. "It's government work, isn't it?"

"Not unless you're thinking of a different government than I think you are."

"Oh, I know you can't say anything about it," said Harriet understandingly. "I'll just bet you're an agent of some kind or other."

"Of some kind or other," Doan agreed. "Other, to be strictly accurate."

"You can trust my discretion, Mr. Doan. I know just what's that queer noise?" She turned around. "There's a dog in your back seat!"

"I noticed that," Doan told her.

"He's awfully big."

"Yes," said Doan.

"He's snoring."

Doan sighed. "Yes."

"He's a Great Dane."

"So his pedigree says."

"I don't like Great Danes. They're stupid, and they're a nuisance."

"You're telling me."

"Then why did you buy this one?"

"I didn't. I won him in a crap game."

"I don't believe in gambling. You might lose."

"I did," said Doan. "The only trouble was that I didn't know it at the time. I thought I'd won something pretty fancy until I got him home and he started sneering at me and snubbing me because I didn't have a ten-room suite in the penthouse of the Park-Plaza Hotel."

"I know. Then, later, you grew so fond of him and he of you that you couldn't part with him."

"What?" said Doan. "Fond? I detest him, and he despises me."

"Oh, no," said Harriet confidently. "Dogs always love their masters."

"Explain that to Carstairs sometime when you're not busy. It would be an interesting new theory to him."

"Does he always sleep like this?"

"Turn around again," Doan said.

Harriet turned around. Carstairs' broad, blunt muzzle was just a half inch from the end of her nose, and his eyes were fiery greenish slits staring unblinkingly into hers.

"Oh!" she gasped.

"Relax, stupid," said Doan.

The rear seat springs bonged as Carstairs hurled himself back into the cushions again.

"Oh," said Harriet, swallowing. "Oh."

"He gets resentful when people make disparaging remarks about him," Doan explained.

"Oh, I'm sorry! I didn't know he could understand…. Why, he can't understand! Dogs can't understand what people are saying!"

Doan shrugged. "Okay."

"You signaled him some way. I know! You mentioned his name!"

"Have it your way."

"Well, I don't like him."

"He'd feel insulted if you did. What did this horrible person who picked you up in Masterville look like?"

"Well, he was tall and skinny and unhealthy looking, and he had a beard that grew in patches in a disgustingly unkempt manner. He was really most unpleasant, and I didn't bother to pay much attention to him. I always say we should ignore the lower elements of the population and concentrate our attention on people of culture and breeding."

"I'll bet."

"Bet what?"

"That you always say that."

After that they rode in silence for awhile. Doan turned on the headlights, and the car moved smoothly and silently through the white tunnel they dug in the night. A few stars came out. In the Mojave the stars aren't coy. They don't twinkle and wink at you. They just stare. Sometimes, when you've been alone too long, you begin to think they're taking an altogether too personal interest in you and your affairs, and then you get sand-silly and start running in circles and screaming.

Carstairs licked Doan on the back of the neck. Carstairs' tongue, spread out flat, was as wide as a four-inch paint brush and had much the same effect when used judicially. It never failed to make Doan jump. Now the car swooped across to the wrong side of the road and back again.

"Damn you!" Doan said emphatically.

"What?" Harriet asked, startled.

"Carstairs," Doan explained. "He has an urgent personal errand to attend to."

He stopped the car and shut off the motor, palming the ignition key as he did so. He got out and opened the rear door.

"Come on. And don't step on a rattlesnake, like I hope you will."

Carstairs looked up the road and down the road and snorted twice disapprovingly and then ambled off into the shadows. Doan walked around to the back of the car and stared up at the stars without much enthusiasm. He looked down after a moment, his eyes caught by the gleam of the chrome handle on the trunk compartment.

It was still turned sideways. Doan attempted to turn it back to the locked position. Something was holding it. It was something soft that gave slightly under pressure.

Doan opened the compartment curiously. It had a light in it that snapped on as he did so and showed the man in the compartment quite plainly. He was sitting down, his knees doubled up, and his head twisted back sideways. It was the middle finger of his left hand that had kept the compartment from locking. The edge of the lock had roweled the skin and flesh across the knuckle, but it wasn't bleeding.

Doan let his breath out slowly and quietly, and then breathed in as slowly. The man had been stabbed expertly in the side of his throat, and blood was caked thick and scaly all over the front of his coat. He was not a large man and not young. His suit, where the blood hadn't stained it, was blue, and it looked as though it hadn't fitted well even when he was alive.

Carstairs came out of the shadows. He paused for a second and then peered around Doan and sniffed once. He backed off two steps, his upper lip curling.

"I know," said Doan. "He's not fresh. I wonder just what kind of a story I'm going to tell Arne that will account for me picking up a three-day dead hitchhiker with a sliced jugular vein."

Carstairs watched him silently.

"The compartment was unlocked," Doan said absently, "and he could have been shoved in there any place I stopped, only I didn't stop any place where there weren't a lot of people around…." He paused and looked toward the front of the car. "Maybe I'm getting softening of the brain."

He closed the compartment, after gingerly shoving the lax, leaden-tinged hand out of the way, and made sure it was locked this time.

"Get in," he said.

Carstairs climbed quickly and silently into the backseat.

Doan closed the door after him and got in the front seat and started the car.

"This horrible person," he said, rolling the car back on the highway, "the one who picked you up, where did he go after he put you down?"

"On along the road," Harriet said. "The same way we've been going."

"He didn't stop or come back, did he?"

"No."

"You didn't see anyone else sort of prowling around in the vicinity while you were waiting, did you?"

"No," she said blankly. "Why?"

"Just wondered," Doan answered. "Did you have any friends with you, back there when I picked you up, someone who might have been temporarily mislaid in the brush or something?"

"Friends?"

"Chums. Acquaintances. Traveling companions."

"Of course not."

"Oh," said Doan. He waited for awhile. "We're coming into Heliotrope in a couple of hours. That's as far as I'm going. Would you take it amiss if I put on my best manners and invited you to have dinner with me?"

Harriet considered. "I think it would be perfectly proper for me to have dinner with you, Mr. Doan."

"I'm glad," said Doan.

CHAPTER IV

HELIOTROPE IS TOO far inland to fall under the restrictions of the coastal dim-out zone, and since the taste of the advertising portion of its population runs toward the more violent shades of neon, it resembles a string of cheap jewelry tucked in against the dark and barren sweep of the Crazy Leg Mountains when approached at night from the floor of the desert. Its main street is four blocks long, paved at the sides but not in the middle, and at close range the signs on the buildings that line it are so blinding that it is hard for the stranger to tell whether he has arrived in a town or at the Fourth of July.

Doan parked the Cadillac in the unpaved section of the street midway between the Double-Eagle Hotel (golden neon eagle flapping its wings in two-four time) and the Bar B Grill (fiendish twenty-foot red flames lapping around a bored blue cow). The combination of colors gave Harriet Hathaway's healthy face a tinge that reminded him urgently of the cargo he was carrying in the trunk compartment.

"Let's try that," he said, indicating the Bar B. "They might really have steaks."

"I'd like one," said Harriet.

Doan opened the door for Carstairs, and the three of them crossed the street and went in through the red bordered swing doors. The place was long and low and L-shaped, filled to capacity with a bar and round, blacktopped tables. The only person in sight was the bartender. He had gold front teeth and only one ear.

"Have you any steaks tonight?" Doan asked.

"Sure," said the bartender.

"Are they good?"

"I dunno, mister. I just cook 'em. I don't eat 'em."

Doan selected a table, and pulled out a chair for Harriet Hathaway. "We'll take a chance. Give us a couple of what you think are New York cuts and some French fried potatoes and a salad bowl."

"Ain't you gonna have anything to drink first?" the bartender asked. "We don't make any profit on our food, you know. We can't run this dive unless we sell liquor."

Doan looked inquiringly at Harriet. "You?"

"I don't drink, thank you."

Doan nodded at the bartender. "I'll have a triple bourbon in a beer glass."

"Why?" said the bartender.

Carstairs had collapsed beside the table, and Doan indicated him meaningly.

"I'm only allowed one drink before meals, unless I want an argument."

The bartender stared. "You mean you let a dog dictate to you?"

"Up-si-daisy," said Doan.

Carstairs got up instantly. Doan pointed toward the bar, and Carstairs swung his head slowly in the direction.

"Hey!" said the bartender. "Hold it, now! I didn't mean any offense. I was just making a remark, and I can see that there's a lot to be said for your point of view."

"Let's have a little less conversation and a little more service," Doan requested.

"Sure. Tell him to lie down again like a nice dog, would you mind?"

"Boom," said Doan.

Carstairs relaxed his muscles and hit the floor all at once.

"One triple bourbon in a beer glass," the bartender said, becoming briskly businesslike. "Yes, sir. Coming right up. Two New York cuts, side of fried and grass. On the fire."

He brought the drink for Doan, making a careful detour around Carstairs, and then went back and began to bustle busily around the hooded grill at the far end of the bar. Doan raised the glass to take a sip of the whiskey in it and then paused, staring at the man who had materialized from somewhere or other and was now standing beside the table smiling at him.

"How do you do?" said the man.

He was small, and he had a round, olive-skinned face with a dimple in each cheek, and his teeth were very white and even under a pencil-line black mustache. His eyes were liquidly dark and sparkling. He wore a brown suit and a brown shirt and tie and had a brown handkerchief peeping artistically out of the breast pocket of his coat.

"All right," said Doan.

The small man turned his head and looked at Harriet. There was nothing insulting about his look. It was courteously calculating, nothing more.

"Would you like to buy a blonde?" he asked, turning back to Doan.

"A what?" Doan said.

"A blonde."

"No," said Doan.

"A brunette?"

"No," said Doan. "Supposing you go away and sit down somewhere."

The small man smiled winningly. "You don't approve of me, perhaps?"

"Not perhaps. Positively."

"You scorn me?"

"That's right."

The small man bowed precisely. "Good evening." He turned on his heel and walked back to the farthest table in the rear corner of the room and sat down.

Harriet said, "He's such a handsome little man, but he must be awfully drunk. I mean, who ever heard of buying a blonde or brunette.... Oh!"

"Yes," said Doan.

"You mean he—they—you.... Oh!"

"Oh," Doan agreed.

"Why, that's terrible! Why, I'm going to call a policeman and have him arrested!"

"It wouldn't do any good. They'd just have to bail him out or pay his fine."

"They! You mean, they pay.... Oh, that's horrible! Oh, I don't believe.... Really?"

"Yes."

"Well, I'm going to…." Her voice trailed away. She was staring glassy-eyed over Doan's shoulder. "Oh, there he is! You!"

Doan turned around. A tall man in khaki pants and shirt and leather jacket was halfway between the door and the bar. He had stopped so suddenly that he had one foot still half-raised to take another step. He was wearing black—not dark, but black—glasses, and he had an unkempt, patchy beard about an inch long at its best points. He was watching Harriet Hathaway with the sort of expression the ordinary person reserves for a nest of rattlesnakes.

"That's the horrible slacker person," Harriet explained to Doan. "You! Come right over here!"

The tall man put the raised foot carefully in back of the one he was standing on. Harriet got out of her chair.

"Don't you dare try to avoid me! You come here! I want to speak to you!"

That last did it. The tall man spun like a top and dove for the door. He hit it and was gone with a double whack-whack to mark his passage.

"Oh, he's not going to get away from me again!" said Harriet, and went right after him.

The doors whack-whacked again, even more emphatically. Carstairs had raised his head and was looking at Doan with an expression of long-suffering annoyance. Doan shrugged and took a big drink of bourbon.

"So you wanna insult my friend, do you?"

Doan looked up slowly. This man was wearing a ten-gallon hat and a blue bandanna and a calfskin vest and brass-studded chaps, and the effect was so startling it was grotesque. His face didn't match the camouflage. It was a fat, florid face with black, beady chips for eyes. It was blurred just slightly. It looked like a face someone had drawn and then half erased. In other words, it looked like a fifth rate prizefighter's face.

"So you wanna insult my friend, huh?" he said again.

"Sure," said Doan, putting his glass down.

The man was as thick as he was wide, and he turned and pointed meaningly toward the back of the room. "That's my friend, what you insulted."

"Go away while you're healthy," said Doan. "Take him with you."

The thick man clipped him with a short right. It was an expertly professional blow, coming without any warning at all. Doan had just time to tilt his head a quarter inch, so that the splayed, thick knuckles landed on his cheekbone instead of on the point of his jaw.

The force of the blow knocked him clear out of his chair and flat on the floor. He rolled over and dove, not for the thick man, but for Carstairs. He was just in time. He got a stranglehold on Carstairs' neck with one arm and jerked his front feet out from under him with the other.

Carstairs sprawled down, half on top of him, making little grunting thick sounds deep in his throat.

"Stop it!" Doan panted, rapping him sharply on the top of the head. "Did I ask for help? Did I? Relax!"

The thick man laughed jeeringly. "Look at this! I hit the guy, so he hits his dog! A screwball!"

Doan got up. "That was a cute trick," he said amiably. "What would you do if I did this?"

He made a fork out of the first two fingers of his right hand and then flicked the fingers at the thick man's eyes. Just exactly like Laurel and Hardy. Only Doan meant it. One of his fingers bit the thick man in each of his eyes.

The thick man screamed and slapped both palms against his eyes. Doan stepped back two paces and then forward one and kicked the thick man six inches below his belt. The thick man stopped screaming right in mid-note and doubled up. Doan hit him in the back of his neck with a full-arm swing, and the thick man followed his nose right down to the floor and squirmed there on his stomach.

Doan stepped back three paces this time and then forward two and jumped. He came down heels first, lumberjack style, on the thick man's back. There was a dull little crack, and then the thick man didn't squirm any more. He didn't do anything. He lay where he was.

Doan stepped off him lightly and looked at the back of the room. "And now I want a word with you."

The small man had lost his neat and glistening smile and the best part of his olive complexion. He looked decidedly ill. He was standing up, flat against the wall, and now he shook a thin clasp knife out of the sleeve of his neat brown suit and opened the blade with a flick of his wrist.

Doan picked up the chair he had fallen out of and walked slowly toward him. The small man threw the knife in a sudden wickering blur. Doan caught it on the bottom of the chair, and it stuck there with a steely thrum. He worked it loose and balanced it in his right hand thoughtfully.

The small man didn't wait for any decisions. He dove head first through the window behind his table. Doan stared at the window as though he had never seen one before. He took three steps toward it, craning his neck, and then suddenly whipped around and dropped into a crouch, facing the other way.

The bartender was standing at attention, both hands raised over his head. "Oh, no!" he said quickly. "No, sir! I'm neutral, thanks."

Doan watched him.

"Mister," said the bartender, "this position ain't very comfortable, but I ain't gonna twitch an eyelid until you say I can."

"All right," said Doan. "Who was the gent who went out the window?"

"Name of Free-Look Jones. No friend of mine."

"Where does he live?"

"I dunno."

"Find out," said Doan, "before I count three. One, two—"

"On Rosewater Lane," said the bartender quickly. "It runs

out north of town. He lives in a shack next to a wrecked dump truck near the end. There's no number."

"Okay," said Doan. "Sweep up the garbage on the floor. I'll be back."

"Don't hurry," said the bartender.

CHAPTER V

ROSEWATER LANE STARTED out with quite a splurge. It was paved, and there were four houses in the first block. The second block was only half paved and contained three houses. The third block didn't have any pavement or any houses, either, and after that the lane circled in a discouraged way around a knoll, and there was the abandoned dump truck like some armored prehistoric bug that had been tipped over on its back and decided to make the best of it.

The shack was low and unpainted and swaybacked, pushed in against the darker blot of the knoll. There were no lights showing, and Doan stopped the Cadillac a hundred yards away from it and opened the rear door.

"Take a look," he ordered. He pointed at the shack and made a circling motion with his forefinger.

Carstairs got out of the car and faded quietly and expertly into the darkness. Doan waited. After about five minutes Carstairs came back and put his front feet on the running board and snuffled over the lowered glass.

"Okay," said Doan.

He got out of the car and went around to the back and opened the trunk compartment. The man inside hadn't changed any, for the better or the worse. Doan took hold of his arm and pulled. The man slid out of the compartment with a horribly fluid laxness and sprawled all over the ground.

Doan said some things to himself in an undertone. He leaned down and picked the man up, trying to avoid the dried blood, and then carried him toward the shack with Carstairs coursing on ahead alertly. The front, and only, door had a padlock and hasp on it, but the padlock had rusted open. Doan maneuvered it off the hasp with the toe of one shoe and then kicked the door open.

He turned sideways and slid through the door, still carrying the dead man. Inside the darkness was as thick and smooth as molasses, but it had considerably more odor. Carstairs snorted disapprovingly. Letting his burden slide down to the floor, Doan struck a match.

The flame reflected in a little sparkle from the unshaded electric light bulb that hung from the ceiling on a limp yellow cord. Doan pulled the string attached to it, and the darkness retired, quivering malignantly, to the corners of the room.

There was a table with a stained and splintered top just under the light, and there were two tin cups and two tin plates and two forks, all dirty, on top of it. Doan regarded the setup thoughtfully for a moment, and then picked up the dead man, and put him in the swaybacked chair in front of one of the plates and maneuvered his arms and legs around carefully until he stayed there.

Doan stepped back to look things over, his head tilted in a speculative way. He was frowning a little. Then his eye caught a battered deck of cards resting between two old gin bottles on a board that had been nailed against the far wall to form a shelf. He picked the cards up and ran through them quickly. They were marked with invisible little nicks along the edges.

Doan smiled. He piled the tin plates and cups at one end of the table and then scattered the cards over its surface, letting a few fall on the floor.

He stepped back and surveyed the scene again. Things looked a little better. He took Free-Look Jones' knife from his pocket and wiped the blade and handle carefully on his handkerchief and then, still using his handkerchief to cover his hand, he put the point of the knife against the purple-edged wound in the dead man's neck and pushed.

The blade went in slickly and easily up to its hilt. Doan let go. The handle of the knife was made of some green composition material that caught the light and glittered sinisterly, sticking out under the lax line of the dead man's jaw.

Doan nodded to himself, satisfied. He pulled the string on the light bulb and felt his way toward the door. He bumped into Carstairs in front of it and said, "Go on. Outside."

He shut the front door and put the rusted padlock back on its hasp, and then headed for the car with Carstairs trailing along behind in disapproving silence. Doan began to whistle to himself in a mildly pleased way.

He pushed Carstairs into the back seat, turned the car around, and headed back for the center of town. Things were looking up a bit now. The signs were brighter, if possible, and parts of the populace, prowling like zombies in the weird light, sauntered aimlessly and stared or merely stood, hip-shot and dejected on the corners, smoking hand-rolled cigarettes and spitting in the gutters. Cars, with sand on their hoods and spades lashed over the front fenders, were parked in thick clusters in the street center.

Doan found a place for the Cadillac, and he and Carstairs got out and walked across to the Bar B Grill. The one-eared bartender was still in sole charge, and he sighed deeply and began to clatter bottles around in a very absorbed manner when Doan and Carstairs appeared.

"Mr. Doan!" Harriet Hathaway called. "You've come back again!"

"I think you're right," Doan said.

She was sitting at the table she and Doan had occupied before, and the man with the black glasses was sitting opposite her. He was eating a steak, but he didn't look as though he were enjoying it. His shoulders were hunched, and he had the numbly suffering air of a man unbearably buffeted by fate.

"This is Mr. Blue, Mr. Doan," Harriet said. "He's eating your steak."

"That's thoughtful of him," Doan remarked.

"I didn't want to eat it," Blue said.

"Nonsense," said Harriet. "Of course you did."

"I don't like steak."

Harriet laughed. "Now isn't that a silly thing to say! Everyone likes steak. And besides, it's good for you. You just go right ahead and enjoy it."

"All right," said Blue glumly. He put another piece in his mouth and chewed with grim concentration.

"You seem to be getting along a little better than you were at last reports," Doan observed.

Harriet laughed again. "It was all a mistake. It was just because Mr. Blue is so ignorant."

Blue looked up at Doan and nodded solemnly, his blacked-out glasses winking in the light. "I sure am. I'm awful ignorant, Mr. Doan."

"Is that so?" said Doan.

Harriet said, "He didn't even know there was a war! He really didn't. He can't read, and he doesn't have money enough to buy a radio, and he's so shy he never talks to people. Isn't that incredible?"

"Yes," said Doan.

"You know," Harriet said, "he thought when I was talking to him before about the emergency that I meant the depression! And when I told him about the WAACs, he thought I was referring to the WPA!"

"Did he?" said Doan.

"But when I explained things, he became very interested at once. Didn't you become interested?"

"Yes, ma'am," said Blue, starting stubbornly on another piece of steak.

"When I told him about our brave boys fighting in all parts of the world on land and on the sea and in the air, he was astounded. Weren't you?"

"Uh-huh," said Blue. "Sure was."

"Won't you sit down, Mr. Doan?" Harriet asked. "I'm just going to describe to Mr. Blue the wonderful work our Air Force has been doing. I'm fascinated by the Air Force, and I know all about it. Wouldn't you like to listen, too?"

"Thank you, no," said Doan. "I have a little business to look after. Perhaps I'll see you later."

He went over to the bar and drummed on it with his fingers.

"Want some whiskey?" the bartender asked, staying at a safe distance.

"No. You. Come here."

"You ain't mad, are you?"

"No."

The bartender slid a little closer, keeping an eye on Carstairs. "What?"

"Where'd you dump the debris I left here?"

"Oh, him. I called Doc Gravelmeyer to look at him, and the doc took him over to his office. I wouldn't want to offer any advice or anything, but if I was you I'd sort of step over and look into that situation."

"Why?"

"Well, Doc Gravelmeyer has been readin' a book again, and when he was over here he was talkin' about acute something-or-other that I didn't like the sound of. He said right away that Parsley Jack—that's the guy you tangled with—looked like a first-class incipient case of it and that he'd better open Jack up and look around a bit. Now the trouble with Doc Gravel-meyer is that he's liable to get so interested when he gets to prowlin' around that it's sometimes fatal."

"I should worry."

"You're right," said the bartender, "you should. Doc's the coroner. The last guy that kicked off while he was operatin' on him got listed as an accidental death due to drowning in a sand storm. Doc is a very humorous guy sometimes."

"He sounds like it. Where can I find him?"

"His office is down the street over the undertaker's parlor. Does the undertaker, too. Just for a laugh, he claims he always gets you, comin' or goin'."

"Ha-ha," said Doan sourly. "Come on, Carstairs." They went out into the street again, but Doan didn't attempt to find Doc Gravelmeyer's office. Instead, he went to the Cadillac, got his two suitcases out of the rear seat, and headed for the Double-Eagle Hotel.

He went up the three slick marble steps at the entrance and through the brass bound doors and right back into the nineteenth century. The lobby was two stories high and featured a crystal chandelier as big as a dive bomber, and potentially as dangerous to any innocent bystanders if it happened to fall. There were rubber plants in all the available corners and chairs with red plush upholstery and gilt-knobbed legs, and shiny brass spittoons with gracefully curved necks. All this was overlaid neatly with an odor of fly-spray that made Carstairs sneeze indignantly.

The only concession to the present was the desk clerk. He was as slick and shiny as a new cocktail shaker, and he owned a smile that hit you in the face like a wet towel.

"Yes, sir!" he said.

"I want a room for myself and my friend. Twin beds."

"Yes, sir!" said the clerk. He twirled a big leather-bound register around on the desk and pointed a pen at Doan.

Doan signed as "I. Doanwashi, Tokyo, Japan."

The clerk didn't bat an eye. "Glad to have you with us, Mr. Doanwashi. I hope you enjoy your stay. Joshua! Joshua! Front!"

A man came out of the door at the rear of the lobby. He was a very small, very frail man, wearing a uniform that would have enabled him to join a Civil War infantry regiment without attracting undue attention. He leaned over the desk and held out his hand blindly. The clerk slapped a key into his palm.

"Two-one-four."

"Two-one-four," Joshua repeated numbly.

He leaned over to pick up Doan's bags and fell flat on his face. He got up carefully, took a deep breath, and picked up the bags. He headed for the red carpeted stairway in a wavering, loose-kneed quickstep. He missed by ten feet and disappeared in the shadows under the staircase.

The clerk smiled amiably at Doan. There was a crash and a thud, and Joshua backed out into the lobby and made another run at the stairs. He hit them this time, and got halfway up before he lost his momentum. He turned around and sat down with a baffled sigh.

"Two-one-four," said the clerk.

"Two-one-four," Joshua echoed obediently.

He got up and picked up the bags again, and made it to the top of the staircase. Doan and Carstairs followed him with due caution. Joshua had dropped the bags halfway down the straight, high-ceilinged hall, and was bent over in front of a door, jabbing at the middle panel with the key the clerk had given him.

"Here," said Doan.

He took the key and unlocked the door. Joshua dove head first into the darkened room. Doan waited. Nothing happened. Finally Doan groped around the edge of the door until he found the light switch and turned it.

Joshua was sitting on the edge of one of the high brass beds. He had his elbows on his knees and his chin resting in his hands. Doan picked up the suitcases and brought them inside the room.

"Thanks, bud," said Joshua. "Open the windows before you go, and leave a call for me at ten-thirty."

"Okay," said Doan.

He took hold of Joshua by the slack of his uniform jacket and marched him to the door and pushed. Joshua fell in a graceful heap in the middle of the hall. Doan shut the door and looked at Carstairs.

"Well, you can't blame me for that, surely," he said.

Carstairs was sitting in the middle of the floor. He watched Doan levelly for a moment and then closed his eyes and sighed with long-suffering patience.

Doan took the .25 automatic out of his pocket and shoved it under the mattress of one of the beds. He straightened his tie in front of the wavery mirror over the dresser, and then nodded at Carstairs.

"Come to, soup-brain. I think we better move around a bit."

He opened the door and looked out. Joshua had disappeared. Doan and Carstairs went down the hall and downstairs to the lobby.

The clerk still smiled. "I hope you found your room satisfactory?"

"Very," said Doan. "Where's Joshua?"

"He went out for a few minutes to get a drink of root beer."

"Root beer?" Doan said. "Joshua?"

"Yes. He makes it himself in the back of a drugstore next door."

"I'll bet," said Doan. "I want to use your telephone to make a long distance call."

"If you'll give me the number, I'll get it for you. You can take it in the booth over there."

"I'd rather use your board. Haven't you got an errand you can run?"

"No," said the clerk. "But I can use these." He took a pair of rubber earplugs from his pocket and inserted them in his ears.

"There's a scorpion on your shirt collar," Doan told him.

The clerk removed one of the plugs. "What?"

"Those are fine," Doan said. He sat down in front of the board and flipped the switch that connected with the exchange, holding the half-headset receiver to his ear.

"Hello Gerald, darling," a feminine voice greeted.

"Gerald's busy not listening to you at the moment," Doan said. "Is there any message?"

"No! What are you doing on the board?"

"Trying to put in a long distance call to Brighton 7-7345. That's an exchange in Brighton outside of New York City. Will you get it for me?"

"I suppose so."

"And don't bother to listen in after you get it. I'm a Japanese spy, and the things I'm going to say are confidential military information."

"Nothing you could say would interest me in the slightest, I assure you. Hold the line."

Doan listened through a long series of clicks and buzzes and dribbles of conversation. Finally the operator said, "Here's your party, and you're welcome to him."

"Hello, hello," said a masculine voice. "Hello. This is A. True-gold, president of Severn International Detectives."

"You won't be for long," Doan said, "if you make any more lend-lease deals with me for the subject or object or whatever."

"Oh. So it's you. Now Doan, nobody asked me to loan you to them. They told me. You want I should argue with the Army and Navy?"

"All right. Send five hundred dollars to I. Doanwashi, care of the Double-Eagle Hotel in Heliotrope, Nevada or California. Telegraph it right away."

"Now Doan, you're already drawn ahead three months. You can't expect to draw any more when you aren't even working for me. Why don't you be reasonable?"

"Why don't you stop arguing? You know you'll lose. Send the dough tonight. I'm trying to raffle off a used cadaver, and I need it for operating capital."

"Doan! A what did you say?"

"Skip it. Just forget the whole matter. Only don't start yelling for me when the cops come rapping on your door and asking about stray bodies."

"Doan! You didn't involve the agency in a murder? That's against our policy! It says so right on our stationery!"

"Show it to the police."

"Doan! Wait a minute! Don't you dare hang up on me! What name did you say you were using?"

"I. Doanwashi."

"Why?"

"I'm a Japanese spy now."

"Don't say things like that! Do you want to get us both shot? Doan! Are you drunk?"

"Stinking. I'm liable to start babbling and drooling at any moment."

"Oh, Doan! Now please. You've got no right to involve me or the agency.... All right! I'll send it. But no more! I warn you! I won't tolerate any further blackmail from you!"

"Okay. Is that little greasy bird who used to collect filthy postcards still hanging out in Des Moines?"

"Meredith? Yes. Why?"

"I want you to call him tonight, as soon as you send me my dough, and tell him to send a telegram to Harriet Hathaway in care of the Double-Eagle Hotel in Heliotrope, Nevada or California, whichever he knows how to spell. Have him tell her in the telegram to stay here until she is contacted for important detached confidential duty. Have him sign it with just his initials and last name, and tell him to put the letters C-A-P-T in front of the name. That stands for capitals."

"It stands for something else, too," said Truegold. "It stands for captain."

"Does it?" Doan asked.

"Doan! I won't do it! No!"

Doan cut the connection and nodded at the clerk.

The clerk removed his earplugs. "Did you get your party?"

"Yes. Put the charge on my room bill. Do you know anyone named Dust-Mouth Haggerty?"

"Not socially," said the clerk.

"I wasn't looking for a formal introduction. Where would I be likely to find him?"

"In jail."

"You mean right now?"

"Almost any time."

"Thanks," said Doan. "I'll go take a look." He snapped his fingers at Carstairs and started for the front door.

A woman, trailed by a faint, dim shadow, came in and stopped short, staring at him. Doan stared back. He couldn't have helped himself had he tried. She was beautifully tall and beautifully slender, and she had shoulder length black hair that gleamed darker and deeper and smoother than polished ebony. She had features so unbelievably perfect they made you gulp and look again, and then keep right on gulping. She was wearing white linen slacks, and a white jacket trimmed with big brass buttons, and white open-toed pumps, and a red sash around her waist. She pulled all the life out of the lobby and focused it on herself, like a little boy sucking soda through a straw.

"No," she said, and her voice was soft and just slightly hoarse. "There couldn't be two pair like you."

"If I wasn't looking right at it," Doan answered, "I wouldn't believe there could even be one like you."

The faint, dim shadow behind the woman tiptoed closer and peered over her shoulder. The shadow owned a pair of wide, worried eyes and a long nose, and sported a white catalogue sombrero with a high crown circled by a purple and red band four inches wide.

"A fat little number," said the woman, "with a big mouth and a bigger dog. Wasn't that it?"

"Now, Sally," said the shadow. "Now, wait. There must be some reasonable explanation."

Susan Sally glided forward three smooth steps. "I don't like fat little numbers. Especially fat little numbers that call me fat." She paused meaningly. "I don't like big dogs, either."

Carstairs promptly walked around behind Doan.

"You coward," Doan muttered. He smiled nervously. "I'm sorry about that. It was a mistake."

"That's okay," Susan Sally said amiably. "Let's shake on it, huh?"

She held out her right hand. Doan reached for it, but didn't take it. Instead he shoved her right elbow back and up with the heel of his palm. She had started to move just as soon as he had. She swung a full roundhouse left at his face. The shove pushed her off balance, and her fist swished harmlessly past in front of Doan's nose. She staggered a little, and Doan caught both her wrists, holding her upright, facing him. He was watching her feet.

The shadow was gibbering and screeching in the background. "Hit her in the stomach!"

"What?" said Doan, startled.

The shadow jiggled both fists in an agony of apprehension. "Not in the face! Don't hit her face! Thirty-five hundred dollars a week!"

Susan Sally was standing perfectly still, perfectly relaxed. Doan didn't let go of her wrists.

"That doesn't fool me, either," he said. "And if you try a faint, I'll just step out of the way and let you flop,"

"You think of everything, honey," said Susan Sally. "Let's have a peace conference, huh?"

"Sure," said Doan, still holding her wrists.

"I mean it."

Doan let go. "Okay. I'm really sorry I said you were fat. I apologize."

She winked at him. "I knew you didn't mean it. After all, you've got eyes, haven't you? I was just griped because you walked off with my special steak. What did you want it ground up for?"

Doan pointed at Carstairs. "For him."

"You mean, he ate it all?"

"Sure."

"Come on out, large and loop-legged," she said, "and let me look at you."

Carstairs sidled cautiously out from behind Doan.

"You're not bad," Susan Sally said. "Only you're not worth a three-pound steak. Walk off with another one of mine, and I'll kick your teeth in."

Carstairs looked impressed."

"MacAdoo!" said Susan Sally.

The shadow with the big hat answered eagerly, "Yes, Sally?"

"Trot out the etiquette."

MacAdoo cleared his throat. "This is Miss Susan Sally, internationally famous star of the stage and screen. And may I ask your name, sir?"

"Just call me Doan for short."

"Miss Sally, may I present Mr. Doan—a humble admirer of your art."

"Hi, toots," said Susan Sally.

"Hi," said Doan. "Who's the echo on my left?"

"Just a stooge," said Susan Sally. "I tote him around for laughs."

"I am Miss Sally's business manager and agent," said MacAdoo. "Elmer A. MacAdoo is the name. I'm very happy to make your acquaintance."

"Pipe down," Susan Sally told him. "What's your line, Doan? Aside from stealing steaks."

"I'm a Japanese spy."

"How's business?"

"All shot to hell. We tried to float a loan, but it sank."

"Maybe you can pump out the Pacific and recover your investment. Let's go have a slug of *sake*, Doan."

"It's an idea," Doan admitted. "We'll toast the Emperor."

"Over a slow fire," Susan Sally agreed.

A new voice said, "Excuse me, please."

The man had come up so quietly they hadn't noticed him. He was the type of person it was easy not to notice. He was small and dusty and shriveled, and he had a long drooping black mustache and round, solemn blue eyes. He had a nickel-plated star pinned to his coat collar.

"Excuse you for what?" Doan asked.

"Excuse me for botherin' you. But I think I'm gonna have to arrest you. Do you mind?"

"Not at all," said Doan.

The man tapped himself on his thin chest. "Peterkin is the name. Ask anybody. I'm the sheriff. Ask Miss Sally."

"Hello, scum," said Susan Sally.

"Right nice to see you again, Miss Sally," Peterkin said humbly. "You went and parked your car in a red zone, and I have to give you a ticket."

Susan Sally snapped her fingers in MacAdoo's direction. He produced a shiny new dime and handed it to Peterkin.

"Thank you, Miss Sally," Peterkin said. "I'll sure tear that ticket right up."

"You sure better had. And remember it gives only a nickel for the next one."

"Yes, ma'am."

Harriet Hathaway ran in through the front door. "Mr. Doan! Oh, I've been looking everywhere! You didn't pay the bill at the restaurant, and Mr. Blue doesn't have any money, and the man won't let Mr. Blue go until the bill is paid, and I'm not through telling him about the Air Force yet, either!"

"It's a problem," Doan agreed. He squinted thoughtfully for a moment and then took out his wallet and gave Harriet a five-dollar bill. "Here. And would you mind taking care of Carstairs for a little while?"

"That nasty, ugly thing!" Harriet said. "Yes, I would!"

Carstairs leered at her malignantly.

Susan Sally slapped him across the muzzle. "Mind your manners!"

Carstairs backed up, staring at Susan Sally with an expression of ludicrously incredulous amazement.

"Yeah," she said. "I mean you."

Carstairs sat down and blinked at her, obviously trying to think of some solution to the situation. He couldn't. He decided to ignore it. He lay down on the floor with great dignity and commenced to snore ostentatiously.

"But I don't want to take care of him!" Harriet wailed. "I hate him!"

"I'll help you," Susan Sally told her. "Doan, who's this fugitive from a select seminary?"

"Harriet Hathaway," Doan said.

MacAdoo stepped forward and cleared his throat. "This is Miss Susan Sally, internationally famous star of the stage and screen. Miss Sally, may I present Miss Hathaway, a humble—"

"How do you do," Harriet said absently. "Mr. Doan, how long are you going to be gone?"

Doan looked at Peterkin. "What am I arrested for?"

"Attempted murder, I guess."

"A couple of hours," Doan said to Harriet.

"Well, I suppose I can—Wh-what? Arrested?"

"Just a formality," Doan soothed.

"A-attempted murder?"

"Not a very good attempt," said Doan.

"But—but—but—Oh, Mr. Doan!"

"Take a deep breath, kiddie," Susan Sally said, "and mama will let you tell her all about the cute little Air Force. See you in jail, Doan."

CHAPTER VI

DOAN AND PETERKIN came out of the Double-Eagle Hotel and walked north along the main street toward the older and dimmer part of town.

"You want I should walk behind you?" Peterkin asked. "So people won't know you're arrested-like?"

"I can stand it if you can," Doan told him. "I was thinking of going to jail anyway as soon as I got around to it. Is Dust-Mouth Haggerty there?"

"I don't know."

"Who could I ask that would?"

"Oh, we'll find out when we get there. Dust-Mouth checks in and out at sort of odd hours."

"I see," said Doan. "Why?"

"He lives there."

"Lives in jail?" Doan asked.

"Yup," said Peterkin.

"All right," said Doan. "Why?"

"Well, he ain't got no place else to live."

"Sure," said Doan. "Why?"

"The government went and stole his claim. That was an awful dirty trick to play on Dust-Mouth. He never did any harm to anybody. He never even voted in his life."

Doan sighed. "Okay. Do you know a character by the name of Free-Look Jones?"

"Sure."

"What business is he in?"

"He's a private detective."

Doan stopped short. "Oh, now wait a minute."

"I guess he has a couple of other jobs, too," Peterkin admitted. "I guess he's a sort of an agent or salesman in his spare time."

Doan started on again. "I should hope so. You know, I'd keep an eye on him if I were you."

"Would you?" Peterkin inquired, interested.

"Yes. He looks to me like the sort of a guy who would cheat at cards."

"Oh, he does. All the time."

"What if someone caught him at it?"

"He'd run, likely."

"Maybe he might not," Doan said. "Maybe he'd haul out that knife he carries and use it."

"Maybe," Peterkin agreed gravely.

"A really alert law officer," Doan said, "would sort of think of those things and go out and look over his shack once in awhile."

"What for?" Peterkin asked.

"To see if he could find any—ah—clues."

"What are them?"

"Clues? Evidence."

"Like in court?"

"Sort of."

"Oh," said Peterkin.

They turned into a narrower street that wasn't quite so fearfully lighted. A small, towheaded boy marched toward them. He had his head down and his shoulders hunched, and he was kicking the walk hard with his heels.

"What's the trouble, Joey?" Peterkin asked.

The boy looked at them with his lower lip thrust out an inch. "Aw, them big kids. They won't let me play with 'em. I don't never have no fun."

"Aw, now," Peterkin soothed. "I'll tell you something you can do that'll just be more fun than the dickens."

"What?" said the boy, skeptically.

"Well, you see that rock over there? Suppose you take that and sneak up on Schmaltz's Variety Store and heave it through the front window. There'll be a big smash and crash, and people will holler and everything."

"Gee," said the boy, entranced.

Doan and Peterkin walked on. The boy was contemplating the rock with glistening, eager eyes.

"You don't like Schmaltz?" Doan asked.

"Huh? Why, sure I do. Schmaltz is one of my friends."

"Why the business with the rock and the window?"

"Oh, that's for the S.E.C."

"Securities Exchange Commission?"

"Nope. Society to Encourage Crime. It's an organization just for police officers."

"Umm," said Doan. "What does it do?"

"Like it says, encourages crime."

"Why?" said Doan wearily.

"Say, did you ever think what would happen if everybody turned honest all of a sudden?"

"No," said Doan.

"All police officers would lose their jobs, that's what! That's why we got the S.E.C. We got to keep a supply of criminals comin' along all the time so there'll be a big demand for police officers. Now you take Joey there. We start 'em out easy, like I did him. He starts bustin' windows. He sees how easy it is. So pretty soon he starts bustin' windows and stealin' the stuff inside. Get it?"

"Oh, sure. Big oaks from little acorns. Does Susan Sally come here very often?"

"Sure. Lots."

"Why?"

"She used to live here. She comes back to sort of show us how wrong we was."

"About what?"

"Well, she used to go around tellin' everybody how pretty she was gonna be when she grew up, and everybody laughed at her because she sure was an ugly little mutt. She ain't now, though."

"I noticed," said Doan. "Who complained on me, anyway? I mean, who asked you to arrest me?"

"Nobody. I thought it up myself. On account of Doc Grav-elmeyer told me he was gonna perform a delicate operation on

Parsley Jack, and when Doc Gravelmeyer gets to operatin', delicate or otherwise, you just can never tell."

"Did it ever occur to anyone to hop him for malpractice?"

"Doc Gravelmeyer? Oh, you couldn't do that. He used to be an abortionist."

"I'm a little slow this evening," Doan said. "Why would that stop me?"

"You couldn't get him convicted. Half the doctors in the state would testify for him. They'd have to. They used to send him patients, and he can prove it. Doc is a very smart fella in his way."

"This is a nice little town you have here," Doan observed.

"Ain't it, though? Here's the jail. I'll bet you'll like that, too."

It was a square, substantial-looking building with white stucco walls and a red tile roof, and the shiny iron bars on the windows blended in pretty well with the Spanish motif. Someone had spent a lot of time and money landscaping the lawn around it and installing floodlights at strategic intervals.

"Nifty," Doan commented. "For a town this size."

"Yup," said Peterkin proudly. "You see, we might belong to either Nevada or California, so we have to collect taxes for both states. But on the other hand, we might not belong to either one, so of course it would be wrong to pay them the taxes we collect. So we spend 'em on improvements."

"Who's we?"

"Well, me."

"I thought so," said Doan. "Don't you have any competition for this job of yours?"

"Well, there was a couple of guys, but they got sick. Doc Gravelmeyer did his best to save 'em."

"He didn't succeed, though."

"Nope," said Peterkin. He pushed open the heavy black varnished door. "Step right in."

It was a reception room and a very nice one. There was a

deep red carpet on the floor and oil paintings on the cream colored walls and a big, flat executive's desk in the far corner. The bald little man behind the desk took off a pair of pince-nez glasses and tapped them against one forefinger in a businesslike way.

"Yes, yes," he said. "Yes?"

"This is Mr. I. Doanwashi, Harold," Peterkin said. "You can call him Doan for short. He's the fella that jumped Parsley Jack. Jack is over to Doc Gravelmeyer's."

"Suspicion of murder," said Harold. He took a big green and gold fountain pen from the desk-set in front of him and wrote in a leather-bound ledger. "Rates are five dollars a day."

"Rates?" Doan repeated.

"Single cell, southern exposure," Peterkin explained. "Home cooking."

"Oh," said Doan. "Will you take a check?"

"On what bank?" Harold demanded.

"The Bank of England."

Harold scowled at him. "Where's that?"

"In England."

Harold nodded. "Oh, I think we can arrange it."

Peterkin said, "Have you got a gun on you?"

"Sure," Doan answered. He pulled the Police Positive out of his waistband and slid it across the desk.

Harold shied back. "Is it loaded?"

"Why, yes. It won't shoot unless it is."

"Take it away!" Harold cried. "Peterkin! You know I've told you I won't have loaded guns around here!"

"I'll keep it," Peterkin soothed, sliding the revolver into his coat pocket. "Well, I got to run along now, Mr. Doanwashi, and see how Parsley Jack is comin'. Harold will show you to your cell. So long."

"So long," Doan answered. He waited until Peterkin had

closed the door behind him and then said, "Where's the nearest pawn shop?"

"There's only one—Uncle Ben's Lend-Lease Emporium."

"How much will Uncle Ben give Peterkin on that gun of mine?"

"Just half of whatever he says he did when you come around to redeem it."

"Thanks," said Doan.

Harold stood up. "Right this way, Mr. Doanwashi."

He opened a door at the back of the reception room and preceded Doan into a corridor painted a cool, clean green that glistened quietly in the indirect lighting. Steel bars made an interesting architectural pattern along each wall.

Harold opened a section of bars and said, "Here you are. Dinner hour is over, but I can bring you a late lunch if you want to pay extra for it."

"I've lost my appetite," Doan said.

"Good night," said Harold, closing the barred door.

He went back up the corridor and closed the door into the reception room. Doan looked around. It was a roomy cell, and the cot had a monks' cloth cover on it. The sheets were clean, too. Doan lay down on the cot and stared at the ceiling, and wondered if he was dreaming or if his brain had given way under some unsuspected stress. He decided that in either case it wouldn't do him much good to worry about it, so he went to sleep.

CHAPTER VII

"HEY! HEY, YOU!"

Doan rolled over and opened one eye. "What?"

"I'm Dust-Mouth Haggerty. Peterkin said you wanted to see me."

He was standing against the cell door with the bars making parallel grooves in his paunch. He had a round, moon face with a fringe of reddish whiskers and a pug nose that was tilted up at an acute angle. He was wearing what had once been a pair of overalls, and a sheepskin vest and a straw hat with the brim torn off in front, and if Doan hadn't been able to see or hear him, he would still have known he was in the vicinity.

"Oh, yes," said Doan, fanning the air in front of his face with the palm of his hand. "I want to make a deal with you on that ore deposit you discovered. I'm representing the Japanese government."

"What kind of a deal?"

"We want to buy the location."

"For cash money? I don't go for none of that Jap yen-sen confetti."

"Cash money," Doan confirmed. "Gold."

"How much?"

"You name it," Doan said carelessly. "We've got lots of dough, and as soon as we invade the United States and capture Fort Knox, we'll have lots more."

"Hmmm," said Dust-Mouth. "How do I know you are a real Japanese agent? How do I know you ain't some traitor that's just pretendin' he's one?"

"Do you think I'd stay in jail if I had any pull with the United States Government?"

"I dunno," said Dust-Mouth. "Them government men are awful tricky. A fella's liable to find them almost any place. There was even one in the asylum. Went around claimin' he was Hitler, but he didn't fool me."

"Sure not. Where's the claim?"

"It's just—aw, no! We ain't agreed yet."

"Let's get started. Name your asking price."

Dust-Mouth rubbed his chin. "Well, now. I can't hardly until I see what this other fella has to say, on account he really has first call."

"What other fella?" Doan asked.

"The other Jap agent. Do you know him?"

"Could be. What's his name?"

"Pocus."

Doan sat still. "Pocus?" he said at last. "H. Pocus? Hangs out in Hollywood?"

"Yeah."

"He's a character I wouldn't trust too far if I were you. Who told you he was a Jap agent?"

"Oh, I knew that on account of the warrant they got out for him."

"Which they?"

"The government. They're gonna hang him because he's a spy, if they catch him, but of course they won't. I mean, they won't catch him."

"I trust not," said Doan. "How are you going about negotiating with this guy, Pocus?"

"I've got an agent of my own on the job. I figure on getting you and Pocus to bidding against each other."

"That will be very interesting to watch," Doan commented.

The door into the reception room opened suddenly, and Harold's bald head glistened eerily in the light.

"Murder!" he shrieked. "Murder, murder!"

He slammed the door shut again.

"Hey, Harold!" Dust-Mouth called. "Who? Who got murdered? Where?" He lumbered down the corridor and opened the reception room door. "Hey, Harold? Who?" He went on into the reception room and closed the door.

Doan sat on the edge of the cot and held his head in his hands. He sat there for about ten minutes, and then the door opened once more and Harold came slowly and shakily down the corridor and peered gloomily through the bars.

"Murder," he croaked. "Just plain murder."

"Who was the victim," Doan asked, "if you can bear to tell me?"

"Poor old Tonto Charlie. Free-Look Jones went and stabbed him in the neck just because Tonto caught him cheating at cards. Why, that's the nastiest thing Free-Look ever did. A man that'll do a thing like that isn't fit to associate with decent people. You come on out now."

"Why?" Doan asked. "Does this business about Tonto Charlie give everybody a furlough from jail?"

"Oh, no. Parsley Jack got away. He was just faking all the time. When Doc Gravelmeyer gave him the ether, Jack just held his breath, and then when Doe turned around to get a knife, Jack hopped off the operating table and jumped out the window. Doc Gravelmeyer is pretty mad. He says Jack has got no business exerting himself like that because he's got a couple broken ribs."

Doan followed him down the corridor and into the reception room. Harold sat down behind his desk and sighed.

"Murder," he said. "Think of that."

"I am," said Doan. "Thanks for the nap."

"No charge," said Harold. "Good-by."

Doan went out the jail's front door and down the street to the corner. He stopped there and, shading his eyes with the palm of one hand, surveyed the signs along the main street. A block and a half to the south there was a ten-foot tall stretch of red neon tubing that said

BURIALS IN THE BEST OF TASTE
AT REASONABLE RATES
CASH

Doan headed in that direction. The sign ran around and over a narrow brick building that had draped, darkened windows on the ground floor. There was a door beside the windows that was labeled conservatively

DOCTOR ETHELBERT GRAVELMEYER
PHYSICIAN & SURGEON
CORONER COUNTY SURVEYOR

Opening the door, Doan went up a long, narrow stairway and into a vintage waiting room that was empty save for some interesting antique chairs and magazines. Another door, at the back, was open, and Doan went through that into a small office lined with glass-doored cabinets full of ferociously shiny instruments. There was a desk in the corner and a man behind the desk. He had big ears and a bald head and a long, drooping, houndlike face. He didn't say anything. He didn't move. He sat still and looked at Doan without much interest.

"Doc Gravelmeyer?" Doan inquired.

The man nodded once slowly.

"I'm Doan," Doan said.

Gravelmeyer nodded again more slowly.

"I came to inquire about a corpse named Tonto Charlie," Doan told him. "Where is he?"

Gravelmeyer put out one hand and pointed a long yellow forefinger at the floor.

"Downstairs?" Doan asked. "In the undertaking parlor?"

Gravelmeyer nodded.

Doan said, "It's a funny thing about this climate around here. Corpses deteriorate very rapidly in it. Don't you think so?"

Gravelmeyer shook his head.

"You don't?"

Gravelmeyer shook his head again.

Doan sighed. "Well, how much would you take to think so?"

Gravelmeyer held up his hand with the forefinger pointing up this time.

"One," said Doan. "One dollar?"

Gravelmeyer raised the hand and the finger.

"Ten?" said Doan.

Gravelmeyer raised again.

"One hundred," said Doan. "And that's where the bidding stops."

Gravelmeyer nodded and dropped his hand on the desk lifelessly.

Doan pointed at the shiny tin alarm clock on Gravelmeyer's desk. "I've been in jail for the last two hours. Tonto Charlie was killed an hour and twenty minutes ago. Right?"

Gravelmeyer turned his hand over, palm up.

"Sure," said Doan. "I haven't got it now, but I'll get it and come back in a minute. Hold everything."

Gravelmeyer smiled.

Doan went out through the waiting room and down the narrow stairs and up the street to the Double-Eagle Hotel. Gerald, the shiny clerk, was still behind the desk in the lobby, and he smiled his nicest.

"Mr. Doanwashi, I'm glad to see you again so soon. There's a telegram here for your friend, Harriet Hathaway."

"Did one come for me?" Doan asked.

"Yes. I gave it to Sheriff Peterkin to deliver to you at the jail."

"Peterkin!" Doan echoed, aghast. "Where's the telegraph office? Quick!"

"On the side street, half a block to your left as you go out the door. It's in the second building."

Doan was on his way. He blew out the front door and down the block, weaving and dodging around startled sightseers. He whirled around the corner, skidded slightly on the turn, and then stopped short.

Peterkin was coming toward him. His head was bent, and he was counting some bills he had in his hand with tenderly absorbed interest.

"I'll take that," Doan said.

"Ah?" said Peterkin, startled. He made an instinctive gesture of concealment. "Oh. What?"

"The money," Doan said.

"Oh," Peterkin said. "The money. You mean—this?"

"That," Doan agreed.

Peterkin sighed and handed him the bills. Doan counted them and then silently held out his hand. Peterkin sighed more deeply and disgorged another twenty-dollar bill. He moistened his lips, watching Doan stow the money in his wallet.

"If you're planning on making an investment," he said, "I could steer you…."

"My gun," said Doan.

Peterkin gave it to him. Doan flicked out the cylinder to make sure it was still loaded and then slipped it into his waistband.

"Say," said Peterkin, "did you know that we was both right about Free-Look Jones?"

"How is that?" Doan asked.

"Well, you said he might use his knife if somebody caught him cheatin' at cards, and I said he'd likely run. He did both."

"Where'd he run to?"

"Somewhere or other," Peterkin said vaguely.

"Have you looked for him?"

"Me?" Peterkin said. "Well, no. Not yet. But I'm goin' to as soon as I get around to it. I probably won't find him, though. Say, do you know you parked that big car of yours right smack in the red zone? I hadda give you a ticket."

Doan took a dime out of his pocket and gave it to him.

"Thanks," said Peterkin. "I'll tear that ticket right up."

"Don't bother," Doan told him. "Save it for next time. Have you seen Dust-Mouth Haggerty?"

"Not since he left for Hollywood."

"What?" said Doan. "Hollywood? When did he do that?"

"Oh, a while back."

"Well, why did he do that?"

"He's gonna kill a fella there."

Doan took a deep breath. "He wouldn't, by any chance, be going to kill a guy named Pocus, would he?"

Peterkin looked surprised. "Why, sure. That's it. How'd you know?"

"I wonder myself," said Doan. "What has he got against Pocus?"

"Oh, he's crazy."

"Pocus or Dust-Mouth?"

"Dust-Mouth. I told him that Free-Look Jones was the one that did for Tonto Charlie, but Dust-Mouth claims that Tonto Charlie went to Hollywood to see this Pocus on a deal Tonto Charlie and Dust-Mouth was hatchin' up, and Dust-Mouth says you told him this Pocus wasn't to be trusted, so he thinks Pocus had something to do with Tonto Charlie gettin' killed. He's just crazy, like I said. You can't talk sense to him."

"Did he say when he'd be back?"

"I don't think he will."

"Why not?"

"Say, you should see the stuff the FBI sent out about this Pocus party. They say he's a Jap spy and a gunman and a murderer and a train robber and all kinds of things. I figure that if Dust-Mouth finds him, this Pocus will snaffle him off so fast it'll be funny. I told Dust-Mouth that, but you can't reason with him when he gets up on his ear."

"Good-by, now," said Doan wearily.

He left Peterkin there and went back to the suggestively fiery area illuminated by Doc Gravelmeyer's neon sign. He went in the side door and up the stairs and through the reception room. Everything in the small office, including Doc Gravelmeyer, looked exactly the same as he had left it.

Doan counted out one hundred dollars on the desk. Doc Gravelmeyer smiled and nodded at him in a kindly manner, and Doan went out again.

Carstairs was sitting on the sidewalk right in front of the street door, looking gloomily bored.

"Now don't you give me any trouble," Doan warned. "I've got enough already."

Carstairs merely snorted in contempt.

"Mr. Doan!" Harriet Hathaway screamed. "Oh, Mr. Doan!"

She came running headlong across the street, dodging through the double line of parked cars in its center, and the nearby loungers stopped smoking and/or spitting temporarily and watched with languid interest.

"I've got a telegram!" Harriet panted, waving the yellow envelope crumpled in one hand. "But I can't tell you what it says! But I didn't want to! I mean—Oh, Mr. Doan!"

"Pit it out in papa's hand," Doan advised. "What's the matter?"

Harriet pointed an accusing finger at Carstairs. "It's all his fault—the nasty, dirty thing!"

"What did he do this time?" Doan asked.

"Well, we were in that restaurant, and that theatrical person and her manager—ha! manager, indeed!—insisted enjoining Mr. Blue and myself in spite of the fact that it was very obvious we didn't want her to and making sarcastic remarks when I was explaining the Air Force to Mr. Blue, and then he"—her finger stabbed at Carstairs again—"kept walking back and forth under the table and tipping over Mr. Blue's beer and snorting and making nasty sounds!"

"Shame, shame," Doan said to Carstairs.

Carstairs burped at him.

"There!" Harriet cried. "Just like that! Right under the table! And that theatrical person said it was because he wanted to go for a walk! Only she didn't say walk, and she's just nothing but vulgar!"

"Yes," Doan said dreamily. "I mean, isn't she, though? Was there anything else?"

Harriet gasped suddenly. "Oh, yes! I mean, I'm so excited—this telegram…. I mean, I got so angry that I just took this awful animal right out of the restaurant and to the hotel, and I was going to lock him in your room! And when I opened the door I saw a duh-duh-duh—"

"Duck?" Doan hazarded.

"No! A dead man!"

Doan groaned. "Oh, no! Not another!"

Harriet gaped at him. "What?"

"A slip of the tongue," Doan said quickly. "This is terrible. Are you sure he was dead?"

"I certainly am! I'll have you know that I graduated at the top of my—"

"Red Cross class in first aid," Doan finished. "Yes, yes. I know. Did you recognize deceased?"

"I think he's that awful little man who sold blondes and brunettes."

"Oh," said Doan in a sick voice. "Just hold still for a minute." He put the palms of his hands against his ears and listened to his brain grind like a rusty cogwheel running around in a rain barrel. He looked up. "All right. Listen closely. Does the name Captain Meredith mean anything to you?"

Harriet opened her mouth and shut it again.

Doan nodded, tapped himself on the chest. "I'm Secret Agent Z-15."

"You!" Harriet said breathlessly.

"In person," Doan agreed. "I had you contacted through headquarters so there wouldn't be any doubt in your mind." He lowered his voice a few dramatic notches. "Are you ready to do, and perhaps die, in the service of your country?"

Harriet stood up straight. "I am."

"Good," said Doan. "Maybe we can arrange it. In the meantime go and sit in the Cadillac. Wait there for me. Take Carstairs with you." He jerked his thumb at Carstairs. "Scram, stupid."

Carstairs eyed him, unmoving.

Doan took a step toward him. "Get!"

Carstairs went, looking back over his shoulder with his upper lip lifted malignantly.

Doan took a deep breath and trudged back up the street and into the lobby of the Double-Eagle.

"Well, good evening!" said Gerald.

Doan didn't bother to answer. He went wearily up the stairs and down the hall. Harriet had used a passkey, and had left it in the lock of the door. Doan opened it, took another deep breath, and looked inside.

The light was on, and Free-Look Jones was laid out neatly on the bed. His hands were folded across his chest, his feet pointed precisely at the ceiling, and he had a knife with a green handle stuck in the side of his throat.

Doan went over and looked at him. He hadn't been mussed up at all. He hadn't even bled on his dapper brown suit or even on the bedspread. His eyes were closed. Doan put his thumb on one of the lids and pushed it open. The pupil of the eye was dilated enormously. Someone had been kind enough to give Free-Look Jones a big slug of morphine before they had operated on him.

Doan went back to the door, looked up and down the hall and listened carefully. After a moment, he took the passkey out of the lock and stepped across the hall to the door opposite and knocked.

The door jerked open, and a red, sullen face peered out at him.

"Well, what?"

"I'm offering a short correspondence course in authorized classics of English Literature—"

"Go away!" the red face snarled. "Shud-up!"

The door slammed emphatically. Doan went to the next one and rapped again. A feminine voice called coyly, "I'm busy right now, dearie."

Doan went on to the next door and tried again. No one answered this time. He rapped again, more loudly. Still he got no results. He tried the passkey in the lock, and it opened at once. He pushed the door open, reached around and flipped the switch.

The room was empty, and the bed was made up. There were no clothes or other odds and ends to indicate that the room had an immediate occupant. Doan went back to his own room and picked up Free-Look Jones as carefully as a mother cradling a baby.

Free-Look Jones wasn't very heavy, and he didn't make any trouble at all as Doan carried him across the hall and deposited him on the bed in the empty room. With his thumb and forefinger, Doan took hold of the green knife handle and pulled the blade free. The skin on Free-Look Jones' neck puckered slightly and then loosened and a few dark drops of blood trickled down on his shirt collar.

The knife looked remarkably like the one that Doan had left appended to Tonto Charlie, and for all he knew it might really be the same one. He was taking no chances. He closed the thin, slanting blade and put the knife in his pocket.

"Nighty-night," he said to Free-Look Jones.

He went out and locked the door. He made another trip into his own room and retrieved the .25 automatic from under the mattress and picked up his suitcases. Carrying them, he went downstairs to the lobby.

"Oh, my," said Gerald. "You're not leaving us so soon?"

"Urgent business," said Doan.

"Well, I hardly feel that we can charge you the full rate for the use of the room for such a short time. Would two dollars be too much?"

"Yes," said Doan. "But here it is. Where's Joshua?"

"Do you want him to carry your bags? I'll call him."

"No. I just forgot to tip him. Where is he?"

"You'll find him in the broom closet at the end of the back hall."

Doan went through the rear door and down a long bare hall.

The door at the end of it was ajar, and one of Joshua's feet protruded out of it in a casual fashion.

Doan opened the door wider. Joshua was sitting on the floor, leaning back languorously on a varied assortment of mops that served him for a pillow. He opened his eyes and blinked at Doan without seeing him at all.

"Hi, Joshua," Doan said. "Lend me your pencil, will you? I want to sharpen my knife."

"Sure," said Joshua. He fumbled around in the pockets of his jacket and came up with a stub of pencil.

Doan made a few passes at it with the green handled knife, and then put the pencil in his own pocket and handed the knife to Joshua.

"Thanks," he said.

Joshua put the knife in his pocket. "Think nothing of it, pal. Want a drink of root beer?"

"No," said Doan. "You take one. In fact, maybe you'd better take two."

He went back to the lobby and picked up his suitcases.

"By the way," he said to Gerald, "that Joshua is rather a strange character, isn't he?"

"Quite," said Gerald.

"Do you ever have any—ah—trouble with him?"

"Oh, no."

"I'm a psychologist," Doan said. "I detect certain traits of homicidal nature there. I'd remember that if I were you, if anything should—happen."

Gerald smiled soothingly. "Oh, nothing will happen here."

"That's what you think," said Doan, going out the door.

He lugged the suitcases over to the Cadillac. Harriet was standing beside it, biting her lower lip and making little jerky, angry motions with her clenched fists.

"Now he won't even let me in! He just growls at me!"

Doan opened both a rear and front door. "In front," he said

to Carstairs. "And no acts if you don't want a pop in the puss. I'm a busy man at this point."

Carstairs took his time about crawling out of the back seat and into the front. He sat on the floor, with his nose pushed against the windshield and glowered sullenly.

"Can you drive this?" Doan asked Harriet.

"With him in there?"

"He won't bother you. He's sulking now."

"Well, why?"

"He has to associate with me because I own him," Doan explained. "But he picks his own friends."

"But I don't want to sit close to him!"

"Are you refusing an order from your superior officer?" Doan demanded severely.

"Well, no."

"Drive," said Doan.

Harriet gulped bravely. "Well, where?"

"To Hollywood. Wake me up when we get there if I don't die in my sleep, I hope."

CHAPTER VIII

SUNRISE ON THE desert is not so terrific as sunset, but it's pretty disconcerting at that when it comes on you unexpectedly. It's awfully bright and enthusiastic in a gruesome way.

"Mr. Doan!"

"Uh?" said Doan. He was tied in a running bowline knot on the back seat. He sat up and looked at the leering bloodshot eye of the sun, and got cramps in both legs and a slight case of *mal de mer* simultaneously.

"Wake up!" Harriet ordered.

"Why?" Doan asked.

"It's going to rain!"

"I don't recall inquiring about the current state of the climate in this hell hole," Doan said, "but just in case I did, what of it?"

"It's against the law!"

"Raining is against the law?" Doan asked.

"No! Telling you it's going to rain is against the law."

"Then why are you doing it?" Doan inquired.

"I just can't understand people who are all blurry and stupid when they wake up. I never am. Of course I didn't mean that my telling you it was going to rain was against the law, but the radio just said it was, and that's against the law. You're not supposed to give out weather conditions in advance. That's a rule laid down by the Defense Command, and it's a very serious offense to violate it."

"All right," said Doan.

"Well, the radio announcer just said it was going to rain. Right out on the air. Suppose a Japanese spy heard him say that? And besides it's not true."

"Sure," said Doan.

"Oh, you're not even listening! Wake up!"

"I'm afraid I'm going to," said Doan. "What's not true?"

"It's not going to rain. It never rains in the desert."

"Is that a fact?"

"Of course it is! The reason the desert is a desert is because it's dry, and the reason it's dry is because—"

"It doesn't rain," Doan finished. "Yes, yes. It all comes back to me now. Where are we?"

"We're coming into Talmuth."

Carstairs put his chin on the back of the front seat, and raised one pricked ear and lowered it, and then raised the other and lowered it, and then raised both and waggled them meaningly.

"Okay," said Doan. "Stop the car, Private Hathaway."

"Why?"

"Because you're going to wish you did if you don't. Carstairs wants to go."

Harriet pulled the car over on the shoulder and stopped. "That dirty thing! He just always has to do something!"

"Ain't it the truth," said Doan, leaning over to unfasten the door for Carstairs. "Out, damned spot, and don't think I'm going to come and supervise you, either."

Carstairs wandered away, sniffing disconsolately at dried brush.

"Mr. Doan," said Harriet, "I think I ought to have had a serious talk with Mr. Blue before I left."

"What about?"

"He didn't know about the war, and I don't believe he'd know about selective service, either. Even if he found out, he'd be too shy to go and register all by himself, don't you think?"

"Yes," said Doan. "I don't think. Did you find out where he lived?"

"On the reservation."

"The what?"

"The reservation. He has to. He's part Indian."

"What brand of Indian?"

"Mohican."

Doan sighed. "Don't tell me that he's the last of the Mohicans."

"Why, yes, he is. That's what makes him so shy. He has no one to talk to on his reservation. I think a person has a duty in a case like that, don't you? I mean, the Indians are wards of the government, you know, and the Government is just nothing less than the people, and the people—"

"Are us," Doan concluded. "Yes, yes." He whistled shrilly between his teeth. "Stupid, snap it up!"

Carstairs came back and crawled into the car.

"No luck?" Doan inquired.

Carstairs grunted.

"Drive on," Doan requested. "Forward. Don't wake me up until you see the whites of my eyes."

CHAPTER IX

FORENOONS IN SOUTHERN CALIFORNIA are wonderful, except when they're not, and in that case there's no use in discussing the matter at all. This one was ordinarily wonderful. The sun was shining and soft breezes were slithering, and there were some small, shy, freshly washed clouds distributed where they would do the least good.

"Mr. Doan!"

"Ahem," said Doan.

"Well, I think it's about time you should wake up! Goodness, it's almost noon! I loathe people who sleep late. I mean, it's not normal, do you think?"

"Ummm," said Doan. "Where are we?"

"In San Fernando Valley. I came that way because there's less traffic. We're just coming to Cahuenga Pass. See?"

"Umm," said Doan. "Where's Carstairs?" He untangled his feet and put them down on what should have been the floor, and Carstairs snarled at him sleepily. "How'd he get in here with me?"

"Well, I put him back there because he was leaning on me and snoring in my ear in a very disgusting way. I don't think people should let dogs ride in cars, anyway."

"Yeah," said Doan. "Take the Cahuenga runway and turn to the left at Sunset."

"Why?" Harriet asked.

"Okay," said Doan. "Turn to the right."

"Well, Mr. Doan, there's no use in getting sarcastic about it, is there? I just wanted to know."

Doan sighed. "I want to go to a drive-in restaurant, and the reason I want to go there is because I'm hungry, and the reason I'm hungry is because Mr. Blue ate my steak last night."

"You should have gotten another."

"Sure."

They went up and down the smooth lift of Cahuenga Pass, and through the underpass, and across Hollywood Boulevard and turned to the left on Sunset.

"Pretty quick now," Doan said. "There it is. Drive on in."

The Cadillac rolled up and stopped under the wooden, pagoda-like awning. The trim little girl in the red pants and the red jacket and the high hussar's hat with the plume in it came out and looked at them and went back inside again. They could see her through the plate glass front of the restaurant. She was arguing with the man behind the cash register. She lost. She came out again.

She slapped a card on the windshield and said, "It would be my luck to be on alone."

"I'm glad to see you again, too," Doan told her. "Do you suppose you could scare up some warm gruel—warm, not hot—all full of cream and junk for poor old Carstairs?"

"Not for a seven-cent tip."

"I'm in the chips now. I'll make it a dime even."

"Four bits."

"I'm bleeding, but it's a deal. What'll you have to eat, Harriet?"

"Make it heavy, honey," said the waitress. "For what you have to put up with, you need strength."

"I don't know what you mean," Harriet said coldly.

"Then I sure pity you. You're going to live but not for long or very well if I'm any judge."

"I'll have an order of hot cakes and coffee," said Harriet. "But are you going to let the dog eat here?"

"We're not any more particular than you are, honey," said the waitress. "What do you want?"

"Same," said Doan.

"And three glasses of water, I suppose"

"Four," said Doan. "Five, counting Harriet's."

"Anything for a gag," said the waitress, going back inside the restaurant.

"She's horribly rude," said Harriet. "I don't see why you didn't go to a better place than this. I don't think it's good policy to eat in cheap places."

"I'm saving the government money."

"Oh, yes!" said Harriet. "I'm sorry. I'd forgotten you had an expense account. I think it's very decent of you to save on it."

"Me, too," said Doan.

The waitress came back with three trays, and gave Doan and Carstairs two in the back seat, and Harriet one in the front. She made an extra trip for the water, and then brought the hot cakes and gruel.

Doan tied into his hotcakes eagerly, pausing only to pour water for Carstairs, and then to shove him off the seat when he tried to climb up on it. He had speared the last portion of hotcake and was carefully mopping up the remains of his syrup with it when Harriet said, "Oh!"

She started the motor, and before Doan could even raise his eyes, she slammed the car into reverse and shot backwards across the graveled lot and straight out into the humming traffic of Sunset Boulevard. Doan cringed. Tires wailed, and horns wapped indignantly from all directions, and then there was a long, lingering, final crunch.

Doan hit the plate on his tray with his face. He straightened up slowly and wiped the syrup out of his eyes with a paper napkin. Carstairs snarled in a manner that indicated that he had had just about enough.

"Double that," said Doan. "Now what—"

Harriet wasn't in the front seat any more. Doan opened the rear door and got out and listened to seven drivers tell him what they thought about things in general.

The Cadillac had traveled clear across the street, and was backed half-up over the opposite parking strip. Doan walked around to the back of it. The Cadillac had pinned another car—a topless, nondescript little roadster—right against the base of a concrete lamp post. It had done the roadster no good, at all.

Blue was standing up in the seat of the roadster, surveying the strips of tin that were pleated neatly fore and aft of him. He didn't seem excited or frightened, just hopeless.

"What did I ever do to you?" he asked Harriet. "Well, I saw you going past," Harriet said, "and I didn't know how to stop you."

"Oh yes, you did," Blue contradicted.

The waitress tapped Doan on the shoulder. "So. Trying to sneak out without paying, and with the trays and dishes, huh? See what happens to people who try to chisel? Let it be a lesson to you."

"All right," said Doan wearily.

"The bill will be one dollar and twenty-one cents—plus four bits."

Doan gave it to her. The waitress tested the coins one after the other with her teeth, and then got the trays and dishes and strutted back across to the restaurant. She went in the door and came right out again. She stuck out her tongue in Doan's direction and made a loud, rude noise.

"And the boss said I could! And he says don't come back!"

They had attracted quite a rooting section by this time, and a policeman came puttering along the boulevard on a blue and chrome scooter, and wheeled around beside them and stopped.

"All right, all right. Now who hit who and why?"

"I hit him," said Harriet. "I wanted to talk to him."

"Talk to me instead," the policeman ordered.

"It's business of a purely private nature," Harriet informed him.

"What do you say?" the policeman asked Blue.

"I can't think of anything," Blue said.

The policeman pointed at the roadster. "Well, what about this?"

"It's my contribution to the scrap metal drive," Blue said. "Tell them to come around and pick it up."

"Oh, that's patriotic!" Harriet exclaimed.

"No, it ain't," said the policeman. "He just thinks he's gonna dodge out of a tow charge, but it don't work."

Harriet snapped around at him. "Are you trying to hinder the war effort?"

"Lady," said the policeman, "do you think it would hinder the war effort if I put you in jail?"

"You wouldn't dare!"

"Just go ahead and dare me, and see," the policeman invited grimly.

"Tweet-tweet," said Doan, holding out a twenty dollar bill between two fingers. "Would this cover the tow charge?"

"Sure," said the policeman, capturing the bill with practiced skill. "And who are you?"

"She's my driver," Doan said, indicating Harriet.

"Man, you sure hold your life cheap," the policeman said. "Now come on, folks. Break it up. Move on. And as for you three playmates, go somewhere else and have fun. I don't want to find you around this district again in the near future."

"I want Mr. Blue to come with us," Harriet said.

"Okay," Doan agreed. "Anything you say, but I drive from here on in."

"Now you're getting half way smart," the policeman told him. "Come on, folks. It's all over. No blood and brains. Move on. Break it up."

Doan boosted Carstairs into the front seat, and slid in under the steering wheel. Blue and Harriet got in the back. There was one last heave and rattle from the roadster as they pulled loose, and then the Cadillac rolled on down Sunset toward Vine.

"Now, Mr. Blue," said Harriet, "I want to talk to you about the draft."

"I don't feel it," Blue said.

"No, no! Not that kind of a draft. It's not really a draft at all. It's selective service, and it's the way the government chooses the men who are to have the honor of serving in our Armed Forces. Are you registered?"

"Nope."

"You aren't! Then you'll have to go and do it right away!"

"Nope."

Harriet gasped. "But why not?"

"I don't wanna."

"You don't want to be in the Army?"

"Nope."

"But why?"

"I don't like war."

"Oh," said Harriet, breathing deeply in relief. "That's just because you don't understand the great issues that are involved in this worldwide conflict between the powers of evil and the forces of freedom. Do you?"

"Nope."

"I'll explain them to you."

Doan turned down Vine Street. "Just a moment before you do. How come you followed us to Los Angeles, Blue?"

"Followed you?" Blue echoed. "I ain't that crazy, Mr. Doan. I came here on business."

"Name it."

"Well, I came to see a doctor."

"Oh, are you sick?" Harriet asked.

"Yup."

"Do you think you're too sick to pass the Army examination?"

"If I ain't, I will be soon," said Blue.

"Now you're just being silly. I'm sure you just don't take care of yourself properly. Do you take deep breathing exercises every morning?"

"Nope."

"You should. I'll show you how."

"All right," Blue said resignedly.

Doan turned off Rossmore, and pulled the Cadillac in at the curb in front of the Orna Apartment Hotel. A round, sleek little man with horn-rimmed glasses and three strands of blue-black hair slicked across the dome of his skull was standing on the steps. He had his hands clasped behind him, and he was teetering up and down on his toes surveying his surroundings with a proud, proprietary smile.

"Mr. Rogan," Doan called.

The bald man's smile curdled. He stared in glazed horror for a split second, and then whirled and dove through the front door.

"Wait here for a moment," Doan told Blue and Harriet. "We'll be back."

He and Carstairs went into the apartment lobby. It was very thoroughly empty. Doan went the length of it to the door next to the back hall that had a neat, enameled plaque saying "Manager" on it.

"Mr. Rogan," Doan said, tapping on the door. "Whoo-hoo, Mr. Rogan."

There was an emphatic silence from behind the door.

"I've come to pay my bill, Mr. Rogan," Doan said.

No answer.

Doan took a twenty-dollar bill from his wallet, folded it lengthwise, and then knelt and thrust the edge of it tantalizingly under the door. Somebody tried to snatch it from the other side, but Doan jerked it back.

"Mr. Rogan," he said.

The bolt snapped, and then the key grated in the lock, and then the door opened just wide enough to show that there was a heavy metal chain holding it from opening farther. One of the lenses of Mr. Rogan's horn-rimmed glasses glittered through the crack.

"You give me my money."

Doan rustled the bill enticingly. "Mr. Rogan, I want to rent my apartment again."

"No!"

"Aw, come on," said Doan. "I'll pay my bill and pay in advance."

"We're full up! We're closed! I'm out of business! Go away!"

"Now, Mr. Rogan, you know what happens to people who tell lies."

"Mr. Pocus, I will not have you in my building. You're a criminal!"

"Oh, no," said Doan. "Not any more. I've changed my character and my business and even my name. My name is Doan now. Don't you think that's an improvement on Pocus?"

"No! Go away!"

Doan looked over his shoulder at Carstairs and said, "Woof."

Carstairs sat down and filled his lungs to capacity, and tilted his head back and bayed. The sound was indescribable. It filled the lobby until the walls bulged, and the echoes whimpered in the corners for minutes after Carstairs had cut off their source.

"He can do that all day," Doan said, taking his fingers out of his ears.

The chain rattled, and Mr. Rogan crept cringingly out into the lobby. He was holding his head in both hands.

"Please, Mr. Pocus—I mean, Mr. Doan—-why don't you go away?"

"I like you, Mr. Rogan," Doan said. "Carstairs does, too. And we both like your apartment hotel. It's so quiet here. That is, it will be unless you refuse to give me my apartment back again."

"Why do these things happen to me?" Mr. Rogan demanded plaintively. "I'm a good citizen. I'm honest. I'm only trying to earn a living for my three divorced wives." He sighed deeply. "What is this new profession of yours, Mr.—ah—Doan?"

"I just go around looking at things."

"An inspector?" Mr. Rogan inquired.

"You could call it that. I collect things, too."

"What things?" Mr. Rogan asked suspiciously.

"Secrets and stuff."

"You give me your word that it's an honorable profession?"

"Certainly," said Doan. "People in my new line of work are much sought after these days."

"All right," said Mr. Rogan. "But in advance, remember. In advance, strictly. Edmund!"

Very slowly Edmund's curly head rose above the level of the desk. He parked his snub nose on the edge of it and looked from Doan to Carstairs, and then back again.

"Ah, Edmund," said Doan. "And how are you, my boy?"

"Mr. Pocus," said Edmund. "I mean, Mr. Doan, I didn't tell those G-men on you. I really didn't. They asked me if you lived here, and I wouldn't tell them."

"That's very nice of you, Edmund," Doan said. "I'll remind Mr. Rogan to give you a raise. Now you two just ready up the receipts and things, and I'll be back flush in a flash."

He went out to the Cadillac. Harriet had Blue crowded into one corner of the back seat, instructing him in a firm and kindly manner on the latest theories of medicine.

"Private Hathaway," Doan said. "We're going to set up temporary headquarters in a couple of apartments here. Come on in."

"You come, too," said Harriet. "I'm not through yet."

"Yes, ma'am," said Blue glumly.

They went back into the lobby.

"Mr. Rogan," Doan said, "I want you to meet Miss Harriet Hathaway. She works for me. I want to rent an apartment for her, too."

"Oh, no!" said Mr. Rogan. "Strictly, no! None of that sort of thing in my building."

"Just what do you mean by that?" Harriet snapped.

"No goings on," said Mr. Rogan.

"Do you dare to stand there and insult your country's uniform?"

"What?" said Mr. Rogan, dazed.

"Shush-shush," Doan said to Harriet.

"Well! Governmental secrecy or not, no one is going to in-sinuate that I—Well, indeed! I'll have you know, Mr. Rogan, that I'm doing confidential work for Mr. Doan and that we're the merest acquaintances in private life. We're not emotion-ally interested in each other in the slightest. Mr. Blue, here, has preempted that position in my heart."

"What?" said Blue hoarsely.

"Well, you know you have. There's no point in being silly and bashful about it."

"Hey!" said Blue.

"Not now. We'll discuss it at some more opportune time, in private."

"Oh," Blue moaned.

Harriet looked Mr. Rogan right in the eye. "Are you going to rent me an apartment so I can continue my work for Mr. Doan, or shall I report you to the authorities as a traitor to your country and a fifth columnist?"

"Excuse me," said Mr. Rogan. "I think I'll go lie down. I don't feel well. Edmund, sign the people up. And remember. In advance, strictly."

CHAPTER X

THE BATHTUB IN Apartment 229 had been cleaned and polished during Doan's absence, and he was sitting in it splash-ing and splattering contentedly when he felt a draft on the back of his neck.

"Yes," said a voice. "You've got all the soap off."

Doan turned around slowly. Arne was standing in the doorway. Barstow was looking over his shoulder.

"Now don't get in an uproar," Doan said. "I've already been to Heliotrope. I just got back."

"Where's the ore deposit?"

"That's a matter we'll have to go into at great length some time. How about next Tuesday?"

"Here," said Arne, handing him a towel.

Doan sighed, turned the drain lever and got up and dried himself.

"And here," said Arne, handing him the bathrobe.

Doan put it on and followed them into the living room. He sat down on the chesterfield. Arne and Barstow sat down and watched him. There was quite a long silence.

"Where's Carstairs?" Barstow asked at last.

"In his sulking corner," Doan said.

"What's he mad at now?"

"He doesn't like the job you gave me. It involves associating with too many people he disapproves of."

"How does he feel about us, anyway?"

"Hey, you," said Doan.

Carstairs' head appeared very slowly above the back of the chesterfield.

"Look who's come to see us," Doan invited.

Carstairs studied Arne and Barstow thoughtfully for about thirty seconds, and then he yawned in a very elaborate manner and pulled his head down out of sight.

"I get it," said Barstow.

"Don't feel hurt," Doan advised. "You should have seen the way he looked when I introduced him to a senator once."

"Let's stop the clowning," Arne said. "Doan, what was the idea of going around telling everybody that you were a Japanese spy? All this cute stuff about I. Doanwashi and the rest of it?"

"You told me Dust-Mouth Haggerty was a whack. When you're dealing with a whack you have to act whacky. If you act normal, he'll think you're on the offbeat. I didn't know how much trouble I'd have finding him, and I was just laying sort of a ground fire."

"It spoiled all the buildup we gave you under the name of

Pocus. We expected you to keep on using that name. Why did you take it in the first place?"

"On account of his fans," Doan said, jerking his thumb toward the back of the chesterfield.

"What fans? Why does he have fans?"

"He trains dogs for the Army. He's been making some movie shorts about how it's done, and all such. They show those not only to soldiers but to dog owners, and then the owners pester the Army until they find out who he is, and then they come around and make goo on him. He'll take only very small doses of goo before he takes a leg back in trade. I got tired of trying to keep him from assassinating fat ladies and cute little tots, so I decided to be H. Pocus and assistant."

"That's what you should have stayed. We put out the buildup about Pocus in Heliotrope because we knew Dust-Mouth hung around the jail there and would pick it up from Peterkin."

"Why not from Harold?" Doan asked.

"Who?"

"Harold. The majordomo of the jail."

"What about him?" Arne inquired coldly.

"Nothing," said Doan. "Only I thought he'd spread the news to Dust-Mouth on account he's FBI."

"How did you know that?"

Doan shrugged. "All private detectives can spot a government man—if they stay in business long. When are you going to pounce on Peterkin and Gravelmeyer and Heliotrope in general?"

"The indictments are all ready now, but we're frying bigger fish first. So let's get at it. You contacted Dust-Mouth. What happened?"

"I convinced him," said Doan. "We'll make a deal as soon as I can find him."

"He'll find you. He'll call you here."

"How do you know?" Doan asked.

"We arranged it."

"Come, come," said Doan. "We're not in a B picture—yet. I'd just as soon know how you arranged it."

Arne said, "I suppose I'd better tell you or you'll butch this all up too. Ever hear of Gower Gulch?"

"You mean the place where all the horse opera cowboys hang out?"

"Yes. Most of them are the genuine article, outside of a few professional rodeo and circus performers. Every Western picture has a few old prospectors and desert rats and such kicking around in it for atmosphere. They're mostly genuine, too. They all hang out together, and Dust-Mouth knows lots of them. We put out the rumor that it would be a profitable idea for him to call you here. We used the name Doan this time. Dust-Mouth will be certain to see some of the boys from Gower Gulch if he comes to town, and they'll relay the information."

"Dust-Mouth has sort of a down on Pocus," Doan said. "Maybe he'll spend his time hunting him instead of calling Doan."

"No. There's a new bulletin about Pocus circulating in Gower Gulch. He's just been shot while he was trying to blow up an airplane factory."

Doan sighed. "Things certainly move fast these days. Sorry to hear about old Pocus. He was a fine chap."

"He concealed it well, though," Arne said. "Now there's another little matter. Just what happened to Tonto Charlie?"

"Who?" said Doan.

"You heard me."

"Yes. But the name's not familiar at all."

"Isn't it? He was sort of a weird character who used to make his living by taking money for smuggling aliens across the line in the desert. We've never been able to get a grip on him because he never actually did it. He used to take the aliens out in the desert south of the line in Mexico and lose them there. Sometimes they didn't die. It didn't make any difference to Tonto

Charlie because he got half his dough in advance, and that's all he wanted. He's been having a tough time since the war because we're hand-in-hand with the Mexican patrols now."

"He sounds like a delightful character," Doan commented. "But I still don't know him."

"Dust-Mouth Haggerty sent him here to contact Pocus. Did you see him? You'd better think about your answer."

"Never saw him in his life," said Doan solemnly.

"He turned up dead in Heliotrope. He wasn't killed there. Someone killed him somewhere else and brought him there."

"How strange," said Doan. "But then, of course a man like that would have a lot of enemies. Desperate people, no doubt."

"No doubt," Arne agreed. "A man named Free-Look Jones was accused of killing him."

"Jones," Doan repeated thoughtfully. "Free-Look Jones…. Oh, yes. I thought the name was familiar. He's that strange person who jumped out the window when I offered to buy him a beer."

"He threw a knife at you before he jumped."

"That was just horseplay," Doan said. "You know how people pull gags in bars just to pass the time away. I thought nothing of it. So he killed Tonto Charlie. Tsk, tsk. I hope he has been apprehended and is on his way to his just and proper punishment?"

"He's dead. Did you ever study medicine?"

"No."

"Art?"

"No."

"Anatomy?"

"Well, yes."

"Where?"

"Oh, on the street on windy days, and at the beaches and at the burlesque shows…. Well, do you want all the details of my private life?"

"This isn't funny," said Arne. "And neither are you. Jones was killed by someone who knew quite a lot about how to operate on a jugular vein so it would drain down into the victim's lungs instead of spurting around."

Doan cringed. "Ghastly. Let's talk about something else."

"All right. What's the idea of the girl named Hathaway in the apartment down the hall?"

"My secretary," said Doan. "And you needn't look that way about it. You've got a secretary, haven't you?"

"Who's the guy with the beard and the black cheaters?"

"Her secretary. There's an awful lot of detail work in this spying business."

Arne watched him in silence for a moment. "You're fast on your feet, but just remember that we've got a long arm and we're awfully long winded."

"You're telling me," said Doan.

Arne stood up. "We won't bore you any more but—"

The telephone buzzed softly.

"Answer that," Arne ordered. "I think it may be Dust-Mouth. Don't drop this one on the floor, or you'll scare him off permanently."

Doan picked up the telephone. "Yes?"

The voice came in a hoarse whisper: "Is this a fella named Doan?"

"That's right."

"Where was you last night?"

"In jail in Heliotrope."

"Who'd you see there?"

"You."

"Uh!" said the voice. It breathed hoarsely for a moment. "Mickey's Wickiup. Eleven-thirty. Say 'Diamond Hitch' to the bull fiddler."

"Right," said Doan.

The line clicked and was dead.

Doan put the telephone down and turned around. "I got him. I'm to be passed on from a joint called Mickey's Wickiup. Now listen. You must have hauled me in this for some good reason, but I'm tired of meeting you every time I take a bath. Why don't you go sit down in some quiet corner and let me sneak up on Dust-Mouth?"

"Okay," said Arne. "Come on, Barstow, we'll move along."

Barstow paused in the doorway. "We'll give you plenty of rope." He made a suggestive circle around his neck with his forefinger and closed the door.

"Funny mans," Doan said sourly. "Hey, you."

Carstairs' head appeared slowly above the chesterfield.

"Did you ever think of what a decoy duck must feel like when it's sitting there waiting for somebody to shoot over its head?" Doan asked. Carstairs stared at him unwinkingly. "Never mind," said Doan. "I know now."

CHAPTER XI

MICKEY'S WICKIUP WAS not so easy to find, but Doan finally ran it down in an alley off Gower, north of Sunset. There was nothing special about the alley, except that it was narrow and dark. Doan parked the Cadillac a half block up the street and got out.

"You stay here," he said to Carstairs. "If you see any G-men around you have my permission to bark or even to bite them." Carstairs watched him suspiciously.

"Only one beer," Doan promised. "On my word of honor." Carstairs sighed resignedly, and lay down on the seat. Doan went back to the alley and felt his way along it cautiously. At the back it widened out, and he groped around in the gloom until he hit a wooden gate that swung back smoothly under his hand. A cowbell went bing-bong in a flat, discouraged tone somewhere ahead.

Doan headed in that direction, and suddenly a door opened

wide in front of him. A fat man wearing a purple silk shirt and
enormous handlebar mustaches beamed at him and bellowed
enthusiastically.

"Howdy there, stranger. Welcome to Mickey's. Light and
set."

"Thanks, pardner," Doan answered. "Reckon I will." He
squeezed through the door into a low, smoky room that had all
the trimmings, even to the smell of horse sweat from the saddle
blankets strung over the rafters. The back of a chuck wagon had
been built into the rear wall. The range cook, complete with
peaked sombrero and leather brush-scarred chaps, squatted in
front of it, manipulating frying pans and iron pots with offhand
skill, over an open charcoal fire that had a protective hood to
suck up the fumes. Several other characters in cowboy outfits
lounged or squatted around him, consuming the results of his
efforts. The tables around the room were made of split logs, and
the chairs of nail kegs.

There were quite a few people here. They were mostly men,
and all in some kind of western dress, from a hundred percent
to a pair of hand made boots. There were some women, and
Doan recognized a serial queen who was wearing a chinchilla
coat over a pair of blue jeans. The bar was made out of plain
pine planks, and Doan shoved up against it and said, "Beer."

The bartender looked like an aged and dilapidated version
of one of the Dead End Kids. "Dime," he said, slapping the
glass down. "You an agent?"

"Agent?" Doan repeated.

"Picture agent?"

"Nope," said Doan. "Tenderfoot."

"Huh!" said the bartender, and went away.

The orchestra started to play in an aimless way. It consisted
of a regular fiddle, a bull fiddle and an accordion, and it was
not so bad, either. They played a roundelay that Doan had never
heard before. He sipped his beer, waiting, and when they had

finished crossed the room to their platform and held out a folded dollar bill toward the bull fiddle player.

"Can you play Diamond Hitch?" he asked.

"Sure thing," said the bull fiddle player. He took the dollar bill leaving a small slip of paper in Doan's palm.

Doan went back to the bar and finished his drink and then walked to the door.

"You ain't a-leavin' us so soon, are you, stranger?" the fat man asked.

"Yup," said Doan. "Gotta go home and shear my sheep."

"Drop in again, stranger. We don't even bar sheepherders here, not unless they start to bleatin'."

Doan went through the gate, causing the cowbell to bing-bong dolorously again, and then down the alley to the street and up the block to the Cadillac.

"See?" he said to Carstairs. "Only one beer, just like I said."

Carstairs grunted and moved over on the seat. Doan slid in under the wheel and snapped on the dashlight. He unfolded the slip of paper. Printed on it in pencil were the words

OLD LISTON LOT COME
PEARL ST ENTRANCE

"Okay," said Doan.

CHAPTER XII

AWAY BACK BEFORE you can remember they made silent motion pictures. This, of course, was too good a thing to last long, and, sure enough, some evil genius cooked up the idea of assaulting your ears as well as your eyes. Everybody took to it with, literally, a whoop and a holler, but the casualties in the business were spectacular, and among the first and the sorriest were the sets that had been used formerly for outdoor shots. Everything was sound staged now, and these veterans of many a catsup-blood battle were retired to odd way-points, like the Liston Lot, and left there to contemplate their celluloid sins.

The Liston Lot in prehistoric times had actually been a place where they shot pictures, and it was still surrounded by a twenty-foot wall that had looked sternly forbidding in its day, but which time and the weather had revealed to be nothing but stucco, plastered over lath and chicken wire. It was dark and forbidding as the mad scientist's castle, as Doan idled the Cadillac along Pearl Street and parked opposite the niche that marked the side gate.

There was not a light showing. Doan got out of the car and jerked his head at Carstairs. Their shadows joggled eerily ahead of them, and Doan's heels clicked in empty, fading cadence as they crossed the pavement. The iron-barred gate was closed, but when Doan pushed at it, it swung back with a rusty mutter of hinges.

Inside Doan could only see the vague, grotesque jumble of half-buildings, piled together like the results of a bad bombing raid. No guard or caretaker was visible. Doan whistled once softly. A breeze moved stealthily past his face and rattled a piece of lath against some boarding, but there was no other sound or movement.

Carstairs nudged his head against Doan's thigh, and when Doan looked down at him, he swung around to peer with pricked ears down a ragged, straggling side lane where the dim light caught and gleamed back from the scummed surface of a ten-foot puddle of water.

"That you, Dust-Mouth?" Doan inquired.

A shadow moved and thickened. "Who's there?"

"Well, now guess," said Doan.

"Doanwashi?"

"You're sharp tonight. Do you want to go on playing hide and seek, or did you have something else in mind?"

"I'm scared."

"We won't let the bad mans hurt you," Doan said.

"We! Who you got with you?"

"My dog."

Dust-Mouth's breath made a tiny whistle. "Dog! Pocus had a dog!"

"Sure," said Doan. "I inherited him when Pocus got blown up. He helps me spy now."

"Pocus got shot, not blowed up!"

"Shot—blown up—what's the difference to him?" Doan asked indifferently. "Or you?"

"I'm scared."

"So we're back there again, are we? What shall I do about it, shiver for you?"

Dust-Mouth gulped. "Well—well, you still want to make that deal?"

"Certainly," said Doan.

"Come on back this way, then."

Doan circled carefully around the pond, feeling the mud squash queasily under his shoes. Carstairs drifted behind him, lifting his feet daintily.

"Through here," Dust-Mouth directed.

Doan couldn't see him any better, but now he could smell him. Dust-Mouth had accumulated a new aroma to blend with the old ones, and it took Doan a moment to identify it as secondhand wine.

He slid in under a pair of deserted stairs that went nowhere in particular, and then a door creaked and let out a flicker of faint light.

"My hideout," said Dust-Mouth.

There was a lantern sitting on a broken crate, and the light that worked its way out of the grimed chimney revealed the ruin of what had once been a siren's boudoir, featuring a faded green and gilt couch big enough for Cleopatra, and a dresser with a broken mirror and some odd broken-down chairs, plus a piano bench with a lath for a substitute leg.

"Shut the door," Dust-Mouth said.

Doan shut it, and the aroma of wine became so intensified that Carstairs made little grumbling sounds to himself. Dust-Mouth settled down warily on the piano bench.

"I'm scared."

"You told me—remember? What are you scared of? After all, you're only selling out to the enemy in time of war. That's nothing to worry about."

"I don't know," Dust-Mouth said doubtfully. "It don't look so good to me no more. I mean, Tonto Charlie gettin' killed…. That had a kind of funny effect on me. I was mad at first, and then I got to thinkin'. A fella can't spend no money when he's dead, you know."

"I hadn't thought of it," Doan said, "but I believe you're right. Why don't you have a drink?"

"Drink?"

"Of wine."

"Ain't a bad idea." Dust-Mouth groped around under the piano bench. "You want some? Here's a cup for you."

It wasn't a cup. It was a horn—evidently a prop for some Viking drinking scene. Doan looked in it, expecting to find at least a spider lurking around somewhere, but it was only slightly dusty. He blew in it and then said: "Okay."

Dust-Mouth poured wine out of a glass gallon jug. "This here's port. It ain't as good as sherry, but it's better than nothin'."

"I guess so," Doan agreed.

"Here's how," Dust-Mouth said. He raised the jug expertly on his forearm, and wine gurgled.

Doan tasted his, and Carstairs growled at him. "This is strictly business," Doan said. "Believe me."

"Glum," said Dust-Mouth, lowering the jug at last. "What say?"

"How about my ore location?" Doan asked.

"I got it all right," said Dust-Mouth. He groped around in

his overall pocket and extended a cupped, incredibly dirty hand. "Samples."

Doan got as close as he dared, and saw a drift of shiny particles hidden among the other visible debris.

"That there," said Dust-Mouth. "That right there will win the war for you. It's carbo-carbo-bezra…. It's the stuff. You can look it up, and then take it to an assayer and ask him if it ain't. And do I know where there's plenty of it! Man, you can scoop it up with a steam shovel. Ain't more'n eighteen inches below surface. Millions of cubic yards. Pure."

"Where is it?" Doan asked.

Dust-Mouth looked all around him cautiously and tilted his head to listen with a sort of groggy concentration. The set had been provided with no windows, but whoever had made a hidey-hole out of it by nailing in a back wall had left a gap in the rough boards about two feet square. It was covered with a mildewed piece of burlap.

"Now we got to talk serious," said Dust-Mouth. "Now we got to strike us a deal. Pull up a little closer."

"I like it here," said Doan. "Go ahead."

"Doanwashi, this is gonna be hard for you to believe, but I'm tired of the desert. Fact. I'm just durned tired of dust and cactus and Gila monsters and all such. I crave to see rivers and creeks and green grass and corn growin' in rows. You ever consider what a purty sight corn is when it grows in rows?"

"I like it better in bottles."

"It ain't bad there, neither," Dust-Mouth admitted. "But what I mean is—I gotta admit it—I wanna go back where I come from and set. I wanta go back to Ioway."

"It's still there," Doan told him.

"You Japs figurin' on conquerin' it?"

"Oh, sure. We'll go through that way on the way to Washington."

"What you gonna do with the people?"

"Kill 'em."

"All of 'em?"

"Oh, we'll leave a few. Have to have somebody to spit on when we feel mean."

"I'll tell you what I figure. I want some of that Ioway land. I figure it'd be nice to have a belt of it runnin' along the Mississippi from about Davenport up to about Clinton and about a hundred miles deep. That'd give me plenty of room to move around in, and I could use the river if I got tired of travelin' on the roads. I'd have to have some people to farm it, too, of course. I ain't gonna work."

"Naturally not," Doan agreed. "I guess we could arrange for you to have some peons."

"What's them?"

"Slaves."

"You mean, I wouldn't even have to pay 'em?"

"No."

"Man, you're makin' this sound like the stuff to me. Just think of me sittin' there like a king.... Could you arrange that for sure, Doanwashi?"

"Right. If this ore deposit is what you say it is. Otherwise we won't even give you ten acres of Texas."

"It's there! There's a million tons of it!"

"Okay. It's a deal. Where's the ore deposit?"

"We got to shake hands first," Dust-Mouth specified cagily.

Doan took a deep breath and held it. "Okay."

"Now we got to drink on it."

Doan let his breath out and sighed. "Okay."

He raised his horn, and Dust-Mouth tipped the jug up on his forearm. The burlap sacking over the back window ripped with a little soggy sound, and in the same split second there was a sharp, smacking report.

The bullet hit the jug of wine and shattered it, and the whole of its contents cascaded down over the lantern. That was too much for the lantern. It went out with a weary gulp, and the darkness moved into the room in a sudden, silent rush.

Dust-Mouth screamed like a lost soul. Doan was up and on his way to the door, the Police Positive ready in his hand. He tripped and fell into the dresser and broke more of the mirror, and then Carstairs snorted, and he followed the sound to the door.

"Right," he said, nudging Carstairs on that side with his knees.

He pulled the door open and dodged to the left. Carstairs faded away in the other direction. Doan fought his way clear of the stairs and staggered into the side of a thatch-covered hut that collapsed with a soggy puff. He stepped over and through the hut, caromed off the edge of a platform, and then was in the open.

"Hi!" he said.

Carstairs' voice bellowed in answer. Instantly there were two more shots. Doan swore loudly and ran straight ahead. He slammed head on into a brick wall that gave way with a tearing crash.

"Hi!" he yelled.

Carstairs bayed. There was another shot. Doan saw the dim, sprayed flash of it this time and fired back, shooting high. The bullet hit something and snapped off into the air with an angry *wheee.*

A door made a hollow thump. Carstairs bayed angrily.

Doan plowed into another brick wall and went through it like Superman, spraying balsa bricks in all directions. Knee-high weeds clutched at him chummily, and he dodged under a hitching rack and rattled the length of a boardwalk. He whirled around the corner of a saloon front and came face to face with a decayed colonial mansion.

Carstairs was on the veranda with both front feet against the closed front door.

"Go around, you fool!" Doan shouted. "There's nothing behind it! It's a set! Left! Left! Hike!"

Carstairs' claws skittered on the porch, and he leaped over the railing at the porch edge and disappeared again. Doan ran the other way. The colonial mansion was edged cozily in against the front half of a yacht, and Doan squeezed in between them, breaking the yacht's anchor chain in the process.

"Hi!" he called.

Carstairs bayed straight ahead. Doan ran along the narrow street of an early English village, detoured around an igloo, and came out on the corner of Broadway and 42nd Street. He paused, blowing, and the iron side gate clanged to his right.

Doan went that way fast. He found Carstairs with his head stuck between the bars, peering vainly out and down the street.

"Get away," said Doan, pulling him back.

The gate opened inward, and Doan jerked at it. It was locked. Doan swore eloquently. He dropped his revolver in his pocket, took hold of two of the iron bars and heaved back. The lock didn't give, but the hinges did. They pulled loose with a shriek of tortured lath, and Doan went down with the gate on top of him.

Carstairs hopped nimbly through the opening and raced down the street. Still swearing, Doan crawled out from under the gate and went out into the street. There was nothing in sight but the Cadillac. Doan sat down on the curb, holding his revolver in his lap, and waited.

In about five minutes Carstairs came ambling out of the shadows and shook himself in a distasteful way.

"It's a damned shame you aren't a bloodhound," Doan told him. "I've got a notion to trade you in on one."

Carstairs merely looked at him.

"I wasn't so hot, either," Doan admitted. "Let's go pick up Dust-Mouth. He's probably having a katzenjammer all by himself in the dark."

They went back through the wrecked gate and down the lane around the mud puddle. Doan leaned under the stairs.

"Hey, Dust-Mouth. The enemy retired to a previously prepared position."

No one answered.

Doan went into the hideout. "Dust-Mouth."

The scent of wine was overwhelming. Doan took a match from his pocket and snapped it on his thumbnail. The sudden spurt of flame reflected gorily from the spilled wine and the pieces of shattered jug, but there was no sign of Dust-Mouth.

"Hey!" Doan yelled.

The echoes came back sullenly—alone.

"Oh, hell," said Doan.

CHAPTER XIII

EDMUND WAS BEHIND the desk when Doan and Carstairs came into the lobby of the apartment hotel. He was working on a new radio diagram.

"A dame called you, Mr. Doan," he said. "I mean, a lady. I mean, she sounded pretty good to me."

"Did she have a name?" Doan asked.

"I guess so, but she didn't tell me what it was. She called you twice, and she said she'd call you back some more. She said it was important."

"Okay," Doan said. "I'll be home for awhile."

"Mr. Doan!" said Harriet.

She came in the front door, her eyes sparkling with eager energy. Blue trailed along disconsolately behind her.

"Have a nice ride?" Doan asked casually.

"Oh, we didn't ride. We walked. It was just wonderful. Wasn't it?"

"I'm tired," Blue said.

"Certainly, but it's a healthy tiredness. It's good for you to feel that way."

"My feet hurt."

"They'll get used to it. Just think of all the hardships our poor soldier-boys are standing all over the world."

"I am," Blue said drearily. He nodded at Edmund. "Get me a taxi, will you?"

Harriet shook her finger at him. "Now you couldn't get a taxi in Africa or the South Sea Islands, you know."

"He probably can't get one here, either," Edmund told her. "But I'll try." He plugged in on the switchboard and dialed expertly.

"Where are you staying, Blue?" Doan asked.

"At the Clark Hotel."

"I'll call you the first thing in the morning," Harriet said. "Now you may kiss me good night."

"Right here?" said Blue.

"Of course, silly. Edmund and Mr. Doan don't mind."

"I should say not," Doan agreed. "We'll find it very interesting."

Harriet put her cheek up, and Blue pecked at it warily. The effort completed his exhaustion. He backed up and sat down on a divan with a weary sigh.

"Tomorrow morning, remember," Harriet said. "Bright and early."

"Yeah," Blue answered hopelessly.

Edmund said, "The taxi company says maybe they'll send a cab and maybe they won't, depending on how they feel about it."

"I'll wait," said Blue.

"Good night, dear," Harriet said. "Sleep tight."

"Yeah," said Blue.

Harriet tripped up the stairs, and Doan and Carstairs followed her. She was waiting for them at the top.

"Mr. Doan, I haven't really done any work for you. I really don't feel that I'm doing my bit."

"You're doing just fine," Doan told her. "Carry on. Chin up. Good night."

"Good night, Mr. Doan."

Harriet went into her apartment, and Doan went on down the hall toward his. He was feeling for his key when Carstairs approached the door, put his nose against the crack under it, and sniffed once.

"Visitors?" Doan inquired.

Carstairs yawned.

"The Gold Dust twins," Doan said in a disgusted voice.

He opened the door. Arne was sitting in a chair facing it, and Barstow was lying on the chesterfield with his hat over his eyes.

"Well," said Arne, "where is it?"

"I don't know."

"What happened this time?"

"Somebody shot at Dust-Mouth and scared him green."

Arne stood up quickly. "Who?"

"That's the sixty-four dollar question."

"Didn't you see him?"

"No. I chased him, but he was too fast on his feet."

"Did he hurt Dust-Mouth?"

"No. And I'd just made him a present of part of Iowa, so I think he'll probably call me up again when he gets through shaking."

Arne breathed hard through his nostrils. "Probably! That's not good enough. We stayed out of the way. We gave you a clear channel. And now look. A fine thing! And you're supposed to be a smart operator!"

"Fire me," Doan suggested.

"We can do better than that," Arne said. "Or worse. You gave the knife that killed Free-Look Jones to the bellboy, by name of Joshua, in the Double-Eagle Hotel in Heliotrope."

"Did I?" said Doan.

Arne stared at him. "Haven't you any conscience at all? Did you want to get that poor devil convicted of murder?"

"We must all serve our country as best we can in these grim times," Doan said. "Is he? Going to be convicted of murder, I mean?"

"No. He has a perfect alibi. He was making root beer in the drugstore next to the hotel. He put some ether in it, and it knocked him cold. He couldn't possibly have been running around loose at the time Free-Look was killed. He couldn't navigate at all. The druggist carried him over and dumped him in the broom closet. Now they're looking for you."

"I thought they would be," Doan admitted. "But of course the government will protect me from being charged with any minor misdemeanors like murder."

"Ha-ha," said Arne.

Doan nodded. "Why don't you two go home and get a good night's rest?"

"We'll give you twenty-four hours more," Arne said. "Come on, Barstow."

"What happens after twenty-four hours?" Doan asked.

Barstow looked back from the doorway. "You were wrong before. *That's* the sixty-four dollar question. Cheer-o." He closed the door softly.

"I've got a good mind to write a letter to President Roosevelt," Doan said to Carstairs.

He sat down on the chesterfield and took off his shoes. He slid the Police Positive under the cushions, and then lay down on his back and stared gloomily at the ceiling. Carstairs stared at the ceiling, too, and then wearied of it and went to sleep in the middle of the floor.

Someone knocked gently on the door.

"What now?" Doan said, not moving.

The door opened, and Harriet looked in.

"Mr. Doan, I forgot to ask you. Did you take care of the matter of that dead man who was in your hotel room?"

"Oh my, yes," Doan said. "I managed things in my customarily brilliant manner."

"Well, why was he killed?"

"That's a military secret."

"Oh, I see. I don't suppose you can tell me who killed him, either?"

"I don't suppose I can," Doan agreed glumly. "You don't know how I wish I could."

"That's all right, Mr. Doan. I can stand the suspense."

"Yeah," said Doan. "But can I?"

The telephone buzzed.

"Ah-ha!" Doan exclaimed, jumping up off the chesterfield. He picked the instrument up. "Yes?"

"This is Edmund, Mr. Doan. At the desk. Woo-woo!"

"What?" said Doan.

"Oh boy! Wow! Whee! You got a visitor. Have you got a visitor! Mr. Doan, it's Susan Sally, and she wants to see you! Woo-woo!"

"Woo-woo!" said Doan. "Send her right up!"

He dove for the chesterfield and got hastily back into his shoes. He slicked his hair down and straightened his tie.

"What is it?" Harriet asked, startled. "Is something going to happen?"

"Probably not," Doan told her. "But you can't blame me for hoping."

Harriet watched him suspiciously. "Is it that theatrical person?"

"How did you know?" Doan demanded.

Harriet nodded slowly and meaningly. "I thought so. She

said she thought you were a very interesting person. I knew what that meant."

"What?" Doan inquired.

"I knew she'd try to see you again. Do you want me to tell her you're busy or not here or something?"

Doan's mouth dropped open. "What?" he repeated incredulously.

"She's not the sort of person you should associate with when you're performing a dangerous and vital mission for your country. I don't approve of her at all."

"Your ballot is void," said Doan. "Would you mind running home and knitting yourself a muffler?"

"You're not going to see her alone? In your apartment? At night?"

"I certainly am," said Doan. "And that reminds me." He nudged Carstairs with the toe of his shoe. "Get. Go with the nice lady."

Carstairs sat up and glared at him in outraged protest.

Someone stumbled in the hall. Doan pushed Harriet aside and opened the door wide. Susan Sally was leaning against the wall opposite, and her eyes were glazed, and she was swaying a little.

"They got me, toots," she said. The muscles in her soft throat tightened suddenly, and the expression on her face changed to one of incredulous, shocked surprise. "Doan!" She coughed. The sound was deep and bubbling in her throat, and then she put out one hand gropingly in front of her and fell forward in a graceful, limp whirl.

Doan caught her before she hit the floor. He stiffened, holding her, staring over her shoulder. On the wall, where she had rubbed against it, there was a wet, red smear.

"What—" said Harriet, scared. "What—"

"Shut up," said Doan. "Take care of her."

He flicked the .25 automatic out of the breast pocket of his coat and ran down the hall. The self-operating elevator was up at this floor, its door open. Doan went down the stairs three at a time.

Edmund was contemplating his radio diagram with a slap-happy expression on his face. He looked up and saw Doan and the automatic, and came to with a startled gulp.

"Who was with Susan Sally?" Doan asked tightly.

Edmund made stiff mouthing motions and shook his head mutely and helplessly.

"Who came in after her?"

"No—no—no—" Edmund said, doing a little better.

"Who was in the lobby when she came?"

Edmund's face was paper-white. He pointed to himself.

"No one else?"

"N-no," said Edmund. "She ain't m-mad, is she? I didn't do nothin'. I juh-juh-just asked her for an autograph, is all."

"Didn't you notice anything the matter with her?"

Edmund swallowed hard. "I thought maybe she was a little drunk. I mean, she staggered. Not much, though."

"What'd she say when you asked her for an autograph?"

"She just said she was in a hurry now, and she'd give me one when she came out."

"Did she use the elevator?"

"Yes. I told her the stairs were quicker, but she said she couldn't make it. That's what she said. 'I can't make it, bub'. So I thought that was why she was drunk. I mean—staggering and—and that…."

"Where are those damned G-men hanging out?"

"D-down in the garage in the janitor's apartment, but I'm not s-supposed to tell anybody…."

"You tell them to get up to my apartment. Now."

"Yes, sir!" said Edmund, plugging in hastily on the switchboard.

Doan ran back up the stairs. Susan Sally was no longer lying in the hall, and he trotted quickly down it to his apartment and pushed the door open.

Harriet stood up beside the chesterfield. There was blood on her hands, and her face was greenish.

"They never taught me anything like this.... I—I think she's...."

Susan Sally was lying face down on the chesterfield. Harriet had taken off her jacket and blouse. There was a little jagged tear, no wider than a man's thumbnail in the softly tanned skin of her back, left of her backbone, just under her shoulder-blade. Dark blood made a thin scribble down toward the hollow of her back.

Doan picked up one hand and felt for the pulse in the wrist. There was none. He pressed his fingers against the side of her neck. Then, very gently, he turned her head sideways and lifted the lid of one eye.

Harriet gulped.

"She's dead," Doan said tonelessly.

Arne came in the room and stopped short. He looked from Susan to Sally to Harriet to Doan. He didn't say anything.

"She was coming to see me," Doan said in the same toneless voice. "Somebody didn't want her to."

Arne touched the flesh around the wound on Susan Sally's back with quick, impersonal fingers. "This is another job by the same one who operated on Free-Look Jones."

"I know!" Harriet cried suddenly. "Oh, I know! Her manager! That's the one! His name is MacAdoo! He did it because he was jealous of her going to see Mr. Doan!"

"What?" said Arne blankly.

"He did! He's a nasty little man! He knew Mr. Doan would win her away from him!"

Arne looked at Doan.

Doan shrugged. "She goes on like that all the time."

"Well, I'm right!" Harriet shrilled. "Of course I'm right! He just couldn't stand the thought of her being interested in anyone else, and so he stabbed her!"

"Elmer A. MacAdoo is the name," Doan said. "In case you're interested."

Arne picked up the telephone. "Janitor," he said when Edmund answered. After a moment he cupped his hand over his mouth and talked in an inaudible voice at some length.

He waited, then. The silence in the room grew and expanded like a living thing. Carstairs stirred uneasily on the floor. Doan looked at him, and he became quiet again.

"Yes," Arne said into the telephone. He listened for a moment and then turned to Doan. "This MacAdoo lives at Malibu Beach. That's about thirty-five miles from here. He's at home. This is supposed to be him on the extension now. See if it is."

Doan took the telephone. MacAdoo's voice was saying angrily, "Hello, hello! Operator! Who is calling? Is this New York? Hello!"

"This is Doan, MacAdoo," Doan said.

"Who? Who did you say?"

"Doan. You met me in Heliotrope."

"Oh! Mr. Doan. Yes. What is it?"

"Susan Sally is here."

"What? She is? Why, she hasn't any business being there! She promised me faithfully she'd go straight home. She has to start a picture tomorrow. She has to be on the set at seven-thirty. Let me talk to her!"

"I can't. She's dead."

"Now, Mr. Doan, I'm her manager, and I'm not going to argue.... What did you say?"

"She's dead."

MacAdoo's voice went up a notch. "Now this is no time for jokes! She has to get her sleep, and she knows very well—"

"She's dead," Doan said patiently.

There was a long silence.

"Dead," said MacAdoo. "Oh, no. Oh, no, no!"

"At the Orna Apartments," Doan said. "On Harkness, just off Vine."

He put the telephone down and nodded at Arne.

Arne said, "She couldn't possibly have driven that far with that kind of a wound. I don't think she could have traveled a hundred yards. A wound of that type is fatal within minutes." He studied Doan for a second. "I'll notify the police. You two stay here and give them a statement. I don't want to appear as yet. There'll be no publicity of any kind—for twenty-four hours. I'll see to that."

He went out and shut the door behind him.

"I don't like him," Harriet said.

"He's getting on my nerves a bit, too," Doan answered absently.

Harriet looked down at Susan Sally. "I—I'll get a blanket and cover her up. It isn't nice for her to lie there…." She paused. "You know, I didn't like her, either, but I don't think anyone should have stabbed her like that."

"I don't think anyone should have, too," said Doan mildly.

Carstairs sat up and looked at him in a worried way.

CHAPTER XIV

EDMUND WASN'T ON duty this time when Doan came down the stairs, and there was no one in the lobby except MacAdoo. He was sitting on a divan in the corner near the door, shoulders hunched, staring dully at the rug between his feet. He had his catalogue sombrero in his hands, and he was twisting the brim with a sort of dull thoroughness. His hair glistened in the light, oily and tightly curled and black, and his eyes were red-rimmed when he looked slowly up at Doan.

"Hello," he said hopelessly.

Doan nodded and sat down in the chair at the end of the divan.

"I came as fast as I could," MacAdoo said.

Doan nodded again.

"They wouldn't let me go upstairs," MacAdoo said. "They told me to stay down here and keep my mouth shut. They told me that Susan Sally's death wasn't to be released to the press. They said I had to stall the studio."

"Who said all this?"

"G-men," MacAdoo said. "F.B.I."

"They're hopping around this joint like fleas in a prison camp," Doan commented.

"I don't understand it," MacAdoo said. "I don't understand what Sally has to do with G-men. She has always paid her income tax right on the dot in full. I know, because I always have made it out for her."

Doan didn't say anything.

MacAdoo glanced at him. "Is she—is she—"

"She's gone. They took her away—to the morgue."

MacAdoo took out his handkerchief and blew his nose loudly. "I don't like that."

"Me, either," Doan said.

"It's not that I'm sentimental," MacAdoo declared. "No, sir. Between me and Sally, it was always strictly business and no nonsense…. Oh, hell."

"Yeah," said Doan.

"I liked her."

"Me, too."

"She shouldn't ought to have been killed."

"That's right."

"She was too damned beautiful."

"You're on the beam," Doan agreed.

"A man would have to be cracked to kill anything as beautiful as that. Am I right?"

"Sure."

"That's going to make it tough to find out who did it, because Hollywood is practically packed with people who are cracked."

"That's no lie."

"You know who did it?"

"No. Not yet."

"I'd like to have a short interview with that party."

"After me," said Doan.

MacAdoo sighed. "Thirty-five hundred dollars a week. And no picture to picture contract, either. Forty straight weeks every year, whether she worked or not."

"How much did you get of that?" Doan asked.

MacAdoo sighed again, more deeply. "Ten per cent for being her agent, five per cent for being her business manager. That amounted to five hundred and twenty-five dollars a week. Oh, it was fair enough. I could have held her up for more. She was green as grass when I found her. And then, I had to spend all my time on her. I mean, she wasn't so easy to handle.

"She got notions. Like I had to save all my gas coupons so she could go to Heliotrope every once in awhile and give the rubes the ritz on account they used to shove her around when she was a kid. And then she was always associating with low characters. No offense."

Doan nodded. "Five and a quarter a week is a nice piece of change. Have you got any more clients like that lying around?"

"I haven't got any more clients, period. I'm flatter than a flounder at this point. I told you she took all my time. As an agent, I'm really not so hot, but you could hardly go wrong with something like Susan Sally, could you?"

"No."

"They come like that only once in a lifetime. I've had my quota."

"How'd you happen to get hold of her?"

MacAdoo began to untwist the brim of his hat. "I've always been interested in the theater. I thought I was an actor once, but nobody else did. I used to be a stagehand, and paint scenery and like that. Then I heard Hollywood was a soft touch, so I came out here. I never even got one job."

"Then what?"

"Well, I thought I'd better be an agent. That doesn't take any brains to speak of, and look at the dough they make. Look at the offices they sport on the Strip."

"Yeah."

"So I set up in business. It didn't work."

"No clients?" Doan asked.

"Anybody can get clients. I couldn't get the clients any jobs. Ten per cent of nothing won't keep you in beans for long."

"No," Doan agreed.

"So I was down to my carfare back to New York. I didn't even have anything to eat on going there. So I was down to the station, waiting for my train. And Susan Sally came up to me and asked me how to get to Hollywood, and the movie studios. She'd just come in on the train."

"What did you do?" Doan inquired.

"I took one look at her, and then went and cashed my ticket in. I got her to sign a contract in the taxi on the way back to Hollywood. I spent most of my ticket money renting an outfit for her, and I took her to the jazziest nightclub in town that night. Half an hour after we sat down in it there were three producers sitting with us, and three more trying to bribe the head waiter to throw out the first three. I mean, you couldn't miss with Susan Sally. I got her a contract that night, written on the front of a producer's dress shirt. It just happens once to one guy, Doan. It won't again for me. I'm all done now."

"Maybe not," said Doan.

MacAdoo nodded gloomily. "I know. Everybody in town has been drooling because I had her. Now they'll give me the brush-off, but quick. I'm back playing with peanuts again. You wouldn't want to let me handle that dog of yours, would you?"

"What?" said Doan.

"He's good. I saw some of the rushes of those defense films he made. Get him released from the government, and I could maybe make you a dime or two or three."

"I'll think it over. It would make him madder than hell though if he thought he was supporting me in luxury. He's old-fashioned. He thinks I ought to feed him instead of vice versa."

MacAdoo got up slowly and wearily. "I guess I'll go home again. It doesn't do me any good to sit here. Will you call me up if you hear anything new?"

"Sure."

"Good-by, Doan."

"Good-by," Doan said.

MacAdoo went out the door, dragging his heels a little. Doan sat still, his face relaxed and bland and peaceful, until the switchboard buzzed softly. He got up, then, and went over to the desk and plugged in one of the outside lines.

"Yes?"

"Lemme speak to Doan."

"You are."

"I'm sure scared good and plenty now, Doanwashi. I sure am."

"That's too bad."

"You ain't gonna go back on your sworn word, are you?"

"Nope. Are you?"

"I guess not. Can you meet me at Hollywood and Cahuenga right away? In your car?"

"I'm on my way."

"Did you see the fella that shot at us?"

"No. Did you?"

"Man, I don't want to see him! Hurry up."

The line clicked, but it didn't hum. Doan waited for a moment, and then said:

"Well?"

Arne's voice said, "Go ahead and meet him. You still have about twenty-two hours."

"Keep out of my tracks," Doan warned. "I'm going to start huffing and puffing now."

CHAPTER XV

THE DIM-OUT HAS done a lot for Hollywood Boulevard. It used to look just as cheap and cheesy as you'd think it would, and the types that clutter it up have been known to turn a strong man's stomach, but now it and they are shadowed discreetly, and it's not so bad. Of course, some very weird things come swimming out of the darkness now and then, but if you have steady nerves and a well balanced personality it is often possible to walk two or three blocks without having hysterics.

Doan rolled the Cadillac across on the signal and pulled in against the curb in the red zone on the far side and opened the door. Dust-Mouth popped out of the shadows and bounced on the front seat.

"Drive on!" he said breathlessly, slamming the door.

Doan pulled out into the traffic. "Somebody following you?"

"If they are, they sure must be dizzy by now. I been runnin' in circles for an hour."

"Where do you want to go?"

"Back to the desert. I wanta show you that there location. I wanta get this here deal all set. I don't like bein' shot at. That ain't good for a person."

"Not too much of it," Doan agreed.

Carstairs snorted twice imperiously from the back seat. Doan reached back and turned one of the windows down. Carstairs put his head outside.

"What's the matter with him?" Dust-Mouth demanded.

"He's a fresh air fiend." Doan said, turning the wing of his own window around so that the wind blew directly in his face. "So am I. You've got a new brand now, haven't you?"

"Of what?"

"Wine."

"Oh, yeah." Dust-Mouth took a round pint bottle out of his coat pocket. "This here is muscatel. It ain't as good as sherry, but it's better than nothin'. You want a drink?"

"No, thanks. Why don't you buy sherry?"

Dust-Mouth looked at him in surprise. "Winos drink sherry. They're nothin' but bums. If I was to go around buyin' it all the time, people would think I was one."

"Oh," said Doan.

"You got any dough on you, Doanwashi?"

"Some. Why?"

"Well, I was thinkin'. I'm still hot on that Ioway deal, but I got to have somethin' to live on until you Japs get there and take it over for me."

"I can spare you some eating money."

"Swell. Say, another thing."

"What?"

"How does the Jap government feel about puttin' people in insane asylums and such like?"

"They never do that. There's only one guy over there they keep a very close watch on."

"Who's he?"

"The Emperor."

"The head gazump, you mean? What's the matter with him?"

"He claims he's God."

"Wow!" said Dust-Mouth, awed. "I've met guys who thought they were Pontius Pilate and Judas and even the Pope, but I never hear of anybody who actually claimed he was God. This boy must be really nuts. Any chance of him recoverin'?"

"Yes," said Doan. "I think that someone will convince him he's wrong one day soon."

"That's good. He ain't runnin' the works in the meantime, is he?"

"No. They keep him under cover."

"I should think so. Even the Japs—no offense—ain't so dumb they'd believe a fandango like that."

"You'd be surprised," said Doan. "How'd you happen to run across this ore deposit?"

"Carbotetroberylthalium."

"What?" said Doan.

"That's it. I mean, that's pretty close to it, anyway. I looked it up again in the library. I can never remember that name."

"What's it good for?"

"I dunno. You put it in steel and it makes it harder or quicker or something. I guess."

"Maybe you'd better stop guessing," said Doan.

"Oh, it's the goods, all right. It's like this. I ran across it one time when I was goin' here and there. It had been washed out of a gully, and it was just layin' around there in the open. Just like them samples I showed you. So I picked up some of it just for hell and took it to this assayer I got credit with. I say, 'What the hell is this junk, Joe? I never see nothin' like it before.' So he foxes around and tests it and looks it up and all that, and then he tells me."

"What?"

"That it's what I tell you a minute ago. So I ask him what it's worth. And he says it ain't worth nothin', because they got mountains of the stuff stuck around here and there in foreign parts. So I forget it."

"What then?"

"So the dirty government cheats me, and we got a war. I still don't think nothin' about the junk until this assayer comes around and asks me about it again. He wants to know where I found it."

"Did you tell him?"

"Ha! Why, he's as big a crook as them guys in the government. Like as not he's hand in glove with 'em. Like as not he'd tell them where it was if I told him. So I let on like I'd forgot and got him to give me a grubstake to go find it again."

"You didn't, though."

"Hell, no. I got drunk. I knew where it was. I didn't have to hunt."

"What happened then?"

"The assayer got mad, but he give me another grubstake. So I got drunk again."

"And neat?"

"He got madder. So the stinker told the government on me, and they give me a grubstake. Only they sent a guy with me to see I hunted."

"What'd you do?"

"We both got drunk."

"Then what?"

"The crooks put me in an asylum. They figured to break down my character, but it didn't bother me a bit. I liked the place. Met a lot of interestin' folks. Had a good time."

"And after that?"

"As soon as the dirty government see I was enjoyin' myself they had me thrown out. They said they'd let me back in again if I showed 'em the deposit. But not me. I got principles."

"Sure," said Doan.

"So I went to Heliotrope. I told Peterkin I'd maybe tell him where the stuff was, so he was lettin' me stay in the jail. Nice jail, huh?"

"Yeah."

"Peterkin was watchin' me sort of, so I sent Tonto Charlie in to deal with this Pocus party."

"Did Tonto know where the deposit is?"

"Naw. I told him where it was, but I didn't tell him the right place. I figured he might not be honest. That's probably why Tonto got killed, I been thinkin'. He probably showed Pocus this place I told him, and there wasn't any ore there. Naturally that'd get Pocus upset."

"Naturally," Doan agreed.

"Oh, well," said Dust-Mouth, taking a drink. "Tonto Charlie ain't much of a loss, is he?"

"No, no," said Doan.

"I'm glad I'm dealin' with you instead of Pocus. He was a little too sudden to suit me. Although I hear you can sort of snort when you've got a mind to. They tell me you sort of run Parsley Jack into the ground."

"He slipped."

"Sure. He's in jail now."

"What for?"

"Evadin' the draft."

"How did that happen?"

"Oh, he was supposed to be inducted a long time ago. He was payin' Doc Gravelmeyer not to have him called. Doc is the head of the draft board in Heliotrope. When Parsley Jack run out when Doc was gonna give him a free operation, that made Doc almighty mad, so he had Parsley Jack pinched. He told Parsley Jack he'd let him go again if Jack would let Doc operate, but Jack said he preferred the Army."

"What's this Parsley Jack's relation to Free-Look Jones?"

"He just used to beat up people for Free-Look."

"For fun?"

"Mostly, I guess. Sometimes Free-Look would give him a beer or something if he beat up a guy real bad."

"I see," said Doan.

"Can you go any faster than this?"

"No. Why?"

"It's gonna rain. They even bust the radio silence on the weather to say so. Afraid of flash floods in the desert, I think, maybe. We got one flat to cross that might give us a bit of trouble."

"We'll worry about that when we come to it."

CHAPTER XVI

THE CADILLAC CRAWLED along like a bug under a bucket, and the simile is all the more apt because this was no ordinary desert day. They are merely unpleasant. This one had a tinge of horror tucked around its edges. The sky was a gun-metal gray with dark, jagged streaks groping through it like a witch's fingers.

The wind was a solid, chill mass of pressure that blew without stopping, and the mesquite bush cringed under it, and even the cactus leaned queasily away. It was strong enough so that Doan had to exert constant force on the steering wheel to keep the car from hopping out of the scarred, straggling ruts to march off into the brush on a tour of its own.

"You sure you know where you are?" he asked.

"Yeah, man," said Dust-Mouth. "Just keep plugging along. Not so far now."

The road wandered up the side of a hill, switching back and forth. The springs hit bottom with a bang, and Carstairs mumbled critically in Doan's ear.

"Shut up," said Doan. "I didn't build this road, and you can be damned sure I didn't invent this desert."

He shifted into second gear. The Cadillac heaved up over the top of the hill, and the desert stretched away in front of them, barren and twisted and empty, with rocks, much too reminiscent of tombstones, pushing up through the sand at odd intervals.

The wind paused just long enough to draw a breath, and then hit them with a bushel of blown sand that scraped like finger-nails on a slate.

Doan winced. "This isn't doing my paint any good."

"Nope," Dust-Mouth agreed cheerfully. "Sand will take it off neat as pie. Probably scar up all your windows so you can't see through 'em, too."

The car crawled down into a valley and twisted back around, through rocks that were cold and black and malevolently twisted. Lights flickered quickly along the horizon, and after a while the thunder bumbled sullenly to itself.

"What happens to the road when it rains?" Doan inquired.

"What road?"

"This one!"

"Oh. This ain't really a road. It's a sort of a path, you might say. When it gets washed out, you just make a new one."

"Fine stuff," Doan commented. "When is it going to rain, or was that just a rumor?"

"Storm's over behind the Crazy Legs now. When she comes around that mountain yonder she won't be drivin' six white horses, but she'll sure be comin'. Keep goin'."

The Cadillac topped another hill, and without any warning lightning flicked at them like a gigantic whip in a green, crackling glare that raised the hair on Doan's head. The thunder hit instantly, not in a roll, but in a blasting report that lifted the Cadillac and slammed it down again.

"Wow!" said Doan groggily.

"Hit back of us in the valley," Dust-Mouth reported. "Reckon there must be some iron in them rocks."

Lightning flicked again, and thunder slammed them back in their seats, and a green spitting ball of fire as big as a house went hopping with terrible daintiness down the slope ahead of them and struck a rock head on and split it neatly in two. The thin, cringing stink of brimstone floated in the wind.

"Did you—see what I saw?" Doan asked.

"Yeah, man," said Dust-Mouth soberly.

A solid gray curtain appeared ahead of them. It marched remorselessly forward over hill and dale, and hit them solidly. It resembled rain just about as much as Niagara Falls does. The Cadillac crouched down under the weight of it, and Doan could see all of a good ten feet ahead of his radiator ornament.

Dust-Mouth pounded him on the shoulder. "Go on! Drown us here!"

Doan turned on the windshield wipers, and effortlessly the wind twisted them loose and threw them aside. It blew out a section of rubber padding around the side window, and rain drops whipped in and hit him in the face like individual needles.

Dust-Mouth pounded his shoulder again. "Stop! Wait!"

Doan halted the car. It rocked ominously. Dust-Mouth was fighting with the door handle on his side.

"What are you doing?" Doan shouted.

"Out. Test road."

Dust-Mouth got the door open and fell out. The wind snatched the door out of his grasp and slammed it hard enough to rock the car even more violently. It spun Dust-Mouth around and knocked him against the front fender. The rain hit him, but it didn't soak in. It bounced.

He fought for his balance, finally got it. Bent over nearly double, he staggered ahead. He was a grotesque shadow stamping and dancing on the road edge. His arms flung and beckoned wildly.

Doan drove ahead in low. The Cadillac slewed gently. Doan fed it more gas, and it caught itself with a jerk and ground on around the edge of a knoll.

Dust-Mouth hauled the door open and fell inside. He was panting brokenly.

"Two hundred foot drop," he said. "On your side. Road edge crumbled under your rear wheel. You feel it?"

"Yes," said Doan.

"Go down now. Faster. Let her roll."

The car heaved and banged down the slope, lurching with a sort of giddy dignity. The road leveled out and straightened, water glimmering cold and metallic in the ruts.

"Faster!" Dust-Mouth yelled. "Faster!"

Doan fed it the gas, and the car rolled stubbornly forward.

Brush crackled damply under the fenders. "Faster!" Dust-Mouth yelled. "Oh, God! We'll never make it!"

Water sucked and gurgled evilly under them, brown streaked with rust-red, surface whipped into a froth of scummed bubbles. It tore at the front wheels and lapped eagerly at the fenders and seeped in coldly along the floor boards. Carstairs yelped indignantly and jumped up on the rear seat, arching his back like a cat.

Doan could feel the sand sliding away under the tires. "Oh, God," said Dust-Mouth numbly.

The Cadillac twitched its rear end like an irritated dowager, and began to climb straight up a cut-bank. It skidded on the top, dipped daintily, made it with a defiant roar. The wheels spun and stopped.

"Well?" said Doan, wiping the perspiration and rain moisture off his face.

"Whew," said Dust-Mouth. "That there was the flat I spoke to you about."

"What was in it?"

"A flash flood. It'll maybe rise ten feet in five minutes. We're safe here, though."

"What'll we do—camp?"

"Naw. There's a shack just beyond that hump. I think we better hole up. I don't think we better drive no further right now."

"I don't think so, either."

They got out of the car and stood against the drive of the rain. The wind rippled the fur on Carstairs' back, and he ducked his head between his shoulders, glaring at Doan in squint-eyed disgust.

"Where the hell are we from that deposit?" Doan shouted, shielding his eyes with a raised forearm.

"Here."

"What?"

"It's right here. We're standing on it. All through this flat here. That's how I spotted it. Another flood washed some out in the flat."

"Where's the shack, then? Let's go."

"Come on—"

Edmund stepped out from behind the car. He had his coat collar turned up, and his left hand grasped it tight around his throat. His hair was plastered flat and slick down over his forehead, and water ran down from it in jagged streaks. He was holding a stubby, shiny revolver in his right hand.

"Well, Edmund, my boy," said Doan. "How are you and all that?"

Edmund's lips looked white and stiff. "Put your hands up."

"Sure," said Doan amiably, raising them.

"Keep your dog close."

"Come here, stupid," Doan ordered.

Carstairs edged in reluctantly against his leg.

"I surprised you," said Edmund.

"Well, yes," Doan admitted. "You might say you did, to some extent. How'd you get here?"

"I came with you—in your luggage compartment."

"Well, well," said Doan.

Edmund lifted his upper lip. "You didn't think, did you, Mr. Doan, that during the course of your nonsensical and childish game of pretending to be an enemy agent that you might run across a real one?"

"I wouldn't want to upset you or disappoint you at this moment," Doan answered, "but yes. I had an idea I might. I must admit that I didn't think it would be you, though. It's too bad, too. I mean, you were a pretty good desk clerk. As a spy, I can't give you so much."

"What?" Dust-Mouth exclaimed suddenly. "Hey!"

Edmund's shiny revolver moved an inch. "I told you to put up your hands."

"Who are you?" Dust-Mouth bellowed.

"Meet my pal, Edmund," Doan said. "He was the desk clerk at the Orna Apartment Hotel in the good old days."

"He said he was a spy!"

"I heard that, too."

"What's he doin' here?"

"Pointing a gun at you. Haven't you noticed?"

"You'd better put up your hands," said Edmund.

"Why, you little stinker," said Dust-Mouth. "Gimme that gun before I make you eat it."

He took a step forward, lowering his head.

"Look out!" Doan yelled.

Edmund fired. The wind took the sound of the report and shredded it and whipped the remnants away. Dust-Mouth turned around and stumbled on legs that were suddenly loose and wobbly under him, and then he went down headlong, and the rain splashed and stained itself on his face.

Edmund's tongue flicked across his lips. Doan stood rigid. Edmund breathed in slowly at last, and Doan relaxed just slightly.

"That is what happens to people who don't do what I tell them," Edmund said.

"Sure," said Doan.

"Roll him over the bank. Keep your hands up."

Doan inserted his toe under Dust-Mouth's body and flopped him over, once and then again. The edge of the cut-bank crumbled, and Dust-Mouth went down the steep side of it like a ragged, molting bundle. The roiled water splashed coldly over him. It heaved his body up once, and he stared at Doan with eyes that were wide and amazed under the red hole in his forehead, and then the water flipped him over much as Doan had done and dragged him greedily down out of sight.

"All right," said Doan. "What's next?"

Edmund felt behind him and opened the rear door of the

Cadillac. "Tell your dog to get in there," he said, sidling away from the car.

"Get in," Doan said, nudging Carstairs with his knee.

Carstairs climbed slowly into the car. Edmund slammed the door.

"Turn around."

Doan turned around. Edmund came closer and pushed the shiny revolver against his spine.

"Don't move."

Doan stood still. Edmund's hand slid lightly over his shoulder and retrieved the .25 automatic from the breast pocket of his coat. The hand disappeared, came back empty, and slipped the Police Positive out of Doan's waistband.

Edmund moved backward cautiously. "Open the door and let the dog out. Keep him close to you."

Doan obeyed. Carstairs sat down on the sand, his ears tucked low against the whip of the wind, and examined Edmund with a sort of speculative interest.

"Well?" said Doan, doing the same.

"We'll go to the shack," said Edmund. "There are some things I wish you to tell me. Walk that way. Walk slowly. Keep your hand on the dog's collar. I'll shoot you instantly if you don't do exactly as I say."

Doan turned around and headed into the wind with Carstairs walking beside him. The rain slashed at Doan's face in slanting flicks, and the sand packed heavily on his shoes. The faint straggle of a path led around a knoll and through scarred, knee high brush, and then the shack loomed at a little higher level across the draw in front of them.

It was small, no more than about twelve-by-twelve, made of odd-size lumber that had weathered and warped, and it had a roof shingled with flattened five-gallon tins and a stovepipe chimney that drooped disconsolately.

Doan stopped when he saw it.

"Go on," Edmund ordered.

"You've got visitors."

"What?"

"There's someone inside," Doan said. "If they're friends of yours, it's okay by me, but I wouldn't like to get caught in a crossfire."

The revolver nudged into Doan's spine again, and he could sense rather than hear Edmund's heavy breathing just back of his ear.

"How do you know there's someone inside?"

Doan pointed down. Carstairs was staring at them but with his ears pricked forward sharply, his head tilted a little. The stunted brush along the sides of the draw clashed and chittered uneasily, and rain ran curiously around among exposed roots.

Edmund moved closer against Doan's back. "Hello!" he shouted suddenly. "Hello!"

A voice came back like a flat, muffled echo. "Hello!"

Edmund sighed noisily. "It's all right. Go ahead."

Doan dug his heels in and slid down the bank. The sand at the bottom of the draw sucked mushily under his shoes, and he climbed up the other side, skidding slightly.

The braced door of the shack moved a little, uncertainly, and then opened back and revealed a square of dim, blue gloom. Rain slapped and spattered on the tin roofing and drooled messily down from the eaves.

"Inside," said Edmund.

Doan and Carstairs edged through the door.

"Why, Mr. Doan," said Harriet Hathaway.

She was sitting down on the floor against the wall at Doan's right with her feet out in front of her. Blue was sitting beside her with his feet out, too. He was studying them with gloomily absorbed interest. He looked like a man who has been suspecting the worst and has just found out that it is all too true.

MacAdoo was sitting on a nail keg against the opposite wall.

His sombrero was spotted blackly with rain, and some of the colors had run from the band across its wide, tilted brim. He looked worried, but not about the rifle he was holding on his lap. He seemed to be quite at home with that.

"Don't tell me," said Doan. "Let me guess. It's old home week."

Edmund shoved the revolver against his back. "Get out of the way."

Doan and Carstairs stepped sideways in concert.

"Hello," MacAdoo said to Edmund.

"So it's you," said Edmund. "What do you mean by coming here?"

MacAdoo moved the rifle to indicate Harriet and Blue. "They were following you. I followed them. I thought I'd best collect them and bring them along."

"What were you following me for?" Edmund asked.

"Oh, you," said Harriet. "What would anyone want to follow you for? I mean, you're just a desk clerk. I mean, we weren't following you at all. We didn't even see you. We were following Mr. Doan."

"Why?" Doan asked.

"You were acting suspiciously. Sneaking."

"Don't blame me," said Blue. "I was agin' the whole idea." He had shaved, and his skin looked new and pink and polished. He still wore his black glasses.

"Well, you know it was a good idea," Harriet told him. "Just look. I mean, it's obvious that there is some kind of a subversive plot going on somewhere. Just why are you neglecting your duties in this frivolous manner, Mr. Doan?"

"Ask Edmund," Doan advised.

"Be quiet," said Edmund. "Speak when you're spoken to." He nodded coldly at MacAdoo. "How did you get here ahead of us?"

"Drove," MacAdoo answered. "I've got no governor on my car. I passed you back at the crossroads."

"Well, why did you come here?"

"I thought—"

"Tchah!" said Edmund contemptuously. "Thought! You do nothing but think. This is a time for action, not thinking. You should have killed them somewhere else."

"What?" said Harriet.

"Who?" said Blue.

"Tchah!" Edmund said. "When you meddle, you die."

"It's no act," Doan told them. "He means it."

"But why?" Harriet demanded shakily.

"Be quiet," Edmund ordered. "Perhaps I will rape you before I kill you, although I don't think it would be worth my time. You." He jabbed the revolver at Doan. "Sit down there beside them. Keep your hands folded in your lap."

Doan sat down and extended his feet. Carstairs sat down in front of him.

"Where'd you get that rifle?" Edmund asked MacAdoo.

"Bought it."

"What kind is it?"

"Mannlicher 6.5 sporter with a five power scope."

"Tchah!" said Edmund. "Austrian. You."

"Present," Doan answered.

"Where is the ore deposit?"

"We're sitting on it."

"No," said Edmund. "The other one, Tonto Charlie, brought me here. There is no ore in this area that could be of any possible use to any government. Right?"

MacAdoo nodded. "Right."

"I'm blanked, then," Doan said. "Why don't you ask Blue?"

"Huh?" said Blue.

"Don't be silly," Harriet said sharply. "Blue doesn't know

anything about ore. He doesn't know anything about anything. Do you?"

"Nope," said Blue.

"Hmmm," said Edmund, watching him. "You are too stupid to be real. You are not even a good actor. What do you know about this matter?"

"Nothin'."

"You'd better answer," Edmund said. "I'm very impatient."

Doan was staring narrowly at the back of Carstairs' neck. Carstairs flicked his ears twice and then finally turned around to stare at him. Doan stopped looking at his neck and began studying the door. It was not latched. The wind moved it slightly, and the bottom edge scraped on the rough floor.

Carstairs began to watch the door, too.

Harriet said, "You're a very silly person. I think you're getting a little above yourself, aren't you? Going around kidnapping people and threatening them. There are laws—"

"If you don't keep quiet I'll kick you in the face," Edmund told her.

Blue sighed drearily. "I dunno why I had to get mixed up with such people."

The wind moved the door back a little more. The muscles along Carstairs' back quivered slightly.

"Edmund," Doan said.

Edmund turned toward him. "What?"

"Which brand of enemy agent are you?"

Edmund's lip curled. "Need you ask?"

"Not any more," said Doan. "What were you doing as a desk clerk?"

"Preparing to get in an aircraft factory."

"I see," said Doan. "That would be—*Hike!*"

Carstairs moved in a blurred streak. He hit the edge of the door with one shoulder and knocked it wider open and slipped through.

Edmund whirled around and fired. Carstairs was in midair, taking off from the threshold. He turned clear over in the air with a breathless grunt, slammed down on his side, and skidded out of sight down into the draw.

"You!" said Edmund to Doan, white-faced. He whirled again and snatched the rifle out of MacAdoo's hands. "I hit him! He won't go far! I'll follow.…Take this! Watch! Make no mistakes!" He thrust the shiny revolver at MacAdoo and ran headlong out the door.

MacAdoo settled the revolver competently in his palm. He still looked worried, but no more so than he had before.

"No more tricks," he warned. "I'm not quite as bloodthirsty as Edmund, but I have some few instincts of self defense."

He got up off the nail keg, holding the revolver carefully leveled, and shut the door tight. He walked backward to the nail keg and sat down again. The rain thrummed noisily on the roof.

"I don't think I like Edmund," Doan said conversationally.

"No one does," said MacAdoo. "Naturally. He's a graduate of the *Ordensburgen.*"

"What are that?"

"Where they train the *Geheim Staatspolizei.* The Gestapo. Their graduates are very clever. They are given a very thorough education in how to assume any particular background they might choose. Edmund's slang and mannerisms are good, I think."

"Very good," Doan agreed. "Do you go around heiling Hitler, too?"

"Adolf? No. Although I've always rather liked him."

"You talk as though you knew him."

"I do."

"I mean, personally."

MacAdoo nodded. "Yes. I do."

Harriet gasped. "You know Adolf Hitler?"

"Certainly," said MacAdoo.

"That's horrible!"

"No, it isn't. He's rather amusing sometimes. Better than the radio. That is, he was. I understand he's run to seed a bit lately"

"How'd you happen to meet him?" Doan asked.

"I ran an art shop in Munich for several years. He used to hang around and cadge coffee money off me. I sold a couple of his pictures."

"They're terrible pictures!" Harriet snapped. "Everybody knows they're just old house-painter's smears."

"No, they're not," said MacAdoo. "They're not bad at all. They're not wonderful, but they're pretty competent jobs of work. I wonder why you Americans always have to try to make anything your enemies do seem ridiculous and bungling. It causes you a lot of needless casualties."

"You ain't lyin'," Blue said.

"Why what do you know about it?" Harriet demanded.

"He was maybe thinking of airplanes," Doan suggested.

Harriet stared at him. "Everyone knows that our planes are the best in the world and that the German planes are nothing but a lot of old junk and ersatz, and that their pilots are all cowards."

"Sure," said Doan. "MacAdoo, if you were kicking around in Munich when Hitler was trying to sell pictures, how come you didn't hitch up with the Nazis when they started going?"

"I did. I've got party card number eleven."

"What does that mean?" Harriet inquired coldly.

"It means there were a total of ten Nazis, including Hitler, when I joined up. I didn't join, really. Hitler presented me with a membership when I asked him to pay me back some of the dough I'd lent him."

"That must have sort of put you in on the ground floor," Doan said thoughtfully.

"Yes."

"You ought to have cleaned up when the Nazis began to get rolling."

"I did."

"How?" Doan asked.

"I was art director of the *Reich*. I—ah—bought pictures from people and—ah—sold them to other people."

Doan said, "You mean you confiscated pictures from Hitler's enemies, and blackmailed people who wanted to be his friends into buying them."

"That's putting it very crudely," said MacAdoo, "but lucidly."

"Did you have a monopoly on that business?"

"Yes."

"You must have put away plenty."

"I did."

"What'd you stop for?"

MacAdoo's lips tightened. "Goering. That big tub of guts. He was building castles all over Germany, and he informed me I should donate pictures for them. He had a list of the pictures. The most valuable ones I had—ah—purchased. Imagine that. I should give him pictures. He wasn't satisfied with stealing all the steel mills in Germany, he's got to cut in on my business."

"What did you do?" Doan inquired.

"Told him to go to hell."

"What did he do?"

"Tried to murder me six times within six days. I had a few bodyguards of my own, of course, but even then he had ten regiments of thugs plus the air force. I had to cut and run for it. I'm going to get even with him for that one of these fine days. I'll probably have to wait until after the war, I suppose."

"Goering is going to be hung after we win the war," Harriet told him.

MacAdoo looked at her. "Don't be silly. The Kaiser didn't have much more than a hundred million dollars, and nobody hung him. Goering is worth two or three billion by this time, and besides that he has heavy influence in England and the United States."

"How do you know?" Doan asked.

"Read the papers. Who do you think is paying for all this bilge about Goering being a harmless, jolly fat man with a love for medals and a heart of gold? Stuff like that isn't printed for free. Particularly not after the guy involved has murdered a half million civilians with his air force. I shouldn't wonder but what he'll wind up as president of the *Reich* under a, pause for laughter, democratic government."

MacAdoo leaned sideways on his nail keg and pulled a leather covered flask from his hip pocket. He snapped the patented top open with his teeth.

"Have some brandy?"

"No, thanks," said Doan. "Edmund's taking a long time, isn't he?"

MacAdoo smiled. "Isn't he? He'll be back, though. Are you thinking about the FBI? Don't. They won't be around. They didn't follow you. I believe they had an idea of scouting for you in a plane, but one couldn't get off the ground in this kind of weather, and if it did no one in it would be able to see anything."

"Hmmm," said Doan. "How'd you get into the country, and stay so long without being spotted? They must have a record and pictures of you."

"There are ways. They do have pictures of me, but in the pictures I was forty pounds heavier, bald, wore a beard, and had a hooked nose."

"Oh. What'll you look like tomorrow?"

"Not like I did then or do now."

"How'd Edmund spot you?"

"Goering. He's never quit trying to find me. He finally did."

"How come he didn't try some more murder?"

"I got in touch with Adolf. I told him to call Goering off, or I'd start talking to the United States Government, and not about pictures, either."

"Edmund doesn't like you very well."

"No. He thinks I'm a party backslider."

"When are you going to kill him?" Doan asked.

"After he attends to you."

The thin, distant crack of a rifle sounded somewhere outside. It was repeated almost instantly.

"That's the end of your dog," said MacAdoo. "He never had a chance. Edmund is an expert killer."

"Too bad," said Doan. "But then, I never liked Carstairs much anyway. Do you think he really could have gotten a job in pictures?"

"I think so."

"How about me?"

"No," said MacAdoo.

Doan sighed. "That's what comes of having brains instead of beauty."

The rain rippled musically on the roof, and the wind brushed tentative, prying fingers along the wall of the shack.

"I don't understand this!" Harriet wailed suddenly.

Doan sighed again. "I might as well tell all, I guess. We might have a long—wait."

MacAdoo chuckled. "Edmund will come back."

Doan said, "The FBI delegated me to find out the location of an ore deposit from a man named Dust-Mouth Haggerty."

"Then why didn't you do it?" Harriet demanded.

"There wasn't any such deposit."

"How long have you known that?" MacAdoo asked.

"Oh, for some time. I'm not as dumb as Edmund."

MacAdoo nodded. "He is very stupid. I don't know what they must be thinking of in Germany. Even Americans aren't complete fools—not all of them."

"Tell me more!" Harriet commanded.

Doan said, "Dust-Mouth claimed to know where some strategically valuable ore was. He didn't. There wasn't any. The FBI were pretty sure of that, but not completely. They used Dust-Mouth and me for bait, and they pulled in quite a haul."

"You shouldn't have taken the job," said MacAdoo.

"Don't I know it? I didn't want to. Every time I work for the government, I get put in jail. I'll bet if I got out of this, they'd slap me away for something."

"You don't have to worry—about jail," said MacAdoo.

"I wonder where Edmund is?"

"He'll come. He's probably burying your dog."

"Well, why did Dust-Mouth say he knew where some ore was if he didn't?" Harriet said angrily.

"He made a business out of it. He got free room and board because people thought they could make a million out of him. He was a very dumb guy. He was playing with fire all the time and didn't have sense enough to know it. He had taken plenty of suckers on phony claims in his day, and he didn't realize that in wartime the suckers might not just laugh it off. He didn't even know what kind of ore he was supposed to have. He had a collection of samples, and he just agreed they contained whatever you said. If you didn't say, he made something up."

"Past tense?" MacAdoo inquired.

Doan nodded. "Edmund."

"Oh," said MacAdoo.

"The FBI thought he might be playing a little deeper game than he was. So did I."

"What were you going to do with him out here?" MacAdoo asked.

"Toast his tootsies over a match flame until he told me who killed Tonto Charlie and Free-Look Jones and Susan Sally."

"Well, who did?" Harriet asked.

"Edmund," said Doan. "Just old Edmund. The fellow we're waiting for. I wonder if he's reading a burial service over Carstairs? Dust-Mouth heard in Heliotrope that I was a Jap agent. The FBI did that. They even furnished my address. Dust-

Mouth was getting short of customers, so he figured he might take a little dough off of me. He sent Tonto Charlie to see me. Tonto ran into Edmund. Edmund bit. That was bad luck for Tonto, because Edmund doesn't have much of a sense of humor. Tonto brought him out here and showed him what was supposed to be some kind of valuable ore." Doan looked at MacAdoo. "Is that when Edmund got in touch with you?"

MacAdoo nodded. "Yes. He wanted samples assayed. I had it done for him. The samples showed no traces of any ore worth a dime to anybody for anything."

"Bing," said Doan. "Good-by, Tonto Charlie. He was hiding out at the Orna in Edmund's apartment at the time, waiting for the assayer's report. Tonto actually thought Dust-Mouth did have something. Edmund got mad and stabbed him, and then he had a body."

"As I said, he is very stupid," MacAdoo agreed.

"Comes the FBI looking for Doan," said Doan. "Edmund gets a little nervous about his body. I mean, Tonto's. The FBI park a car in front of the door where Edmund can see it and go away. Edmund finds gas ration books made out in my name in the car. A light dawns. He sends the garage attendant or janitor or whoever away on an errand, drives the car into the basement garage, gets Tonto Charlie's body and sticks it in the luggage compartment, and drives the car back to the front of the apartment and parks it. Now Doan has a body."

"Oh!" said Harriet.

"I thought it belonged to you," Doan told her. "I thought your pal, here, stuck it in the car when I stopped for you in the desert. That's why I wanted to keep you sort of under my eye for the time being."

"Oh!" said Harriet.

"I'm cold," said Blue. "Sure wish I was back on my reservation."

"Don't these horrible things you've been hearing make you

want to join the Army and fight, fight, fight?" Harriet demanded. "No," said Blue glumly. "You're a coward!"

"I sure am," said Blue. "I guess you hate me now, huh?"

"Well…" said Harriet. "No. I—I don't."

"Oh," said Blue, sighing.

"And then there was Free-Look Jones," said Doan. "He was the sort of gent who would lay his hand to anything. He had been sniffing around behind Dust-Mouth and his make-believe ore. Edmund snared him, too, and signed him up. That's why he jumped me. He wanted me to get into a riot and get my car searched. He missed, and when Tonto Charlie mysteriously turned up with Free-Look's knife in his throat, he got too hot. Edmund put him away. How did Edmund get to Heliotrope?"

"With Susan Sally and me," MacAdoo said.

"I thought so. That's what she wanted to tell me, wasn't it?"

"Yes. Edmund talked too much in front of her. I may have done a little of that myself, at one time or another."

"Edmund killed her. Very neatly, too. She didn't know he had done it until she was dead"

"Very neatly," MacAdoo agreed. "They teach you those things at the *Ordensburgen.*"

"He took her up in the elevator," Doan said. "He tripped her when she got out, didn't he?"

"Yes," said MacAdoo.

"And when she fell he fell on top of her, hard."

"Yes," said MacAdoo.

"He knocked the breath out of her and stabbed her in that instant. He knew just how and where. Then he picked her up and brushed her off and apologized. She was dying right then, but she didn't know it. It takes a little while, with that kind of a stab wound, for the pain to catch up with you."

"Yes," MacAdoo said woodenly.

"She thought she was just breathless and bruised a bit. Edmund steered her toward my apartment and then ran downstairs and started figuring on his radio diagram. That was very clever. He was so obviously right on the spot that he figured I wouldn't believe it. Aside from that, he's a swell actor, and he's just stupid enough to take all kinds of screwy risks without counting up the odds against him. He knew what I was going to do before I did it most of the time. He listened in on all my telephone conversations and spied on me in every other way he could find. He was in the luggage compartment again when I went to see Dust-Mouth first last night. At that time he still thought Dust-Mouth might have something. He prevented Dust-Mouth from telling me what it was. And then he tried to point the finger at you."

"Me?" said Blue.

"Yeah. He knew you were a phony, but not what kind of a one."

"Do you know?" said Blue. "Sure. Since you shaved."

"What?" Harriet snapped.

"Haven't you spotted him yet? Blue is just his nickname. His real name is Roger Laws. Blue Laws, they call him."

"Whu-whu-whu-what?"

"How are the eyes now?" Doan asked Blue.

"Okay. I'll be able to ditch these glasses soon."

Harriet screamed.

Blue glanced at her with distaste. "What now?"

"You're the ace! The fighter pilot! Tuh-twenty-five enemy planes!"

"Twenty-seven," Doan corrected.

"You're a huh-hero!" Harriet wailed. "You were sh-shot down in flames!"

"Three times," Blue agreed sourly. "And don't talk to me about German planes and pilots. I don't fall five miles for fun. Anybody that knocks me down has to be better than I am, and I'm damned good."

"Oh—my—yes!"

"Shut up."

"Oh! You're won-wonderful!"

"Oh, nuts," said Blue.

"Why the dumbbell act?" Doan inquired.

Blue jerked his thumb at Harriet. "After this performance, you can ask?"

Harriet reached out her hand and touched his sleeve reverently with her fingertips.

"Get away," said Blue. Harriet stared at him, shiny-eyed.

"Oh, my God!" Blue snarled. "Will you stop that? Listen. I like to fly. I like to shoot planes down. It's very interesting work. It pays well. I even get a pension when I retire."

"You mean—if," said Doan.

"Ooooh," said Harriet.

"Get away from me! Damn you, I acted as dumb as I could to get rid of you, but no matter how I tried I couldn't act one tenth as dumb as you can without trying!"

"Yes, Blue," said Harriet, entranced.

"You've got no more brains than a rabbit."

"No, Blue."

"You make me sick."

"Yes, Blue. I love you."

"Oh, shut up."

"Now I can die happily—with you."

"Dying is no fun," Blue said. "I've already tried it a couple times."

MacAdoo was looking more worried now. "I wish I'd known. I wish I had."

"What eats him?" Blue asked Doan.

"Goering," said Doan.

"Come again?"

"You shoot down Goering's men. MacAdoo loves you like a brother for that."

MacAdoo nodded. "I only wish I'd known. I'd have thought of something else. Now it's too late."

"Maybe not," said Doan.

MacAdoo said, "I'll shoot if you move your hands again."

"Edmund, dear Edmund," said Doan, "please come home to me now."

"Where is Edmund?" Blue inquired slowly.

"Ah," said Doan knowingly.

Watching Doan, MacAdoo took a drink out of his flask and put it down again carefully on the floor beside him.

"Of course," Doan said judicially, "MacAdoo wouldn't have to wait for Edmund. He could just shoot us."

"Could he?" said Blue.

There was a little film of sweat on MacAdoo's forehead. "Sit still," he said.

"I'm not moving a muscle," said Doan. "Neither is Blue. Are you?"

"Nope," said Blue. "I wonder if Edmund got lost."

"Sure," said Doan. "That's it. He's wandering around in the desert, with nothing to drink but a flash flood."

"Too bad," said Blue, "but then MacAdoo was going to kill him anyway. Why?"

"He killed Susan Sally," said Doan. "He shouldn't have done that. She was worth five and a quarter a week to MacAdoo."

"Shut up," said MacAdoo thinly.

"Why, sure," said Doan.

The rain clattered nerve-rackingly on the tin above them and gurgled and choked under the eaves.

MacAdoo sighed a little and got up from the nail keg. He began to move toward the door, side-stepping carefully. He reached it and felt for the latch with his left hand, keeping the revolver leveled in his right.

The latch clicked, and MacAdoo pulled the door open and turned his head quickly. He didn't have time to do anything else voluntarily. Carstairs must have been about ten feet away, waiting, and he had started to run as soon as the door moved. His chest hit MacAdoo shoulder high with the force of a battering ram, and his jaws snapped across MacAdoo's face with an ugly, sliding squeak of teeth on bone.

MacAdoo went clear the length of the shack and hit the back wall hard enough to bulge it. He slammed down full length on the floor with both hands clapped over his face and the blood running red and thick through his fingers. He began to shriek in a high, bubbling voice, writhing around in blind circles on the floor, arching his body up in the middle.

Doan was on his feet instantly. He caught Carstairs by the collar and hauled, exerting all his strength.

"Back! Back!"

Carstairs allowed himself to go back one reluctant step.

Doan nodded to Blue and then pointed at MacAdoo. "Hold him down."

Blue got up and then knelt with one knee on MacAdoo's chest. MacAdoo kept right on shrieking. Doan measured carefully and then kicked. His toe caught MacAdoo in the temple. MacAdoo's head jarred sideways, and then his body loosened and went limp. He stopped shrieking.

"He was right," Doan said thoughtfully. "Come to think of it, I don't believe he will look the same tomorrow."

"Oh, oh, oh, oh," Harriet moaned.

"Shut up," said Blue. "Did you want him yelling like that all the way back to town?"

Harriet made little gulping sounds.

Blue sat down beside her and put his arm around her shoulders. He pulled her head against his chest.

"Okay. It wasn't nice to see. Don't look any more."

"I was scu-scared."

"Hell, so was I."

"I love you."

"Sure," said Blue.

There was a silence.

"Go ahead and say it," Doan ordered. "She deserves it."

"I love you, too," said Blue reluctantly. "Oh, Blue. Oh."

"Let's take a look at you," Doan said to Carstairs. "Oh-oh. Too dumb to duck, huh?"

There was a deep red groove through the muscles of Carstairs' shoulder, and blood had run down from it and formed in ugly clots on his chest and leg.

"What happened to Edmund?" Blue asked.

"They probably taught him about tracking in the spy school," Doan said absently. "But I guess they forgot to tell him that when you're tracking something like Carstairs, you should watch behind as well as in front. Carstairs just circled and jumped on his back when he went by. I'm afraid dear old Edmund is deader than a doornail."

"How can you be sure of that?"

"It makes Carstairs mad to be shot. Offhand I can't think of anyone who ever did it that lived to talk about it, and Edmund wouldn't be the exception. Hold still."

Doan picked up MacAdoo's flask and straddled Carstairs, one leg on either side of him.

"This'll hurt, maybe."

He poured from the flask carefully. Carstairs grunted and arched his back violently. Doan sat down hard on the floor, carefully holding the flask right side up.

"Okay," he said. He sniffed once and then grinned. "Ahem. Have you been drinking, my friend?"

Very slowly Carstairs turned his head toward his shoulder and sniffed. Just as slowly he turned his head back to look at Doan.

"Aw, now," said Doan. "I was only clowning."

Carstairs turned around and started for the door. Doan

scrooched along hurriedly, bump-bottom fashion, and grabbed him by the tail.

"Wait! Can't you take a joke?"

Carstairs sat down with his back to him.

Doan scrooched around in front of him. "Now, look. I had to put something on that groove, or it'd have gotten infected. Would you like to go to a dog hospital and associate with a lot of curs with only ordinary pedigrees?"

Carstairs turned his head aside.

"Look, Carstairs," Doan said. "Look."

He tilted the flask and swallowed in big gulps. He choked and then held the flask over his head and sprinkled liquor over himself like a shower.

"See? Now if you just stay close to me everyone will think I'm drunk and they're smelling me. Get it? I'm drunk. Whoopee. Wheee."

Carstairs looked at him for a long time in a thoughtful, dispassionate way. Doan beamed back. Carstairs fetched a sigh from the bottom of his heart and then lay down and closed his eyes in soul-weary resignation.

CRY MURDER!

Introducing Carstairs, who's almost human…
Doan, who's almost bloodhound… and a road which
stretched through the night to—trackless murder!

CHAPTER I

CANINE COPPER

THE STATION WAGON trundled around the corner into the narrow, deeply shaded street, idled down the block with scarcely a whisper from its motor, and parked in at the curb. This was no ordinary station wagon by any manner of means. It was a custom job, and in the good old days when you could buy such things it had set its owner back just $3,987.92 F.O.B. Michigan plus tax.

It looked something like a sportily streamlined combination of a limousine and a high-class hearse.

Doan was driving it. He was plump and not very tall, neatly and soberly dressed in a gray business suit, and he had a round, unlined face and a complexion like a baby on a supervised diet. He was a very innocent and nice and harmless appearing person, but that was all strictly camouflage. He was innocent and nice only when it paid him, and he was as harmless as a rattlesnake.

"We're here," he said, looking over his shoulder.

The back seat of the station wagon ran around in a semi-circle to fit the rear contour of the body, and it was designed to seat six persons comfortably. Carstairs was filling it all up, now, and dangling over the edges here and there. He was snoring with gentle gusto.

"Hey, stupid," said Doan.

Carstairs opened one eye and watched him.

"Come on," said Doan. "You've slept long enough."

He opened the door beside him and slid out into the street

and then opened the rear door. Carstairs mumbled under his breath and began to assemble himself in sections, cracking his joints and grunting with the effort.

Carstairs was a dog, but it would be impossible just to let it go at that. In the first place he was a Great Dane, and in the second place he was enormous. Standing on four feet, after he had untangled himself and climbed out into the street, his back came up even with Doan's solar plexus. Had Carstairs worked up energy enough to stand on his hind legs he could have looked right over Doan's head, hat and all, without the slightest effort.

"You see that wall over there?" Doan asked.

Carstairs examined the wall across the street from them with disapproval. It was really something in the way of a wall. It was two stories high and made of gray granite blocks that looked cold and sullenly unyielding in the morning sunlight.

"There's a prison behind it," Doan said.

"A prison is a place where they put criminals—well, not all of them, as you very well know, but the ones they catch. Keep that in mind in the future."

Carstairs grunted and sat down. The sun hadn't risen high enough to shine on the pavement as yet, and it was cold. Carstairs stood up again, muttering disgustedly deep in his throat.

Doan pointed. "That small door there is where they let the criminals out after they're through with them. Keep your eye on it."

CARSTAIRS watched the door without any noticeable signs of interest. The street was very quiet, and the tree shadows made motionless, dappled patterns along the base of the prison wall. Somewhere a clock began to strike the hour with sullen, rumbling booms. It was ten o'clock.

"Just right," said Doan.

There was the cold rattle and snap of bolts, and then the recessed door in the wall opened and a man stepped out through it and stood hesitantly on the sidewalk. The door closed behind him with a sharp clack. The man winced slightly. Then he pulled in a deep breath of free air and started up the street.

"Hey, you," Doan called.

The man stopped short and half turned, and Doan crooked his ringer invitingly. "Come here."

The man hesitated again and then walked slowly across the street. He was young, and he was dressed in a brown tweed suit that had cost quite a lot some time ago. He had black, close-cropped hair and heavy black brows and contemptuous brown eyes with little greenish flecks in them. His lips were thin and hard and twisted down a little at one corner. He stared silently at Doan.

"Are you Bradfield Owens?" Doan asked.

"Yes."

"I'm Doan," said Doan. "This is Carstairs. He's my assistant, or else I'm his. We've never straightened out the relationship."

"Very interesting," Owens said. "So what?"

"Colonel Ephriam Morris got you paroled," Doan told him. "It was quite a job. Parole boards are a little leery of guys who go around sticking knives in people and stuff like that. He wants to see you."

"What if I don't want to see him?"

"Just go right over and rap on that door," Doan answered. "They'll let you back in."

Owens shrugged. "Okay. Where's Morris?"

"Where he always is. On his farm. That's where we're going to take you."

"What am I supposed to do when I get there?"

"Run the damned place," Doan said. "What did you think Colonel Morris got you paroled for—just because he liked your pretty brown eyes?"

"No," Owens said grimly. "I didn't think that. Well, let's go."

IT WAS dusk now, and Doan was still driving. The road looped in long, loose curves through country that was just slightly rolling.

"I've only driven this road once before," Doan said. "We're pretty near there, aren't we?"

Owens nodded. "Yes."

"I don't hear any loud cheers from you."

"No," said Owens glumly.

Carstairs grunted and complained to himself, shifting around

"I'll give you five minutes to scram before I loose Carstairs," Doan said.

in the back seat, and then snuffled meaningly just behind Doan's right ear.

"Okay," said Doan. "Screw-loose, back there, wants a drink and a walk. Is there any place we can stop near here?"

"Yes. Cleek's Mill is just around that curve ahead. It's abandoned, but there's still a dam and a mill pond."

Carstairs snuffled more urgently.

"All right," said Doan. "I hear you."

"He's a nice dog," Owens remarked.

"Well, no," Doan said. "Not exactly nice. As a matter of fact, he's meaner than hell."

"I meant that he was a good specimen. He's one of the finest Great Danes I've ever seen."

"He is the finest you've ever seen. He's got four hundred and eighty-nine blue ribbons to prove it, but they weren't judging him on his good disposition. He doesn't have one."

"Did he cost a lot?"

"He didn't cost me anything. I won him in a crap game. Of course the up-keep is a little heavy. He eats three times as much as I do. I wouldn't mind that so much if he'd only act a little grateful when I give him my meat coupons."

"Doesn't he?"

"No. He goes around sneering because I'm not allowed more. He acts as if rationing is something I dreamed up just to annoy him."

Carstairs made an ominous, rumbling sound.

"All *right!*" said Doan.

The road swung around in a sharp curve, and the mill loomed to their right, blending into the thick shadow of the trees close behind it. It was a two-story brick building with a steeply peaked roof, the harshness of its outline blurred and melted by the thick growth of vine that covered it. The windows gaped like dark, empty eyes. The creek that ran along the road had been dammed to make a pool that gleamed deep and smoothly stagnant.

Doan bumped the station wagon along a weed-grown lane that ran up to the wreck of a loading platform, and then he stopped with a sudden jerk. They could see on the far side of the building now, and there were two figures facing each other in the shadow. One was crowded in against the wall, and the other loomed over it in gaunt and gangling menace. They were too interested in each other to have seen or heard the station wagon.

Doan turned off the motor. "What's all this?" he asked.

The figure crowded in against the wall was a woman—short and dumpy in a shiny black silk dress and wearing steel-rimmed glasses set a little askew on her pudgy nose. She was holding a short, crooked stick in her hand.

"Aw!" said the gangling figure, making little tentative grabs at the stick. "You're scared! You don't even dare hit me! Yah!"

This one was what could be roughly called a youth. He had

hulking shoulders and a lop-sided, out-of-proportion face with loosely blubbering lips. He wore an old pair of overalls and a stained shirt and a dirty slouch hat with the brim ripped off on one side.

He feinted again at the stick in the woman's hand and then suddenly grabbed it and twisted it away from her.

"Now," he said, malignantly gleeful. "Now what you gonna do, huh?"

"**THAT'S** Toady Turnbull," Owens said. He flipped the catch on the station wagon door and stepped out. "Joady! Quit that! Leave her alone!"

Joady Turnbull swung around with a sort of awkward grace. He stared unbelievingly, his lips loose and slack in his smeared caricature of a face.

"Brad Owens," he said. "Brad Owens. They went and let you out of the jail."

"Yes," said Owens.

Joady Turnbull made a thick, choking noise. "And you got the nerve to come back! You think you're gonna get away with that?"

"I think so," said Owens. "And I think that you're going to stop annoying Miss Carson."

"You gonna make me?"

"Yes," said Owens.

"How?" Joady Turnbull jeered. "You think you're gonna stab me, too? In the back?"

"No," said Owens evenly. "I'll just break your neck."

"But not now," said Doan, getting out of the car. "I'll tend to that if it's necessary. Listen, goon, run along and haunt some other neighborhood."

"I know you," Joady Turnbull said. "You're that city detective old Morris brought down. You don't scare me none."

"Then you're even more simple than you act," Doan told him. He opened the rear door of the station wagon, and Carstairs got out. Joady Turnbull backed away two steps. "I heard about that there damned big dog."

Doan nudged Carstairs with his knee and said, "Woof."

Carstairs bayed suddenly. It was a solid, rocking blast of sound with a deep undertone of savagery in it. Joady Turnbull backed away three more steps, stumbling a little. Carstairs watched him with eyes that gleamed greenish in the dusk.

Doan said, "If you're not out of sight in five seconds, I'll have him give you a little demonstration that his bite is worse than his bark. Get on your horse and gallop."

It took Joady Turnbull the count of two to absorb that. Then he whirled around and fell over a bush and scrambled to his feet and ran. His feet slashed through the drift of fallen leaves, and then he disappeared in the thicket on beyond the mill.

Carstairs grunted contemptuously, shook himself in an irritated way. Then he strolled over to the mill pond and lapped the water, making a noise like rain on a tin roof and sending the ripples scurrying in frightened haste.

"Would he really have attacked Joady?" Owens asked.

"Sure," said Doan. "He likes nothing better than to bite people. He won't hurt you, lady."

The woman was still crowded back against the mill wall. She had been watching Carstairs with a sort of fascinated horror, and now she looked at Doan with her eyes wide and dilated behind the steel-rimmed spectacles.

"D-dogs frighten me," she said with a little catch in her voice. "I—I thank you for—for interfering...."

"Aren't you going to say hello to me, Norma?" Owens asked.

"Yes! Of course, Brad! I'm so upset—Joady and you and the dog...."

"I'm here, too," Doan reminded her.

"This is Mr. Doan, Norma," Owens said. "Apparently he is my—ah—guardian for the time being. Doan, this is Norma Carson. She teaches the lower grades in the Ramsey village school."

"Pleased," said Doan. "Who was the ghoul we just chased off?"

Norma Carson looked uneasily at Owens and then away again. "That was Joady Turnbull."

"I suspected that," said Doan. "Is this the way he usually goes on, or was he celebrating some special occasion today?"

Norma Carson said, "You see—I refused to have him attend any longer the grades I teach in school…."

"I may be wrong," Doan remarked, "but he looked a little elderly to be attending the lower grades."

"He's a moron," said Norma Carson. "I mean, really he is. He just can't learn anything, and he's so much older and larger than the other children, and he does things in school he shouldn't and—and—"

"And," Doan agreed. "I get the picture. If he bothers you again, tell him Carstairs and I will pay him a social call. We love morons. We feel right at home."

"Are you a parole officer?" Norma Carson asked.

"Right now," Doan said. "It's nice work if you can get it—I hope."

Owens said, "Norma, can we give you a lift into town?"

She shook her head. "No, thank you, Brad. I have my coupe. It's parked up the road. I came to the mill, here, because I'd heard there were some swallows nesting in it. I wanted to show their nests to the children. But Joady came while I was watching for them."

Carstairs came back to the car and sat down with a self-satisfied sigh.

Doan rapped him on top of the head with the knuckle of his forefinger and said, "Get in the car, dumbness."

Carstairs climbed in and dumped himself on the back seat so enthusiastically that the springs groaned in protest.

"Brad," said Norma Carson hesitantly, "are you going back to The Square?"

Owens shrugged. "Apparently I am."

"After all that has happened?"

"I don't have any choice, Norma."

"Jessica is there."

Owens frowned. "I was hoping she wasn't."

"I *hate* this town and all the nasty, mean-minded people in it for what they've done to you, Brad!" Norma said. "And that goes for Jessica Morris, too."

"I lived through it," Owens said. "Forget it. We'll have to run along. Good night, Norma."

THEY got back into the car and Doan turned it around and bumped out along the lane again to the main road. Every once in a while Owens silently pointed out the turns to be taken in the roads.

"You might sort of explain this and that to me," Doan requested, "just so I can pretend I know what the score is here."

"You know, of course, that I murdered a man," Owens said.

"That's nothing to brag about," Doan told him. "I've finished off a couple of dozen more or less in my time."

"I stabbed this one in the back."

"I've never used that method," Doan said. "I'll have to give it a ring some time. What was this party's name, as if it mattered?"

"It does matter. His name was Turnbull."

"So?" said Doan. "Any relation to the mental giant we just met?"

"Yes. His father."

Doan nodded. "Well, that might explain the way he acted when he recognized you, although if heredity means anything I'd say you did the boob a favor. Was the old man as stagnant in the head as the kid?"

"Even worse. He was stupid in a sort of mean, vicious way that grated on everyone's nerves."

"What did you kill him for?"

Owens sighed. "We gave him work sometimes as an extra hand when we were short of help. This particular time he was harrowing with a tractor over in the north field. It was a new tractor. I told him several times to watch the oil and water and not let it get too hot. He let the water boil out, and then he was too lazy or too contrary to walk two hundred yards to get some more. He ran the tractor until the engine seized. When I came around to see what he was doing, he was pounding the block with a wrench. The motor was ruined."

"What'd you do?"

"I lost my temper."

"Imagine that now," Doan commented. "Just over a little matter like that. What then?"

"I bawled him out, plenty."

"Did it kill him?"

"Not that, no. He got nasty and threw the wrench at me."

"The Turnbulls are certainly an attractive family," Doan said. "Did he hit you?"

"Yes. In the head. I don't remember a thing that happened after that."

Doan glanced at him sideways.

Owens shrugged. "Believe it or not, I honestly don't. When I came to, I was in the hospital under police guard."

Doan said, "I had an idea when this started that we were going to talk about a murder."

"We are. According to the evidence, Turnbull started to run after he threw the wrench at me. I threw my knife at him and hit him in the back when he was about twenty feet away."

"Whose evidence?" Doan inquired.

"There were no witnesses. The field is not close to any houses, and there was no one else near. The evidence was the tracks on the ground, my knife in Turnbull, and the positions we were lying in when we were found."

"Uh," said Doan. "It seems to me that the matter of self-defense might come in there somewhere."

"No," said Owens. "Turnbull was running away when the knife struck him. He wasn't attacking me."

"Uh," Doan repeated. "It seems to me, just offhand, that there's something missing in this little tale."

Owens nodded slowly. "Colonel Morris."

"How does he fit in?"

"He's very unpopular around here. He's accumulated about five thousand acres of the finest farm-land in the state through some pretty sharp deals in mortgage foreclosures. He owns the bank in Ramsey."

"He runs the bank, so they put you in jail," said Doan. "Well, maybe it makes sense."

Owens cleared his throat. "You see, lots of people are anxious to get back at him for one thing and another—and, well, I was supposed to be his prospective son-in-law. It seemed a good chance to hit him through me."

"A little tough on you," Doan observed. "This son-in-law thing. Let's look at that a little more closely."

"I was engaged to his daughter."

"Was?" Doan said.

"Yes."

CHAPTER II

CARSTAIRS ACCEPTS A CASE

"OPEN UP A little," Doan invited. "Are you engaged to Colonel Morris' daughter now?"

"Certainly not," Owens said.

"Did she give you the brush-off when they put you in the pokey?"

Owens stared at him, narrow-eyed. "Is this any of your business?"

"Oh, hell no," said Doan amiably. "I just ask questions because I've got nothing else to do until I get to this farm."

"Then what are you going to do?"

"Ask more questions—of other people."

"Ask them of me, instead."

"You're a hard guy to please," Doan observed. "That was just what I was doing. Did this party of the second part give you the brush-off?"

"Her name is Jessica Morris, and she did. Now are you happy?"

"Oh, very," Doan said. "Are you?"

Owens said slowly, "You're going to carry this matter a little too far, friend."

"Probably," Doan admitted. "I've got no sense of discretion. Are you? Happy, I mean?"

"No, you fool! Would you be?"

"All depends," said Doan. "How does this Jessica stack up? Bowlegged? Knock-kneed? Halitosis? Poisonous personality?"

"No!"

"I only asked," Doan said. "I didn't see her when I was down here before. What kind of a brush-off did she hand you?"

Owens breathed deeply. "Very kind. Very polite. Very diplomatic. She believed in me. She trusted me. She blubbered all day long at my trial. She wrote me nice letters when I was in prison—affectionate at first and getting less and less so all the time. Finally I received a clipping from the Ramsey paper. She was engaged to a man named Gretorex."

"Cute," said Doan. "Is she married to him now?"

"I don't know."

"Who is he?"

"He's a gentleman farmer—so he says."

"Oh," said Doan.

"He hunts foxes—on a horse."

"Tally-ho," said Doan. "Does the dame go for that brand of daffiness?"

"I suppose so. She evidently goes for him. And the colonel likes him."

"There's no accounting for tastes," Doan comforted. "This Norma Carson, the school-ma'am, doesn't seem to think so highly of Jessica."

"She's prejudiced. You see, she and I were raised in the same small town. We've known each other all our lives. She thinks the setup here prejudiced the jury against me and that if it hadn't been for the colonel and Jessica, too, that I would never have been convicted in the circumstances. Jessica didn't seem to care about what happened to me."

"What do you think?" Doan asked.

Owens scowled. "I don't know. The colonel is hated. I don't think he's technically dishonest, but he's very sharp and slippery in a business deal, and he doesn't have any more mercy than a weasel."

"Well," said Doan, "it looks like things are a bit complicated here. It's a good thing the colonel hired me to sort of straighten them out."

Owens snorted. "How do you think you're going to do that?"

"I'm a genius. I don't have to think. I just sit down and wait for an inspiration."

"You'll need one," Owens said sourly.

"Where do we turn?" Doan asked.

"The next block to the right."

"There it is," said Owens after awhile. "The show place of the county. All lit up like a wedding cake, as usual."

The house sprawled across a fold of ground up and back from the road. The architect who had designed it had taken a good long look at Monticello and Mt. Vernon and other colonial show places before he had started working.

Fine gravel rattled under the station wagon's fenders as Doan wheeled up the long, curving drive, and stopped opposite the front door.

"Ah, there!" a voice boomed at them. "Hello!"

The man was at the top of the veranda steps, looming huge and solidly confident, with the light gleaming sleekly on his bald head. He was dressed in tan trousers and a tan tweed jacket and a darker tan shirt. He looked like the country squire in a whiskey advertisement. He beamed and rubbed his hands joyfully and came hurrying down the steps.

"Ah, there, Doan. It's a pleasure to see you again. And you brought him with you? Ah, yes! I knew you would. I had every confidence in you. Brad, my boy! Brad! Welcome home, lad!"

"Hello, Colonel," Owens said, getting out of the car.

Colonel Morris clapped him on the shoulder. "Why, you're looking fit, lad! Yes, you are! And it's good to see you! Indeed, it is! I could hardly curb my impatience. I swear, I've been pacing the floor all day."

"I've done that a few times, too," said Owens.

"Eh? Oh, yes. Of course. But it's past now, my boy! Past and done with and better forgotten. Now just step right in here, lad, and…. Eh? Oh, yes. Here's Jessica."

She was standing on the veranda, a little out of the pathway of light thrown from the front door. She was wearing a white dress, and her hair gleamed darkly lustrous in the shadow. She made no move to come closer.

"Jessica," said Colonel Morris. "It's Brad Owens come back from… well, come back."

"She knows where I've come from," Owens said.

"Hello, Brad," Jessica said evenly.

Owens nodded politely. "Hello."

"Eh!" said Colonel Morris. "Well…."

"Ahem," said Doan.

"Oh!" said Colonel Morris. "Yes. Surely. This is Doan, the

detective fellow, Jessica. You remember I told you he was fetching Brad from the… from the city."

"Hi, Jessica," said Doan.

"What?" said Colonel Morris, startled. "Here! This is my daughter!"

"I wouldn't even count that against her," Doan assured him. "Are you going to leave her all your dough when you croak?"

"Well, of course I— What do you mean, sir?"

"I was only asking," Doan said. "I wouldn't know as much as I do if I didn't ask people things. Are you married, Jessica?"

"No," said Jessica.

"Somebody should do something about that," Doan said. "Aside from the dough you're a pretty neat little number just as you stand. Don't you think so, Owens?"

"That's immaterial," said Owens coldly.

"Not in my book, it isn't." Doan denied. "You don't find girls with figures like Jessica's and dough, too, on every street-corner. I know, because I've looked."

"Here, you!" the colonel bellowed furiously. "Stop your infernal insolence! I'm your employer, sir!"

"You'll find that out when I present my bill," Doan assured him. "Well, let's go inside where it's comfortable and sit down and have a long chat about the political situation. Jessica and Owens probably want to talk, too."

"We have nothing to talk about," Owens said coldly.

"No," said Jessica. "Good night."

SHE WALKED across the porch and through the front door.

Colonel Morris scowled at Doan. "Sir, I resent your attitude and your words. Hereafter, if you find it necessary to address my daughter at all, do so with more courtesy."

"Okay," said Doan. "But I'll have to charge more for special service like that. Are we going to stand out here and gab all night? I'm tired."

Colonel Morris breathed deeply. "Come in the house, please.

I have some matters to take up with you, Doan. Brad, your clothes and personal effects are in your old room in the left wing."

"I'll go there now," Owens said. "This has been rather a long and busy day for me."

"Would you like Cecil to get you something to eat?"

"No, thanks," Owens said. He turned to his left and walked on along the veranda.

Colonel Morris nodded at Doan. "Come with me."

They started toward the front door, and then Colonel Morris stopped and pointed a stiff, accusing forefinger.

"Do you propose to take *that* into the house?"

"Carstairs?" Doan said. "Yes. He's afraid of the dark, and when he's scared he howls."

"Well, let him howl!" Colonel Morris sputtered.

"Oh, no," said Doan. "You've never heard him. The last time he let loose he broke three plate glass windows and stopped a grandfather clock dead in its tracks."

Carstairs settled the argument by pacing dignifiedly through the front door into the hall. Colonel Morris followed him, muttering to himself. Doan trailed along behind them down the hall and into a room that had been fixed up as a combination study, den, and office by someone who had expensive, if not very original, taste.

There was a fireplace with a high, broad mantel cluttered up with ship models and hunting prints on the wall and an enormous flat executive's desk in one corner and deep leather chairs.

Doan sat down in one of the chairs, sighing. "I could use a drink now," he observed.

"Humph!" said Colonel Morris. He picked up a square, cut-glass decanter from the stand beside the desk and looked at it. It was empty.

"Cecil!" he shouted. *"Ce-cil!"*

The rear door of the study opened, and a man put his head

inside. He was bald, and he had a limp, corn-colored mustache and eyes that were just slightly crossed.

"You're gonna bust a gut sometime, yellin' like that," he said. "What you want?"

"There's no whiskey in the decanter!"

"Of course not," said Cecil. "You drank it."

"Bring some more!"

"I was goin' to in a minute. Just keep your pants on, will you?"

He pulled his head back, and the door swung shut.

Colonel Morris slammed around behind his desk and sat down with a thump. "Insolence!" he seethed, the veins in his cheeks standing out in bright, cherry-red knots. "Nothing but insolence. The world is going to the dogs, sir!"

"If it does," Doan said, indicating Carstairs, "I'll get my share."

Carstairs was sitting in the middle of the floor, examining the room with an air of supercilious disapproval. Cecil opened the door and came back in the room. He was carrying a white crockery jug. He pulled the cork out with his teeth and poured liquor from the jug into the decanter. The liquor was just off the color of water, slightly yellowish, with an oily, smooth thickness.

When the decanter was full, Cecil upped the jug in the crook of his elbow and took a long pull out of it.

"You the detective?" he asked, glaring at Doan.

"Right," said Doan.

"I don't like detectives," Cecil said flatly.

"Oh, you'll like me, though," Doan said. "I'm something special."

"You'll be something dead if you don't stay out of my kitchen," Cecil assured him. "I'm the cook around this dump, and I don't like snoopers, and what I say goes. The dead-line of my bailiwick is right at that door there. Don't cross it."

"That'll do, Cecil," Colonel Morris said.

"Don't interrupt me," Cecil ordered. "I don't have to work here, you know. I can get a job any time for twice the dough you're paying me and meet a better class of people at that. I suppose I've got to feed that cross between a water buffalo and a giraffe, too."

"Yes," said Doan, "but you'll love him when you get to know him. He has a beautiful character."

"Hah!" said Cecil skeptically. "What does he eat?"

"Steaks," said Doan.

"What kind?"

Doan stared. "You mean you've got a choice?"

"Hell, yes," said Cecil. "I've got a couple of cows hung out in the freezer. I can hack off any kind of a piece you want."

"OH, FOR the life of a farmer," Doan commented. "I think a filet would do nicely for him. About two pounds. Grind it up and just warm it in the oven. Don't cook it. You might dig up one for me, too, when you get through with him."

"Okay," said Cecil. "Come on, clumsy."

"Go with the nice man, Carstairs," Doan ordered. "He's got a steak for you. Steak. Meat." He licked his lips elaborately.

Carstairs stared at him incredulously.

"Fact," Doan assured him. "Real meat."

Carstairs instantly heaved himself to his feet and started for the door, eyes narrowed in anticipation. Cecil held the door open for him and then nodded meaningly at Colonel Morris.

"Don't go and drink yourself dumb, now. You know the doc told you to lay off the stuff."

"Get out of here!" Colonel Morris shouted furiously. "Mind your own damned business!"

"Pooey to you," said Cecil, closing the door emphatically behind him.

"Insolence," Colonel Morris muttered. "Unmitigated, infernal insolence, no matter where I turn!"

"It's enough to drive a man to drink," Doan agreed. "Are you going to?"

"Eh? Oh, yes. Here."

Colonel Morris took two out-sized shot glasses from the rack under the stand, poured liquor into them, and handed one to Doan. Doan drank it.

The liquor felt as smooth and slick as plush in his throat.

"Like it?" Colonel Morris asked.

"Sort of tasteless," Doan said. "Pretty weak stuff, too, isn't it?"

Someone suddenly set off a small charge of blasting powder in Doan's stomach. The room tipped up at one corner, spun around three times, and settled back slowly and gently.

"Weak?" the colonel repeated softly.

"Wow!" said Doan, swallowing hard. "No. I take that back. What is it, anyway?"

"Just corn liquor. Cecil makes it. That's why it's necessary for me to put up with his boorish impertinence. He has a still hidden somewhere here on The Square. He won't give me his recipe or even show me his methods."

"Can't you find the still?"

Colonel Morris chuckled. "No. Cecil is an old-time moonshiner. Sheriff Derwin has caught pneumonia twice sitting out all night on Fagan's Hill watching with night glasses and trying to spot Cecil visiting his hide-out. Derwin would like nothing better than to bring a moonshining charge against Cecil and against me as his employer. Will you have another drink?"

"No, thanks," said Doan. "That stuff goes a little rough on an empty stomach."

"Then to business," said Colonel Morris. "Do you know why I hired you for this particular job?"

"Sure," said Doan. "Because I've got such a world-wide reputation as a brilliant detective."

"No," said Colonel Morris. "Hardly. I made many inquiries

from official sources. I was informed that you were shrewd, violent, tricky and completely unscrupulous."

Doan shook his head sadly. "That's nothing but slander. I devote all my time to good works."

"I can imagine," said Colonel Morris dryly. "However, if you can curb your blasted impudence, I think we will get along." He leaned forward and tapped his stubby fingers impressively on the desk top. "I anticipate trouble, Doan. A lot of it."

"Trouble is my business," said Doan.

"I SUPPOSE you've had sufficient initiative to make inquiries of Brad Owens about the death that occurred here?" the colonel asked.

"We talked about it some."

"Good. That was a most vicious miscarriage of justice. If the jury hadn't been composed exclusively of half-wits and enemies of mine, he would never have been convicted in the circumstances. As it was, it took me two years and every bit of influence I have to secure his release even on parole. There is a great deal of bitterness in the neighborhood because I was even able to do that. You are to see that the bitterness doesn't take any—ah—material form."

"I get it," said Doan. "If anybody opens his mouth, I bat him down."

"That is putting the idea crudely but lucidly," Colonel Morris agreed. "I feel that Owens is almost a son to me, and I will not have him persecuted further."

"And besides," Doan added, "you need him to manage your farm."

Colonel Morris' red, overripe face darkened slightly. "That is the kind of remark I would prefer that you keep to yourself. Such cynicism sickens me."

"Me, too," Doan agreed. "All right, I'll sort of walk around behind Owens and interview anybody who sticks out his tongue. How long does this go on?"

"If there is trouble—and I believe there will be, as I said—it will come soon. Resentment of the sort felt against Owens—and me—shows itself immediately."

There was a furious, strangled yell from the rear of the house, and an instant later the door burst open and Cecil raged into the room.

"What kind of an animal is that you own?" he yelled at Doan. "Was he raised in a pigsty?"

"Yes," said Doan, "but a very clean one. What did he do this time?"

"He sneezed in my cake dough! After I fed him! What kind of manners is that? He sneezed right in it on purpose and blew it the hell all over the drain board!"

"What did *you* do?" Doan asked. "Before he sneezed, I mean?"

"Why, I just took a short snort of corn, is all."

Doan sighed. "That was it. Carstairs disapproves of drinking—violently. The smell of alcohol gives him the pip."

Cecil gasped. "You mean to say he won't even let me drink in peace in my own kitchen?"

"Probably not," Doan admitted.

"The hell with that noise!" Cecil shouted. "Then he ain't gonna eat in my kitchen! You hear me, Colonel? After this, that damned dog-eats in the dining room!"

"Here, here!" Colonel Morris echoed, aghast. "That infernal beast in the dining room? Impossible!"

"Impossible or not, that's where he gets served," Cecil snarled. "And he'd damned well better keep his nose out of my cake dough after this. You! Come out of that kitchen!"

Carstairs strolled unconcernedly through the door into the study. Once inside, he stopped short and turned his head slowly and ominously, glaring at the glass still in Doan's hand. Doan put it down quickly.

"I've only had one," he said.

Carstairs snorted in utter and contemptuous disbelief. He

walked over to the corner and lay down with his head in it and his back to the room.

Doan shrugged. "Oh, well. Since he's going to sulk about it, anyway, I might as well have another drink or two or even three. Roll out the barrel."

CHAPTER III

MURDER IN THE NIGHT

DOAN WAS LYING flat on his back in bed, gurgling peacefully in his sleep and blowing alcohol fumes at the ceiling, when an object that was cold and gruesomely moist pressed itself against his cheek. Doan woke up, but he wasn't startled at all. This had happened many times before. Carstairs' nose, properly applied, was a very effective alarm clock.

"All right," Doan said. "What's your trouble now?"

It was pitch dark, and he rolled over and fumbled for the reading lamp on the bed-stand and snapped it on. Carstairs was sitting on the floor at the head of the bed, watching him narrowly. Seeing that he had Doan's attention, he paced over to the door of the bed-room and stood looking at it.

"Listen, lame-brain," Doan said, "if you think I'm going to get up in the middle of night and escort you on a tour of the trees outside, you'd better start thinking all over again."

Carstairs looked over his shoulder, his ears flattened tight against his head. He growled very softly.

"So?" said Doan. "Some matter that needs my attention?"

Carstairs turned his head back to stare at the door.

"Coming right up," Doan said.

He got out of bed. He was wearing only the top of a pair of pajamas. He pulled on his trousers, put his suit coat on over his pajama jacket, and slid his bare feet into a pair of old moccasins he used for bedroom slippers. He jerked the bed covers back and unearthed a .38 Colt Police Positive and dropped it into his coat pocket.

"Let's go," he said.

He opened the bedroom door and bumped Carstairs in the rear with his knee, commandingly. They went out into the hall. It was darker even than the bedroom had been. Doan fumbled along the wall, and then Carstairs nudged in against him. Doan put his hand on Carstairs' spiked collar, and the dog led him, Seeing-Eye fashion, down the length of the hall toward the front of the house.

At the stairs, Carstairs stopped, and Doan felt out cautiously with one foot until he located the top step. They went on down into the smooth, stagnant blackness of the lower hall. Carstairs headed straight for the front door and stopped in front of it.

Doan snapped the night latch and opened the door. Outside, the moon was fat and red and bulging, low over the rim of hills that enclosed the valley, and in its thin light familiar objects assumed brooding, weirdly twisted shapes. The air was dry and cold and sharp in Doan's throat.

"If this is just a gag to give you a stroll in the moonlight, I'll beat your brains out," he threatened.

Carstairs ignored him. He was testing the faint stir of wind, head held first on one side and then the other. He went down

*The lumpy figure
lay very still.*

the steps of the veranda and trotted in a circle, muzzle lifted high. He stopped suddenly and looked back at Doan.

"Lead on," said Doan. "I'm with you."

Single file, they went along the front of the house and on past the west wing. Carstairs stopped again, made up his mind, and then angled down the back slope. There were shrubs here, high and shaggy in the moonlight, and they worked their way through them. A row of barns and out-buildings stretched, solid and sturdily white, ahead of them, and Doan could hear faintly the stab of hoofs on board and the rolling wet crunch of corn in animal teeth.

"I'm getting damned good and tired of this," Doan stated angrily. "Just what…."

A CREEK meandered across the pasture beyond the barns, and Carstairs was standing near a bend where it looped lazily back on itself in the lee of a dense, close-cropped clump of brush. His ears were pricked forward, and his shadow lay thin and spindly and black on the ground in front of him.

Doan came up to him quietly, alert now, his hand grasping the revolver in his coat pocket.

"What?" he whispered.

Carstairs rumbled deeply and softly in his throat.

Doan saw it, then, too. It was an object pushed in under the brush, lumpy and motionless and limp, with the dim light gleaming a little on the paleness of what could only have been a face.

Doan drew his gun. "I see you, bud," he said. "Just speak up nicely."

There was no answer, and the lumpy bundle did not stir. Doan cocked the revolver and then Carstairs moved in cautiously, his head lowered. He snorted suddenly and loudly.

"The hell," said Doan.

He moved in, too, shoving Carstairs aside with his knee. He leaned down and poked the bundle with the barrel of his revolver. It was a slack and solid weight. Doan poked harder, and the head rolled back so that the moon shone on the pallidness of the face.

"Joady Turnbull," said Doan softly. "Fancy meeting you here."

Joady Turnbull's eyes stared dully and sightlessly up at him. A trickle of blood, glistening black and jagged in the moonlight spread over his chin. Doan lifted him slightly and saw the knife handle sticking up, grimly solid, from his back just over his heart.

"Very neat," Doan commented.

He took hold of the handle and pulled the knife free with a little grunt of effort. He dropped Joady Turnbull, and the body rolled loosely back under the brush. Doan stood up and examined the knife. It was not graceful or deadly or designed for murder. It was a work-knife with a thick, broad blade that could be used for almost anything from pulling nails to cutting down a tree.

Doan stared at it, whistling noiselessly to himself, and then he stopped that and looked at Carstairs. Carstairs had turned his head and was watching a clump of willows that made a thick, dark clot on the far side of the pasture where the creek ran out into the next field. He began to pace toward it, stiff-legged, and Doan trailed right along behind him, the knife still open in his left hand, the revolver in his right.

They approached the willows slowly, circling a little, and then a voice said wearily:

"I'm right here, if you're looking for me."

"Well, well," said Doan. "Good evening and all that. We're not intruding. I trust."

"You are," said the voice. "But I don't suppose there's anything I can do about it. There's a path just to your left."

Carstairs found it, and Doan followed him along the tunneled blackness with the branches whipping stingingly across his face and the dried leaves whispering slyly together. There was a little opening here with the dappled, dark sheen of the creek moving slowly past. Owens was a bulking shadow seated on a fallen log beside the water.

"I saw you coming across the pasture," he said. "What did you find back there?"

"Three guesses," Doan answered. "On the other hand, let's not play games. I found Joady Turnbull, and he's deader than a salted smelt, and just what the hell do you propose to do about that?"

Owens' body jerked. "Joady...."

"Turnbull," Doan finished. "Remember him? He's the one who was lying out there with a knife in his back."

"Knife," Owens whispered in a shocked, thick voice.

"This one," Doan agreed, holding it out.

Owens moved back. "That—that's mine. That's the one—I—his father...."

Doan stared, trying to see his face in the dimness. "You mean that this is the same number you stuck into his old man?"

"Yes. It—it's called the 'Farmer's Friend.' I always carried...."

"THIS is a pretty dish of goulash," Doan remarked. He knelt down on the creek bank and, holding the knife under the chilling water, scrubbed its blade and hilt with his fingers vigorously. "How did you get hold of it again?"

"Me? Why, I've never had it since the day that Joady's father and I...."

"Huh!" said Doan. He found a handkerchief in his pants' pocket and dried the knife carefully. Then he snapped the blade shut and put the knife in his pocket.

Owens said incredulously, "What are you going to do with that?"

"Never you mind," said Doan. "And as of now, you've never seen it, and neither have I."

"Do you mean you're going to conceal...."

"Look," said Doan. "Remember me? I'm the guy who was hired to keep you out of trouble. If you have to be consistent when you murder people, I wish you'd be a little more careful about it."

"But you can't just...."

"Oh, yes, I can," said Doan. "But after this, if you're going to murder people at night, I'm going to charge Colonel Morris time-and-a-half for overtime."

Owens came up to his feet suddenly. "Do you think.... Are you saying that I killed Joady Turnbull?"

"What am I supposed to think?" Doan asked.

"Why, what reason...."

"You tell me," Doan invited.

Owens leaned forward dangerously. "I had nothing whatever to do with it, you fool! I had no idea he was anywhere near here, alive or dead!"

Doan stared at him speculatively.

"Don't you believe me?" Owens demanded.

Doan sighed. "The hell of it is, I think maybe I do. You don't strike me as being completely nuts. Oh, this is a fine state of affairs. I think I'll resign."

"Resign?" Owens repeated blankly.

"It wouldn't be so bad," Doan explained, "if I only had to keep the police, or whoever, from proving you did the dirty work. But now I'll have to dig around and find out who is really guilty, or else they'll certainly hang you for it."

"Hang..." Owens said dully.

"Somebody wants to see your neck stretched," Doan said absently, "and he strikes me as one of these gents who believe that if at first you don't succeed you should try, try again. It's all very discouraging at this point. If you weren't killing Joady Turnbull, just what were you doing out here at this hour of the night?"

"I couldn't sleep," Owens said. "After two years in a cell.... I just thought I'd walk down here and sit for awhile. It's quiet, and we—that is, I—used to come here often...."

"Which way did you come?"

"Through the north gate. It's on the far side of the pasture from where you came in."

"Uh," said Doan. "How do you let the cows and horses and junk out of those barns?"

"Why do you want to do that?" Owens demanded.

"We'll track up the pasture. We'll let the animals run back and forth a while and confuse the issue."

"But—but that would be destroying evidence!"

"Don't worry," Doan said gloomily. "I've got an idea the guy that thought up this little caper will strew some more around."

Carstairs growled warningly. Doan turned around quickly, the revolver poised in his hand. Dried leaves rustled somewhere close in the shadow, and then a voice whispered:

"Brad! Are you here?"

Owens stiffened. "It's Jessica!" he breathed.

"Hail, hail, the gang's all here," Doan said sourly. "I hope she brought something to eat. We'll have a picnic lunch. Come join the band, Jessica."

SHE STILL wore her white dress, and she was plainly visible groping her way cautiously closer. "Brad," she said uncertainly. "I was sitting up, and I saw you come down here, and I thought—thought…."

Owens said to Doan, "As you've probably gathered by this time, we used to meet here quite often and sit and look at the moon."

"A harmless pastime," Doan said.

"You used to like it," Jessica said.

Owens nodded curtly. "I used to be stupid, too."

"What do you mean 'used to be'?" Doan asked. "You're giving a pretty good imitation of it now."

"Mind your own business."

"Okay, okay," Doan agreed. "But it wouldn't hurt you to talk to the girl."

"I don't want to talk to her."

"Why not, Brad?" Jessica asked.

"I'm not interested in making polite conversation with the future Mrs. Gretorex."

"I'm not the future Mrs. Gretorex," Jessica said steadily.

"The paper said you were."

"The paper was wrong. Gretorex comes here quite often, and some busybody called up the editor and told him that Gretorex and I were going to be married. The editor called Gretorex and asked him if it was true, and Gretorex said that was his intention, so the paper printed the story. I didn't know anything about it until I saw it. I could have made the editor print a retraction, but what could that possibly have brought about?"

"H'm," said Owens doubtfully.

"Brad," said Jessica. "Don't you remember asking me to marry you? I said I would. I intend to."

"What?" said Owens.

"He's a nice fellow," Doan said to Jessica, "but he's a little slow on the up-take."

Owens said, "Jessica! You don't know what you're saying!"

"Oh, yes I do."

"But you can't. You couldn't possibly—"

"Take a deep breath," Doan advised helpfully.

"Shut up!" Owens snarled at him. Then: "This is all the most ridiculous nonsense. Why, you don't even love me, Jessica!"

"I'm the best judge of that," Jessica informed him calmly. "You offered to marry me, and I intend to hold you to it."

Owens turned on Doan. "Now see what you've done!"

"I told you I was a genius," Doan said. "Since I'm stage managing this reconciliation, I'd advise you to kiss her about now."

"Oh, be quiet! Jessica, your letters to me didn't sound as if you still loved me!"

"It's a little hard to write love letters to someone who won't answer you or even let you visit him."

"I couldn't… I didn't want you to think…."

"He's dumb," Doan observed, "but he means well."

"All right," Owens said. "Since you're so clever, just explain to her what you found in the pasture."

"Yes," Jessica added. "I saw you come across from behind the barns. What did you find?"

"Nothing to get excited about," Doan told her. "Just a body."

"Joady Turnbull!" Owens snapped. "And he was stabbed with my knife!"

Jessica stared. "Your…. The same knife…."

"Yes! Now I suppose you'll tell me you don't believe I did it!"

"I'll believe what you tell me, Brad."

"You're the only one who will!"

"Don't forget me," Doan said.

"Oh, you!" Owens said. "You don't count."

"I do so," said Doan. "My opinion on a matter like this is vital."

"What—what are you going to do?" Jessica asked faintly.

"He thinks he's going to conceal the evidence that links me with the murder!" Owens blurted. "He's crazy!"

"Like a fox," Doan said amiably. "Now look. Let me explain things to you in simple words. You are out on parole. If you are even faintly suspected of being involved in anything slightly illegal, your parole will be revoked. Aren't you tired of jails?"

"But it's only a matter of time before they suspect me anyway!"

"That's what I want," Doan said. "Time. Now you scram over and let the cows out of the barn. I would myself, only they might moo at Carstairs and scare him. And just keep in mind that you weren't here tonight and you don't know anything about any bodies or pastures or knives or what-the-hell. You were in your room the whole time, and I was with you. So was Carstairs. So was Jessica."

"You can't involve her—"

"She's already involved," said Doan. "Didn't it ever occur to you that she might need an alibi herself?"

Owens breathed in noisily. "Don't you dare insinuate that she—"

"Oh, run along," said Doan.

"Do what he says, Brad," Jessica directed.

"Now there's a woman with brains," Doan observed.

Owens spun around, muttering fiercely in an undertone, and slammed out through the brush.

Jessica came a step closer to Doan. "If he says he didn't—didn't have anything to do with Joady…."

"I don't think he did," Doan said. "I wouldn't be sticking my neck out like this if I thought so. I'm not completely cracked. Someone wants people to think Owens is out to eliminate the Turnbulls."

"Then—then it might be that Joady's father…."

"Say," said Doan admiringly, "you are pretty smart at that."

"If you could prove—if you *could*—I'd give anything…."

"I hate to bring up these commercial matters," said Doan, "but how much would anything be worth in cash? A thousand bucks?"

Jessica swallowed. "I—I haven't that much. My father gives me only an allowance…."

"I'll shake it out of him," Doan said, "with a slight assist from you. Let's get out of here before the cows get in."

CHAPTER IV

"YOU AIN'T SEEN NOTHIN' YET"

SUNLIGHT, COMING THROUGH the open front door, made a bright, slanted outline on the rug in the front hall as

Doan came down the stairs with Carstairs shambling along, limp-legged, behind him. Doan started toward the back of the house and then heard angry voices from the porch. He turned around and went outside.

There was a long, swoopingly low convertible with a right-hand drive and high, slanted fenders standing in the drive. A man stood in front of it, his head held high and arrogantly, his hands pushed deep in the pockets of a tailored suede sport jacket. He wore boots and riding breeches, and he had a voice that sounded as though it came from directly behind his beaked nose.

"This is a situation," he said, as though that settled it, "which is absolutely intolerable."

Jessica was standing on the edge of the porch, and Owens was leaning against a pillar beside her, scowling darkly. Colonel Morris teetered back and forth from heel to toe at the top of the porch steps, looking unhappy about it all.

"Intolerable," the man with the beaked nose repeated. "A man of your sensibilities, Colonel, should have realized that. You should have consulted me."

"We didn't think it was necessary," said Jessica.

The man looked amazed. "Well, naturally it was. A man of my experience is able to give sensible advice on such matters. Who is this person with the—ah—dog?"

"Doan," said Doan. "You could only be Gretorex. This is Carstairs. Don't mistake him for a fox. He probably wouldn't react properly."

"Naturally he's not a fox," said Gretorex. "He's a Great Dane."

"He means you," Doan said.

Carstairs sat down and scratched himself absentmindedly.

"He thanks you kindly," Doan said. "What were you beefing about?"

"Ah?" said Gretorex. "Beefing? Oh. I was objecting to the presence of this person—Owens—in this vicinity at this time.

As I said, the situation is intolerable. People simply won't stand for it. There'll be serious trouble. I warn you."

"Consider us warned," said Doan. "Why don't you go chase a fox?"

"What?" said Gretorex. "Well, really, this isn't the season for fox hunting, you know."

"Then chase yourself," Doan advised.

"Here!" Colonel Morris intervened.

"Doan! Mr. Gretorex is a respected neighbor of mine, and I put great value on his opinions. I didn't realize the repercussions…. I rather feel…."

"I'll leave right away," said Owens.

"Wait until I pack my things," Jessica requested.

"Eh?" said Colonel Morris.

"What?" said Gretorex.

"If he leaves, I leave," said Jessica.

"Oh, I say!" Gretorex blurted in horror. "You really can't do that, you know. I mean to say…."

"Go ahead," said Jessica. "What do you mean to say?"

Gretorex swallowed. "Well…. The Owens person is a criminal—a convicted one. You can't just go away with him."

"Try me and see," Jessica invited.

"But, my dear girl, *think!*"

"I'm through thinking. Now I'm going to do something about it."

"Wh-what are you going to do?" Gretorex asked warily.

"Marry Brad."

Gretorex went back a step, shocked to his core. "Oh, but this is unbelievable! Colonel Morris, do you mean to say you will allow this bounder to abduct your daughter into—into a life of crime?"

Colonel Morris sighed. "There's no respect for parenthood any more. She's stubborn and defiant."

"What's more," Doan added, "she's of age."

Colonel Morris nodded gloomily.

"WELL!" said Gretorex. "My dear Jessica, think of the terrible consequences of such a rash act. And you mustn't feel too broken-hearted over the little quarrel we had regarding that item in the paper. You were sarcastic and rude and—quite impossible, but I'll forgive you. I'll marry you myself!"

"Thanks," said Jessica. "Some other time."

There was an echoing yell from behind the house. It vibrated in the still air, and then there was the hurried pound of feet running.

"Here we go again," said Doan.

A man in overalls swung himself frantically around the corner of the house. "Colonel Morris! Down there—in the p-p-pasture—"

"Here, here!" Colonel Morris snapped. "Get a hold on yourself, man! Speak up! What is it?"

"There's a fella," said the man, gulping. "And he's there in the pasture—lyin' there. And he's dead with a stab in the back. And—and he's Joady Turnbull!" The man's eyes, round and avid and horrifiedly fascinated, stared at Owens.

"Mercy me," Doan commented. "A murder. And so early in the morning."

Colonel Morris made a strangled sound. "Murder! Joady Turnbull!"

Gretorex had got back his arrogant confidence. "I don't think, Colonel, we need worry about this bounder and his attentions to Jessica any longer."

Colonel Morris' face was leaden-colored. "Show me!" he shouted incoherently, lunging down the steps. "Show me where you found…."

He disappeared around the corner of the house with the farm hand thumping along behind him.

"Maybe we'd better notify what passes in this neck of the woods for the police," Doan suggested.

Gretorex smiled thinly. "I'll attend to that. Personally. And with pleasure." He slid under the wheel of his car and headed it for the highway in a sudden ripping blast of power.

"Bad news sure travels fast," Doan remarked.

Cecil came out on the porch and pointed a finger at Doan. "Listen, you. If you want me to get you your breakfast, you get up when the rest do around here. All my help has run out on me on account they're afraid of gettin' their throat cut, and I'm runnin' the whole damned she-bang, and if you want your bed made, make it yourself."

"Okay," said Doan, following him back into the house. "Did you hear that Joady Turnbull has been found murdered?"

"I can't think of anybody I'll miss less," Cecil informed him. "What does clumsy eat for breakfast?"

"Just gruel. With lots of cream and sugar and no lumps in it. I eat ham and eggs. I'll bet Joady Turnbull and his old man were good hunters, weren't they?"

Cecil stopped short and turned around. "They hunted rabbits and stuff some."

"Did they ever hunt stills?"

Cecil's gaunt shoulders hitched up threateningly. "If they had, they wouldn't have found none, and if they had found one, they wouldn't have been stabbed in the back. They'd have been shot right between the eyes. Just keep that in mind. Now sit down and eat your breakfast and keep your big mouth shut."

DOAN was staring, glassy-eyed, at the ceiling. In front of him, on the dining room table, were the scant and tattered remains of what had been the equivalent of six restaurant orders of ham and eggs. Carstairs was lying under the table, gurgling and grunting in surfeited content.

Colonel Morris came into the room, followed by a second man who walked with a limply disconsolate slouch, long arms dangling loosely. His pants were baggy at the knees, and his coat was rumpled in front, and his whole posture gave the impression that if you patted him on the top of the head he would slump into a small heap.

"This is Sheriff Derwin, Doan," Colonel Morris said in a worried tone.

Doan burped. "Excuse me," he said. "How are you, Sheriff?"

Derwin leaned down and looked him right in the eye. "I know you, all right. I heard plenty about you. Don't try to put none of your slick tricks over on me."

"Not right after breakfast," Doan said. "Not, anyway, this breakfast. Cecil is certainly a whiz-bang."

Color surged up into Colonel Morris' face. "Doan! There's been a murder, do you understand that?"

"Sure," said Doan, sighing contentedly.

"Well, don't sit there like a stuffed toad! This is serious! *Do* something!"

"He ain't gonna do nothin'," said Derwin. "Not if he wants to keep walking around outside my jail, he ain't. I got this case sewed up, and I don't stand for no monkey-work from the likes of him."

Colonel Morris' face was turning purple. "Doan! This—this imbecile claims that Owens murdered Joady Turnbull! He proposes to arrest Owens!"

"Let him," Doan advised lazily. "Owens has been arrested before. One more time won't hurt him. We'll get him right out again."

"Oh, you will, will you?" Derwin inquired. "And just how do you think you're gonna do that?"

"You haven't the slightest shred of evidence connecting him with the crime," Doan said. "We'll be on your trail with a habeas corpus for him in a half hour."

"Humpf!" said Derwin. "If he didn't do it, then who did do it?"

"That's your question. You answer it. What time was this murder put together?"

"Doc Evans says Joady's been dead about ten hours."

Doan nodded. "Some time around midnight. Owens has an iron-clad alibi."

"What?" Derwin demanded.

"Not what. Who. Me. I was with him all the time. We were talking things over in his room."

"Hah!" Derwin jeered. "You think anybody'd believe that? You'd say it, anyway."

"Jessica was there, too," Doan said.

Colonel Morris made a gurgling sound. "Jessica! Was she in—in—"

"Don't get excited," Doan advised. "I told you I was there with them."

"When?" Derwin asked skeptically.

"From ten o'clock last night until four o'clock this morning, more or less, as the case may be."

"Jessica!" Colonel Morris bellowed furiously.

Jessica came in the dining room. "Yes?"

Colonel Morris gestured wildly. "Doan has the infernal insolence to say you were with Owens last night!"

"I was," said Jessica.

"It was all very proper," said Doan. "We were playing cards. Five card stud. A fascinating game. By the way, I won a thousand bucks from Jessica. She said you'd pay."

"A thousand…." Colonel Morris repeated numbly.

"One thousand and three dollars and ninety-one cents, to be exact," Doan said. "But I'll skip the small change."

"Shut up, all of you," Derwin ordered. He looked at Jessica. "Was you with Owens like he says?"

"Yes."

"All right," said Derwin grimly. "All right, for now. But I got my ideas. That stab in Joady looked mighty like the one his pa got, but this time I ain't found the knife—not yet. And somebody let the cows out so they'd trample up the ground. And I bet I know who."

"I never bet," said Doan. And then he added hastily, "Except in poker games."

"Your time's comin'," Derwin promised. "You think you're pretty smart, but you ain't seen nothin' yet. Colonel, you're responsible for Owens. I'm leavin' him here now, but I'll be back, and I wanta find him here." He pointed his finger at Doan. "And you, too."

CHAPTER V

THE PARTY OF THE FIRST PART

TWILIGHT MADE SHADOWS that were thick and gloomy in the study where Doan was napping when someone twisted his foot and woke him up.

"Umm?" he said, rolling over on the couch and blinking sleepily.

"The master-mind at work," Cecil sneered. "Listen, dopey, here's someone who wants to talk to you, and you'd better pry open your ears and listen."

Norma Carson's steel-rimmed spectacles made shiny circles in the dusk. Her face was pallidly drawn, and her hair straggled loosely down over her forehead.

"Oh, Mr. Doan!" she said. "You've *got* to do something! They're coming here! They *are!* And it's partly my fault!"

Doan sat up. "Who's coming, and what's your fault?"

"Those—those loafers and bums from town! It was that beast of a Gretorex. He talked to them and worked them up and gave them drinks, and then when Sheriff Derwin didn't arrest Brad Owens for Joady's murder, he said that they should take the law into their own hands!"

"Think of that, now," said Doan.

"They'll come here!" Norma gasped. "They—they'll *lynch* Brad!"

"How would that be your fault?" Doan asked.

"Joady told all over town that Brad had you send your dog after Joady. There at the mill. He said the dog attacked him, and he barely got away with his life. They're talking about tarring and feathering you!"

"Don't worry about it," Doan soothed her. "I'll handle things. You run on back to town now. It wouldn't be so good if the school board found out about this Paul Revere act of yours. Cecil, here, won't say anything, though."

Norma left reluctantly. Cecil went through the door, and slapped it shut emphatically behind him. Carstairs was lying on the floor with his head in the corner. He had slept through all the disturbance.

Doan got up and kicked him in the rear. "Up on your feet, brainless."

Carstairs sat up and yawned and then stared at Doan with an air of cynical expectancy. With Carstairs padding silently behind him Doan went through the hall and out on the front porch in time to see Norma Carson's dingy coupe turn out into the highway and head back toward town. Doan sat down on the front steps. He took the Police Positive out of his pocket, flicked the cylinder open to make sure it was loaded, and then slid the gun into the waist-band of his pants under his coat.

He sat there, looking dreamily thoughtful, while the shadows thickened and deepened and crawled softly across the sweep of the lawn. A few early stars made bright pin-pricks in the darkening purple haze of the sky, and then there were other bright pin-pricks, lower down, that moved and jittered jerkily in pairs and that were not stars.

Doan nudged Carstairs in the ribs with his thumb and pointed. "Company coming," he said.

Carstairs grunted, and his claws scraped a little on the porch flooring. Doan sat unmoving while the pin-prick headlights of the cars crawled closer on the town road.

Suddenly the front door banged deafeningly behind him, and Colonel Morris raged out on the porch. "Scum!" he bellowed. "Infernal, impudent swine! Do you see them?"

"Yup," said Doan.

The colonel stamped down the steps past Doan and stood at the top of the drive.

Doan jerked his head at Carstairs and then got up and sauntered quietly around the side of the house and down the back slope through the thick hedge. Light showed mellowly through the windows of the barns, and there was the high, thin whine of a cream separator. Following the sound, Doan went around to the front of one of the buildings and in through the wide doors.

Jessica was tending the separator, and she snapped the switch and stared at Doan.

"We're having some visitors," Doan told her. "The unwelcome variety."

Owens came in from the back carrying two shiny tin pails. He set them down, and milk spilled a little, frothily thick, on the cement floor.

"Don't tell me you've finally decided to lend us a hand?" he said to Doan.

"In a manner of speaking," Doan said. "There are some rough and ready parties on the horizon who have the idea of hanging you on a tree like a Christmas stocking. You and I and Carstairs are going for a hike in the woods and study bird life and all that."

"Run away?" Owens asked incredulously.

Doan nodded. "Just that."

"And you," he told Jessica, "are to run back and put on a little diversion for the boys. You weep and wail and wring your hands and tell them that Owens has left you flat."

Jessica stared at Owens for a moment, biting her lower lip,

and then she turned wordlessly and ran out of the building and up the slope toward the big house.

"They might trail us," Owens said. "If they should have dogs...."

Doan smiled and indicated Carstairs. "He likes nothing better than a light snack of well-buttered bloodhound. Let's be on our way."

THIS was thick timber, on the north side of the valley, and it was darker than the inside of a cat. Doan bounced his chin off a low-hanging branch, stumbled backwards, and nearly stepped on Carstairs. Carstairs growled warningly.

"The thing I don't like about woods at night," Doan said, rubbing his chin, "is that they're dark. Do you know where we are?"

"Certainly," said Owens. "Keep close behind me, and, that way, you won't have much trouble."

"Okay," said Doan. "Is there any place near here where we can park and watch our back-trail?"

"Yes. Fagan's Hill is on ahead a ways."

"You can see the farm from there?"

"Yes. You can see the whole valley."

"Is there any place else like that?"

"No. All the other hills are timbered thickly. Fagan's Hill was once, but some early party dug a big quarry out of the side of it. It's not in use now, but the cut and the erosion made a sort of a cliff out of it. It drops off steeply, and there are no trees to cut off the view."

Doan said, "You told me that you don't remember stabbing Joady Turnbull's father."

"I don't."

"I know," said Doan. "Would you remember doing it if you had?"

Brush crackled against Owens' legs, and he was much closer suddenly. "What do you mean by that?"

"I mean, I think the reason you don't remember stabbing him is because you didn't do it. Someone else handled that end of it for you."

Owens' breath made a harsh noise in his threat. "What are you—"

"Easy," Doan said. "Take it easy. I've got a gun, and Carstairs is right behind you, and we're nervous people."

Owens said, "I don't know what you're talking about."

"It's simple," said Doan. "You didn't kill Joady Turnbull or his old man, either. I want to know if you know who did."

"If I knew, do you think I'd have gone to jail for it?"

"Maybe," said Doan. "Just maybe."

"You fool! Why?"

"To protect the person who did do it."

Owens' shadow contracted a little. "You—"

"Don't try to jump me," Doan warned. "That won't work. Answer my question. Do you know who did the dirty deeds?"

"No!"

"I do," said Doan. "And I don't think you're going to like my answer."

Owens was breathing heavily. "What kind of a trick are you trying to pull off now?"

"I'm trying to earn a bonus," Doan told him. "A little matter of one thousand bucks, and I see it fluttering prettily right in front of my snoot. Turn around and lead us to Fagan's Hill."

"Why?"

"Because I'm telling you to," said Doan, "and, brother, I'm not fooling. Lead on, or I'll dump you here and find the place myself."

Owens stood there for leaden seconds, leaning forward, trying to see Doan's face, and then he turned without any more words and headed through the tangled darkness. They went on steadily in silence, climbing slightly. Doan had his left arm in front of his face to protect it from invisible slashing branches. He was holding the revolver in his right hand.

At last Owens' face made a pallid blob as he paused and looked over his shoulder. "It's about a hundred and fifty yards ahead," he murmured.

Doan reached back and got hold of Carstairs' spiked collar and hauled him ahead. "Go ahead. Go on. Watch."

Carstairs slid on ahead of them, his head swinging alertly from side to side.

"Follow him," Doan ordered. "Don't make any more noise than you have to."

OWENS walked on slowly, picking his path, and Doan kept in step right behind him. Owens stopped again. Doan looked around him. Carstairs was standing still, his head tilted, testing the night air with noisy little sniffles. He growled in a low rumble.

Doan sighed. "I'm on the beam tonight." He stepped past Owens and nudged Carstairs with the revolver barrel. "Go on. Get him. And take it easy. Hold. Hold, you hear?"

Carstairs mumbled sullenly and then seemed to fade away silently into the shadows. There was no further sound, and Owens and Doan waited, listening to their own breathing. Then a man yelled frantically.

Instantly Doan cupped his hands around his mouth and shouted, "Don't run! Don't try to get your gun! Don't move, and he won't touch you!"

He threshed his way ahead up the slope with Owens pounding along behind him. The timber thinned into stunted brush, and they broke through it into a small clearing. There was a man sitting on the ground, both his hands raised protectively.

Carstairs was crouched squarely in front of him, his head thrust forward until his muzzle was no more than a foot from the man's face. His fangs glistened, white and shiny, in the dimness, and he was growling in a continuous, ugly mutter.

"Okay," said Doan. "Relax, stupid."

Carstairs quit growling and yawned in a bored way. He backed off and sat down.

"Gaah!" said the man in a choked voice. "He come without no warning and—and jumped at me…."

"Hi, Sheriff," Doan said.

Derwin caught his breath.

"I sent him on ahead," Doan said, "because I thought you might hear us coming and sort of shoot before you looked."

"Huh?" said Derwin. "Why?"

"I thought your conscience might be bothering you."

"Huh?" Derwin repeated. "Conscience?"

Doan pointed. "On account of that."

The valley stretched out in a long, smoothly graduated scoop ahead of them, rolling up on its sides into the timbered shadows of the hills. The Square was immediately ahead and below, far down, as small and miniaturely perfect as an expensive doll house with lights bright and tiny in its windows. Other lights, mere pin-pricks, moved and churned around it—in front and on the sides and in back among the smaller, lower outbuildings.

"Friends of yours?" Doan asked.

"What do you mean?" Derwin demanded.

"Look," said Doan. "We're grown up. We know the facts of life. No one could gather up a mob that size in a little joint like Ramsey village without the sheriff knowing all about it. You knew all about it. You just didn't want to stop them, so you kept out of their way."

"Humpf," Derwin said sullenly. "Well, damn it, I—I figured…."

"You figured maybe the mob would scare Owens so that he might confess to something."

"So maybe I did," said Derwin. "And he's guilty!"

"And you're so dumb it's pathetic," said Doan.

Carstairs suddenly stood up and growled.

Doan swore in a bitter whisper. "No, I'm wrong. I'm the dumb one."

"What is it?" Owens demanded.

"I figured Derwin would come up here to see what was going on. I never thought that the murderer might, too."

"What?" said Derwin. "Hey!"

"Shut up," said Doan, watching Carstairs.

Carstairs lowered his head, staring into the darkness at the back of the clearing. A stick snapped loudly there. Carstairs started forward.

Doan kicked him in the ribs. "No!"

"Why not?" Owens whispered.

"This is different," said Doan. "This party sees us. I don't want Carstairs full of buckshot. You out there! Come on in! I know who you are!"

Doan shoved Owens. "You and Derwin go to the left. Run for it! Circle around and drive back in toward the cliff here!"

Then he nudged Carstairs with his knee.

"Come on!" He ran across the clearing and crashed into the brush on the right side of the clearing.

THE DARKNESS closed in tightly. Doan felt for Carstairs, grabbed the spiked collar. Carstairs lunged ahead, and Doan smashed and clattered along behind him, swearing in a bitter monotone.

"Make some noise," he ordered. "Woof!"

Carstairs bayed savagely, and the sound rolled and echoed ahead of them. Doan fell into a gulley, and Carstairs dragged him, willy-nilly, up the other side, going ahead in great, heaving jumps. He bayed again and then stopped short. Doan fell over the top of him and scrambled to his feet. He stood tensely, listening.

"I know you're close to me," he said. "You're not going any further in this direction."

There was the whistling sound of an in-drawn breath.

Carstairs leaped in that direction, and Doan got him by the tail and hauled back, digging in his heels.

"No! Take it easy, lame-brain! I like you without holes in your hide better!"

He got a new grip on the collar, and they went ahead in a weirdly tandem fashion with Doan caroming off trees and wading sightlessly through brush that crackled angrily.

"Derwin!" Doan yelled. "Owens!"

"Here!"

"Here!"

"Circle back this way!"

Carstairs stopped uncertainly, started in one direction, turned and went in another.

"Make up your mind," Doan panted.

Carstairs slowed up, and Doan hauled on the collar, gasping for breath, and then the darkness seemed to thin a little, and the undergrowth fell away ahead of them.

"Ah," said Doan. "This is it." He slapped Carstairs on the muzzle. "Back! Keep back."

Carstairs grumbled and grunted indignantly, but he edged in back of Doan's legs. Dean went ahead slowly, the Police Positive poised.

The ground sloped steeply down, and then they were abruptly in the clear, looking out over the empty black space of the valley. There was a figure right on the edge of the drop ahead—dark and wavering there, unsteady.

Doan said, "There's the party of the first part."

"Who?" Derwin said. "Who…."

A small, soft breeze from the valley ruffled the brush-tips and touched the figure on the cliff-edge, and her skirt ruffled and moved a little.

"Why," Owens said in a numb, incredulous voice, "why, it's Norma Carson!"

Her spectacles glinted a little, turning toward them, and then she turned and gathered herself.

"Hey!" Doan yelled.

There was nothing on the cliff-edge, and then like an echo to his yell there was a thin, chilling shriek that tapered off into the rolling, rumbling smash of rocks rolling.

"She jumped!" Derwin shouted.

He ran toward the cliff and threw himself down on hands and knees and crawled forward.

"Oh," he said in a sickened voice. "Oh…. Clear down on those sharp rocks, and she's all twisted and smashed…."

He got to his feet and ran back across the clearing, heading for the smoother slope farther along the hillside.

"Norma…." Owens said. "I don't—I don't understand…."

"She killed old man Turnbull and Joady."

"Killed?" Owens repeated, still numb. "I can't believe she would…."

"It took me quite awhile to get the idea, too," Doan admitted.

"But why?"

"Well, did you ever notice the way she looked at you or the way she looked when she talked about you?"

"What?" said Owens.

"She loved you, you dope. You thought no one saw old man Turnbull smack you with that wrench. But Norma did. She thought you were killed, and she gave herself away completely. Probably got hysterical and took on at a great rate. Old Man Turnbull got the idea. He was scared because he had socked you, and he put the pressure on her. She was supposed to say you hit him first or something. He threatened her.

"That was about the end of him. Your knife had probably fallen out of your pocket, or else she found it while she was trying to find out how dead you were. She gave it to Turnbull— in the back. Then, when she found you were only knocked cold, she scuffed out her footprints and scrammed."

OWENS swallowed. "But then, when I was arrested…."

"I'm afraid you won't like Norma so well after this," Doan said. "I'm afraid she figured that if you were in jail, she wouldn't have you, but neither would Jessica."

"Oh," said Owens slowly.

"Norma probably figured on gathering you in when you got loose," Doan went on. "She never dreamed that Jessica would stick to you—especially after she maneuvered that little phoney rumor of her engagement to Gretorex and sent you the paper so you'd know."

Sheriff Derwin's voice came to them faintly from below. "Doan! Owens! She—she's dead. Oh, lordy! What—what will I do now, huh?"

"Go get a doctor or an ambulance or a hearse or something," Doan ordered.

"But about Joady…." Owens said.

"Joady was mean," Doan said. "Joady was dumb like his old man. He was so mean and dumb he died. He was mad because Norma wouldn't let him go to school. Probably people needled him about it. He took to following her around and pestering her—like at the mill. He followed her once too often. She had to come, you see, and find out if you and Jessica were going to get together again. She *had* to know that. She was sneaking around the joint last night, and Joady followed her, and she caught him at it. He would have told on her. She couldn't have you—and everyone—know she was sort of a Peeping Tom."

"The knife…." said Owens.

"After it was used at the trial, it would just be filed away in some drawer in the courthouse as an exhibit. No one would suspect a schoolteacher of anything if she was around the court-house, and certainly no one would ever dream she would pinch a knife."

Doan took the knife from his pocket, opened it and wiped the blade and hilt on his coat front. He flipped it over the cliff edge, and a thin metallic rattle echoed back.

Owens drew a deep breath. "You—you know, it's a little hard for me to grasp all this...." He hesitated uncertainly. "You—you are a pretty clever detective after all!"

"I'm the best there is," said Doan. "I told you that in the first place. You better run on back to Jessica. The mob has beat it by this time."

"Well...." said Owens. "Thanks."

He turned and started back.

"Have Cecil put on a couple of steaks for us!" Doan called. "And, hey! Don't forget that thousand dollars!"

Owens ran on, unheeding.

"Love," said Doan, nodding to Carstairs.

Carstairs slowly and thoughtfully licked his chops.

Doan nodded. "Yup. Steaks are good, too."

V

OH, MURDERER MINE

CHAPTER I

HERE IT WAS spring again, and the bees were buzzing and the buds were bursting and the doves were cooing, and the sun was beaming on all these and lots of other activities in a benignly obscene way. It was just the same old tedious show that has been playing return engagements at regular intervals for a million years or more and certainly nothing to get worked up over, but nevertheless it seemed new and splendid and fine to Melissa Gregory, because she was happy. She was a simple and uncomplicated sort of a person, and it didn't take much to put her in that state.

She walked along the edge of the Old Quad now with her head up and her shoulders back and her heels tapping in what she considered a briskly competent manner. She was slim and tall enough, and she had brown hair with copper-gold glints in it. Her blue eyes tipped a little at the outer corners, and her nose had three freckles on its bridge and turned up at the end. She was wearing the wrong shade of lipstick.

She was being happy at this particular moment because she had been promoted to a better job as the result of her outstanding merit and her faithful record of attendance at faculty tea parties. She was now an instructor. In the odd hierarchy of college faculties, an instructor rates somewhere between the head gardener and the lowest professor, if anyone can determine which one he is. An instructor is not allowed to lecture—or, for that matter, to talk loudly anywhere—but is entrusted with conveying the more elementary truths in certain subjects to beginning students.

Melissa taught anthropology, and she did this at an institution of higher learning called Breckenbridge University, Western Division, which specialized in the mass production of graduates of a standard size and competence. It was an efficient and impersonal sort of a place, but unfortunately one of its founders had once been on the campus of a well-known Eastern college and hadn't forgotten it. Consequently the campus of Breckenbridge had as much functional design as a bunch of dice dumped out of a hat. The buildings were scattered in all directions and hidden under ivy and behind bushes.

Melissa's headquarters was a building known as Old Chem because there were three beginning chemistry laboratories on the first floor. Old Chem was a solid, two-story, gray granite building with an ugly front and a splayed-out rear, and its architect had evidently had the theory that windows were designed to shoot Indians out of and not to facilitate the entrance of fresh air or light.

Melissa went up the block stone steps and through the arched entrance and then up the stairs to her right into the dimness of the upper corridor. Her office was the second one down, and she was fumbling in her purse for the key when she noticed that the door was slightly ajar. She pushed it open wider and looked in.

This was a fairly representative example of a college faculty office. It was quite a lot larger than a hall closet and ventilated about as well, and the furniture probably would have brought a comparatively good price at a fire sale. Melissa loved it in a proud and fiercely possessive way because it was the first one she had ever had that was hers and hers alone.

At present there was a man in it. He was sitting in Melissa's chair. He had papers spread messily all over Melissa's desk. And, in addition to all that, he was a young man.

Which was something to give Melissa pause, because when

she thought about men—which was neither too often nor yet too infrequently—she thought about young men. As a matter of fact, when she was doing thinking of this sort and enjoying it most of all, she thought about a young man who looked almost exactly like this one.

Unfortunately, however, this was neither the time nor place for Melissa's dream-man-come-to-life to suddenly appear. Obviously, she couldn't go swooning at him even if she wanted to—and she told herself sternly she had no such desire—because he was an intruder. Worse than that, he had all the earmarks of being one of the vilest criminals the university faculty produced—an office snitcher—and here he was caught red-handed in an attempt to move into Melissa's quarters even before she'd had an opportunity to get settled herself.

"Well," said Melissa in a cutting way. "Good morning."

"Uh," said the young man. He was making some very involved mathematical computations on a scratch pad, and he didn't look up. "Uh," he said, and pulled a large, indistinct map toward him and made a careful, wavy line on it with India ink and a drawing pen. He was extremely handsome. He had blond hair that curled in ringlets and a straight, short nose. His eyes were blue, shaded with long, dark lashes. The effect of this collar-ad perfection was tainted a little by the way his mouth twisted down at one corner and the way he was scowling, but even at that he missed being pretty only by a very small margin.

Melissa stepped through the door. "I beg your pardon."

He looked up sideways at her. "What do you want?"

"Well, really," said Melissa. "It so happens that this is my office."

"Not any longer."

"What?" said Melissa blankly.

"It's mine now."

"What?" said Melissa.

The young man scowled. "Are you hard of hearing, or don't

you understand English? I'm going to use this office from now on—exclusively."

Melissa swallowed hard. "Well, you can't just move in like this!"

"I already have."

"Well, who gave you the authority to do it?"

"The president of the university."

"Oh," said Melissa.

The young man eyed her coldly. "Was there anything else?"

Melissa's voice was shaky. "But—but all my files and notes are in here."

"Not now, they aren't," said the young man. He pulled one of the desk drawers open to illustrate that it was empty.

"My files!" Melissa shrilled. "My class notes! What have you done—"

"Nothing," the young man said shortly. "I didn't touch them. Some dusty, beefy party who makes noises like a tin mouse took them away."

"Do you mean Professor Sley-Mynick?"

The young man shrugged. He had custom-built shoulders.

Melissa took a deep breath. "Now look here, this is all wrong, and I don't care what the president of the university said. This office is mine. It was assigned to me. You haven't any right to just walk in and take it."

"What's your subject?" the young man asked indifferently.

"Anthropology."

"Oh, that silly stuff. You don't need any particular office for that. Go find one somewhere else."

Melissa swallowed again. "What is your subject?"

"Meteorology."

"Hmmph," said Melissa contemptuously. "And just why do you need this particular office for that?"

The young man jerked his thumb toward the ceiling. "It has a trap door. My instruments are on the roof."

"What instruments?" Melissa asked. "I thought you people used crystal balls to predict the weather."

The young man didn't answer. He just curled his lip. He reached down and rattled the weather map. He was waiting very pointedly for Melissa to leave.

Melissa changed her tactics. "Now, listen," she said, smiling. "I really want this office. This particular one. I like it. And I was here first. Let's make a deal."

"Let's not."

Melissa lost her smile. "Well, damn you anyway, you supercilious imitation of a Greek statue. This office is the only one in the building that has a private ladies' powder room. Do you think I'm going to come here and knock on the door and ask your permission every time I—well, every time?"

"I know you're not. I have to make progressive calculations, and it's important that I'm not interrupted in the middle of them when I'm plotting a front. You'll have to make some other arrangements."

Melissa breathed hard through her nose, staring at him. He stared back.

"I've seen you somewhere before!" Melissa stated accusingly.

To her amazement, he cringed. There was no other word for it. Melissa watched him narrowly, sensing her advantage, but not knowing what it was.

"Yes," she said, feeling her way. "I *know* I've seen you somewhere before. Your face is very familiar."

He was blushing, very painfully. The flush crawled in red waves up from his collar.

"What's your name?" Melissa demanded.

He moistened his lips. "Eric Trent."

It didn't mean a thing to Melissa. She was baffled.

Eric Trent knew it, and he sighed lengthily. "If you don't mind, I'd like to get on with my work. Good day."

Melissa scrambled around frantically in her mind looking

for an inspiration. She didn't find one. "Oh, all right." She shot her hand out suddenly, forefinger pointed rigidly. "But I'll remember where I've seen you! And then, you'll find out!"

She stepped back into the hall and slammed the door violently, and then she marched down the stairs and back along the lower hall to the office door opposite the largest of the chemistry labs. She hammered on the dark, scarred panels vigorously. There was no answer. Impatiently Melissa tried the latch. It clicked, and she pushed the door open and looked in the office. It was larger and considerably more cluttered than hers, and dust motes stirred and glinted uneasily in the sun beams that pried their way through the narrow windows. There was no one in sight.

Melissa shut the door, and then she had a sudden hunch and opened it again very quickly. She caught Professor Sley-Mynick in the act of crawling cautiously out from under his desk. He froze there on his hands and knees and made wordless little pip pipping noises.

Also, he seemed to be stuck, for he was by no means a small man and the space he was in looked to be about three sizes too small. He was fat, as a matter of fact—fish white and jelly fat—but despite his size, the fierce, jet-black mustache he was wearing was still too big for him and Melissa got the impression the mustache was leading him around willy-nilly. He was bald and wore tiny rimless spectacles so thick they were opaque.

"Good morning, Professor," Melissa said.

"Oh," said Professor Sley-Mynick. "Yes, it is. Good, I mean. Isn't it?"

It was strange hearing such a pipsqueak voice emerge from such a roly-poly body. By dint of great exertion, the professor extricated himself from the trap he was in.

"What were you doing under your desk?" Melissa asked.

"Desk?" Professor Sley-Mynick repeated blankly. He spoke with an accent that gave his words a just noticeable blubber.

"Under it? Oh. My fountain pen. I mean, it dropped and rolled, I guess. Didn't it?"

"No," said Melissa. "It didn't. You were hiding."

"I?" said Professor Sley-Mynick, amazed.

"Yes, you."

"From—from what?"

"Me."

"Why?"

"Because you are the senior professor in this building, and you are in charge of assigning offices in it!"

"Oh, dear," said Professor Sley-Mynick.

"Just what," said Melissa, "do you mean by giving my office to that matinee-faced moron upstairs?"

"Oh, he's not a moron. He's a meteorologist. It's the science of the weather—storms and the climate and—and things. It's very important work. He said."

"Never mind what he said. Answer my question. Why did you give him my office?"

"Oh, that," said Professor Sley-Mynick. "The president! T. Ballard Bestwyck. He's the president of the whole university. He talks to rich people—face to face—and they often give him some of their money. That's very vital. He wrote a letter. To me—personally. It said that the moron—I mean, the meteorologist—was to have an office in this building. I'll find it. The letter. It's right here. Isn't it?" He burrowed busily among the papers on his desk.

"I don't care about the letter," Melissa told him. "Why did you have to give this seasonal swami my office?"

"He said he wanted it."

"Oh, he did? And that was reason enough?"

"Yes," Professor Sley-Mynick admitted. "I mean, he's a very handsome young man, but I'm afraid he's not very nice. He snarls. Doesn't he?"

"Yes," said Melissa, sighing. "All right, Professor. Have you given any thought to finding another office for me?"

"Indeed, yes!" said Sley-Mynick. "Number 5. All your files and notes are in there. I was very careful of them. You'll like Number 5. It's nice. Isn't it?"

"It most certainly is not! It stinks!"

Melissa was speaking the literal truth. Number 5 occupied an unused corner of one of the chemical labs, and its partitions were porous. It is a moot question whether students like to make stinks because they take chemistry or whether they take chemistry because they like to make stinks. In any event, they invariably do.

"It's not right," said Melissa. "The whole thing is nothing but an injustice. You know that, don't you?"

"Oh, dear," said Professor Sley-Mynick.

"And do you know what I'm going to do one of these fine days?"

"What?" Professor Sley-Mynick asked.

"I'm going to spit right in one of his beautiful eyes!"

"Oh!" said Professor Sley-Mynick, deeply shocked.

Melissa slammed his door and started down the hall in the general direction of Number 5. She had gone about ten paces when something stirred sluggishly in the shadows. Melissa stopped with a startled gasp. It was too early yet for students to be lurking about, and anyway this couldn't possibly be mistaken for one.

It was a dog. It was the most enormous dog Melissa had ever seen. It sat right down in the hall in front of her in a leisurely and self-possessed way and proceeded to look her over from head to foot in a manner that was not far from insulting.

Melissa caught her breath. "H-hello," she said timidly. She snapped her fingers in a feeble attempt at friendliness.

The dog studied her fingers as though he had never seen any before and wouldn't care if he never did again. He was a fawn-colored Great Dane.

"Hello," said a voice.

Melissa jerked around. There was a man leaning against the wall, watching her. He hadn't been there two seconds before. He was small and plump and pleasant-looking. He was wearing a double-breasted pin-striped blue suit with outsize lapels and a dark blue hat. He had a naively appealing smile and a smooth, roundly pink face. He moved his head to indicate the dog and said:

"I use him for a decoy. While people gape at him, I sneak up behind them and pinch them."

"P-pinch them?" Melissa repeated, shying away.

"A slang expression," the man explained. "I mean, I arrest them. I'm a detective. What are you?"

"An anthropologist."

"Oh," said the man. "You study apes and like that?"

"No! Certainly not! Anthropology is the study of mankind. We study apes only because you can learn a lot about men from them."

"I'll bet that's the truth," said the man. "My name is Doan. What's your name?"

"Melissa Gregory."

"Hello," said Doan. "That's Carstairs in front of you. He works with me—that is, when he's not working against me or just not working."

"He looks like a very good dog."

"That's what he looks like," Doan agreed. "I've got a word of warning for you."

"A what?" Melissa asked, staring at him.

"A word to the wise. Lay off the bird in your office. He's not for sale or for rent."

"What?" said Melissa.

"Eric Trent," Doan explained. "Mustn't touch."

"What?" said Melissa.

Doan sighed. "You must not make passes at Eric Trent. That is verboten."

Melissa's eyes narrowed. "I don't believe I like the idea you're selling. Suppose you elaborate on it"

"It's simple," Doan told her. "I keep females from making love to Eric Trent."

"Well, why?"

"Because I've been hired to do it. And, believe me, it's a full-time job. Women fall for him in squads. I mean, they would fall over backwards—if I didn't stop them."

"I understand the words you're saying," Melissa said. "But they don't seem to make sense. Are you seriously telling me that this—this person has a bodyguard to keep women from falling in love with him?"

"That's right," Doan agreed. "And I'm it."

Melissa shook her head groggily. "Well, why? I mean, I'll agree, just for the sake of argument, that there might be one or two women in the world hard up enough or dumb enough to want that insolent imbecile, but they're the type who would deserve him if they got him. Why should either he or you worry about them?"

"We're not," said Doan. "But his wife is."

"Oh. He's married?"

"And how."

"Hmmm," said Melissa. "Now wait a minute. I'm just catching up with you. You have the barefaced insolence to warn me. I think I'll slap your face."

"Don't," Doan warned. "Carstairs will bite you if you do. Not that he cares anything about me, but he would feel it was a reflection on him."

Melissa looked at Carstairs. He was lying down on the floor with his eyes shut.

"Don't let him fool you," said Doan. "He's ready to go into instant action. He's just pretending he's not interested."

"Hmmm," said Melissa. "You know, this is all sort of fascinating in a repugnant way, and I know I've seen this Trent party before, but I can't remember where. Have you any idea where I could have seen him?"

"Yes," said Doan.

"Well, where?"

"His wife is Heloise of Hollywood."

"Heloise," Melissa repeated. "Of Hollywood. Oh!"

"Oh," Doan agreed.

"Now wait," said Melissa. "Now wait a minute... I know! He's Handsome Lover Boy!"

"Yup," said Doan.

"Stay right here!" Melissa ordered. "I'll be right, back!"

She ran down the hall and through the malodorous gloom of the chem lab. The door of Number 5 was open, and her notes were arranged in well-ordered confusion all over the floor and the swaybacked desk. Melissa dug through them, spewing lecture fragments in all directions, until she found the current issue of a large and slick and all too popular woman's magazine. She trotted back to the hall, thumbing eagerly through the back pages of the magazine.

"Wait, now," she said. "I know I saw one... Here!" It was a full-page ad. In the upper left-hand corner there was a portrait photograph of a very handsome young man in a naval officer's dress whites. The very handsome young man was Eric Trent. Under it there was a message in artistically slanted and swirly facsimile handwriting.

"*... and I can hardly bear the thought of the endless, weary days that must somehow pass before I can find safe haven once more in the dear circle of your strong arms... but I too know my duty, dear one... and I shall keep alive the beauty that charmed you... keep it alive and glowing until your return, my own handsome lover boy....*"

"Doesn't that make you feel like you just picked up a dead fish?" Melissa asked.

"Sort of," Doan agreed.

"I thought it was just an advertising gag," Melissa said. "I had no idea that anyone in the world would have a strong enough stomach to aim drool like that at an actual person and do it in public. Is this really a picture of Heloise of Hollywood, too?"

"Oh, yes," said Doan.

A second portrait, three times the size of Eric Trent's, filled up the lower right of the ad. This was a woman. It was taken in profile, and she had her head tilted back to show the long, smooth line of her throat. She had blond hair, and a cold, smooth, ice-frosted beauty. She looked as artificial, but just as well-designed, as a wax orchid. There was a message beside her picture, too, but this one was in printing, not in handwriting.

"... Heloise of Hollywood, fifty-four years young, at the supreme pinnacle of gracious, mature beauty—poised, assured, alluring— waits with calm confidence for the return of her own young hero- husband. Heloise of Hollywood has the glamour that is the rightful and easily obtained heritage of the Woman-Over-Forty. Heloise of Hollywood Beauty Prescriptions, compounded exclusively for the mature woman, are on sale at all the really discriminating shops from coast to coast...."

Melissa tilted her head judicially. "Fifty-four? And she looks like this?"

"Well, pretty near," Doan said.

"And she hired you to watch her husband?"

"Yes," Doan agreed.

"I still want to know why. It doesn't sound reasonable. It isn't the sort of thing a normal person would do."

Doan shrugged. "I'm just a hired hand, myself."

Melissa watched him curiously. "Well, what is Trent doing here? That nauseating junk Heloise of Hollywood peddles is piled neck-deep in every department store in the country, and it's expensive. She must make millions, and I've got a good idea what Trent's salary is. Did she throw him out?"

"No," said Doan.

"Oh-ho!" said Melissa suddenly. "Now I get it? He walked out on her, didn't he?"

"No," said Doan flatly.

"He did, too! That explains everything." Melissa tapped the magazine. "She has run hundreds of these ads in all the big women's magazines in the last couple of years. Every one of them had a picture of and some sort of a sticky message to Handsome Lover Boy. She must have spent millions of dollars promoting that angle."

"I wouldn't know," said Doan.

"Oh, yes you would. The whole point of that campaign was and is that if you're anywhere under ninety years old and use her stuff, you'll make yourself irresistible to men—just like *she* is! Yes, and you can catch yourself a handsome young husband, just like *she* did!"

"You're probably wrong," said Doan.

"I am not. And now he's walked out on her in spite of all her mature allure. *Oh-ho!* And now her pretty advertising campaign is about to backfire right in her face! No wonder she hired you to keep women away from him. If he falls for some twenty-year-old twirp and starts a divorce action in all the headlines, she wouldn't be able to sell that stuff of hers for axle grease."

"Have you ever heard of something called slander?" Doan inquired.

"Hmmph," said Melissa. "That doesn't prevent me from laughing at him and at her, too. And that's just what I'm doing. Ha-ha-ha-ha! I'm just practicing now, waiting for the next time I see that gloomy gigolo upstairs."

"What's the joke?" a voice asked. Its owner was a woman. She had sleek, carefully groomed gray hair, cut short, and she wore a tailored blue suit. Her face slanted from above and from below, culminating in a beak of a nose that made her look like an intelligent and slightly sinister eagle in search of a free meal.

"Oh, hello," said Melissa. "This is Mr. Doan. This is Beulah Porter Cowys, Mr. Doan."

"Hello," said Beulah Porter Cowys to Doan. "What do you do? You look too stupid to be a student, if you'll pardon me for mentioning it."

"Quite all right," said Doan. "You're being deceived by my detecting expression. I put it on to fool desperate criminals. I'm actually very clever, indeed. In fact, many people, including me, think I'm the smartest detective in the world."

"A detective," said Beulah Porter Cowys. "Now I've seen— What on earth is that?"

"A dog," Doan told her.

"Is he dead?"

"No. Just bored."

"His name is Carstairs," Melissa volunteered.

"Gaaah," said Beulah Porter Cowys. "It would be. I hate dogs."

"That's all right," said Doan. "He hates people."

"Was he what you were laughing at?" Beulah Porter Cowys asked Melissa.

"No," said Melissa. "Look, Beulah. See this picture? Handsome Lover Boy? He's upstairs."

"What?"

"It's a fact," Melissa told her. "Really. He actually exists, and he's really married to this Heloise. He's a meteorologist, or so he claims. Isn't it horrible?"

"Isn't what horrible?"

"Why, she must be almost twice his age."

"Just twice," Doan said. "He's twenty-six."

"Ugh!" said Melissa.

"Melissa," Beulah Porter Cowys said, "did you ever try stopping to think before you started talking?"

"What?"

"It just so happens that I admit to being forty-nine, myself. What's so repulsive about that?"

"Oh!" said Melissa. "Well—well—well, you don't keep a gigolo."

"That's because I can't afford one."

"Oh now, Beulah," said Melissa. "You're just saying that. What I meant was that it's sort of ugly to think about old people having—having—well, having ideas."

"There are some aged male movie comedians who don't seem to agree with you."

"Oh, them," said Melissa. "They're just sexual neurotics. It's a transference of the youth-longing. Shirley Parker explained it all to me. It's the same sort of urge that makes nasty old men peep into grade-school girls' playgrounds."

"That Shirley Parker," said Beulah Porter Cowys. "She can always give me the creeps in five seconds flat. She makes life sound like an unsupervised pigsty. She and her Freudian theories of motive analysis are enough to turn anyone's stomach. But what I want to know right now is, why is this alleged detective hanging around here?"

"Beulah," said Melissa, "that's simply priceless."

"Remember what I said about slander," Doan warned.

"Pooh! Beulah, this old hag—Heloise, I mean—hired him to keep women away from her pretty husband. I mean, actually. Isn't that a scream?"

"Oh, I don't know," said Beulah Porter Cowys. "Knowing what I know about the morals of the younger generation—and do I know!—I think it's a good idea."

"Oh, Beulah! You're just pretending—"

Something dropped and made a tinny battering clatter inside the second chem lab.

"It's that damned janitor eavesdropping again!" Beulah Porter Cowys snapped angrily. "Morales! Come here!"

A man eased himself out of the lab and looked at them in

an elaborately surprised way. He was short and solid and lack-adaisically stoop-shouldered, and he made each move as though it were the last allowed him and he intended to draw the process out as far as possible. He wore a battered black hat and a shirt with strategic holes in it and overalls that bagged improbably in the rear. He was carrying three galvanized pails in one hand and a floor brush over his shoulder.

"Hallo, peoples," he said in a liquidly lazy way. "You want something of Maximilian Morales, no?"

"No," Beulah Porter Cowys agreed. "Go away somewhere."

"Wait a minute," Melissa intervened. "Morales, can't you do something about the smell in Number 5?"

"I?" said Morales. "No."

"Yes, you can. You can calcimine those partitions or something—at least, that'll give the place a new kind of an odor."

"Calcimine?" said Morales. "I? I have eight children, senorita."

"What has that got to do with it?"

"Senorita, it is very hard to have eight children. It makes a man tired. I, Maximilian Morales, am tired."

"Well, stop having children then."

"Senorita, you are unreasonable."

"Eight children are enough."

"No," said Morales. "You will pardon me, senorita, but eight children are not enough."

"Why not?"

"Because none of them are any good. That is why it is necessary for me to arrange to have a ninth. Perhaps it will be smart enough to provide a comfortable old age for its honored father and jobs for its stupid brothers and sisters. One can only hope and keep trying."

"For how long?" Beulah Porter Cowys inquired.

Morales shrugged wearily. "That, of course, becomes a question one often considers at our age."

"Just be careful, now, Morales," Beulah Porter Cowys warned.

"I am always careful, senorita. It becomes an established mannerism in one of my breeding. You have, no doubt, heard of my great-great-great grandmother?"

"Too many times."

Morales nodded politely at Doan. "My great-great-great grandmother was regarded with a certain amount of favor by the great Maximilian, Emperor of all Mexico."

"Congratulations," Doan said.

"Thank you, senor. Is that your dog lying on the floor which is my care and responsibility?"

"Yes."

"Has the dog been trained, senor, to avoid—ah—accidents of an intimate nature?"

"He's very well educated," Doan said.

"You relieve my mind, senor. It is easy to see that with a dog of such great stature, an accident might be overwhelming."

"He never slips."

"He is to be congratulated. Now, if you will excuse me, I will resume my duties."

"Here," said Melissa. "Wait a minute. Aren't you going to do anything about fixing up Number 5?"

"Naturally not," said Morales, disappearing into the lab.

"Why all this sudden concern about Number 5?" Beulah Porter Cowys asked.

"Handsome Lover Boy has appropriated my office."

"Well, didn't you remonstrate with him?"

"Certainly. He just sat and sneered."

"Did you kick to Sley-Mynick?"

Melissa shrugged. "Yes, but you know how he is. Handsome Lover Boy evidently sneered at him, too, and that threw him into an outside loop."

"Is Sley-Mynick the puffy guy who pip-pips at people?" Doan

asked. "What goes with him, anyway? He acts like someone had just given him a hotfoot."

"He's troubled with international spies," Beulah Porter Cowys said.

"Beulah," said Melissa, "it's not really right to make fun of him. He's a refugee, Mr. Doan. He's a very brilliant research biochemist. He was a professor at some university near Budapest with a name I can't pronounce. I don't know just what he did, if anything, but when Hungary threw in with Hitler, Sley-Mynick was arrested and put into a concentration camp. They must have treated him terribly there. Apparently it wrecked his nervous system."

"Did he escape from the place?" Doan asked.

"No. They decided, after they had half-killed him, that he was harmless and let him go. After that, though, he did sneak out of Hungary and get to Mexico some way or other. Then he nearly starved down there waiting for a passport permit to get into the United States. Once he got here, he ate so much he got bloated. He's had a rough time of it, and he's so jumpy and jittery yet that he can't even give lectures. He hates to meet strangers, and if anyone starts staring at him, he tries to crawl inside his clothes. It's a shame, because I think he must have been a nice man before all this happened to him."

"He was anyway a damned good biochemist," Beulah Porter Cowys added.

"What do you teach?" Doan asked.

"Elementary physics. Very dull stuff."

A man came running up the front steps of the building and bounced through the front door. He sensed that there was someone in front of him, and he stopped so quickly he skidded, peering at them in a myopically eager way. He was all hands and feet and freckles, and his red hair was slicked down painfully flat except for three clumps at the back that stuck out like an un-trimmed hedge. He spotted Melissa and gave another bounce and an embarrassed gulp.

"Oh! Hello, hello! Hello, Melissa! I was just going to drop into your office and—and say hello."

"You'd better say it here," Melissa advised. "My office has been liberated."

"Really?"

"Yes. The enemy is in possession."

"What enemy?"

"A party known as Handsome Lover Boy, alias Eric Trent."

"Trent," said the newcomer. "Oh, yes. He's the new meteorology man. I met him at the faculty lunch yesterday. He's very nice."

"He is not!"

"Isn't he?" the man asked anxiously.

"No! He's a boor and—and a cad!"

"Really?" said the man. "Was he rude to you, Melissa? Shall I go up and hit him in the face?"

"Never mind," Melissa said. "Mr. Doan, this is Frank Ames. He's an assistant professor of English. Mr. Doan is Handsome Lover Boy's bodyguard, Frank."

"How odd," Ames said absently. "Melissa, you haven't forgotten, have you? Tonight, I mean? Our date?"

"No, Frank. Just see that you don't forget."

"I certainly wouldn't forget anything that concerned you or— Oh! Your letter!" He commenced to fumble through his pockets. "It was in your slot over at Administration…. I put it somewhere I wouldn't lose…. Here!"

Melissa took the letter and opened it. "Well, well. A personal missive from the president's office, if you please. And signed by T. Ballard Bestwyck in person or a rubber stamp…. Oh! *Ooooooh!*"

"What?" asked Beulah Porter Cowys.

"Gluck-gluck-gluck," Melissa said in frustrated incoherence. "Cluck! It says I have to exchange apartments in Pericles Pavilion with that—that—that—with Handsome Lover Boy because the one I'm in is a double and his is a single and he needs more room! Just after I've gotten mine decorated to suit me! I won't do it! I—will—not—do—it!"

"Oh, yes, you will," said Beulah Porter Cowys.

"Why?" Melissa demanded defiantly.

"Because T. Ballard Bestwyck told you to, and T. Ballard Bestwyck sits at God's right hand."

"Oh, damn!" said Melissa. "Oh, double damn-damn-damn!"

THE MOON was riding high, red and fat and swollen with its own importance, when Frank Ames' dusty little coupe puttered up the hill and pulled into the curb opposite the Pericles Pavilion.

Frank Ames turned off the coupe's motor. He swallowed and took three long, deep breaths and then turned and stared at Melissa in a portentously concentrated manner. Melissa sighed and wiggled a little on the slippery seat. She knew what was coming. It always did.

"Melissa," said Frank Ames, "I have a very serious matter which I wish to present to you for your consideration. I wish to ask you—to entreat you—"

"Thank you for the dinner and the movie," Melissa said.

"No," said Frank Ames. "I mean, it was a pleasure, but that isn't what I wanted to—"

"I had a very nice time," Melissa told him.

"What? Oh; that's nice, but Melissa, I feel that you and I are ideally constituted to embark upon—"

Melissa opened the door on her side. "Don't bother to come in with me, Frank. It's late, and I know you're as tired as I am. The first day of the quarter is always a bore, isn't it?"

"What? Yes. Yes, indeed. But, Melissa, I haven't had a chance to tell you how I feel about—"

"Good night, Frank," said Melissa. "I've really got to run."

"But—but—but—"

"See you tomorrow!" said Melissa.

"Oh," said Frank Ames glumly, "Drat."

Melissa ran across the street. The Pericles Pavilion, in spite of its classically resounding title, was nothing but a small apartment house, a little ragged and run down at the heels. There was no point in keeping it up to snuff, because it had no competition, and besides no one but a few instructors and assistants lived there. It belonged to the university, and hence it came under the autocratic direction of T. Ballard Bestwyck, who subscribed to the theory that the payment of the most rent possible entitled the payer to the least comfort feasible because it was obvious to him that no one but an idiot would pay rent in the first place.

Melissa pushed through the squeaky double door and went on through the narrow L-shaped lobby and up the scuffed stairs to the second floor. She hadn't moved out of her apartment as yet. She knew very well that there was no question of whether she would move—just a matter of when. But nonetheless she was determined to fight as stubborn a delaying action as possible.

She was directly in front of the apartment, fumbling for the key in her purse, when she noticed that the door was not quite closed. Melissa drew in her breath slowly. She thought of a great many lurid words and applied them all to a personality known as Handsome Lover Boy.

Very quietly she pushed the door open wider. The light in her living room was not on, and the furniture looked distorted and unfamiliar. The door of her bedroom was open, and there was a light in there—dim and bluish and indistinct. Melissa knew that this light came from the reading lamp clamped on the head of her bed, and she began to seethe inside at the mere thought.

She tiptoed across the living room and stopped in the bedroom doorway. The light did come from her reading lamp, and it reflected from the brightly patterned spread on her bed and from the brightly painted face of the little Spanish clock on her night table. Melissa saw, without noticing, that the gilt hands of the clock were lined up at midnight exactly.

There was a man standing in front of her dresser with his back to her. Melissa opened her mouth, but she didn't speak. There was something queer about this man.

Melissa swallowed against the sudden tightness in her throat. The man's head was black—all black—and it was distorted in back into an ugly knotted lump. His hands were black, too—a different kind of black, smooth and shiny and ridged. He was staring down at a pair of Melissa's nylon stockings that dribbled limply between his black, clumsy fingers.

The Spanish clock whirred very softly to itself and then tinkled out its dusty-sweet little Andalusian peasant tune. The black man made a startled sound deep in his throat. He whirled half-around, and one of his shiny hands reached out for the clock.

"No!" Melissa cried involuntarily.

The black man kept right on turning until he faced her. Melissa knew now what made the blackness of his head. He was wearing a stocking mask, pulled tight and knotted at the back of his neck. There were eyeholes in it, and he was watching her through them. He was wearing black leather gloves on his hands.

He made no sound at all. Melissa backed up a step, and then he moved, coming at her with a deadly, animal-like swiftness.

Melissa screamed—once.

CHAPTER II

IT WAS TWENTY-THREE minutes after eleven when Eric Trent closed the textbook he was reading with a sharp, disgusted snap and said, "I've been reading the same page for the last half hour, and it still doesn't make sense. Let's go get a beer."

Doan had been lying on his back on the chesterfield with

his hands folded across his chest. He sat up instantly and started hunting around for his shoes.

"Now you're talking," he said enthusiastically.

Carstairs was sprawled all over the floor in front of the door. He sat up, too.

"Trent and I are going to the library and get some books," Doan told him.

Carstairs watched him.

"Don't look so damned skeptical!" Doan shouted. "I can read. And dogs aren't allowed in the library, so just relax and lie down again. You're staying here."

Carstairs stood up and turned his back and put his nose against the door.

"All right, all right," Doan said. "Hurry up, Trent. The bars close up in this cockeyed state at midnight."

He opened the door, and Carstairs preceded them down the long hall. This apartment was on the third floor, and there was no elevator. There were no elevators in any of the university buildings with the exception of those frequented by T. Ballard Bestwyck. He did not believe in pampering the lower classes. Doan and Trent, with Carstairs still ahead of them, went down the stairs past Melissa's floor, and on down the first flight and out through the lobby.

Trent's car—a small and shabby two-door sedan—was parked at the curb fifty yards north of Pericles Pavilion. Doan opened the door on the right side and hitched the seat forward.

"Get in back," he ordered. "Snap it up."

Carstairs climbed in distrustfully.

Doan popped the seat back into place and slid into it. "Hurry up. It's half-past eleven."

Trent started the car, and they drove through the narrow, sharply curved residential streets that bordered the university and then out on the smooth, wide sweep of the boulevard that ran south of the campus.

"There's a place," said Doan. "Kerrigan's Klub Kar. Under the green neon sign ahead."

"All right," said Trent absently. He drove the car into the empty graveled lot beside the building and parked.

"Roll your window up about three-quarters of the way and get out and shut your door," Doan said casually. He was lounging back in the seat with his hands folded back of his neck.

Trent looked at him curiously. "Okay."

Doan waited until Trent's door was shut, and then he slipped the catch on the door next to him with his knee. In one smooth motion, he darted out of the car and slammed the door shut behind him. He was not a split second too soon. Carstairs broad, moist muzzle slapped against the inside of the glass an instant after the door thumped shut. His eyes glared through at them, greenishly malignant.

"What's the idea?" Trent asked.

"He's a dry," Doan explained. "He hates liquor. I don't like to take him in bars because he raises hell. He sneers at the customers and barks at the bartender and tips over tables. Hurry up. It's twenty minutes to twelve."

They went up three steps and into a long, dreary room with a bar running along the length of one wall. The place was empty except for the bartender and one chummy customer. The chummy customer hailed them with a loud and lonesome cheer.

"Hiya! Hi there, fellas! Have a drink, huh?"

"Now, Bert," said the bartender.

"Well, I know that guy there," said Bert. "I sure do know that guy. I sure seen his face before lots of times. Sure. Now wait a minute. Don't rush me." He came weaving along the bar. "Hi, fella! I seen you before, ain't I, huh? Huh?"

"Lay off, Bert," said the bartender.

"Yee-hoo!" Bert yelled joyously. "I got it! I know where I saw you! In all them ads for all that face cream junk! Sure! How are you, little old Handsome little old Lover little old Boy? Woo-woo-woo!"

Eric Trent hit him on the side of the neck with the edge of his palm. Bert came apart at the seams. He hit the floor so hard he bounced. After that he didn't move at all.

"Here!" the bartender said indignantly. "What's the idea? He's my best customer. I recognize your face myself. If you want to marry some old crow for her dough and advertise it in all the magazines, you've got no right to get sore if people rib you about it. What did you do to Bert?"

"This," said Trent.

The bartender's jaw smacked against the edge of the bar, and then he slid gently and slowly down out of sight behind it.

"Let's get out of here," Trent said.

"I think maybe that's a good idea," Doan agreed reluctantly, looking at the electric clock behind the bar.

It was thirteen minutes of twelve.

They went back outside, and Doan opened the left door of the sedan.

"Oh, stop snorting at me," he ordered. "I didn't have anything to drink—not even a beer. Get in the back."

Carstairs climbed over the seat, muttering to himself.

Doan got in. "We'll have to hurry," he said. "It's almost midnight."

Trent pushed the starter. "I've lost my thirst."

"Well, I haven't," said Doan. "Drive around fast and find a place where I can pick up a pint."

Trent drove out on the boulevard. "I've got a bottle at home you can have."

"Where?" Doan demanded. "I searched that apartment from stem to stern the other morning when I was suddenly taken with a hangover."

"That big green book in my bookcase—the one with the Greek lettering on it—is a fake. It's hollow. There's a fifth of bourbon in it."

"Do tell," said Doan. "Have you got any more literature like that?"

"No. I wouldn't have that except for the fact that my wife bought it for me."

"She's very thoughtful of you," Doan told him. "She not only gives you liquor, but she also provides you with a party named Doan to drink it."

"Yes," said Trent.

They drove back through the winding residential streets. Trent parked the car at the curb near the Pericles Pavilion, where it had been before. Garages are an affectation in Southern California and aren't used except by people who wish to impress, or don't trust, their neighbors.

"Come on, stupid," Doan said, holding the door open for Carstairs.

The three of them were on the steps of the apartment building when the chimes in the university chapel tower began to boom lugubriously.

"Twelve o'clock," said Doan, pushing through the doors into the lobby, "and all's well."

And then the three of them stopped short.

"What was that?" Trent demanded.

"A dame screaming," said Doan. "There must be a wife-beater hidden around this rat trap somewhere."

He was watching Carstairs. Carstairs had his head raised alertly. His ears were pricked forward, and a muscle quivered nervously in his shoulder.

"Find them," said Doan.

Carstairs and Doan both moved so fast then that Trent was caught flatfooted. Carstairs was at the top of the first flight of stairs and Doan was halfway up before Trent could get started. He pounded after them, taking the steps three at a jump. He turned out into the hall at the top.

Doan was halfway along it, standing in front of an open apartment door. He had his right hand inside the front of his coat. Trent pulled up behind him and stared over his shoulder.

Melissa was lying in a bedraggled heap in the middle of the living room floor. Her eyes were shut and her mouth was open and her legs were sprawled immodestly. Carstairs was just inside the door, watching her with his head lowered and one huge paw raised.

"What?" said Trent. "What was…. Why, it's that homely girl who wanted me to give her my office! What's the matter with her? What happened to her?"

"Somebody popped her on the jaw," Doan said absently, "and knocked her cold. See where her heel dragged in front of the bedroom door?"

Trent looked at the heel mark and then he looked down at Melissa. "Well, not so homely." He twisted his head around and took a step across the room. "In fact, considered from the proper angle, rather nice. I've seen the time when I could use something like this. I'd prefer her conscious, of course."

"Huh," said Doan. "From what I hear, when she's conscious she doesn't prefer you."

Carstairs swung about to stare up at Doan and give him an inquiring look.

Doan nodded. "Yeah. Let's find the bird who did the bopping."

Carstairs walked out into the hall, still eyeing Doan.

"Go on," said Doan. "Get him."

Carstairs started with a lunge and headed down the hall toward the back of the building like an arrow out of a bow.

"Pick up the doll and paste her together," Doan said to Trent. "We're busy."

Doan turned and ran back down the front stairs. He skidded to a stop in the lobby, listening. He was holding a .38 Colt Police Positive in his right hand now—Carstairs bayed from the back of the building.

"Yeah!" said Doan.

He ran back through the lower hall, whirled around a corner with the revolver up and poised. Carstairs was standing up against a closed door further along, pawing at its panels with the claws of both front paws.

"Get away," said Doan, shouldering him aside. "This is the cellar, I think. Watch it."

He pulled the door open, staying partially behind it. There was nothing on the other side but pitch darkness. Carstairs dove heedlessly right into it. There was a rumble and a bump as he hit a lower level and then the skitter of his claws on cement.

"Wait until I find the light, you fool," Doan ordered.

Carstairs began to bellow in furious frustration.

"All right," said Doan.

He pushed ahead into the blackness, located steps under his feet, and went stumbling and sliding down them, waving both arm's wildly over his head. He hit bottom and fell headlong over something that rattled and rolled tinnily.

Carstairs was raising racketing echoes somewhere in front of him.

Doan scrambled to his feet and groped blindly forward until he bumped into Carstairs and then into another closed door. He found the catch and pulled the door back. Fresh, cool air puffed into his face, and Carstairs lurched up a half flight of cement steps and out into the open. Doan ran up after him and came out in the back areaway of the apartment house. It was surrounded by a high, thick hedge.

An opening showed dimly at Doan's right, and he headed for it. A clothesline brushed his hair neatly and eerily, and then he burst through the opening and stumbled on the rough surface of a narrow alley. Carstairs made a motionless, stilt-legged shadow ten feet away. He snorted at Doan in a disgusted way.

"Lost him, huh?" said Doan. "Well, don't just stand there with your teeth in your mouth. Get out and beat around in the weeds in that lot. Go on. Hike."

Carstairs faded silently into the darkness.

Doan began to walk very cautiously down the alley, slipping silently along with his head half-turned so he could watch in both directions, searching each shadow. He had gone about twenty yards when something whispered spitefully past his ear and something else twitched the cuff of his coatsleeve and a third something drew a line across the telephone pole he was touching with his left hand.

Doan was falling by that time, and as he dropped he heard the reports—three of them very close together, but sharp and nastily distinct. He flattened himself on the dirt, hiding his face in the crook of his elbow. He was swearing at himself in a mumbling undertone.

Carstairs came down the alley, running low and very fast and making fierce little grunting sounds. Doan thrust out his arm and caught Carstairs halfway up his front legs. Carstairs did a complete somersault in the air and came down flat on his back with a breathless "Ga-whoomp."

Doan hitched forward and fell across him. "Be still!" he snarled. "Quiet!"

They lay there in a rigid, motionless tangle. In a couple of moments, a car starter ground somewhere close. The engine caught with a choked roar, and then tires made a long wailing protest as the car whirled around a corner. The sound died away.

"Wow," said Doan softly, sitting up.

Carstairs sat up, too, and glared at him.

"Oh, relax," said Doan. "Why do you act so stupid? That boy had a gun, and he certainly knows how to use it. He was just on the other side of that street light ahead. If you had run out under that light, he'd have picked you off like a duck on a rock."

Carstairs grunted.

"The same to you," said Doan. "I certainly get a lot of thanks for all the care and attention I lavish—what's the matter with you now?"

Carstairs rumbled deep in his throat. His head was turned away from Doan, and he was watching an apartment-size trash can on the other side of the alley. The lid of the can was tipped drunkenly to one side.

Doan was on his feet instantly. The hammer of his revolver made a soft, metallic click.

"Come out of that," he said.

There was no answer—no sound.

Doan approached the can, circling. Close to it, he put his right foot against the upper part and heaved. The lid fell off with a rattling clangor. The can tilted past its balance line and fell suddenly on its side.

Doan's breath hissed through his teeth. A foot protruded from the open end of the can—a man's foot clad in a tan sport shoe. The foot was queerly limp.

It didn't move.

Leaning down suddenly, Doan took hold of the foot and jerked hard. The rest of the man's body slid loosely and easily out of the can.

"This is nice, too," said Doan. "Oh, this is just dandy."

He found a match and snapped it on his thumbnail. The man's throat had been cut with one deft, neat slash that began under his ear and slanted down and across. His face was smeared thickly with blood, but Doan recognized him at once. He was Frank Ames. He was dead.

Doan dropped the match and nodded solemnly at Carstairs. "The bird we were chasing so merrily carries a knife and a gun, and he operates in a very fancy way with both or either. I don't think we would care to know him any better, but I'm afraid we're going to."

Carstairs began to scratch himself.

DOAN and Carstairs came into the apartment building through the front door. The lobby was as empty and shabby as it had been before and would be again, and they were heading for the stairs when the first door on the lower hall opened and two faces peered out at them.

That is, Doan saw two faces. Or, rather, he saw one face multiplied by two—one above the other. It was very uncanny. The two faces duplicated each other exactly. They were round, pink-cheeked, feminine, middle-aged faces. They had braided gray hair tied with blue ribbons. They had blue, frightened eyes that peered at Doan through identical pairs of pince-nez spectacles.

The short hairs at the back of Doan's neck rose and prickled alarmingly. Carstairs made a startled noise through his nose and ducked behind Doan's legs.

"Hello," said the faces.

Doan swallowed. "Hello," he said faintly.

"We are the Misses Aldrich," said the faces.

"Are—are there two of you?" Doan asked.

"Yes. We're twins."

"Oh," said Doan, breathing again. He looked back and down at Carstairs. "You big coward."

"We are specialists," said the Aldriches in fascinating unison, "in the emotional and social conditioning of pre-school-age children. We teach that at the university. To students of education."

"I see," said Doan.

"We heard noises. We heard screams and loud, raucous shouting. We were frightened."

"I'm sorry," said Doan.

"We think we even heard some shots. Do you think you heard some shots, too?"

"Yes," said Doan. "I think I did."

"Do you think there might be some intoxicated persons at large on the premises?"

"I couldn't say," Doan told them.

"Do you think we are in danger?"

"I hardly think so," said Doan.

"Thank you," said the Aldriches, "for reassuring us. You are very kind."

"Thank you," said Doan.

"You have a very large dog."

"Yes," Doan admitted. "Unfortunately."

"We do not have a dog."

"You're lucky."

"But we like dogs very much. Will you be so kind as to allow us to pet your dog at some more appropriate time?"

"I will," said Doan, "but of course the important question is whether or not he will. He doesn't like to be petted. He thinks it demeans him. And now, if you'll excuse me, I'll go up and look into the screaming at a little closer range."

"Be very careful."

"Indeed, I will."

"Good night."

"Good night," said Doan.

He nudged Carstairs with his knee, and the two of them went up the stairs and along the hall to Melissa's apartment. The door was ajar, and Doan pushed it open wider and looked in.

Melissa was lying on the chesterfield, propped up with some wadded pillows. Her hair straggled dankly down over her cheeks, and her mascara had run in futuristic streaks. She looked very repulsive. She was holding an ice bag against the left side of her face, and in the other hand she held a tall glass of murkily powerful looking liquid. She sipped the liquid with little blubbering sounds and glared at Doan. Her eyes weren't focusing very efficiently.

Beulah Porter Cowys was hovering over Melissa, twitching at the pillows and making little croaking sounds that were meant to be soothing. Eric Trent was standing against the opposite wall, trying to appear at ease and find a place to put his hands.

"Well!" said Beulah Porter Cowys. "The great, late detective! What have you been doing all this time—hiding in a dark closet?"

"No," said Doan, "but there was a moment there when I wished I had one to hide in." He nodded at Melissa. "How do you feel now?"

"How do you suppose?"

Beulah Porter Cowys said, "That decorative dimwit dumped a barrel of water in her face."

"It was a glass of water," Trent corrected coldly.

"It was too much, anyway."

"I thought that was the proper remedy in the case of mild shock."

"Well, stop thinking," Beulah Porter Cowys advised. "You aren't equipped for it."

"Mild shock!" Melissa echoed thickly. "What are you talking about? I didn't faint. I was knocked out."

"I'm sorry," said Trent. "I was trying to help you the best way I knew."

"Oh, yeah? What are you doing here, anyway? Lurking and throwing water at people? I suppose you think you can put me out of my apartment while I'm too weak to resist."

"What?" said Trent blankly.

"Oh, stop trying to act innocent. I'm nauseated enough already."

"I don't know what you're talking about," Trent told her.

"It's not important now, anyway, is it?" Doan said quickly. "I mean, there's the matter of this prowler to consider."

Trent looked at him. "I heard some shots. Were you shooting at him?"

"No," said Doan. "On the contrary."

"Oh, phooey with an olive," said Beulah Porter Cowys. "It was probably just a car backfiring."

"Then this car backfired bullets," Doan told her, "and that's not all it did, either. I'm afraid we're going to have to call the police."

"I already have," said Trent. "The first thing."

"Uh!" Doan grunted. "Which police did you call?"

"The sheriff's office—the university substation."

"Oh—oh," said Doan. "Oh—oh—oh."

"What's the matter?" Trent demanded.

"A guy named Humphrey is the deputy-in-charge there. And he doesn't like me any at all."

"Why not?" Beulah Porter Cowys demanded. "Aside from the fact that liking you is a pretty difficult thing to do."

"You're kind to say so," Doan said. "Humphrey has a grudge against me because he hates Carstairs. Carstairs spends nine-tenths of his time alienating people and making enemies. He humiliated Humphrey, and that's a thing that no cop can take. At least, no cop named Humphrey."

"How did he do it?"

"Well," said Doan, "it's like this. Since my youth I have been subject to periodic attacks of vertigo, during which I find it difficult to walk straight. Many callous and uninformed characters—like Carstairs, for instance—think these attacks are due to drinking alcohol in large quantities, but of course that's nonsense."

"Oh, certainly," said Beulah Porter Cowys.

"At the time I'm talking about, by the merest and sheerest coincidence, I was seized by one of my attacks while I was sitting at a bar. So I started home, and I was sort of tacking and veering down the street when Humphrey spotted me. Carstairs, the cad, won't even walk with me when I'm in the throes of one of my attacks for fear people will connect the two of us. He pretends he doesn't know me. This time he was tagging along about fifty yards behind me."

"This is getting good," said Beulah Porter Cowys. "Go on."

"Humphrey grabbed me. He was in plainclothes, and he was

connected with homicide then, and it was none of his affair whether I was drunk—I mean, sick—or not. That's what I told him, and so he started to shove me around, and Carstairs came up and bit him in the pants."

"In the pants?" Beulah Porter Cowys repeated.

"Yes. He didn't touch Humphrey. He just tore the seat clear out of his pants. It was broad daylight on a busy street, and Humphrey collected quite an audience. That made him mad. He's still mad."

"Oh, well," said Beulah Porter Cowys, "maybe he won't be on duty tonight"

"He's always on duty. He never sleeps, for fear he might miss out on a chance to arrest someone. He loves to arrest people. He'll arrest me as soon as he sees me."

"That's nonsense," said Trent. "Policemen don't go around arresting people just because they have a grudge against them."

"Ha?" said Doan. "May I use your telephone, Melissa?"

HUMPHREY was as round and smooth and soft as a custard pie. He came huffing importantly into the apartment, flapping his hat indignantly in his hand, with three uniformed deputies trailing right behind him.

"Now!" he barked. "What's all this nonsense about a prowler—"

He saw Carstairs. There was a pregnant, crackling silence, and then Humphrey's neck began to puff pinkly above his shirt collar.

Carstairs was sitting down, leaning against the wall with his eyes shut, dozing. After awhile he opened one eye and regarded Humphrey in a critical, coldly detached way, and then shut the eye again and went on dozing.

Humphrey turned his head slowly and carefully, with the air of a man who knows there is a coiled rattlesnake near him somewhere. Doan was sitting sprawled out in the lounge chair in the corner.

"There he is," said Humphrey. "That's the guy. Put the cuffs on him."

One of the deputies stepped forward alertly, pulling his handcuffs from their leather case on the back of his belt. Doan held out his hands amiably, and the cuffs snapped around his wrists.

"Search him," Humphrey ordered.

"It's in my waistband," Doan volunteered.

The deputy found the revolver. "It's a .38 Police Positive," he reported.

"And I've got a license to carry it," said Doan.

"You won't have long," Humphrey told him. "All right, you people. You'll have to appear at his arraignment. That'll be in the court in downtown Los Angeles, probably on Wednesday morning. The district attorney's office will get in touch with you. Bring him along, boys."

"Here!" Eric Trent shouted. "What do you think you're doing?"

Humphrey looked at him. "Who're you?"

"My name is Eric Trent. Doan warned me you'd act like this, but I was stupid enough to think you'd have better sense. Doan ate dinner with me, and he was with me continuously from that time up to the time we heard this woman—What's your name, you?"

"It's Melissa Gregory, in case it's any of your business, you."

"Up to the time we heard this Melissa Gregory scream," Trent went on, paying no attention to her tone.

"Trying to alibi him, eh?" said Humphrey. "That just makes you an accessory, bub. And you've got a record, too, haven't you? I've seen your picture before."

"Sir," said one of the deputies.

Humphrey looked at him. "What do you want?"

"He's Handsome Lover Boy."

"What?"

"He's the guy in those cold cream ads."

"Well, I'll be damned," said Humphrey. "So you pose for ads when you're not prowling, eh?"

"Sir," said the deputy.

"Now what?"

"He's really married to that woman—that Heloise of Hollywood. It was in the papers—in the society news—a couple of years back. My wife read it to me."

"Hmmm," said Humphrey, staring at Trent. "Is that a fact? Are you really her husband?"

"Yes," said Trent tightly.

"Hmmm," said Humphrey. "Hmmm." He spun around suddenly and pointed at Doan. "Who hired you?"

"You'll find out," said Doan, "in due course."

"I'll find out right now!"

"My wife hired him," Trent said.

"To do what?"

"To watch me."

"Ah," said Humphrey. "And of course he's playing both ends against the middle as usual. He always does. When anyone hires him to watch someone else, he always runs around to the second party and tells them and then collects from each of them for watching the other. Don't you?"

"Sure," said Doan.

Melissa sat up on the couch. "Listen, you," she said loudly and clearly. "You were called here to investigate a masked prowler who attacked me. Are you going to do that, or are you going to get the hell out of my apartment?"

"Melissa!" Beulah Porter Cowys gasped.

"I mean it," said Melissa. "I'm serious. I've had my nose rubbed in this teak-headed Trent's nasty personal affairs until I'm good and sick of him and them."

"Doan is the prowler," Humphrey told her.

"He is not!"

"Well, then Trent is."

"He isn't, either!"

"How do you know—if the guy was masked?"

"Because he wasn't as tall as Trent nor as fat as Doan."

"You're just trying to make things difficult for me," Humphrey complained.

"I'll make them more difficult," said Doan. "There's a murdered man in an ashcan out in the alley in back."

"Ah-ha!" Humphrey gloated, rubbing his hands. "You heard that confession, all of you? You're witnesses. I've always hoped for a chance to peek at you in the gas chamber, Doan. Who'd you kill? You might as well tell the truth, because I won't believe what you say, anyway."

"I didn't kill anyone," said Doan. "The prowler did it on his way out."

Humphrey waved his hand. "A detail. I know you're the prowler. Who is the guy, and why did you knock him off?"

"His name is Frank Ames."

"Oh!" Melissa gasped.

"Frank," said Beulah Porter Cowys, swallowing with a little croaking sound. "Gee."

"Frank Ames," Trent repeated thoughtfully. "I met someone by that name at the faculty lunch…. Isn't he a red-haired chap? English assistant?"

"That's the one," said Doan.

"Why did you murder him?" Humphrey demanded.

"I just got through telling you I didn't. The prowler did."

"Sure, sure," said Humphrey. "Don't quibble. Just tell me why it happened."

"I'm not sure why. Ames doesn't live here, but I think he must have been visiting someone in the building."

"M-me," said Melissa. "He took me to dinner and the m-movies."

"That's it," said Doan. "Which way did he bring you home—did he drive up the hill?"

"Yes."

Doan nodded at Humphrey. "Here's what happened, then. He swung his car around in a U-turn in the middle of the street. His headlights swung across that alley just as the prowler was coming out of the back areaway. Ames saw him. I think probably the prowler either had taken off or was taking off his mask. He wouldn't want to run around the streets with it on."

"You mean, Ames recognized you?" Humphrey asked.

"I think he must have recognized the prowler. Otherwise Ames wouldn't have gotten out of his car, and he did. His car is headed into the curb ten feet this way from the alley with the door still open. He jumped out and went to find out what the prowler was up to. If he hadn't known the prowler and recognized him, the prowler would just have batted him one like he did Melissa, instead of cutting his throat."

Humphrey nodded at two of the deputies. "Go take a look. See how much of this he's making up."

The two deputies ducked out the door.

Melissa was bent double. "It was my—my—my fault...."

Humphrey pounced. "What? What's that? Speak up."

"Shut up," said Beulah Porter Cowys. "Don't pay any attention to this fat boob, Melissa. Don't say anything at all if you don't want to."

Melissa said slowly, getting the words out with enormous effort: "He tried to ask me to marry him. He had many times—before. I liked him, but... this time I avoided—I slipped away. Oh, Beulah!"

Beulah Porter Cowys seized her competently by the shoulders. "Right in here, honey. Come on." She boosted Melissa to her feet and headed her for the bedroom.

"Wait, now!" Humphrey shouted. "About this prowler. What kind of a mask did he have on?"

"A stocking—a silk stocking. Black. Over his whole head."

"Whole head," said Humphrey. "Whole head…. What about the hands? Did you see them?"

"Gloves. Black shiny gloves."

"That's all," said Beulah Porter Cowys, shepherding Melissa into the bedroom and slamming the door.

"Who is that dame?" Humphrey asked. "The old scrawny one?"

"Beulah Porter Cowys," Trent told him.

"Where'd she come from?"

"She lives down the hall. She heard Melissa Gregory scream and came to see what was wrong."

"She did, did she?" said Humphrey. "Does she ever wear slacks?"

"No," said Doan.

"Yes," said Trent at the same time. He looked at Doan, startled. "What?"

Doan said wearily: "Humphrey is going off into another of his dreams. The prowler wasn't Beulah Porter Cowys because I was chasing the prowler."

"Oh, yeah?" said Humphrey. "It could have been her—with gloves to hide her nail polish and a stocking over her noggin to hide her long hair."

"Smoke another pipe," Doan advised.

"Okay, smarty," said Humphrey. "Did you see this prowler? I mean, did you pass a mirror on your way out?"

"No," said Doan, "but I can give you a handy item of information about him. He packs a gun as well as a knife. It's a .22, and it's an automatic, so it's probably a Colt Woodsman. He's very handy with it. If you'll look, you'll find three ejected shells on the other side of the street light north of the building."

"Now you're dreaming. Why would he want to pack a pea-shooter like a .22?"

"If you can shoot like he can, you don't need anything bigger."

Beulah Porter Cowys came out of the bedroom. "You'll have to adjourn this bull session. Melissa is all shot to pieces. Scat."

"Not so fast," said Humphrey. "Just how well do you know Doan, eh?"

"Just as well as I want to," said Beulah Porter Cowys, "and that's hardly at all."

One of the uniformed deputies squeezed through the front door. "The body is there, sir, and so is the car. It's registered in Ames' name. But look what I found back of the seat."

In front of him, balanced like a tray, he was carrying a very large, thick book with a flossy hand-carved leather cover. The deputy was supporting it with the tips of his fingers. On the cover, stamped in gold, was the legend: THE PATHWAY TO PERFECTION—HELOISE OF HOLLYWOOD.

"I peeked in it," said the deputy. "It tells how to get rid of your wrinkles if you're an old dame and got lots."

"Hmmm," said Humphrey. "Did your wife know Ames, Trent?"

"I don't think so," said Trent.

"She did," said Doan. "He was working for her."

"What?" said Beulah Porter Cowys incredulously. "Frank working for Heloise of Hollywood? You're just completely nuts!"

"Not this time," Doan told her. "She's getting together a new advertising campaign. It's going to be all about middle-aged women who had a big influence on history—had poems written to them and lakes named after them and wars started on account of them and all like that. Ames was doing the research for her."

"How do you know?" Beulah Porter Cowys demanded.

"Because Heloise told me so."

"Hmmm," said Humphrey. "Hmmmm. This case is beginning to develop some angles. Now suppose Ames was getting chummy with Trent's wife, and Trent found it out from Doan and hired Doan to hide in that alley and then lured Ames…."

"Here we go again," said Doan.

Humphrey ignored him. "Or suppose Doan told Heloise that her husband was getting chummy with this Melissa Gregory, and Heloise dropped in here to look around. Of course, Doan would cover for Heloise, because he could shake her down for plenty, and this Melissa would try to throw me off because she doesn't want any scandal. And Ames recognized Heloise and tried a little shaking down of his own, and Doan got mad about that...."

"Is this man crazy or something?" Trent demanded.

"He's certainly something," Doan agreed.

The telephone rang in the bedroom, and Humphrey and Beulah Porter Cowys made a simultaneous dash for it. Melissa was lying face down on the bed, her face buried in her arms. Beulah Porter Cowys leaned over her and grabbed the phone.

"Here!" Humphrey shouted. "Give me that! I warn you now—"

"Shut up," said Beulah Porter Cowys, kicking at him. "Get away.... Hello.... Yes.... Is he a fat, pig-faced character with a big mouth?... Yes, he's here." She extended the telephone toward Humphrey. "It's for you."

"Hello!" Humphrey bellowed. "Who are—Who?.... Yes, sir.... Yes, sir.... Yes, sir.... T. Ballard Bestwyck and the mayor and the president of the Chamber of Commerce and the district attorney—all of them? But Doan doesn't know them.... Yes, sir. I know they know you.... Yes, sir.... Yes, sir.... But there's been a murder, and Doan is involved—Yes, sir.... Yes, sir.... At once, sir."

Humphrey handed the phone back to Beulah Porter Cowys. He looked a little wilted. He went back into the living room and stared at Doan with his shoulders hunched and his lower lip stuck out.

"Hello there, Humphrey," said Doan.

Humphrey grunted. "Take the cuffs off him," he said drearily.

The deputy who wasn't carrying the book unlocked the hand-cuffs.

"Give me my gun," Doan requested.

Humphrey nodded reluctantly, and the deputy handed over the Police Positive. Doan put it in his waistband.

"I don't know yet how you got all that big noise to front for you," Humphrey told him bitterly, "but, oh, you just wait. There'll come a day. And in the meantime—"

Humphrey spun around suddenly and kicked viciously at the spot where Carstairs had been sitting an instant before. Carstairs wasn't there now. Humphrey's foot went through the space he had been occupying and hit the wall hard.

"Oooh-woooo!" Humphrey bellowed.

Carstairs looked out from behind Doan's chair and regarded him with an air of polite inquiry.

Melissa appeared in the bedroom doorway, holding on to both sides of it for support. "You get out of my apartment—all of you!"

Humphrey was standing on one foot, holding the other with both hands. "Now wait a minute. I've got to look for clues—"

"Get out of here!"

Eric Trent said, "I don't think you should stay alone—"

"Shut up, you! Get out!"

Beulah Porter Cowys said, "I'll stay with—"

"Beulah, no! I don't want *anyone* here! I just want everyone to leave me *alone!* Now, go away! Go home! All of you! Get out!"

"Let me leave Carstairs here," Doan said. "He won't bother you, and he won't let anyone in you don't want in."

"All right, all right, all right!"

Doan pointed his finger at Carstairs. "You stay. Do you hear? No one comes in unless she says so."

Carstairs was leaning against the wall again, dozing. He didn't open his eyes.

Trent said: "I still don't think—"

"Get out, get out, get out!" Melissa screamed.

She ran at them and pushed and shoved indiscriminately. They all bumbled and stumbled out into the hall, and she slammed the door and locked it and then propped a chair under the knob.

She sighed shakily, then. Her knees didn't feel like they belonged to her. She went into the bedroom, dragging her heels, and began to undress.

She was unhooking her brassiere when there was a sudden loud and juicy plop from the direction of the kitchen. Melissa stiffened rigidly, feeling her heart inflate like a balloon, and then she whirled around and ran through the living room to the kitchen doorway. She snapped on the light.

The refrigerator door was wide open, and on the floor in front of it there was a large glass bowl of potato salad, wrong side up. Carstairs was regarding this last phenomenon with an air of incredulous amazement.

"You—you!" Melissa shouted. "You thief! You food robber!"

She slashed at him with the brassiere. He dodged that with negligent ease. Melissa's knees gave out entirely, and she sat down and began to bawl, pounding the floor with her fists. Carstairs stared at her, aghast at this unseemly display of emotion, and then stalked into the living room, picking up his feet queasily.

After awhile, Melissa's sobs tapered off in to whimpering sniffles. She got up wearily and picked up the potato salad and wiped the floor.

Shutting the refrigerator door, she went back into the living room. Carstairs was nowhere in sight. Melissa went into the bedroom.

"You!" she shrieked. "Get off that bed! You're not going to sleep—Get off! Get out!"

Carstairs retreated into the living room.

"On the floor!" Melissa shouted. "That's where you're going to sleep! Lie *down!*"

Carstairs bent his legs slightly and then let himself go and hit the floor hard enough to rattle the windowpanes. He rolled over on his side and commenced to snore instantly.

"Oh," said Melissa. "Oh, dear."

MELISSA slept without the hindrance of pajamas or nightgowns or other such impedimenta, and consequently she was in the best condition possible to get the full benefit of Carstairs' nose when he placed it precisely between her shoulder blades. She came out of the dim, pleasant shadows of her private dream world in one hair-raising leap.

"What—what—what—" she gabbled, sitting up and kicking frantically at the covers.

Carstairs backed away from the bed. The sun was pushing bright, inquisitive fingers through the half-closed slats of the Venetian blinds.

"You!" said Melissa. "I'll break every bone— Oooooh!" She felt the side of her face in a gently experimental way. Her jaw was hot and puffed and sore. It felt awful. Her mouth didn't taste at all good, either.

"Oh—oh—oh," said Melissa miserably. She dug at her eyes with her fists and then squinted painfully at the little Spanish clock. "Ten minutes of seven! What do you mean by waking me up at the crack of dawn, you stupid brainless monstrosity?" Carstairs continued to regard her with an air of urgency. "What's wrong with you?" Melissa demanded. Carstairs lifted one forefoot and then the other in a painfully anxious way.

"Oh!" said Melissa. "You want to go, don't you! And the door downstairs is closed…. Oh, damn! All right, all right. Wait until I get dressed."

She went into the bathroom and looked in the mirror and nearly frightened herself to death. Her cheek was inflated ludicrously, and along the lower side it was beginning to exhibit an interesting tinge of purple.

Carstairs whiffled from near the front door. "All right," said Melissa, hurrying.

She put on some slacks and moccasins and a sweater and swiped at her hair with a comb and then went out into the living room. Carstairs was standing with his knees bent and his nose pressed against the front door.

Melissa opened it for him, and Carstairs shot down the hall and raised rumbling echoes on the stairs. He was waiting unwillingly at the front door of the building when Melissa got there. She opened the door for him. Carstairs slipped through and dove gratefully into the shrubbery that circled the building.

Melissa sat down on the steps. She found a cigarette and a match in the pocket of her slacks. The cigarette tasted like underdone steel filings.

It was one of those spring mornings in Southern California that are so incredibly beautiful they seem indecent in some vague way. The sun was just clearing the last of the night mist out of the sky, and the palm trees—like king-sized, upended feather dusters—nodded and dipped in polite unison at the urge of a softly caressing breeze.

Carstairs peered out the shrubbery to make sure Melissa was still waiting for him and then disappeared again. The door clicked in back of Melissa, and the Aldrich twins appeared. They looked at Melissa, taking in the slacks and the cigarette and the straggling hair and the swollen cheek. They smiled in a patient, forgiving way.

"Good morning," they said.

"Morning," said Melissa.

"It's a nice day."

"Is it?" Melissa asked.

Carstairs came out of the shrubbery and sat down on the steps beside Melissa with a luxurious, replete sigh.

The Aldriches said, "That is the large dog which belongs to the plump, pleasant-spoken man who rooms with Mr. Eric Trent."

"Yes," Melissa admitted. "His name is Doan. The man's. The dog's name is Carstairs."

"Mr. Eric Trent is very handsome," said the Aldriches.

"So they say."

"We understand that he is married."

"I understand that, too."

"Hmmm," said the Aldriches. They watched her for a moment, and then they looked at Carstairs. "Mr. Doan intimated that we might pet him."

"Go right ahead," Melissa invited.

"Here, Carstairs," said the Aldriches. "Here, nice dog."

Carstairs watched them for a moment, obviously weighing alternatives. Finally he got up and stepped over to them. He permitted them three pats each, and then he went back and sat down with the air of a person who has done his duty.

"We must go now," said the Aldriches. "We always walk before breakfast. Early to bed and early to rise, you know."

"I know," Melissa agreed.

They went down the steps and along the walk. They were exactly the same height, and they walked in step.

The door clicked again, and Beulah Porter Cowys came out.

"Are they gone for good?" she asked. "They're a little too plural for me at this hour."

"What are you doing out so early?"

"I've got to set up the lab for my 1-B class. I was too busy to do it last night. I'm sorry about Frank, Melissa. Were you going to marry him?"

"No."

"Why not?"

"He wasn't very grown up—I mean, in the head. He used to quote me poetry—Herrick and Lovelace and that sort of stuff."

"They're good poets."

Melissa shrugged. "They're more in the Aldriches' style. You know, they're sort of an interesting pair. They're identical siblings. That's why they talk and even think alike. It seems that the one fertilized gene splits—"

"Pah!" said Beulah Porter Cowys. "That's Shirley Parker and her Freudian interpretation of biology again. I can recognize her touch. The Aldriches talk and think alike because they've lived within arm's reach of each other for sixty years, and that's the only reason. I'll see you later, Melissa. Keep your chin up."

She walked down the steps, and Carstairs leaned over and growled confidentially in Melissa's ear.

"What do you want?" Melissa demanded.

Carstairs licked his chops.

"Oh, dear," said Melissa. "Do I have to feed you, too? What on earth do you eat for breakfast? Orange juice, oatmeal, bacon and eggs?"

Carstairs tilted his head back and bayed joyously.

"Stop that!" Melissa ordered. "You'll wake up the whole town! Can't you wait until I finish this cigarette?… Stop it, I said! I'll feed you…. Yes, right now. Come on."

CHAPTER III

THE STUDENTS WERE beginning to stir when Melissa walked diagonally across the Old Quad with Carstairs tagging dutifully along behind her. The students gathered in cackling flocks or walked alone brooding upon the pitfalls in academic life, as is their wont. Strangers are apt to be disconcerted by their odd mannerisms, but Melissa was accustomed to them and knew that all they needed was to be ignored.

Eric Trent was sitting on the front steps of Old Chem. He stood up quickly when he saw Melissa and Carstairs and then, realizing that they had already seen him, sat down again reluctantly and stared into space.

"Hello," said Melissa.

"How do you do," Trent said warily.

"I'm tired," Melissa told him. "Will it distress you if I sit here on the steps?"

"Not at all," said Trent.

Carstairs sat down, too, and regarded Trent in a speculative way. He received no signs of recognition in return, and after a moment he snorted once, loudly, and then lay down and went to sleep.

There was a prolonged and weighty silence, and then finally Trent said:

"I'm very sorry about last night. About your own experience, and about the death of your friend."

"Thanks," said Melissa.

"In regard to your apartment. Doan spoke to my wife about getting a larger one. He has to sleep on my chesterfield, and he says it gives him bad dreams. My wife knows T. Ballard Best-wyck. She arranged things with him. I had nothing to do with it at all. I didn't know anything about it. Of course, I'm not going to appropriate your apartment. Doan can get himself a hotel room if he doesn't like my chesterfield."

"That's very sweet of you, sweet and generous," Melissa said and she looked at him with eyes that shone. "Maybe you aren't a bad guy after all—that is, not as much of a dope as I believed you to be at first after reading those sticky-icky things your wife said about you in her advertisements…. However, before I can be sure, I'd like proof."

"What kind of proof?"

"Proof of how really sweet and generous you are. For instance, if you gave me back my office as well as my apartment, then I could believe some very fine things of you—practically any fine thing you wanted me to believe."

Trent regarded her with a puzzled frown. There was guile in her face but there was also sincerity. "Well," he said in a relent-ing tone. "Well…." But then he stopped relenting and lifted his chin with the air of a man who's been taken in by a female before and has no intention of being a two-time sucker. "No," he said firmly. "You don't need that particular office and I do."

"Hmmph," said Melissa, "so that's the way it is. And I'll bet I know why. You think Doan would figure you for a sissy if you gave in to a woman."

"That's not so."

"It is too. I know it is. Why do you put up with Doan, anyway? I mean, tagging you around and sleeping on your chesterfield and all that?"

"There's no way I could prevent him from following me around. There's no law against it. So I thought I might as well make the best of it. As a matter of fact, I like Doan. He's very good company. He's very adaptable. If I want to talk, he listens. If I want to study or work or read, he goes to sleep. Apparently he can sleep anytime, anywhere. Of course, there's always Carstairs. He's a bore."

Carstairs mumbled to himself.

"Why don't you assert yourself?" Melissa asked. "I mean, why don't you tell Doan you'll sock him in the eye if he doesn't go away?"

Trent looked at her. "Doan? That wouldn't have the slightest effect. He's not afraid of violence at all. In fact, I think he enjoys it. I think that's why Carstairs likes him. Everyone else is afraid of Carstairs—at least, a little. Doan is not—not a bit."

"Well, they're rather odd chaperones. I should think they'd cramp your style."

"They don't. I'm not interested in women."

"Is that a fact?" said Melissa.

"Yes."

"Oh."

A shaky voice said, "P-p-please…."

Trent and Melissa looked up. There was a girl standing on the walk in front of the steps, facing them. She was wearing a plaid skirt and a red sweater, both turned inside out. She was wearing her left shoe on her right foot and her right shoe on her left foot. There was a circle painted in lipstick on one of her cheeks and a double cross drawn with eyebrow pencil on the other. Her hair was drawn right straight up from her head into a topknot and stiffened with soap or grease. She was holding a magazine in one hand and a fountain pen in the other.

"Please," she said, staring at Trent with dilated eyes, "will you autograph this—this for me?"

She held out the magazine open to one of the Heloise of Hollywood ads.

"What?" said Trent.

"Oh, please," said the girl. "If you don't, they'll take me back to the house and paddle me on my b-bare skin. And they paddle awfully hard."

"Who?" said Trent incredulously.

The girl rolled her eyes mutely to indicate a group of girls standing about twenty yards away. These were all normally dressed—that is, normally for girl students. They were watching with a sort of sly, breathless anticipation.

"What's the meaning of this?" Trent demanded.

"She's a pledge," said Melissa. "This is Hell Week for sorority pledges. She's going through her initiation. They always make pledges do embarrassing things like this—or worse. Let's see your pledge pin…. She's a Delta Gamma. Go ahead and sign her ad. She really will get paddled unless you do."

"All right," said Trent.

The girl handed him the pen and the magazine. "Will you," she said, cringing, "will you sign it Handsome Lover Boy?"

Trent made a strangling noise.

"Oh, go ahead," Melissa said. "Give her a break."

Trent was white around the nostrils, but he signed.

"Aw, creepers," said the girl, breathing again. "Thanks a million, and I'm sorry."

Trent handed her the magazine and the pen. "Are any of your

cute sorority sisters—any of the upperclassmen—taking meteorology?"

"Why, yes," said the girl. "Four or five of them."

"Tell them," said Trent, "not to bother about studying or
turning in any papers I assign, because every one of them is
going to flunk the course."

"You mean it?" said the girl. "Oh, good—good!"

She ran back to the group of girls. They opened up to receive
her, giggling. The girl said something. The group stopped giggling. Their heads turned in unison in Trent's direction. They
huddled and argued. They looked at Trent again. They turned
around and walked away very soberly. The pledge, trailing
behind, looked over her shoulder and leered gleefully.

"You cooled them off," said Melissa. "That house has been
up before the Dean of Women once already this year for lousy
grades. Are you really going to flunk them?"

"Yes."

"They'll send a delegation of seniors to apologize to you
tomorrow."

"They'll still flunk."

"They'll wail at the Dean of Women and probably at T.
Ballard Bestwyck."

"And they'll still flunk."

"You're sort of a determined character," said Melissa. "And
awfully touchy."

"You're entitled to think so, if you like."

"Now don't get mad," Melissa said. "I know it's none of my
business, but you can't blame me for being curious."

"What about?"

"Well, you act sometimes like you have half-good sense. You
certainly knew what anyone intelligent would think about those
ads. Why did you let your wife put them in all those magazines
in the first place?"

"I didn't let her. I didn't know she was doing it."

"You can read, can't you?"

Trent looked at her, exasperated. "For the last four years—up until a few months ago—I was sitting on an ice pack in the middle of the Arctic Ocean. All my supplies and mail were delivered by jeep plane. I didn't order any women's magazines, and consequently I never saw one."

"What on earth were you doing in the middle of the Arctic Ocean?"

"That's where the weather makes up—the weather that affects the flying conditions on the Great Circle route through Alaska and Siberia. There were quite a few isolated weather stations up around there."

"Oh. Who was up there with you?"

"One Aleut and two Eskimos."

"Males?"

"Yes."

"I'm an anthropologist," Melissa said. "I know what they use to cure the furs they wear. Did these use it?"

"Yes."

"Ugh," said Melissa. "They must have been very sweet-smelling companions. I had the idea that you'd only been married about two years."

"That's right."

"Well, how *did* you manage it?"

"Do you know where Point Barrow is—on the extreme northern tip of Alaska?"

"I know now."

"Well, I came south to there from my station, in the supply plane, to get a tooth filled. There was a Navy port authority at the Point, and a Navy dentist called on them once in awhile. Heloise—my wife—was there at the time."

"What? What was she doing clear up there?"

"It seems that in her cosmetics she uses some very exotic materials of one sort and another. The juices from arctic lichen

d walrus blubber and all that sort of thing. This
llected at Point Barrow. She had a big batch of it
. It was worth a lot of money, and the naval port
:r refused to assign shipping space for it. She got
ı a transport plane—she has a great deal of influence—a..d went up to see about the matter. She was still arguing
with the commander when I arrived."

"I see," said Melissa. "How many white women were living
at Point Barrow?"

"At this time she was the only one there."

"Hmmm," said Melissa. "You'd been up on that ice floe for
two years before that?"

"Yes."

"I see," said Melissa slowly.

"See what?"

"Oh, nothing. Just a little matter I was curious about."

"Heloise is a very attractive-looking woman."

"Did I say she wasn't? Is she actually fifty-four?"

"She doesn't look it."

"Not, anyway, after two years on an ice pack."

"That had nothing whatsoever to do with it!"

"Well, all right. Don't be so huffy. I'm not arguing with you."

"What are you doing?"

Poking my nose in your business," Melissa admitted frankly.
"You can snub me now, if you like."

"I can't snub everybody in the world."

"That's true enough. Can I ask you something else?"

"I don't know of any way I can stop you."

"Well," said Melissa, "isn't it true that when you got back
here again and found out about those ads and sort of surveyed
the rest of the feminine population—"

"No!"

"You don't even know what I was going to ask."

"I certainly do."

"Well, I'm not blaming you."

"Blaming me for what?"

"For getting smart and walking out on her."

"I didn't!"

"Oh, phooey," said Melissa. "She agreed to let you go peacefully if you'd lay low and let Doan keep tabs on you until she buried that Handsome Lover Boy drool and started another advertising campaign."

"You know," said Trent, "judging from your unconventional visitor last night, I should think you'd have enough troubles of your own to sort of keep you busy."

"I guess you're right," Melissa admitted. "What happened after I ran you out of my apartment last night?"

"Nothing, actually. I mean, they didn't find out anything except what Doan had already guessed. That Humphrey is so interested in getting something—it doesn't matter what, apparently—on Doan that he hardly has time for anything else. They went up to my apartment last night, and he and Doan both got drunk. The only change that rings in is that they argue more loudly. If you know who that prowler is, you're the only one who does or is likely to find out."

"Doan called your wife, didn't he? When he thought Humphrey would be likely to arrest him?"

"Yes."

"She must really know a lot of influential men in these parts."

"No. She knows their wives. You've seen that enormous monstrosity of a beauty salon of hers out on Sunset Boulevard, haven't you? Her headquarters? That place is staffed like a battleship.

She doesn't make any money out of it—even though the prices are something terrific. She keeps it for prestige. She lures motion picture stars into the place and fills them up with liquor—it's easy to get drunk in a steam cabinet—and then finagles free testimonials out of them."

"I don't think I'd like her."

"Nobody—I mean, perhaps not."

"I'd like to meet her, though."

Trent said, "If you ever do—and tell her that you know me—you're likely to get a reception that will surprise you."

"Why?" Melissa asked.

"Never mind. Just don't tell her."

A new voice said, "Hi, Melissa."

"Hello, Shirley," Melissa said.

This girl was small and slim and dark, dainty as a new doll. She had very large, mildly vague brown eyes and black hair gathered into two thick braids that dangled forward over her shoulders and down over an attractively prominent chest. She was wearing a sloppy-joe sweater with the sleeves pushed up and moccasins and a pair of blue denim jeans with three fountain pens in the right hip pocket.

"You look, terrible," she said to Melissa. "I heard about your prowler from Beulah Porter Cowys. That must have been a very interesting experience."

"Oh, it was."

"How did it make you feel? Now don't just tell me you were scared. I want to know specifically. Did you feel a tingling sensation in—"

"Shirley! Now, stop it! I didn't feel any tinglings, and I'm not going to talk about it any more."

"Well, why not?"

"Just because," said Melissa flatly and finally. "Shirley, this is Eric Trent—meteorology. This is Shirley Parker. She's a special—doing graduate work for a master's in psychology."

"How do you do," said Trent.

"You're Handsome Lover Boy," said Shirley.

"And what if I am?"

Shirley shrugged. "Now there's no point in reacting toward me in a hostile manner. The name is simply a word association picture with me. I don't feel any contempt toward you on account of it."

"Well, thanks very much," said Trent.

"Your attitude shows an obvious repression there. You ought to work it out. How do you feel when you approach your wife?"

"What?"

"You heard what I said. Wasn't the question clear?"

"It's clear that it's none of your business!"

"Oh, yes, it is. I'm writing a monograph on the subject—to get my master's. It's going to be published by the university press."

"I don't care to be in it."

"I wouldn't use your real name," Shirley assured him. "You'd just be an anonymous case history."

"No, thanks," said Trent.

"You're not showing the scientific attitude."

"You're right," Trent agreed.

"People make things very difficult for me," Shirley complained. "I mean, they're all so stupidly touchy on the subject of sex."

"Hi, everybody," said Doan. He was wearing a brown tweed sport coat now and brown tweed slacks and a dark green sport shirt.

"Hello, Mr. Doan," said Melissa.

"How do you feel this morning?" Trent asked.

"Not too bad," Doan told him. "I mean, I'm breathing—I think."

"Two of our third floor neighbors complained this morning about the noise last night."

"Humphrey always talks loud when he's drunk."

"You were doing all right in that line yourself."

"Self-defense," said Doan. "You have to talk loud to Humphrey, or else he won't pay any attention."

"He didn't, anyway."

Doan nodded. "Humphrey is very stupid, I fear. Who's this, here?"

Melissa said: "Shirley, this is Mr. Doan. He's a detective. This is Shirley Parker, Mr. Doan."

"You're cuter than a bug's ear," said Doan.

"I know it," said Shirley.

"She's writing a monograph," Eric Trent warned. "On sex."

"No," Shirley corrected. "Sex comes into it just incidentally. It's on psychotherapy. Psychosomatic therapy."

"That's nice," said Doan. "I bet."

"Do you have a sex life?" Shirley asked.

"Sure," said Doan. "But it's private."

"That's the way everyone acts," Shirley said. She stared at Carstairs in a speculative way. "What about him?"

"He does very well," said Doan. "He's different from most males. He gets paid for his services, and they're very much in demand. The owners of lady Great Danes have to write months ahead to get an appointment with him."

"Would you mind changing the subject?" Trent asked.

"Why?" Doan asked. "Sex is very interesting, and personally I think it's here to stay."

"**HALLO,** peoples," said Morales, coming out of the front door of Old Chem and shaking the dust from a mop gently over them all. "Nice day, no? Yes?"

"Did you paint my office?" Melissa demanded.

"Senorita, I have eight—"

"Yes, I know. Just forget it."

"Senorita, if you had eight children, you would know that forgetting them is difficult—not to say, impossible. Ah! And how do you do, Senorita Shirley?"

"Hello," said Shirley.

"Senorita Shirley, last night I had a very surprising experience."

"I don't want to hear about it."

"Senorita, this is a matter of immense scientific interest."

"How do you know?"

"Senorita, when a man has eight children, he acquires a certain flair in this field which gives him superior judgment."

"I'm not interested," Shirley told him.

"Senorita, in my opinion you are discriminating against me. I would bear it in silence, except for the fact that my experiences are of enormous scientific value. Just regard the matter objectively, Senorita. Incorporated in your book, my unparalleled performances would make your reputation."

"No doubt," said Shirley. "But they're not going to be—incorporated in my monograph, I mean. You're too disgustingly normal."

"Senorita, I resent that."

"Go ahead and resent."

Morales glowered darkly. "There is very little justice in this world, in my opinion." He hitched the mop up over his shoulder and marched back inside the building.

Shirley looked at Doan. "Did you ever kill anyone? I mean, either indirectly—by getting them hung, or directly—by doing your own dirty work?"

"Both ways," Doan answered.

"Do you rationalize your sadism when you do? I mean, in the manner judges do—by claiming they are ridding society of a menace and all that stuff?"

"No," said Doan. "I do it because I get paid for it. It's nice work."

"I'm afraid you're normal, too."

"I'm sorry," Doan told her.

"Do you know many murderers?"

"Hundreds."

"Are they paranoid or cycloid? It's my opinion that all of them are paranoid to some degree."

"What does that mean?"

"They're paranoiacs," Shirley explained. "It means they live in a subjective world of their own. They rationalize their destructive impulses by a cockeyed logic that has no relation to reality. Hitler was a marvelous one."

"I've never met a murderer who went in for it on such a big scale as he did," Doan said. "Although I did run across a nice old female party who knocked off twenty people with nicotine distilled from bug spray."

"Were her victims all of one sex?"

"Nope. Men, women, and children. She wasn't a bit choosy."

Shirley nodded indifferently. "Generalized transference of a subconscious repressed aggression. It's very common. Well, I'm going in and try to get something out of Professor Sley-Mynick."

"Oh, Shirley," said Melissa. "Leave him alone. You know you terrify the poor man with your questions so much you make him ill."

"It's good for him," said Shirley. "He's got to work out those experiences—get them up and out in the open. He'll never get well if he keeps them seething in his subconscious the way they are."

A fat shadow waddled out from the doorway and on emerging into the sunlight turned out to be Professor Sley-Mynick himself. He blinked behind his heavy glasses and then, settling his gaze on the group standing and sitting on the steps, twisted around suddenly and looked as though he was going to scurry back from where he'd come.

"Just a minute, Professor," Shirley Parker called to him. "You're the very man I want to see. We were talking about abnormal psychology—about murderers and...."

The professor threw up his hands. "Oh, dear," he said. "Did you say murderers? Who's a murderer? I'm not a murderer, am I? I don't know any murderer. Or do I?"

Shirley tripped up the steps and patted Sley-Mynick on the shoulder. "Now don't be alarmed," she told him. "Our discussion was purely objective, no personalities involved. We were talking about murderers and sex. As you know, I'm writing a monograph and in order to do it I have to interview people and get material on their sex experiences. I wanted to ask you…."

If the professor had seemed startled before, now he looked positively horrified. "Oh, dear," he said. "Sex. Do I have any sex? What sex am I? Male, of course. And you're a female. Oh, dear!"

The poor man retreated back into the building. Shirley had a grip on his elbow now and she dragged along after him until they were both out of sight in the lobby.

"She's pretty, isn't she?" Melissa asked.

"And how," Doan agreed. "Is she married?"

"Shirley? No. She doesn't believe in marriage."

"Is she a communist?" Trent asked warily.

Melissa laughed. "Of course not. Shirley wouldn't go in for anything as old hat as that. She's a philosophical anarchist."

"Oh," said Trent. "Well, excuse me. I have a ten o'clock class." He looked to make sure Shirley was not in sight in the hall and then went in and up the stairs.

"You know," Melissa said to Doan, "he's not so bad, after all. I mean, I thought he'd be an awfully icky sort of a wolf until I got his side of the story. He's sort of cute and innocent, isn't he?"

"Well," said Doan, "I suppose that all depends on your point of view. Don't let his face fool you. He gets mad quick, and when he does it's not a good idea to be standing around within arm's reach of him. He's a judo expert among other things, and he's hard as nails. Since I've been following him around, he has put away about twenty characters who made cracks of one sort or another to him about those Heloise ads, and so far he hasn't even gotten his hair mussed. I talk soft and smile loud with him. I don't want him mad at me. Even Carstairs detours around him."

"That reminds me," said Melissa. "Thank you just oodles for letting Carstairs stay with me."

"What did he do?" Doan inquired.

"It would take two hours to tell you, but right now you can have him back."

"Look," said Doan seriously, "I know he's a pest, but I think you'd better keep him with you. He does have sense enough to guard you."

Carstairs stood up. He looked levelly and coldly at Melissa and then at Doan. After he had done that, he went down the steps and along the walk about twenty paces—just out of earshot—and lay down on the grass.

"It irritates him to have people discuss him," Doan explained, "because he can't talk back—thank God. You'd better let him follow you around."

"Well, why?"

"Look," said Doan. "There was a prowler in your apartment last night. Remember?"

"That was just an accident. I mean, that he was in my apartment."

"Do you think Frank Ames cut his own throat by accident?"

Melissa shivered.

"That's more like it," said Doan. "That bird was no hallucination, and he's no joke. He carries both a knife and a gun, and last night wasn't the first time he's used them."

"Who do you think he was?"

"I don't know. Do you?"

"No!"

"Think back," Doan requested. "Think of the way he looked—the way he moved. Have you got a mental picture?"

"Y-yes."

"Could it have been a woman?"

"What?" said Melissa, staring.

"Humphrey had a hunch in that direction, and sometimes—by sheer accident—he gets a grip on an idea that makes sense.

Do you think this prowler could have been a woman dressed up as a man?"

Melissa felt her jaw. "No."

"That blow doesn't mean anything either way. Some women can hit mighty hard. It's just a matter of knowing how, not of strength. Keep thinking. Was there anything off-center or unusual about this party?"

"Well," said Melissa, trying. "Well…."

"Go ahead."

"Nothing I can put my finger on. But something about the way he moved…. Something queer and strange and yet horribly familiar…. Something sort of out-of-focus…."

"How well do you know Beulah Porter Cowys?"

"Oh, don't be ridiculous!"

"I'm not," said Doan. "I'm worried. I tell you, this is a very bad boy we're dealing with. He's got lots of confidence. He uses a .22, which is a very light gun, but it really doesn't matter how big a hole you get punched in you if it's in a vulnerable place. Last night he was shooting in the dark—he couldn't see his sights—and he couldn't have seen more of me than just a blur, and he shot awfully fast, but even at that he would have hit me all three times if I hadn't moved in the wrong direction at just the right time. I'd hate to meet him when he could see well."

"You're scaring me now."

"I'm trying to. Think back again. What was he doing when you first saw him?"

"It sounds silly, but he was looking at a pair of my stockings as though he'd never seen any before."

"He didn't take anything?"

"No."

"What else did he disturb—besides your bureau or dresser or whatever?"

"Nothing. Just that one drawer."

"Yeah," said Doan absently.

"Are you really considering Beulah as a suspect?"

Doan frowned. "I don't see how it could have been her. She had the time, all right. You were still unconscious when she turned up, and Trent thinks it was about seven or eight minutes after I started chasing. But he was so busy dithering around over you it might have been an hour for all he'd know. I made some experiments. In her apartment, with the door closed, it would be hard to hear a fire siren in your apartment. None of the other tenants heard you. We did because your door was open, and the hall funnels the sound. But if Beulah Porter Cowys has a stocking mask around, she's carrying it with her. Along with an automatic and a knife, and that doesn't seem reasonable. She does have a pair of black leather gloves, though."

"Did you search her apartment?"

"Sure."

"How'd you get in?"

"The locks in that building are easy to pick. Of course, too, she could have circled around and gone in the front of the building after she shot at me—it's physically possible—but I don't believe she could have done it without Carstairs spotting her."

"Why don't you let Carstairs just sniff around until he locates whoever it was?"

"Carstairs?" Doan said. "He's not that kind of a dog. He can't smell any better than I can. He operates with his ears and his eyes."

"Look here," said Melissa. "Why are you so interested in me and in my prowler?"

"Why, Melissa," Doan chided. "I love you. Did I forget to tell you?"

"Pooh," said Melissa. "We can't use that. Come on. I've co-operated. Now, give."

Doan said slowly, "I noticed something I don't think Humphrey spotted. You know that directory in the lobby of the Pavilion? The one that lists the names of the tenants opposite the number of the apartment each lives in? Well, the manager or someone had already put Trent's name opposite your apartment and yours opposite Trent's last night. You know, because Trent insists on exchanging apartments with you and—"

"I know all about who wants to exchange apartments and why."

"Oh," said Doan. "Well, that chesterfield in Trent's apartment is too damned short. Now if you'd just let me sleep in that pull-down bed in your living room...."

"I wouldn't care for that arrangement."

"Okay," said Doan.

"Just a minute here!" said Melissa. "Don't try to get off the subject. You're so concerned about this because you think—on account of the directory—that the prowler made a mistake in the apartments. You think he intended to get into Trent's apartment instead of mine!"

"Yes," Doan admitted. "And I think that's why he was staring at your stockings in such a dumbfounded way when you came in, he naturally didn't expect to find a drawer full of women's stuff in Trent's apartment."

"Well, what do you think he did expect to find?"

"I don't know. That's what I'm worried about. This bird is no ordinary prowler—no garden variety of sneak thief. And anyway, Trent has no dough, aside from a big gob of back Navy pay which is in the bank. He hasn't any rajah's rubies or any secret plans for atomic bombs. I can't figure out what the prowler was after, and why he was willing to go to such lengths to keep from being caught. I mean, look at it this way. Suppose I had caught him—or rather, suppose Frank Ames had. The prowler hadn't stolen a thing. All he could possibly have drawn would be a couple of years for breaking and entering. And yet, he was willing—and ready to commit murder to dodge that. It doesn't make sense."

"So you think it was a woman."

Doan grinned. "Not for that reason. But sometimes they do

funny things when they get bitten by the love bug, and Trent
is dynamite in that direction."

"*Oh-ho!*" said Melissa suddenly.

"What now?" Doan demanded warily.

"I'm just getting the drift of all these sly, snide questions of
yours. I know who you're eyeing."

"Just relax, now," Doan advised.

"I won't. You're thinking about somebody whose name starts
with H and who hangs around in Hollywood."

"There's still a law against slander," Doan warned.

"Pooh. No wonder you're worried. You're afraid you might
be guarding Trent against your own boss."

"You've got an evil mind, Melissa," Doan told her.

"Haven't I, just? But it works, doesn't it? So Heloise is a crack
shot with a pistol, is she?"

"I don't know," said Doan, "but she used to juggle knives."

"She did? Really? Where?"

"In carnivals and at county fairs."

"How do you know?"

"I investigated her. I always investigate the people who hire
me. I want to know whether their checks are good."

"She must have millions!"

"Maybe, now," Doan said. "But back in the thirties there was
a time when she was on the ropes financially. Her outfit nearly
foundered under her."

"What happened?"

"Her husband forged her name and misused a limited power
of attorney to dribble all her assets into the stock market."

"Her *husband?* You mean, another one? Has she been married
before?"

"Oh, yes. To a guy named 'Big Tub' Tremaine. He was a spieler
on a sick pitch."

"What does that mean?"

"He sold medicines at carnivals and fairs—Kickapoo Joy

Juice and Colonel Ouster's Calibrated Cure-All and stuff like that. Heloise was his come-on. She used to dress in spangled diapers and a necklace and juggle knives to attract a crowd so Big Tub could work them over. He was good at it, from all accounts."

"What happened to him?"

"He died."

"Ah-ha," said Melissa. "Mysteriously, I'll bet."

"Nope. He dunked himself in the drink of his own free will and accord—and right in front of about a hundred witnesses who were all chasing him to stop him."

"Why did he do that? Kill himself, I mean?"

"Because he was smart," said Doan. "He stole money from Heloise. That's just about as serious an offense as there is. If she could have laid hands on him she'd have had him boiled in oil or, at the very least, drawn and quartered.

"Have you ever heard about the other guy who stole money from Heloise?"

"No," said Melissa, "I haven't heard. Tell me about the other guy."

"I've forgotten his name but he worked for her as a book-keeper. He figured out a complicated and what he thought was a foolproof system for rigging the books. He'd embezzled the magnificent sum of one dollar and seventy-six cents when she got wise to him. He was bonded and Heloise forced the bonding company to prosecute, although they didn't want to. The court, however, threw the case out. They said stealing a dollar seventy-six was hardly a misdemeanor, much less a felony. Where-upon, Heloise decided to prosecute in her own way—not through the courts...."

"Did she fire the fellow?"

"No, she kept him on—raised his salary, in fact, so high that the poor guy's wife wouldn't let him quit. Heloise wanted him right under her thumb where she could torture him. But she didn't let him keep books any longer. She made him the manager of her complaint department, and if you want to live a life of hell and damnation just go get yourself a job in the complaint department of a cosmetics manufacturer."

"I can imagine," said Melissa.

"I wonder if you can," Doan told her. "This poor ex-book-keeper, with the sensitive soul you'll find in most embezzlers, had to take lip from women all over the United States and some foreign countries who'd bought Heloise of Hollywood's beauty preparations and hadn't turned out as beautiful as the advertisements said they would. They stormed the poor guy by letter, telegram, telephone and in person. All of them were mad, some of them madder. His nerves gave out."

"What finally happened to him?"

"He went off his bat, which is what Heloise had counted on. They've got him stuck away now in a nuthouse somewhere in a room wallpapered with mattresses. The doctors say he'll never get any better."

"Ugh," said Melissa. "This Heloise must be plenty tough."

"She is that," said Doan, "but a good businesswoman. She built up her business all on her own, although she did and does use the sap bait Big Tub taught her. He had nothing to do with the management of it. She supported him in relative luxury until he started giving her money to the stockbrokers."

"Where did he kill himself?"

"At Ensenada. He dove off a fishing pier after loading himself down with most of the liquor in the nearest bar and bidding all the patrons a fond farewell. They just thought he was crocked, until he actually did heave himself overboard, and then they had a hell of a time fishing him out again. When they did, he was deader than a kippered herring."

"I'd really like to see Heloise," Melissa said ruminatively. "I mean, in person. She interests me."

"Is that a fact?" Doan inquired politely. "Heloise interests you?"

"Don't get funny."

"You'd better forget Trent. He's out of your league."

"Oh, is that so?"

"I'm just telling you," Doan said. "I'm your friend."

"Ha!"

"Now just think. Suppose by some freak of chance you did manage to land him. He looks just as good to other gals as he does to you, remember."

"I could handle that angle, all right. And without hiring a detective to watch him. Does Heloise give her personal attention to that salon of hers on the Strip?"

"Yes," Doan admitted. "But if I were you, I wouldn't show up around there."

"I will if I please, and I think I please."

"Well, take Carstairs with you, anyway."

"I can't. I haven't a car. It's against the law for dogs to ride on buses."

"Let him handle that situation. I've never yet run across a bus driver who could keep him off a bus or put him off once he got on…. Carstairs!"

Carstairs raised his head languidly.

"Go with her," said Doan. "Watch it." Carstairs lifted his upper lip and sneered at him in an elaborately bored way.

CHAPTER IV

THE SUNSET STRIP is a section of the county, not incorporated into the city of Los Angeles, which points like an accusing finger directly at the heart of Hollywood. It is inhabited by actors and actresses and their exploiters or victims, and by people who have been run out of Beverly Hills, and by bookmakers, saloon keepers, unsuccessful swindlers, antique dealers and interior decorators of one kind or the other, but mostly the other. It is considered quite fascinating by the sort of people who like to go on bus rides through the Bowery.

Heloise of Hollywood had a building all of her own in the

center of this streamlined slum. The building featured glass brick and chrome and pink plaster and dainty gestures in the air, and taken over all it was as slick and as screwy as one of Salvador Dali's copyrighted hallucinations.

There had been a certain amount of opposition to Carstairs' presence on the bus, and Melissa was feeling a little frazzled out when she went up the steps and pushed open the pink, padded door that was billed as "The Pathway to Perfection—Entrance."

"Well, for goodness' sakes, come on," she said impatiently.

Carstairs ambled up the steps and looked inside. He grunted, and the hair stood up on his back.

Melissa kicked him. "Go on!"

Carstairs went in reluctantly. Melissa followed him, and her hair stood up, too.

The foyer was a passageway about five miles long and lined with mirrors. These weren't distortion mirrors—not quite. They were just very, very clear and brilliantly lighted, and they magnified matters just enough. Melissa watched herself walk, because there was nothing else she could do. She saw herself highlighted from fore to aft and from top to bottom and from some other odd and interesting angles. It was the most sadistically efficient sales promotion for beauty treatments she had ever run across.

Even Carstairs had begun to cringe by the time he had reached the mirror door at the end. Melissa held it open for him, and they entered a plush-lined cubicle which featured a tall, round ebony desk placed in its exact center. There was a girl behind the desk, and she was beautiful. She really was. She had black, glistening hair and a corpse-like pallor and a face so perfectly contoured it was frightening.

Women who look like this usually sound like crows, but this one had been trained. Her voice was soft and insinuatingly confidential.

"How do you do?" she said, as though she were actually interested. "May I help you?"

"I think so," said Melissa. "Can you do something about my cheek?"

"Your cheek?"

"Yes. Right here. My husband beat me last night."

"Of course. Do you wish it to look worse or better?"

"What?" said Melissa.

The girl smiled at her. "Those incidents happen so rarely to some of our more unfortunate clients that they often wish to capitalize on them when they do."

"Capitalize?" Melissa repeated.

The girl moved her right hand casually, and the big diamond on her fourth finger sparkled.

"Oh," said Melissa. "No. I want it to look better. It always irritates my boyfriend when my husband beats me, and I want the two of them to stay pals."

"Naturally. May I have your name?"

"Susan Halfinger."

"And who is sponsoring you?"

"Sponsoring? Oh. T. Ballard Bestwyck. He's the president of—"

"Oh, we know T. Ballard here."

"You do?" Melissa said, startled. "Oh, of course. His wife "

"Wife?" said the girl, just as startled. "Oh, yes. Yes, indeed. His wife."

"Hmmm," said Melissa thoughtfully.

"Would your dog like something to play with while he is waiting? We have some very enchanting rubber mice that squeak."

"No," Melissa said judicially. "I don't believe he'd care for that sort of thing."

"Then if you'll just step into the anteroom…. Through that

door.... Yes.... Our bruise specialist will be prepared for you in just a few short moments."

"Thanks," said Melissa.

She opened the door and ushered Carstairs through it into a long, narrow room cluttered with dusty pink lounges with scrolled gilt legs.

There were three fat women sitting in a row on one of the lounges. The nearest one bounced up and down and pointed a pudgy, admiring finger at Carstairs.

"Ooooh! Look!"

The middle one patted her hands and cooed.

"Darling!" said the third one. "Just delicious!"

Carstairs backed up against Melissa. Melissa pushed him away and sat down on one of the lounges. Carstairs crept up and huddled against her legs.

"He's so pretty!" said the nearest fat one.

"Ippy-ippy-ippy-tweeeeet," said the middle one.

"Those divine brown eyes," said the third one.

Carstairs moaned in a soft, terrified way.

Another door opened, and a girl looked in. This one was a cool tall blonde. She was dressed in a white uniform, but it was white silk, and it had been made just for her. She looked like nurses should look but never do.

"Miss Halfinger," she said. She waited for a moment and then said more pointedly: "Miss Halfinger."

"Eh?" said Melissa. "Oh! Yes."

She got up and started for the door. Carstairs started right after her.

"You stay here," Melissa ordered.

Carstairs stared at her in incredulous dismay.

"Lie down," Melissa said. "Wait."

Carstairs whimpered piteously.

Melissa stamped her foot. "Lie *down!*"

Carstairs began to fold himself up reluctantly.

"Ippy-ippy," cooed the middle fat one.

"Just too precious," said the third fat one.

Melissa closed the door and followed the blonde down a passageway that had dark brown cork flooring and beige walls and a yellow ceiling. Along each side, at staggered intervals, there were doors curtained with white oiled silk. From inside of the rooms came sharply distinct slaps, the grisly cracking of reluctant joints, retchings and gaggings and moans, and sobbing pleas for mercy.

Melissa and her guide turned a corner and went past a hideous place full of malignantly coiling serpents of steam vapor and pinkly parboiled things that squeaked and jibbered in their agony.

"Right in here," said the blonde, swishing aside one of the oiled silk curtains.

This wasn't a cubicle. It was as large as an ordinary hotel room. It contained a desk and a chair and a couch equipped with smelling salts and a telephone. It was as obtrusively antiseptic as an operating amphitheater.

"Just take off your clothes," said the blonde. "The shower is behind that door."

"What?" said Melissa. "Wait a minute. My husband fights fair. He just pasted me one. He didn't kick me after I was down."

"The Pathway to Perfection," said the blonde, "lies in the complete realignment of all the component parts of the body to express the poetry of true beauty."

"Okay," said Melissa.

"The towels are on the table. The water is electronized and energized. I will return."

"Do that," said Melissa.

She took off her clothes and put on a rubber bathing cap that came in a sealed cellophane container. She opened the frosted door the blonde had pointed out. The shower was about eight by eight, all black shiny tile, and was worked by a control panel as complicated as a transport plane's. Melissa twisted some knobs and turned others for a while and finally got the right combination. There were approximately one thousand water jets of varying capacity and intensity, and some of them apparently gave out with cologne instead of water.

Melissa walked right in and luxuriated. She stayed until she began to feel washed away and then came out and selected one of the towels. It was as big as a bed sheet and as fluffy as a cloud. Melissa was all tangled up in it when she heard the first scream.

She didn't pay any attention.

Immediately there were some more screams. They were very loud, very terrorized screams in different voices that blended in a sort of chromatic progression that was not unpleasing to the ear. Melissa stopped rubbing to listen. The screams kept mounting in volume and in pitch, and now there were some other noises—metallic clanging and the crash of shattered glass.

And through all this—as a sort of a minor undertone—something was howling. Melissa suddenly isolated that last sound and identified its source. She ducked out into the hall dragging the towel behind her.

The screams now were multitudinously deafening. They had begun to echo and meet each other in midair. The air began to quiver and palpitate.

Carstairs spun around the corner down the hall, leaning far over and scrabbling for his footing. His mouth was wide open, and he was making a lot of noise.

"Here!" said Melissa, waving the towel.

She wasn't wearing any clothes, and she still had her bathing cap on. She was just another naked woman. Carstairs wailed and skidded and hiked back around the corner. The screaming redoubled.

Melissa ran, trying frantically to wrap the towel around herself. She reached the corner. There were screams to her right and screams to her left and screams in front of her, undulating in weird concatenation. Their intensity seemed to center toward the left. Melissa went that way.

She turned into a long low room where sun lamps coiled like chromium cobras among women who screamed and squirmed and clutched at themselves. She ran through another room where women writhed helplessly in the metallic grip of permanent wave machines. She got out into another hall in time to see Carstairs hurdle gracefully over a pile of whooping casualties.

Melissa fought and clawed her way over cringing, sweaty bodies and made it out into the clear again. Carstairs had hit a dead end and was on his way back, running with desperate, driving effort.

"Stop, you!" Melissa shrieked. She swooped at him, arms spread.

Carstairs dodged and whipped sideways through a curtained doorway, and Melissa went right after him. It was a low-ceilinged, dank room with a white tiled floor and walls that glistened damply. Carstairs was headed for the door at the other end.

Right in front of this door there was an oblong opening in the floor—a little longer and a little wider than a grave. It was filled to the brim with something black and malignantly slick. Carstairs intended to jump over it. His foot slipped.

He yelled—one last, lorn note of utter despair. He fell full length in the mud bath, and the mud bath went off in an explosion that splattered the whole room and everything in it, including Melissa.

Carstairs was incapable of making any more noise, but he wasn't defeated, even now. He scrambled frantically to get out. Melissa wiped the mud out of her eyes and hit him with her fist in the approximate spot she judged his head was.

"Stop, stop!"

Carstairs couldn't stop. He got out of the mud bath, carrying most of its contents on him. He got out through the door, staggering, and bumbled down another hall with Melissa scrambling and grabbing behind him.

The door at the end of the hall was closed. Carstairs lunged and hit it with his remaining strength. The door popped open. Carstairs fell into the anteroom. The three fat ladies were long gone. Carstairs was trying feebly to crawl under one of the dusty pink lounges when Melissa landed on him.

"Carstairs!" she shouted furiously. She dug through the mud and found an ear and jerked it hard. "I'm me! I'm here!"

Carstairs blubbered at her in pitiable relief. He tried to sit in her lap.

Melissa punched him. "Behave yourself, you fool!" There were knees digging into her back, and Melissa brushed at them absently. "Get away and give me room to…. What?" She turned her head slowly.

Eric Trent was sitting on the lounge. His mouth was open.

There was one of those silences.

Melissa suddenly remembered her towel. She pulled it up higher. That was bad. She pulled it down lower. That was not good, either.

"Turn around, you gaping idiot!" she snarled.

Trent behaved as though he hadn't heard her. There was a look on his face that was half a smile of amusement and half an expression of artistic appreciation. "Gosh, Melissa," he said, "you've got a pretty nice—er—you look pretty wonderful— er—what I mean is…."

"I know what you mean!" Melissa spat. "So this is what those years on an icicle or iceberg or whatever did to you, is it? Ogling helpless unclothed women!" She scraped a handful of mud off her thigh and hurled it at him. "Didn't you hear me? I said *turn your head!*"

A glob of mud struck Trent on the nose. He turned his head so fast his neck clicked.

Melissa rewound the towel. "All right," she told him.

Trent looked at her and swallowed. "Did you have an accident or—or something?"

"Me?" said Melissa. "Oh, no. I do this sort of thing all day every day."

Trent swallowed again. "I—see."

Melissa took off her bathing cap and slapped at him viciously with it. "Why do you always have to be sneaking around and spying on me?"

Trent blocked the blow with his arm. "I am not sneaking around and I am not spying on you."

"You liar. Doan told you I was coming here, so you had to come snooping."

"Doan didn't either tell me you were coming here. I had no idea you were."

"Pooh-bah! I suppose you came to get a permanent wave? You don't need it. The one you have hasn't grown out yet."

"I came here," said Trent evenly, "because my wife sent for me."

"That was very nice of you, Eric," said a new voice. It was a voice that was hoarsely hollow and smooth at the same time. It sounded a little like a billiard ball rolling down a rain spout.

Melissa turned her head slowly again.

This was Heloise of Hollywood. She was tall and erect and sleekly slim, and she had jade green eyes. There wasn't a line in her face or a wrinkle in her neck, but she was fifty-four years old. No one could possibly have gotten as hard as she was in less than that time. The hardness wasn't a mask—it wasn't even striated. It was smooth and icy from outside in and from inside out. She radiated as much warmth as a diamond.

She studied Melissa for a moment. "Is that your dog?"

"I'm responsible for him."

Heloise nodded. "I wondered if you'd lie—again."

"What do you mean by that?"

"Your name is Melissa Gregory—not Halfinger."

"My name is what I choose to call myself."

Heloise shrugged indifferently. "Quite. I know the dog. It

belongs to Doan. It should be shot. It's mad, I think. It started on this rampage just because one of my more stupid customers, who was waiting in here, tried to tie a pink hair ribbon around its neck."

"That would make me mad, too."

Heloise studied her again and then looked at Trent. "I'm afraid your taste is deteriorating, my dear. She's a mess. Even her feet are dirty."

They were.

Trent wiped the mud off his nose with a finger and said: "I wouldn't go too far, if I were you, Heloise."

"Wouldn't you, Eric?" Heloise asked, idly interested.

"No."

They watched each other, and Melissa shivered.

The receptionist came in from the foyer. "Madame, there are two men outside."

"How very interesting," said Heloise.

"Both of them say they are detectives. They are handcuffed together."

"Send them in."

"Yes, Madame." The receptionist had really tried hard, but temptation overcame her. She rolled her eyes in Eric Trent's direction and twitched her hips at him.

In one smooth, deadly motion Heloise picked up a heavy crystal ashtray and threw it. The receptionist shut the door quickly. The ashtray made a dent in it and then clattered dully on the floor.

"Doan must be in trouble again," Heloise said casually.

Humphrey shouldered through the door, dragging Doan along behind him.

"Hi, everybody," Doan said amiably.

"Shut up," Humphrey ordered, jerking on the cuffs that fastened his left arm to Doan's right. "What's going on in this joint, anyway? I heard a lot of screaming."

"A couple of my customers got a little hysterical," Heloise told him.

"It sounded more like—" Humphrey stopped and stared incredulously. "Wheee-hooo! Look at that, will you? Wheee-hooo-hooo-hooo!" He collapsed against the wall, shaking help-lessly with laughter.

Heloise said impatiently: "Take the dog inside and clean it. And you'd better do a little work on yourself at the same time."

Melissa groped through a crust of mud and located Carstairs' collar. She led him toward the inner door. When they reached it, Carstairs suddenly twitched the collar out of her grasp and turned around. His eyes were bright red.

Humphrey stopped laughing.

Carstairs turned around again and preceded Melissa through the door. Melissa slammed it emphatically behind her.

"Say," said Humphrey uneasily, "I didn't like the way he looked at me just then."

"You thought about that a little bit too late," Doan said. "Don't ever let him catch you up a dark alley. People who laugh at him often have fatal accidents."

"He caused plenty of accidents here," Heloise said. "He ran wild through this place. He must have damaged a thousand dollars worth of equipment."

"That was naughty of him," said Doan. "I shall speak to him severely."

"Not only that, but he caused a general attack of hysteria among the customers."

"Charge them for it."

Heloise stared at him. "You know, sometimes you act quite bright." She snapped her fingers.

The receptionist opened the door and looked around its edge cautiously. "Yes, Madame?"

"Double all the bills this afternoon."

"Yes, Madame."

In the back room one of the girls started the old screaming routine again.

Heloise's nostrils flared. "If that dog…."

The scream whooped down the corridor in their direction, and then the door of the anteroom burst open.

"Gad," said Humphrey in an awed murmur.

The screamer was pink and enormous and bare as the day she was born.

"Murder!" she squalled at them. *"Murr-durr!"*

She collapsed, then, in a suety quivering heap.

"Gad," said Humphrey, even more awed.

A white-clad attendant came down the hall carrying a sheet. She dropped the sheet over the screamer, and the sheet began to quiver uncannily, too.

"Madame," said the attendant, "there is a corpse in one of the massage rooms."

"What?" said Humphrey, suddenly coming to. "What was that?"

"Is it a customer?" Heloise asked.

"Yes, Madame."

"Hey!" said Humphrey. "Corpse? Did I hear you say— corpse?"

Heloise stepped over the quivering sheet and started down the corridor. "What number?"

"Seven, Madame."

"Here!" said Humphrey. He darted after Heloise, tugging Doan along in his wake.

Eric Trent got up from the lounge and followed them. Heloise went to the right at the first turn and to the right again and then stopped and pushed aside a white curtain.

It was a room similar to the one Melissa had used, except that in this one a long white rubbing table with gleaming tubular legs was fastened to the floor under the drop light in the center. There was a woman lying on the table completely covered with a massage sheet except for her bony, beaked face and her long, crook-toed feet. Her tongue was sticking out in a last sardonic gesture of defiance. She was laid out just as though she were in a morgue, and she was just as dead.

"It's the old scrawny dame!" Humphrey blurted. He jerked on the handcuffs. "What's her name?"

"Beulah Porter Cowys," said Doan.

Heloise stepped forward and pulled the sheet down a little. They could all see the spreading blue-black splotches on the lined throat.

"Strangled," said Eric Trent.

Humphrey shot out a pointed finger. "And you were here at the time! I've had an eye on you all the time, bub! You were afraid the old scrawny dame would squawk to your wife about you and that Melissa number, and so you followed her here and planted Doan outside for a lookout and sicked that damned Carstairs on the customers to create a riot, and then you wrung her neck for her!"

"What's your name?" Heloise asked coldly.

"Huh? Humphrey."

"He's the same one," said Doan.

Heloise walked over to the couch and picked up the telephone. "Get me the sheriffs office. His headquarters."

"That's not going to do you one bit of good," Humphrey informed her, "because this is a very clear-cut case of conspiracy to—"

Heloise spoke into the telephone: "Hello. This is Heloise of Hollywood. I want to speak to your boss. Hello, Mouthy? This is Heloise. I had some of my friends speak to you last night about one of your trained apes. He's here at my place now, annoying me. I'm getting a little tired of this character, Mouthy. I want you to talk to him. This time make things clear." She held out the phone toward Humphrey.

Humphrey took it gingerly. "Hello." The phone buzzed at him like a rattlesnake. "Yes, sir. But—Yes, sir.… But I—Yes, sir…. No, sir…. But there's been another murder right here in— Yes, sir…. Yes, sir…. Yes, sir…. Yes, sir…. Yes, sir." The phone popped and quit rattling.

"Well?" said Heloise. "Have you got things straight now?"

"Yes, ma'am," said Humphrey soberly.

Two uniformed deputies from one of the sheriffs radio prowl cars shouldered into the room.

"Oh, hello," said one of them, recognizing Humphrey. "Some dame phoned in and said there was a murder—"

"Shut up," said Humphrey. "Don't even mention the word. It's all a mistake. The dame, here, committed suicide."

"Huh?" said the deputy. "Suicide? She's got finger marks on her gullet."

"So she choked herself to death!" Humphrey snarled. "Is it any of your business? Do you want to disturb the customers? Beat it! Go home!"

The deputies backed off reluctantly. One said, "Well, we'll have to make a report…."

"Yeah," said Humphrey. "To the sheriff, and I want to be right there when you do. I want to hear that. I'm coming with you now."

He started down the hall.

Doan jerked him to a halt. "I don't want to walk around with you any more."

"You'll walk or get carried."

"Wait a minute," said Trent. "What did you arrest him for this time?"

"For loitering and suspicion of grand larceny—auto. He was loafing out in front in a car that wasn't his."

"That's my car," said Trent, "and I told him to wait in it while I was in here."

"Take those handcuffs off him," said Heloise.

"Yes, ma'am," said Humphrey, obeying.

"Get out," said Heloise. "And stay out."

"Yes, ma'am," said Humphrey.

THE SHADOWS were stretching long and thin over the mathematical segments of lawn when Doan and Eric Trent walked diagonally across the Quad. They found Humphrey sitting and brooding on the front steps of Old Chem. He was hunched up, with his chin resting grimly in his hands. He looked like he had been sitting for quite some time and intended to keep on doing it until he got what he wanted.

"Look who's loitering now," Doan said.

"Shut up," said Humphrey. He was watching Trent. "What are you doing here? You've got no classes at this hour of the day."

"I don't think it's any of your business," Trent informed him, "but I don't mind telling you. I came over to take a sundown reading on my instruments."

"What instruments?"

"Various weather recording instruments. You wouldn't know what they were if I told you."

"What are you doing here?" Doan inquired.

Humphrey nodded at him. "You're a very clever lad, Doan."

"This is so sudden," said Doan.

"Yeah. You're clever, and you've got lots of heavy artillery in the shape of influence lined up behind you. But I'm clever, too."

"No kidding?" Doan asked, surprised.

"Yup. And I'm mad."

"Dear me," said Doan.

"And I've got an idea."

"Oh, boy."

"Do you want to hear it?"

"No."

"You're going to, though," said Humphrey. "My idea is this Melissa Gregory."

"Why don't you just relax for a while, Humphrey?"

"Shut up. Melissa Gregory is at the bottom of this pileup, and you're not going to lure me off on any of your false trails."

"I suppose she popped herself on the jaw?"

"No. I don't mean she's the murderer. I mean, she's the motive. Trent is the one who popped her."

"What?" said Trent incredulously. "Are you saying I popped her? Now look here, you. You can't go around making accusations like that about me or about Melissa either. She's a nice girl and I won't stand for anybody talking about her."

"I knew it! I knew it!" Humphrey chortled. "You're talking up for her and that means only one thing—you're crazy for her."

"I am?" said Trent. "For *her?*"

"Yup. This business about your wife hiring Doan to watch you is a gag. Your wife is completely in your power. She does exactly what you tell her and nothing else. She wouldn't dare hire a detective to watch you."

"This one is going to be really something extra," Doan observed. "Keep on, Humphrey."

"Your wife may be paying Doan," Humphrey said to Trent, "but it's you who tells him what to do, and what you told him to do this time was to watch Melissa Gregory."

"Why?" Trent asked blankly.

"I told you. You're crazy for her, and you suspected she was falling for this Frank Ames. There wasn't any masked prowler last night. You have a key to her apartment, and you were waiting for her when she came home. You popped her one for going out with Ames."

"I did this?" Trent asked, stunned.

"Yes, you. She squawked before you popped her, and this Beulah Porter Cowys came blundering in and saw and heard enough to know what really happened. You called the cops in an attempt to cover things up with that nut-wagon story about a guy with his head in a silk stocking. You didn't fool Beulah Porter Cowys any. She went over to Hollywood this afternoon to shake your wife down by telling your wife about you and

Melissa Gregory. She wouldn't have gotten any change out of your wife, like I said, but you had to knock her off anyway because Doan had knocked off Ames, and Beulah Porter Cowys might have sounded off about that."

"I wondered when I was going to appear in this," Doan observed.

"You'd been following Ames and Melissa," Humphrey told him. "You were out in front of the building, lurking around like you usually are. Ames saw or heard something, and he got out of his car, intending to go on up and take this Trent all apart for batting Melissa Gregory around. That damned dog of yours took out after Ames and ran him into the alley and cornered him, and you cut Ames' throat."

"Who shot at me?"

"Nobody. You had two guns. You fired one off in the air and then gave it to that damned Carstairs, and he buried it in one of those vacant lots around there."

"I congratulate you, Humphrey," said Doan.

"This is incredible!" Trent choked. "This is the most absolutely fantastic tissue of criminal nonsense that I've ever listened to!"

"That's all right, bub," said Humphrey, nodding at him meaningfully. "I just wanted you to know I'm on to you. And I always get my man."

"Crime doesn't pay," Doan added.

Something slid through the air between Trent and Doan with an ugly, slicing hiss. It hit the sidewalk right at Trent's feet and shattered into shrapnel-like splinters. It was a heavy, grooved roof tile.

"Gug?" said Humphrey, staring up.

"Just remember," said Doan, also looking up. "That Trent didn't throw that tile, and neither did I."

"Ah," said Humphrey. "Nobody threw—"

Somebody yelled, though. It sounded thin and high and far away. Glass tinkled faintly.

"My instruments!" Trent gasped. He lunged up the steps.

"Wait a minute, you!" Humphrey shouted. He tore into the hall and up the stairs after Trent, flipping up his coattails and fumbling for the revolver in his hip pocket.

Doan spun on his heel and ran back along the side of the building. He had his revolver out. The turf was soft and spongy and silent under his heels He shoved heedlessly through a hedge and faced the narrow, shadowed rear door of the building.

He waited, puffing a little. Nothing happened. Nothing came out. And then a snarling, half-muffled uproar drifted down to him. Humphrey's yapping voice rode on the crest of it.

Doan darted inside the building. He found the narrowly twisting back stairs and went up them four at a time. He whirled around a corner at the top and out into the main upper corridor and ran down it toward Melissa's old office. He stopped short in the doorway.

The office was well on its way to being torn to pieces. Morales and Professor Sley-Mynick occupied the vortex of a sort of a whirlpool in the middle of it, caroming first one way and then the other and screeching like men possessed. Professor Sley-Mynick had a constrictor-like grip around Morales' waist. Morales was pounding him on the top of the head with both fists and trying to kick him at the same time. Trent and Humphrey ran around and around the two of them, trying to get a grip somewhere.

Doan fired his revolver at the ceiling, and for the space of a heartbeat the furious action froze dead still.

Then Humphrey got Morales by the neck. "What do you think you're doing? What goes on—" He shook Morales like a rag.

Trent was trying to disengage Professor Sley-Mynick. The blubbery man's glasses were gone—trampled underfoot—and his fat face was twisted hideously, lumpy mustache twitching and writhing like a live thing.

"What is it?" Trent demanded. "What happened?"

Professor Sley-Mynick collapsed into a half-sitting position. *"Geheim Staatspolizei!"* he cried, pointing a wavering finger at Morales. *"Geheim Staatspolizei! Yah, yah!"*

"Christian pig!" Morales spat at him.

Humphrey shook him again. "Shut up! What's the old guy saying?"

"Geheim Staatspolizei is German," Trent said, puzzled. "It means German State Security Police, I think."

"Sure," said Doan. "The Gestapo."

"Gestapo?" Humphrey repeated. "Them guys is all in jail or hung or something."

"Nein!"

Professor Sley-Mynick screamed. "No! He is! Him! That one!"

"Offspring of a she dog," said Morales.

Humphrey gave him another shake. "Keep your trap shut, or you're going to be missing some teeth. Trent, ask the fat guy what's going on."

Professor Sley-Mynick swallowed, groping furiously for words. "Always they do it! Yes! *Geheim Staatspolizei!* They break things—smash them! Scientific things! They did mine in Hungary! Now he does it! This one! He smashes them on the roof! Yes, yes! Believe me! I saw him! On the roof!"

"My instruments!" Trent blurted.

The stepladder was still propped up in the corner under the square trap door in the ceiling. Trent swarmed up it and squirmed through and out of sight. Instantly his face reappeared, red and congested, peering down at them.

"My barometer and my anemometer are smashed, and there is something in my precipitation calibrator that certainly isn't dew!"

"Yes, yes!" said Professor Sley-Mynick, "I told you! Always they do it—*Geheim Staatspolizei!* Always they smash and break scientific instruments!"

Trent slid down the ladder. He advanced on Morales with his eyes narrowed dangerously and his upper lip lifted at one corner.

Humphrey jerked Morales back. "Get away from him," he warned Trent, "or I'll slap you one with this pistol. I'm running this bazaar. This crum bum doesn't look like any Gestapo to me. Did you smash those instruments and shy a tile at Trent, dope?"

"Yes," said Morales.

Humphrey stared at him, taken aback. "You did? Well, what the hell for?"

"He is a blasphemer."

"Huh?" said Humphrey.

"What?" said Trent. "What am I?"

"A pig," said Morales. "A blasphemous, illegitimate Christian pig."

"Well, why?" said Trent. "What did I do?"

"Your existence and your pretensions are an impious mockery. By your very presence you deny the existence of Quezatepequez."

"Who?" said Humphrey groggily. "What?"

"Quezatepequez," said Trent. "That sounds like an Aztec word."

"Mayan, illiterate fool!" Morales snapped. "Quezatepequez is the great and only lord of Tegucigalpa—lord of the dark sky and the thunder bird. And you—you!—attempt to read his mind and predict his moods! I can do that—only I—a hereditary priest of the clan of Tegucigalpa!"

"Where does Maximilian come into this?" Doan inquired.

"Faugh! I spit on his name! I use it only to mock Christian pigs!"

"This guy is a nut," Humphrey stated. "I can see that without going any further. He should be locked up, and that's just what's going to happen to him. Come on now, screwloose, or you'll think the thunder bird laid an egg right on your noggin."

"I'm coming along, too," said Doan. "Take care of Sley-Mynick, Trent. I'll holler up some help for you below-decks."

"What was all that the old guy was yipping about the Gestapo?" Humphrey asked.

"They pinched him once," Doan explained. "They evidently wrecked his laboratory as well as him when they did it. When he saw Morales working out on Trent's instruments, he made a connection."

"There are too many nuts around here," Humphrey said darkly, "and them that ain't are worse. What do you want to come along with me for?"

"You're going to succeed in arresting me sooner or later. I want to see what kind of service I can expect. Besides, this guy strikes me as sort of violent. Maybe you'll need some help."

"And I suppose you'd give me some if I did?"

"You'd be surprised."

"Oh, no, I wouldn't," said Humphrey.

CHAPTER V

IT IS WELL recognized by the authorities responsible for law enforcement that students very seldom commit any very serious crimes, with the exception of attending college, and that a jail is not quite in tune with the reverent inattention to worldly matters current on a campus. Consequently the sheriff's office, university substation, was tucked away unobtrusively on a residential street north of the campus and camouflaged under a green tile roof and behind spotless off-white walls. Even the steel bars on the windows were fluted and painted black to imitate ornamental iron grilles. But then, in Hollywood they have a habit of disguising the functional purposes of many buildings, both public and private, as witness a movie house that looks like a Chinese temple, a movie star's home built in the style of a Venetian bordello, gas stations designed on the igloo principle and a funeral parlor, the facade of which might be mistaken for the entrance to a race track or an amusement park.

Humphrey dragged Morales, who was very much on his dignity now, up the neat, narrow walk and in through the polished oak doors. Doan trailed negligently along behind them.

The receiving room of the substation was as clean and barren and impersonal as a military adjutant's office in a staging area. There were some chairs and a bench and a uniformed deputy sitting behind a long, low desk with four telephones, a ledger, and an interoffice communicator on it. The deputy had the air of a man who wouldn't know quite what to do about it if something did.

Morales advanced to the middle of the room and stopped short and looked around to make sure he had everyone's undivided attention. "Now," he said impressively.

He reached inside his shirt and brought out an oblong packet of yellow oiled silk. The silk rustled slickly as he unfolded it. He handed the papers inside to Humphrey.

"What?" said Humphrey.

Doan looked over his shoulder. The top sheet contained a photograph of Morales, some fingerprints, and a very impressive gold and ebony seal.

"This is in Spanish," said Humphrey.

"Can you read it?" Morales asked.

"No."

Morales snorted. "Is there no one in this pigsty who has any culture?"

Humphrey glared at him and then nodded to the desk deputy. "Call Hernandez."

The deputy flipped the switch on the communicator. "Hernandez! Front and center!"

One of the doors at the rear of the room opened, and a thin, gray-haired man came in and peered at them through thick hornrimmed glasses.

"Read these," Humphrey ordered, handing him the papers. "They belong to this bird."

Hernandez scanned the top sheet. "Well!" he said suddenly. He looked curiously at Morales. "He's a captain—that's a heavy rank—in the Coahuila State Police."

"What?" Humphrey said incredulously. "What police?"

"Coahuila. It's a state in Mexico. Right below the border." Hernandez was reading the next sheet. "Hey! Here's a letter from the Mexican ambassador to the United States asking that the guy be extended all aid and courtesy. And here's another saying the same thing from the American ambassador to Mexico. And here's one from the State Department—and one from the Mexican Department of State! And whoops! Here's one from the FBI. You'd better drop this guy quick—before he burns your fingers clear off!"

"Are those about a bird named Morales?" Humphrey inquired, still incredulous.

Hernandez flipped back to the top sheet. "Nope. The guy's name is Sebastian Rodriguez y Ruiz. But Sebastian Rodriguez y Ruiz has this guy's face and this guy's description."

"I am Sebastian Rodriguez y Ruiz," said Morales. "Morales is merely an alias I adopted. Are you satisfied now as to my real identity? If you like, you may call the Mexican Consul for Los Angeles. He knows me."

Humphrey stared at him, goggle-eyed. "Well, what's the big idea? I mean, going around acting like a janitor and a thunder bird and whatever?"

"May we have a little more privacy?"

"Sure. Come along."

Humphrey led the way through another door at the back of the room and along a short hall into a smaller office.

"Take that chair," he said. "Now what.... Wait a minute." He pointed his finger at Doan. "We can't use you. Scram."

"No," said Sebastian Rodriguez y Ruiz. "I want him to hear what I say. I have my reasons."

"Oh, all right. Get going."

"I am concerned with a matter of very great importance. I repeat that so you will understand it clearly—*of very great importance.*"

"I get you," said Humphrey.

"In the State of Coahuila there is a very ancient, very revered religious shrine. I will not identify it further for reasons that will become clear as I proceed. The shrine was built and blessed in the sixteenth century. In it there were a number of sacred parchment scrolls."

"Yeah," said Humphrey eagerly.

"These scrolls are enormously valuable for a number of reasons. Historically, because of their contents. Commercially, because they were ornamented in gold leaf by several of the greatest artists then living. Religiously, because they are believed to have miraculous powers by the people who worship at the shrine."

"Yeah," said Humphrey. "Yeah."

"The scrolls were stolen."

"Ah-ha!" Humphrey exclaimed.

"They must be recovered. I repeat—they must be recovered."

"You bet," said Humphrey. "Positively. I can see that. Who hooked them?"

"Horace Trent."

"Yah-ha!" Humphrey chortled, "I knew all the time—What? *Horace Trent?*"

"Yes. Eric Trent's brother."

"Well, well, well," said Humphrey.

"Horace Trent," Sebastian Rodriguez y Ruiz said. "Claims to be an archeologist. He specializes in the theft of ancient objects of art of one sort or another. If he can't steal them, he fakes them. Eric Trent sells them for him."

"I knew it," said Humphrey. "I knew it all the time."

"Horace Trent," Sebastian Rodriguez y Ruiz went on, "is in jail now in Mexico. But he sent those scrolls—disguised as weather maps—to Eric Trent before I could find him and arrest him. Again, I must emphasize that it is of much more vital importance to get those scrolls than it is to arrest these two criminals. Eric Trent is perfectly capable of destroying them to clear himself—and, incidentally, his brother. That is why I assumed the identity of Morales, the idiot janitor. I wished to watch Eric Trent without him having any suspicion of me."

"Why did you bust his instruments?"

"That fool of a professor caught me searching Trent's office, so I broke the instruments to take his mind off the search. It did. Then I had to explain breaking the instruments by that nonsense about thunder birds, so Eric Trent wouldn't get suspicions of my actions. Eric Trent is very clever and very dangerous."

"And how," Humphrey agreed. "But, say? You shouldn't have said all this in front of Doan. He's probably in on that scroll deal. If he isn't, he'll try to steal them himself from Trent. I'd better lock him up right now."

"No. He is the one who is going to get those scrolls for me."

"He is?" Humphrey asked.

"Yes. He is in Trent's confidence. He can find out where Trent has hidden them—that is, if he doesn't already know."

"Man alive!" Humphrey protested. "You can't trust Doan. He's no straighter than a snake."

Sebastian Rodriguez y Ruiz smiled in a very sinister way. "This time he will be honest. Because if he does not get me those scrolls I will testify that I saw him kill Frank Ames."

"What!" Humphrey yelled, coming half out of his chair. "You saw—Doan, I hereby arrest you for murder!"

Sebastian Rodriguez y Ruiz sighed wearily. "Please restrain yourself. I am not going to testify that he killed Frank Ames if he returns the scrolls."

"You're not—" said Humphrey groggily, floundering around two laps behind. "You're not going to—"

"No! Must I keep repeating and reiterating that the recovery of those scrolls is of absolutely paramount importance? The murder is a minor matter."

"But—but you saw Doan—"

"Certainly. I was the prowler."

"Ugh," said Humphrey, completely lost now.

"Kindly pay attention to what I am saying. I was searching for the scrolls at the time Melissa Gregory surprised me. I thought Trent might have persuaded her to hide them for him."

"But you saw Doan—"

"Yes!"

"Oh, boy," said Humphrey, blowing out a long, gusty sigh of relief. "At last. I've got him. You'll have to testify against him whether you want to or not."

"I think you are a complete fool," said Sebastian Rodriguez y Ruiz. "You had better refer again to that letter from the Mexican Department of State. I have diplomatic immunity."

Humphrey stood up and threw his chair into the corner. He raised his fists and shook them impotently at the ceiling.

"Why does everybody I pinch have to have friends or immunity or drag or influence or some damned thing? Why? Why? What have I done to deserve this?"

When no one answered him, Humphrey lowered his fists to his sides and for a moment he looked beaten. But then a crafty light came into his eyes and he regarded Sebastian Rodriguez y Ruiz intently.

"There's one thing your diplomatic immunity doesn't protect you against," he said. "If I accuse you of murder—unless you testify against Doan—there's nothing you can do about it."

Sebastian Rodriguez y Ruiz gave a loud and long Latin laugh. He hooked out an arm pointed a finger at himself. "Me of murder? *Me?* Tell me, please, who have I murdered?"

"Frank Ames," Humphrey said. "As a matter of fact I could whip up a pretty good case against you. Already you've confessed being the prowler. That puts you on the scene. All I really need to prove now is intent and motive."

Sebastian Rodriguez y Ruiz started laughing again. When he had finished, he spat out one word: "Ridiculous!" And then, drawing himself up, crossing his arms on his chest and patting one foot impatiently, he said, "And what about Beulah Porter Cowys? I suppose I am supposed to have killed her too? Maybe I disguised myself as a sunlamp or a permanent waving machine and sneaked into Heloise of Hollywood's Beauty Salon?"

"Maybe," said Humphrey.

"And maybe not," said Sebastian Rodriguez y Ruiz with a positive air. "Do you happen to know a most attractive young graduate student at the university named Shirley Parker? Well, whether you do or not makes no difference. Miss Parker is a special. She is taking her master's in psychology. She is writing a thesis on sexual behavior—at least sexual behavior has something to do with it—and I am trying to help her by providing her with material…. Well, it so happens that at the precise time and moment when Beulah Porter Cowys was killed, I was embarked on a little matter of research for my friend Miss Parker. I was, in fact, in the company of a most attractive young blonde who, though for the moment shall be nameless, could be induced I am sure, in view of the pleasure she seemed to derive out of the assistance she gave me in the research, to testify at the proper time that…."

"What?" Humphrey interrupted. "Get to the point."

"I have an alibi," Sebastian Rodriguez y Ruiz told him. "An iron clad alibi, as you stupid Americans say. Accuse me of killing anybody or anything and I'll sue you for libel, slander, false arrest, both malfeasance and misfeasance in office, but mostly for malicious prosecution. Accuse me of something—just you dare! I'll sue you for one hundred thousand dollars or maybe one million dollars!"

"Rot!" Humphrey came back at him. "Nonsense! If you refuse to testify against Doan, I'll arrest you just as fast as that...." And he snapped his fingers. "In fact," he shouted, now completely beside himself with rage and frustration, "I'll arrest anybody I want to for anything I want to so long as I—as I wear this badge." He pointed to the shield on his vest.

With an unobtrusive but nevertheless lightning quick motion, the Mexican reached over, jerked off the shield and threw it to the floor.

"Your outbursts are distasteful to me," Sebastian Rodriguez y Ruiz informed Humphrey. "I shall leave now, but I advise you to remember everything I told you and to act accordingly. I do not propose to be thwarted by your stupidity. Come with me, you."

Doan followed him meekly along the hall and out through the receiving room.

Sebastian Rodriguez y Ruiz stopped on the steps and nodded coldly. "I shall expect you to search out those scrolls and turn them in to me at once."

"You just go right ahead and expect," Doan invited.

"Aren't you going to do it?"

"No."

"Did you hear what I just told Humphrey?"

"Yes."

"Well?"

"That was a very interesting story," said Doan. "Of course, there was one little discrepancy in it. Eric Trent doesn't have a brother named Horace. In fact, Eric Trent doesn't have any brothers at all. Good-by for now, Sebastian. I'll be seeing you."

IT WAS nine o'clock when Doan came in the front door of the Pericles Pavilion. He had just spent a couple of hours talking long distance to Mexico City. This is a hazardous occupation which, besides time and money, requires persistence, patience, a loud voice, an extensive vocabulary, and a strong constitution. Right now, Doan was dragging his heels.

The door of the Aldriches' apartment opened, and the duplicate Aldrich faces, superimposed one above the other like carbon copies, peered disapprovingly out at him.

"Good evening," said Doan.

The Aldriches continued to peer—in silence.

Doan tried again. "Good evening."

The Aldriches said: "We do not approve of murder. We do not feel that we can longer acknowledge your acquaintance." Their door closed. Immediately it opened again. "Or that of your dog," said the Aldriches. The door closed.

Doan shook his head and went on up the stairs. He knocked on the door of Melissa's apartment. There was no answer. He went on up to the third floor and tried Trent's apartment. The door was unlocked, and he opened it.

Carstairs was lying on the chesterfield with his head dangling over one end and his tail over the other. He was snoring.

Doan went in and looked around. There was a note fastened to the lamp shade with a bobby pin. Doan read it. It was from Melissa, and it said:

I am going to the Get Acquainted Dance at Dullwich Hall with Eric Trent. I persuaded Carstairs that I didn't need a bodyguard just for that, because after all, Eric isn't the murderer, is he?

Under this, in different handwriting, was the one word: No.

Doan studied that "No" uneasily. He was wondering just who wrote it. After a moment, he put the note down and took the large volume with the Greek title from Trent's bookcase. He opened it with an air of wistful anticipation. It was empty.

"Oh, hell," said Doan.

The telephone rang.

Doan picked it up. "Yes?"

"Is Eric Trent there?"

"No. This is Doan."

"This is Heloise of Hollywood. Where is Eric, Doan?"

"I don't know."

"Well, suppose you find out."

"Okay," said Doan.

"And when you do—tell him I want to see him. I mean, tonight."

"Okay."

"Up at my house. Tell him he can bring that Melissa Gregory mess along. I know he's with her."

"Okay."

"And after that—you're all through."

"What?" said Doan.

"I won't be needing you any more. I'll pay you up to the end of next week if you don't hike your expense account too high."

"Before I exit smiling, I should maybe give you an item or two of information I uncovered."

"I have all the information I need. Just turn in your bill."

"Okay," said Doan.

"Go find Eric now. Don't stop to get drunk on the way."

"What do you mean—drunk?"

"You probably know the meaning of the word better than anybody I ever came across, Doan. I mean soused and stinko and looping and polluted like I've seen you more times than I can count on both the toes and fingers of all my customers."

"You're maligning me," said Doan. "My mother wouldn't like to hear you talk about me like that—that is, if she could hear."

"Get going."

"Okay."

Doan hung up, and then he reached down and put his thumb across Carstairs' nostrils. Carstairs reared up on the chesterfield, snorting like a grampus.

"I'm not me, really," Doan told him. "You're having a nightmare and I'm a part of your bad dream."

Carstairs looked at him incredulously, raising his eyebrows.

"You're still asleep," Doan said. "The only reason you aren't resting peacefully is that you ate something that disagreed with you."

Carstairs yawned, settled back down on the chesterfield again and closed his eyes.

"Dope!" Doan shouted, and Carstairs jumped up alertly. "Dope, dope, dope, dope, dope. You'd believe anything anybody told you…. Come on, we've got business."

SOMEWHERE or other T. Ballard Bestwyck had picked up the idea that the student serfs under his sovereign sway would like to know each other at least slightly. This naive notion was treated with the contempt it deserved by the normal members of the student body, but that didn't stop T. Ballard Bestwyck from throwing contests he called Get Acquainted Dances everywhere, anywhere and incessantly. No one ever attended them but the bedeviled members of the faculty who were drafted into supervising them and assorted coveys of drips and drools who, upon their arrival, chose up sides according to their sexes, threw out battle lines on opposite edges of the dancing arena, and spent the evening smirking and sneering at each other in frantic frustration.

Things were going normally when Doan and Carstairs arrived at Dullwich Hall, which was a dreary sort of a place, very appropriately named. Several of the faculty couples had ventured out into the no man's land between the battle lines out of sheer boredom and were pushing each other pointlessly around to a natty arrangement of *Japanese Sandman* played by two feeble fiddles and a rheumatic piano.

Melissa and Eric Trent were among them. Melissa wasn't exactly beaming, but Trent was making very heavy weather of it. His blond hair was sweatily matted, and he was breathing through his mouth, and his eyes roamed ceaselessly in search of succor. He saw Doan and stopped short. Melissa half-tripped. Trent straightened her up and pointed at Doan. They came across the floor, avoiding the other rhythmic navigational hazards.

"Mr. Doan," said Melissa, "do you want me to be frank with you?"

"Sure," said Doan.

Melissa pointed. "He can't dance worth a damn."

"I told you I couldn't," Trent said. "Who do you think I could have practiced with the last few years—polar bears? You're the one who insisted that I try."

"I thought you were a man," Melissa said. "I thought you could stand on your own feet."

"I didn't step on you."

"Just because I'm exceptionally agile, you didn't."

"I can't dance."

"Well, all right," said Melissa. "I'm agreeing with you. That's what I just got through telling Doan. Why are you arguing with me?"

"I'm not."

"You are. And if you don't stop, I'm going to call you something I told you I wouldn't call you."

"And if you do, I'll do what I told you I'd do if you did."

"Do you think he would?" Melissa asked Doan.

"Yes," said Doan. "If you're thinking of calling him what I think you are. Whenever he hears that name, his strength becomes as the strength of ten."

"All right, then," said Melissa. "I won't call you that, but you can't stop me from thinking it at you."

"Oh, yes, I can," said Trent.

"Let's postpone this matter," Doan suggested, "before we get too metaphysical. I have a message for you both from Mrs. Heloise of Hollywood Tremaine Trent."

"Is it printable?" Melissa asked.

"Oh, yes. She wants to see you both up at her house—right away or anyway, pretty quick."

"We're not going," said Trent.

"Yes, we are," said Melissa. "I've got a few conversational tidbits I've dreamed up to try out on her. She got the jump on me last time. I can't think well when my feet are dirty. And, anyway, I want to see her house. I'll bet it's something, isn't it?"

"I don't know," said Trent. "I've never seen it."

Melissa stared at him. "What?"

"I started getting mad at Nome, Alaska, where I ran across the first newsstand I'd seen in four years. By the time I got to Seattle, I was steaming, and I boiled clear over before I arrived in Hollywood. We did our sparring in her lawyer's office."

Melissa patted him on the shoulder. "You're a good boy."

"Thank you. Doan, what happened to Morales? Melissa says those names he used were just nonsense words. No such clans or gods or whatnot exist."

"That's only the half of it," Doan informed him.

"Morales doesn't exist, either."

"What?"

"His real name is Sebastian Rodriguez y Ruiz, and he's a detective from Mexico."

"Well, why did he smash my instruments?"

"This one will stop you," said Doan. "He smashed them because your brother, Horace, stole some scrolls from a church in Mexico."

Trent just stared at him.

Doan nodded. "That's what he told Humphrey and Humphrey believed him."

"But why?"

"Because this Sebastian Rodriguez y Ruiz is a genius. I suspected that, and so I called up Mexico City, and they confirmed it. He is a positive, certified genius at detecting things. If you don't believe it, ask him."

"Another detective," Melissa groaned. "They're getting as thick around here as fleas on a chihuahua. When I started teaching here I thought this was a general arts university, but now it looks as though it's turning out to be a school for rookie cops. If I don't watch myself I'll wake up one day in a police matron's uniform with my name changed to Maggie O'Flaherty."

Trent turned to Doan. "But about this Morales, or Sebastian Rodriguez y Ruiz or whatever he calls himself. Why was he pretending to be a janitor?"

"I told you," said Doan. "He's a genius and genius is inscrutable."

Melissa tugged at Trent's arm. "Come on. I want to go see Heloise."

"Good-by, forever," said Doan.

"What?" said Melissa.

"Carstairs and I have now taken our humble place among the faceless army of the unemployed and unwelcome. We have been fired."

"Oh," said Melissa. "But we want to say good-by to you—I mean, in a big way. Wait here until we get back. You can dance with some of these girls."

Doan shivered. "Thank you," he said. "Thanks a million. But no thanks."

"Well, wait at Eric's apartment, then."

"It's a deal," said Doan. "That is, it's a deal at the moment. But I'm feeling sort of restless and I have a lot on my mind and I don't know where I may end up eventually."

THE ROAD up the canyon wasn't particularly steep, but its designers had done the best they could to make it appear so. It switched back and forth and doubled on itself like a snake with a stomach ache. The headlights of Trent's car illuminated it only about one tenth of the time; during the other nine tenths they swept pretty but aimless swaths in the night off to the right or left. The engine grumbled and complained to itself in a deeply outraged way.

"For goodness' sakes," said Melissa. "Shift into second before you pull a bearing."

"I might have known it," said Trent.

"Known what?"

"That you'd be one of these females who aren't satisfied with just backseat driving. In addition, you've got to run in a lot of senseless lingo you picked up hanging around garages. Pull a bearing!"

"Well, people do!"

"Not people named Trent."

Melissa looked miffed. "I'm not as bad a backseat driver," she said, "as you are a dancer."

"I told you I don't like to dance," Trent informed her. "Also I'm out of practice." He took his eyes off the tortuous road for a moment and gave her a little smile. "But let's stop quarreling. As far as not liking dancing is concerned, I have this to say. I almost enjoyed dancing with you. If there hadn't been anyone else there, and even if there hadn't been any music and we'd been just standing there, I think I really would have enjoyed it."

Melissa turned to him but her lashes covered her eyes. "I wonder why?"

"Yes," Trent said, "I wonder." The smile disappeared from his face and for a moment he looked painfully serious. "I don't suppose it had anything to do with the fact that you were very close to me and I had my arms around you and all of a sudden I had the feeling…."

"Does Heloise of Hollywood make you feel that way too?" Melissa interrupted impishly.

"Oh, stop it!" Trent said. "Can't a guy get even a little bit sentimental with you without—well, just without?"

Melissa had to turn her head. Her shoulders were shaking with chuckles. "I suppose you'd get even more sentimental if I called you Han— Oooh! Don't you dare choke me! Look out! Grab the wheel! What are you trying to do—kill us both?"

A cliff jumped out at them and then jumped back in place when Trent, whose hands had been off the steering wheel and around Melissa's throat, grabbed the wheel again and gave the car a twist back into the road.

The headlights swished around like a scythe, and the tires squealed on a cutback curve.

"Go slower!" Melissa cried. "We're going to pass Heloise's place without seeing it."

"I can't go slower," Trent said, "without backing up."

"Wait, wait, wait!" Melissa shrilled. "I think that must be it! Clear back up there. Look for the gates, now."

"That's what I am doing."

"You missed them!"

"I did not."

"Oh, why do you have to be so stubborn and stupid? You must have missed them. You just weren't looking. Well, you'll just have to turn around—"

Two fat, high white-brick pillars swam smoothly at them out of the night.

"Yes?" said Trent gently. "Yes?"

"Oh, shut up."

Trent turned off on smoothly oiled macadam. The road dipped down, and then went up in a rush. Trent shifted into second, and they ground dismally upward.

"Gee," said Melissa. "Look."

They were up on the top of the butte now, and the house was waiting right there, poised and ready to pounce. It was enormous, squared off solid and dark against the sky, throwing a sullen shadow in deference to the moon. Trellised vines crawled sinuously black over the side walls, and the few lighted windows were like sly, peeping eyes.

"There's one thing I'm missing," Melissa observed, "and it bothers me. I wonder where Boris Karloff is?"

The road circled and widened at the front of the house. There was no veranda or porch. There were six wide stone steps leading up to an immense arched doorway sunk deep in the smooth stone. There were lights behind the thick-walled porthole windows on either side.

Trent stopped the car, and he and Melissa got out. The wind was soft and cool in their faces, and the moon seemed very far away. Their heels clicked lightly on the macadam and scraped a little on the stone steps.

"What do we do now?" Melissa asked. "Yell 'Ahoy, the castle' or blow ourselves a fanfare?"

"This seems to be a bell," said Trent.

Chimes played a lingering, low melody somewhere inside. The house brooded and waited in utter silence.

"Well," said Trent, after a while, helplessly.

"Well, hell," said Melissa. She raised her fist and smacked the door one.

It swung back noiselessly.

"Glug," said Melissa. "Aren't we just having more darned fun, though?"

They were looking the length of a hall. It was a story and a half high, and the walls and ceiling were painted a dead white. The floor was black polished oak and there were white rugs spread along it like grotesque giant footprints.

"Homey," Melissa commented. "Let's go in."

They started along the hall, and their footsteps started following behind them in tapping echoes. Melissa took hold of Trent's arm.

There was a door to their right, and a door to their left. Both were closed. Trent and Melissa went reluctantly past them, and then Melissa said, "Wait. There's a light behind that one."

She rapped on it. The silence seemed to stir itself slightly, but there was no real sound. Melissa tried the long, wrought-iron latch on the door. It clicked, and the door moved back, softly reluctant.

The room was a library. The walls from ceiling to floor were lined with shelves of books. The books looked like they had been taken out often—and dusted and put right back again. Facing the door, at the end of the room, there was a desk that was a solid block of black wood as big as a dining room table.

Heloise of Hollywood was sitting behind the desk. She was wearing a blue tailored dress, and her hair was meticulously unswept. Her head was tilted a little to one side, and she was staring at them with an air of polite, dead interest.

"Oh," Melissa murmured. "Oh."

Trent whispered to himself.

Very slowly they advanced, holding hands like reluctant children. One of Heloise's hands—the nails were a polished, appropriate purple—was lying on the desk top with the lax fingers just touching a fat, ugly automatic with a snub nose. Trent and Melissa were closer now, and they could see the very small, neatly dark hole in her left breast. Blood had darkened the cloth of her dress below it, but it was hardly noticeable.

"She shot herself," said Melissa. Her voice croaked ridiculously on the words, and she swallowed hard.

"No, she didn't," said Trent. "There's no powder burn on her dress. And that's an 8 millimeter Mauser on the desk. It would make a much bigger hole."

"Would—would a .22 make a hole like—like...."

"Yes."

"Oh, my," said Melissa. "Doan said my prowler had a .22."

"Well, there's one thing," said Trent slowly, "Humphrey can't claim Doan did this. He's not here."

"But you are," said Melissa. "And, what's more, so am I."

The telephone rang. It was on a circular stand at Heloise's left hand. Trent and Melissa waited with a sort of dread fascination for her to answer it. She didn't.

It rang again.

Melissa walked gingerly around the desk and picked it up. "Hello."

A voice like thick plush said: "Good evening. This is T. Ballard Bestwyck. May I speak to Heloise?"

"Well," said Melissa, "no."

"I beg your pardon?"

"You can't speak to her. I mean, she can't speak to you, which amounts to the same thing, doesn't it?"

"I don't think you understood me, young woman. I am T. Ballard Bestwyck. I'm the president of—"

"I know. I work for you."

"What was that?"

"I teach at the university."

"What's your name?"

"Melissa Gregory."

"Well, it's about time?"

"What?" said Melissa blankly.

"I was just calling Heloise to apologize for your brazen behavior. Now that you're up there, you can do it yourself. And you'd better be very humble about it, young woman. There's a moral turpitude clause in your contract, and if you don't let other women's husbands alone you're going to find yourself involved in a serious situation."

The line suddenly crackled. T. Ballard Bestwyck hadn't hung up. There was no dial tone. The line was dead.

Melissa turned her head slowly to look at Trent.

"What's the matter?" Trent demanded.

"Somebody—cut the line."

The lights went out.

"Eric!" Melissa cried. "Oh, Eric—"

She grabbed him and clung to him desperately, both arms about his neck.

"I'm so sc-scared," she whimpered, "and you shouldn't mind.

J-just a few minutes ago you s-said you liked to be close to m-me and have your arms about m-me...."

"My arms aren't about you," Trent said, obviously trying to remain calm. "Yours are about me, but it's all right, Melissa. Heloise won't mind now—not any more."

The half door boomed shut and the lock clicked coldly and Melissa gasped.

"All right," Trent said. "Start screaming. That's just what we need at this point."

"I've never screamed in my life!" Melissa retorted, and immediately afterward began screaming her head off. "Eeeh! Oow! Eeeh! Eep!"

Trent slapped at her. He missed her face in the darkness and hit her on the back of the head. Melissa stopped screaming.

Something scraped very gently in the hall, and then without warning there were three shots—very close together, sharp and bitingly distinct. Instantly there was another shot. This was a heavier, louder thud.

After that there was silence. It was not a pleasant or comforting silence. Melissa breathed against Trent's coat collar with her mouth open.

Something tapped lightly on the hall door.

Doan's voice murmured, "Trent. Melissa."

"In here," said Trent. "The door is locked."

The lock clicked again and the shadows moved vaguely.

"Are you two all right?" Doan asked.

"I guess so," said Trent.

"Come closer to the door here. I want to watch the hall. I chased the guy back inside. He's holed up in the house somewhere now."

Trent and Melissa shuffled forward cautiously. They could see a vague, bent outline that was Doan. The barrel of his revolver gleamed a little in the dimness. He had the hall door almost shut and was watching through the narrow opening.

"He'll run out the back," Trent said.

"He'll maybe try. Carstairs is out there."

They waited tensely.

"Heloise is dead," Trent said in an undertone. "Over at her desk. She was shot."

"Yeah," said Doan. "I thought I'd better come up and warn her even if she didn't want me to. She thought she could handle the guy. She could just as well wrap up a tiger in a paper napkin."

"She had a gun."

"Sure. She had twenty servants, too."

"Where did they go?"

"They're locked up downstairs somewhere—probably in the wine cellar. I've got no time to go fishing around for them now. I've got a hunch I'm going to get myself killed as it is. This guy is hell on wheels with that pistol of his. He mistook a tree for me a minute ago, or I'd be past worrying at this point."

Carstairs let go with a bellowing halloo. The .22 cracked twice precisely. Carstairs bellowed angrily right back at it.

"He's under cover," Doan breathed. "If he only has brains enough to stay that way."

The pistol cracked futilely again. Carstairs let his bellow out another notch, and the whole night began to throb with it.

"Stay in here," Doan ordered, "I'm going a-hunting, and I'm going to shoot at anything that even looks like it might move. I'm scared green of this guy." He opened the door wider. "Stay right here. I mean it. Oh, why do I get myself into situations like this? I must be crazy."

He faded noiselessly into the darkness.

CHAPTER VI

TRENT AND MELISSA waited tautly. The silence pressed in on them as thick as black butter. One century crawled past. And then another.

Doan's revolver thudded. Trent jumped involuntarily, and Melissa whimpered against his coat.

The silence crept back and surrounded them. Doan's revolver thudded again. The .22 cracked back at it spitefully this time. Someone yelled, fiercely incoherent. Feet raced across bare flooring. Something fell over with a crash that made the air shudder. A door slammed dully.

"I can't take this," Trent said. "I've got to help him. You stay here."

"Oh, no! Oh, no!"

"Stay right close behind me, then. Walk in step with me."

They went out into the hall like a queer four-legged bug. Melissa was clutching the back of Trent's coat in both fists. She could feel the muscles in his back, rigid and tensed. They moved slowly, and the darkness moved right with them, unchanging.

"Steps," Trent whispered.

They went up them—a lot of them. And then there was a cold, slow click just over their heads.

Doan said: "Trent?"

"Yes."

"You're lucky," said Doan. "That's the time you didn't get killed. Come on up here."

They were in a hall.

"Did you hit him when you shot?" Trent asked.

"Hell, no. I did run him into the bedroom there, though. The one behind that door. And if he thinks I'm going in there after him, he's crazy."

Carstairs barked from somewhere outside on an inquiring note.

Doan cupped his hands and bellowed through them. "Yes! I'm still with you! Stay out there! Watch!"

Carstairs barked again, momentarily pacified.

"Well, what are we going to do now?" Trent asked.

"Call the cops," Doan said, keeping his gun pointed at the bedroom door. "Let them root him out. They're expendable."

"The telephone line is cut. It was cut at the same time the lights were switched off. Melissa was talking on it."

"This guy," said Doan, "thinks of everything. Okay. We'll starve him out. How are we fixed for supplies? Have you got a drink on you?"

"No."

"All right. Go on down and unlock the servants. Send a bottle back up here by one of them. We'll fight it out on this line if it takes all summer."

Trent said uneasily: "Maybe he'll shoot through the door at us."

"Not that door. It's a two-inch hardwood slab. A .22 won't punch through it."

The .22 smacked from inside the bedroom. Carstairs yelled in furious indignation. The .22 smacked again instantly. Carstairs bellowed right back, but the tone of his voice was slightly muffled now.

Doan let his breath out. "He got under cover again. He's going to get his brains blown out if he doesn't stop playing around.... Carstairs! Stay where you are! Down! Keep down!"

Carstairs barked once, defiantly. Then he cut loose in a continuous, urgent, racketing uproar.

"What now?" said Doan, listening tensely.

Wood creaked faintly.

"He's climbing out the window!" Doan exclaimed.

He aimed his revolver at the lock on the door and fired and then fired again. Wood splintered, and the smell of burned powder was sharp and acrid in the hall. Doan slammed his heel against the door above the lock, slammed it again below the lock. He shouldered into the door hard, hammering at the lock with the butt of his revolver.

Metal gave with a sudden rasp, and the door banged violently open. Doan fell flat on his stomach, half in and half out of the bedroom, revolver pushed ahead of him. He stayed that way, rigid, watching.

"What?" Trent whispered, crouched against the wall beside the doorway. "What?"

Doan spoke without turning his head. "I think he's on the trellis outside the window."

Moving vines made a leafy, ripping sound.

"Yeah!" said Doan, lunging to his feet. "Carstairs! Carstairs! Guard!"

Carstairs roared willingly from outside and below. The vines crackled.

"Now what will I do?" Doan demanded. "If I poke my head out that window, he'll pop it off for me. If I run outside, he'll come back in this way."

"Another bedroom…." Trent suggested.

The vines rattled and slithered more loudly.

"Back!" Doan ordered urgently. "He's coming back up! Get out of the doorway!"

Something crawled up eerily at the lower corner of the open window. Moonlight glinted on the long, pencil-like barrel of the .22 pistol. It groped around blindly and then suddenly spat. Flame streaked slantwise toward the ceiling.

"Ah," said Doan.

He was aiming carefully with his revolver, steadying his right wrist with his left hand. He fired. The .22 automatic spun up into the air, glistening sleekly, and then thudded loosely on the floor.

"I did it!" Doan chortled. "I've always wanted to, and I did it! I shot a gun out of a guy's hand! Come in off that vine, screwloose! And don't try any funny work! I'm as good as Red Ryder!"

Wood suddenly tore loose in a long drawn, ripping screech.

"What—" said Doan.

He raced across the bedroom to the window with Melissa and Trent stumbling along behind him. The moon was ghastly bright now, and in its light, suspended incredibly in space ten feet out from the window, was something large and black, black and crouched and malignant that screeched at them.

The lattice work was propping it up there, unbelievably, like a weirdly extended, clumsy stilt. Then the lattice swayed further and lost its last hold on the wall with a series of popping reports and began to fall, crumpling in on itself, away from the house.

The black figure mouthed incoherent, terrified sounds, twisting in the air. And directly under it, gleaming like quicksilver, was the slickly sullen surface of Heloise's swimming pool. The lattice hit the edge of the pool, and the water opened up with a resounding boom.

Carstairs raced his shadow across the lawn and skidded on the edge of the pool.

"Carstairs!" Doan shouted. "Stay out of there! Let him drown, and save the state money! Stay out—"

Carstairs dove into the pool.

"Oh, hell's fire!" Doan exclaimed angrily.

He whirled away from the window and ran out of the bedroom. Trent tore down the stairs after him, jerking Melissa along behind with a viselike grip on her wrist. They drummed along the hall and out the front door and around the side of the house.

Doan pulled out ahead of them going down the slope of the lawn. His heels grated on the tiled edge of the pool. The surface of the water was ripped and torn to froth, and then Carstairs' head heaved up out of it. He had a black, chunky, limp arm gripped in his jaws, and he was coughing in half-strangled snorts.

"Let go!" Doan yelled. "Let him drown! Who cares? Come here! Here! Here!"

Carstairs kept his grip and plowed away determinedly at the

water. He came agonizingly closer. Doan leaned far out and grabbed the arm.

"All right! So you're a hero! Let go!"

Doan heaved back, and the black, ugly form slithered wetly out on the edge of the pool. Doan kicked it aside.

"Sit on him for a minute," he ordered no one in particular. "Carstairs! Now, come here, stupid! Here!"

Carstairs floundered against the side wall, and Doan got him by the collar. He hauled. Carstairs' forelegs flopped out on the tile. His back legs churned powerfully at the water. He came up and out suddenly, snorting and dripping.

Doan fell over backwards. "Now, watch out! Don't—Ow!"

Carstairs walked right over his prone form. He stepped aside, but not far enough aside, and shook himself.

"Floosh!" Doan sputtered. He sat up, wiping his face. "I'm going to kill you someday. I mean that seriously."

Carstairs stopped shaking and sat down and began to pant victoriously.

Melissa said in a small, stunned voice: "Mr. Doan, this— this—this is Professor Sley-Mynick."

"Yup," said Doan, getting to his feet. "Let's see if he's still working."

He knelt down beside the wet, black form. Professor Sley-Mynick's thin face was bluish and distorted, and little bubbles burst frothily on his lumpy mustache. Doan probed with exploring fingers.

"Cracked his skull," he stated. "Must have hit the bottom of the pool. He'll probably live, though."

"But—but did he...."

"He did," said Doan cheerfully. "He's your little old prowler in person."

"Oh!" Melissa exclaimed. "Then there was something awful and familiar.... But what was he doing in my apartment?"

"It's just like I told you. He thought he was in Trent's apartment."

"What did he want in my apartment?" Trent demanded.

"I think he was going to fix up a nice little booby trap for you. That's why he had both the knife and the gun with him. He probably had a strip of rubber inner tubes and some nails with him, too. He was going to fasten the knife to the tube and the tube to the nails in such a way that when you opened the drawer, the tube would stretch and then flip the knife in your face. It's easy to fix up a trap like that if you know how."

"With a knife?" Trent said doubtfully. "That seems sort of uncertain."

"He didn't want to kill you. I mean, he didn't care whether he did or not. He just wanted to remove you from the campus. It didn't matter whether you were removed to the hospital or to the morgue."

"And Frank Ames?" Melissa said.

"There he was turning his car around when Sley-Mynick walked right out into the alley—and into Ames' headlights—busily engaged in peeling off that stocking mask. Ames recognized him at once. He stopped the car and got out to see what in the devil he was up to. You can see the fix that put Sley-Mynick in. There wasn't any story he could dream up that would pacify Ames permanently, because when Ames found out that the prowler had socked Melissa one, Ames was going to sound off like a fire siren. Sley-Mynick is not a man who takes long to make up his mind. He hadn't used his knife yet, and so now he did. He cut Ames' throat and dumped him in that garbage can, hoping to be able to drive in the alley and pick him up and tote him off somewhere and bury him. But he couldn't put that last idea over. Carstairs and I came snooping around after him. He shot at us and then he had to scram."

Melissa said, "And—and Beulah?"

"Remember what I said about how I went into her apartment and listened around? She couldn't have heard you yip if her door had been shut. I think she had her door open a little. I think she was snooping, just like the Aldriches were. I think she wanted to see whether or not Ames came up to your apartment with you."

Melissa nodded slowly. "Beulah was a little like that. She was nosey."

"And this time it was fatal. She saw the prowler. He ran past her door on the way out. I don't think she recognized him positively, or she would have said so. But she saw enough to make her wonder, because she was already wondering. Remember what she said when we were first talking about Sley-Mynick? She said he *was* a good biochemist—meaning he *had been.* Physics is sort of close to biochemistry, and Beulah Porter Cowys must have spotted something that Sley-Mynick did or said that made her a little leery. I mean, I suppose she was just sort of wondering about it vaguely, and this was something added. In any event, I'm sure she went around and talked to him the next morning, and he must have told her something that pacified her for the moment."

"What?" Trent demanded.

"I have no idea. He's a slicker. Anyway, Beulah Porter Cowys made a very bad mistake after that. She went to Heloise's place. That cooked her goose. I don't know whether she went there just to get her face fixed or whether she had some other reason. Neither did Sley-Mynick, I suppose. But he couldn't take a chance on her talking to Heloise about him. Carstairs' riot gave him his chance, although he would have managed it by some hook or crook anyway. That sort of wiped things up for Sley-Mynick. He'd had bad luck running into Ames and getting spotted by Beulah Porter Cowys, but now they were cleared away, and he went back after you again. He shied that tile at you. That probably wouldn't have killed you unless it hit you in the head, but it wouldn't have done you much good, either."

Trent said, "But *why*—"

Carstairs growled. Doan whipped around alertly, jerking the revolver from under his coat.

There was a man walking down the slope of the lawn toward them slowly and portentously, his shadow jigging eerily thin ahead of him.

"It's Morales!" Melissa gasped.

"Not any more," said Doan. "Now it's Sebastian Rodriguez y Ruiz, the great detective."

"How do you do," said Sebastian Rodriguez y Ruiz. "I see that, by sheer luck, you have managed to capture my quarry. You probably have no admissible evidence against him, so it is fortunate that I have arrived."

"What evidence have you?" Trent demanded.

"An unassailable case. I always make certain I have an unassailable case before I make an arrest. This man is demonstrably and unmistakably guilty of the murder of Herbert 'Big Tub' Tremaine in a cottage on the outskirts of Piedras Negras, State of Coahuila, Mexico, seven months and eleven days ago!"

"Who?" Trent said sharply.

"What?" said Melissa. "Big Tub Tremaine!" She stared accusingly at Doan. "You told me he had committed suicide!"

"I thought he had," said Doan. He looked at Sebastian Rodriguez y Ruiz. "Your authorities should file a little clearer reports."

"I suppose they do seem a little complicated to the dull-witted," Sebastian Rodriguez y Ruiz answered indifferently.

Doan said to Melissa: "The report said just what I told you—that Tremaine had heaved himself in the drink in front of a lot of witnesses, and that they'd had a lot of trouble fishing him out again. Well, the trouble was that it took them four days to recover his body, and by that time he was all chewed to pieces."

"But you said—he said—"

"I will explain the matter," said Sebastian Rodriguez y Ruiz, "because it involves some very brilliant feats of scientific detection. Big Tub Tremaine wished to flee to Mexico because he had embezzled some money from his wife. He had formerly worked in carnivals. He went down to Skid Row—a region in Los Angeles frequented by many vagrants—and located a character, a man he had known formerly in his carnival days, called Bumbershoot Bennie."

"Bumbershoot Bennie," Trent said numbly.

"Yes. Big Tub Tremaine hailed him with great joviality as a dear old pal. Big Tub Tremaine was going on a vacation trip to Mexico, he said, and nothing would do but that his old friend, Bumbershoot Bennie, should accompany him. But first he must buy Bumbershoot Bennie a new outfit of clothes. To show his great generosity and good heart, he would buy Bumbershoot Bennie an outfit as good as he was wearing himself. In fact, he would buy Bumbershoot Bennie an outfit exactly like the one he was wearing. He did."

"Oh," said Trent.

"Then," said Sebastian Rodriguez y Ruiz, "they started in Big Tub Tremaine's car for Ensenada. Somewhere along the road—as yet I don't know just where—Big Tub Tremaine killed Bumbershoot Bennie by beating him over the head with a tire iron. Then he tied a rope around Bumbershoot Bennie and threw him in the surf where there were some sharp rocks. He let Bumbershoot Bennie grind against the rocks for two days, until he was completely disfigured. Then he pulled the body in and put it in the rumble seat of his car."

"Oooh," said Melissa sickly.

"And then," said Sebastian Rodriguez y Ruiz, "he drove to Ensenada. He picked an appropriate spot and, secretly and by stealth, threw Bumbershoot Bennie in the ocean again. Next he put on a noisy performance in a bar, threatening loudly and dramatically to drown himself. Then he ran forth into the darkness, pursued by the people in the bar, and dove into the ocean. There was a wind, and the water was rough. It was at night, you remember. He swam under water away from the searchers, came ashore, and went his way. The police kept on searching until they found Bumbershoot Bennie's body, wearing Big Tub Tremaine's ring and his wrist watch, with Big Tub Tremaine's wallet in the pocket of a suit that obviously fitted the body and exactly matched the description of the clothes Big Tub Tremaine was wearing. It is quite understandable that in the circumstances they identified Bumbershoot Bennie's body as that of Big Tub Tremaine."

"And—and what next?" Melissa asked.

"Big Tub Tremaine wandered around, under various aliases, in Mexico for some two years. Finally he came to Piedras Negras, where he fell in with the murderous Sley-Mynick. And you can see what a temptation he offered to Sley-Mynick. He was already supposed to be dead, and in any event he was wanted as a criminal. He still had some of the money he had embezzled. Sley-Mynick murdered him and buried him in the patio of the cottage."

"Oh!" said Melissa. "But what in the world—"

"Pardon me. I am not finished yet. Sley-Mynick came to the university, thinking his murderous secret was safe forever, but he reckoned without Sebastian Rodriguez y Ruiz. I followed him relentlessly. And all would have been well if you had not appeared."

"Me?" said Trent.

"Yes. Naturally Sley-Mynick's evil conscience bothered him. He thought that Big Tub Tremaine's wife had gotten some inkling of his guilt and had set you to spy on him. He tried to get rid of you as he brushed aside the other fools who got in his way."

"Wait a minute," said Trent. "Why did you break my instruments?"

"I didn't. Sley-Mynick did that in an outburst of rage because he missed you with that tile he threw."

"Why didn't you say he did it—at the time?"

Sebastian Rodriguez y Ruiz said, "Sebastian Rodriguez y

Ruiz has a reputation. I did not intend to have Sley-Mynick arrested until I was ready to do it myself."

"Sley-Mynick murdered Heloise. You caused her death by not speaking up about him when you should have."

Sebastian Rodriguez y Ruiz shrugged magnificently. "What of it? She is not Mexican. She was only an American."

"Well, so was Big Tub Tremaine."

"That is an entirely different matter. It must be known to all evildoers that they cannot murder anyone—not even an American—in the State of Coahuila without answering to Sebastian Rodriguez y Ruiz. Now I have wasted enough time here. You, Doan. Pick up the culprit and carry him to my car. I will go through the formalities and then return him to Mexico to meet his fate."

"He's wanted here for a few murders," Doan said.

"That is immaterial. I have a federal warrant certified and cleared by the state department. It takes precedence over local authority."

"Who is the warrant for?" Doan asked.

"For Sley-Mynick, naturally."

"Then it's no good, because this guy on the ground isn't Sley-Mynick."

"Are you insane?" Sebastian Rodriguez y Ruiz demanded.

"No. You did all right with your detection, but you didn't look hard enough at matters before you started. Just consider for a moment. On the one hand we have Big Tub Tremaine— a carnival tough guy, an embezzler and a murderer at least once. I think he'd done in several here and there before Bumbershoot Bennie, because you don't learn as much as he knew about murder just overnight. And on the other hand you have Professor Sley-Mynick—a poor beaten-up biochemist on the run from the Gestapo. Sley-Mynick and Big Tub Tremaine met in Piedras Negras, and one did the other in. Which one would be most likely to be the murderer?"

Sebastian Rodriguez y Ruiz said some things to himself in firecracker Spanish.

Doan smiled. "Sure. You slipped because Professor Sley-Mynick turned up and took his job as big as life."

"What are you talking about?" Trent demanded.

"Professor Sley-Mynick didn't kill Big Tub Tremaine. Big Tub Tremaine murdered Sley-Mynick. That's Big Tub Tremaine dying right there."

"Oh!" Melissa gasped. "Oh!"

"Don't you see what a wonderful deal this was for him?" Doan asked. "Big Tub Tremaine wanted to get back to the States. Probably he was fed up with Mexico and tortillas and enchiladas and frijoles and everything else Mexican—even the senoritas. That's the way with most fugitives. Before they commit their crimes they gloat over the dough they're going to grab and the life of luxury they're going to lead in some far away clime, but once they beat it out of the country they get homesick and the thing they want most in the world is to get back."

"I'm beginning to catch on," said Melissa.

"Of course," said Doan.

"Big Tub was afraid if he came back and the cops didn't spot him, his wife would—a fate worse than arrest."

"Exactly," said Doan.

"So he needed some place to hide," Melissa went on. "Also he needed some identity other than his own and a means of occupying himself respectably so that no one would suspect who he actually was."

"Smart girl," Doan told her. "Sley-Mynick's identity was ready-made for Big Tub. It included a job at a good salary and a nice refined, quiet place—the university—to hide as long as he wanted to. It was ideal. The fact that it was quite near, to where his wife had her beauty salon made little or no difference. When people are looking for something they're less likely to find it when it's stuck right under their nose."

"But Big Tub Tremaine wasn't a biochemist," Trent objected. "How could he hope to get away with such a disguise?"

"You forget," said Doan, "he was a onetime medicine show spieler. He could talk the lingo of drugs and chemicals and bell jars and test tubes right out of the pharmacopoeia. Whether or not what he said would make sense is something else again, but who were his undergraduate listeners to question whether the stuff their eminent European professor was giving them was straight from the shoulder fact or carnival doubletalk?"

Carstairs moved about restlessly, stopped in front of Doan, looked up and yawned.

"I know," Doan told him, "I bore you. But there are others present and they are interested, so keep still for a minute until I'm finished."

Carstairs lay down, crossed his paws and closed his eyes.

"Sure," said Doan, "for a long while Big Tub's disguise was perfect. He always had the Gestapo to fall back on, remember. Maybe he didn't know quite as much as he should about biochemistry. Well, his mind was confused and had been ever since he left Hungary. The Gestapo had knocked a good part of his knowledge out of him. And suppose he didn't look just exactly like the old Sley-Mynick. The Gestapo had disfigured him. And suppose he dodged people. The Gestapo had made him shy. Any possible slip he made, he could blame on the Gestapo, and no one would question him because his nerves were in such bad shape, poor man."

"I noticed he was pretty jumpy," Eric Trent said. He was standing talking to Doan but looking at and leaning close to Melissa and there was an expression on his face which seemed to indicate that he was thinking about something entirely different from what he was saying. "I noticed he was exceptionally jumpy every time that Shirley Parker was around. He avoided her like the plague."

"He had a reason there," Doan told him. "Shirley's a psychologist, isn't she? At any rate, a graduate student in psychology, and these psychologists and psychiatrists and the like have a way of seeing right through fakers and spotting a liar as soon as they talk to one. This guy was afraid of Shirley for that reason. It's a wonder he didn't murder her too, which would have been a shame, because aside from being a psychologist she's a remarkably pretty girl.... Thinking the matter over and remembering the difficulty she was having getting together her material on sex, I wonder if I couldn't be of some help to her—maybe in a personal way. Do either of you happen to know her telephone number?"

"Never mind that now," Melissa said. "You tell us the rest—quick!"

"There isn't much rest. Everything was going along as smooth as silk for Big Tub—he knew nothing about Sebastian Rodriguez y Ruiz—alias Morales trailing him—and then Trent had to turn up. That blew things sky high. Big Tub knew who Trent was. He'd been keeping track of Heloise. He knew Trent was separated from her, but he knew very well that wasn't the end of the story. He knew Heloise didn't let go of things that were hers that easy. He knew she'd start hanging around the university, and if she did, sooner or later she was going to spot Big Tub. No disguise would fool her for an instant. If she spotted him, she'd have him in jail before he could wink, and that would mean getting it in the neck for Bumbershoot Bennie and Sley-Mynick on top of the embezzlement rap. He had to get Trent away from the university, and that was just what he was trying so hard to do."

"You told us about that," Melissa said. She, too, was talking to Doan, but she was looking at Trent who was still looking at her, and between them there seemed to be an intimacy born of a new discovery or a new thought. "That's what started the whole thing off. Sley-Mynick or Big Tub or whoever was fixing up a booby trap for Eric when I waltzed in and caught it in the noggin."

"That's right," said Doan.

"But Ames—and Beulah…."

"They got in his way. He was desperate. He had two murders—and probably more—behind him. He couldn't take any chances at all. He couldn't afford to have any attention directed toward him. He swatted them like the ordinary person would a couple of flies—Ames because Ames had seen him and Beulah Porter Cowys because she was nosing around and might say something to Heloise that would point Heloise at Big Tub, alias Sley-Mynick. He could easily prowl around in the beauty salon. He used to loaf there all the time. He knew the place like the palm of his hand, and Carstairs gave him a nice assist."

"I still want to know," Trent said, "why he smashed my instruments."

"You and your silly instruments," said Melissa, but there was no malice in her voice.

"They are not silly, and they are damned expensive."

Doan said, "He did that to cover himself after he missed with the tile and spotted Sebastian Rodriguez y Ruiz watching him. He was going to play his goofy blame-it-on-the-Gestapo game. Sebastian Rodriguez y Ruiz saved him the trouble by inventing that business about thunder birds."

"And another thing," said Trent. "What about my so-called brother, Horace?"

"Sebastian Rodriguez y Ruiz told Humphrey that because he thought Humphrey might possibly be bright enough to figure out that if Sebastian Rodriguez y Ruiz hadn't busted those instruments, only one other person could have. Sebastian Rodriguez y Ruiz did not intend to let Humphrey arrest the bird he thought was Sley-Mynick, so he pulled a herring in the shape of some nonexistent scrolls across the track."

"And you went off with the two of them and left me alone with Big Tub Tremaine—after he just got through trying to cave my head in with a tile! You're one hell of a bodyguard!"

"You were as safe as if you were in church," Doan assured

him. "He wouldn't have dared make a move after that close shave. If he had killed you, even Humphrey would have known who did it."

"That would have been a big consolation," said Trent.

"Oh, Doan," said Melissa, "how awful. To think you could have been so heartless as to leave poor Eric alone and unarmed and unprotected in the company of this awful, awful person. I wouldn't have believed it of you. I've a good mind to strike your name off my list of nice people."

Doan looked at her blankly. "Your attitude," he said, "towards this guy—Eric. What's happened to change your attitude?"

"Never mind," said Melissa. "I want to know about Heloise."

"Sebastian Rodriguez y Ruiz went around to see her," Doan explained. He turned to the Mexican. "Didn't you do that?"

"Naturally," said Sebastian Rodriguez y Ruiz. He was looking very gloomy and very sullen and as though he had lost his last friend in the world somewhere far south of the Rio Grande.

Doan said, "Sebastian Rodriguez y Ruiz here wanted to know if there had been any previous connection—before Piedras Negras, I mean—between Big Tub and Sley-Mynick. And while he was at Heloise's, he showed her a picture of the fake Sley-Mynick. So much is my assumption. Now let's see if I'm not correct." Again he turned to the Mexican detective. "Isn't that what happened?"

"Naturally."

"But Heloise fooled you. She didn't admit she knew him, did she?"

"No."

"But she did," said Doan. "And how she did. She recognized her dear departed husband's puss instantly. But Heloise never did anything without figuring what effect it would have on the business of Heloise of Hollywood. And this was something to chew on—two murders and a dead husband turning up. But more to the point, a husband she'd feel fine about never seeing again inasmuch as she'd already proclaimed to the world her marriage to Eric and his great love for her despite her age, not to mention the amount of money she'd invested in an advertising campaign emphasizing just those features...."

"Wait a minute! Wait a minute!" Trent shouted suddenly and loudly. "I knew there was something if I could just think of what it was, and now I've got it."

"I've got it too!" cried Melissa joyously. "Oh, Eric, Eric, isn't it wonderful, wonderful?"

Carstairs woke up suddenly and stared at them in amazement. They were dancing around like children at a Maypole.

"Well, I'll be a double-dyed Mexican blanket if I know what's going on here," Doan said.

"Naturally," spoke up Sebastian Rodriguez y Ruiz, alias Morales, a worried and puzzled look on his dark face.

"Oh, you dopes!" Melissa taunted them. "Oh, you two big stupid lumps who call yourselves detectives! It's perfectly obvious. Can't you see it? Why, Eric isn't married—isn't even a widower—hasn't been married at all. With Heloise married to Big Tub, who wasn't dead like everybody thought, then her marriage to Eric couldn't be legal. Oh, wonderful! Wonderful!"

"Yeah, yeah," said Doan. "I get that, but really the excitement—the cause for all this celebration.... Well, really, it escapes me unless...." He stopped talking and smiled broadly.

"Not married," said Trent dazedly. "Think of that. A bachelor. Never married at all."

"Don't fret about it, darling," Melissa told him. "You soon will be.... But go on, Doan. I forgive you for everything. I'll even go so far as to put your name back on my list."

Doan sighed a deep sigh and started all over again. "So Sebastian Rodriguez y Ruiz went to see Heloise and got himself played for a sucker. Then Heloise got rid of him and started figuring. She thought she could handle Big Tub. She had twenty servants and a gun, and she was tough. She called him up and told she'd give him a twenty-four hour start or some kind of a start. She wanted to get rid of him without scandal. Big

Tub started, all right—in her direction. She had lots of jewelry, and he needed some fast dough. He came in the back way and gathered up the servants—singly or in batches—and locked them away in the cellar. Then he interviewed her—with his gun. He must have been getting the shakes pretty badly by this time. He was playing in hellish luck. I don't think he heard you two arrive. About that time he was up in the back bedroom fiddling around in Heloise's wall safe. The first he knew about you was when the phone rang there's an extension in the bedroom. He heard you talking and hiked down and cut the wires and switched off the lights and locked the door on you and was waltzing out the front when he met me."

There was a sudden raging roar in the night, and Humphrey came billowing down the lawn toward them, pumping his legs furiously and waving his fists in the air.

"You!" he shouted. "As soon as I heard over the radio that there was some kind of a riot up here, I said to myself 'It's that damned Doan again,' and sure enough here you are! I've had enough of you! I've had all I'm going to take! What have you done to poor Professor Sley-Mynick? Look at him lying there all wet and cold and unconscious, if not dead. Don't try to lie, Doan. I warn you. You're under arrest right now!"

"Oh, relax," Doan advised. "I've just caught your murderer for you. He fell off the trellis, there, into the swimming pool and—"

"What?" Humphrey blurted. "Fell in the pool?" He ran to the edge and peered tensely in. "Where? Where?"

There was a sudden streak of fawn-colored shadow. A big body ran through Trent's legs and brushed past Melissa and made for Humphrey with the speed of a maddened goat, horns lowered, who's been waiting a long, long time for just the right opportunity.

"Carstairs!" Doan yelled frantically. "Don't you do it! Don't you dare…."

Humphrey shrieked and leaped right straight ahead, clutching his rear with both hands. The water swallowed him up with a cold and gleeful gulp.

"Carstairs!" Doan yelled. "You imbecile! You know he'll blame me for that! Do you want to see me in the gas chamber? Do you want to see me in jail for life?"

Carstairs ignored him. Carstairs was contemplating the frothy, turgid water in the pool with the remotely sadistic indifference of a scientist studying a pinned-down bug.

And Eric and Melissa ignored him too. For the moment they were too occupied with each other to have any interest in external affairs. Melissa's arms were about Eric's neck and he was holding her so closely that no biochemist or meteorologist or physicist or psychologist or any other scientist could have presented a logical explanation of how it was that she could breathe.

But she could, even though her lips were pressed close to his lips, and when their kiss was ended she sighed rapturously and long.

"Not married," Eric told her in a perfectly audible whisper. "Not married and never married to that old crow—God rest her. Now I have a right to ask you…. Without any strings tied to it, I can offer you my name. You can be…."

"Stop! Stop!" Melissa cried, hugging him to her. "It's going to make you mad, maybe, but I can't help myself. I've just got to say it. It's too funny. If I don't say it I'll burst…. Now I can be—can be *Mrs. Handsome Lover Boy!* There! I've done it! Don't strike me, Eric…. Don't…. Oh, oh! You aren't striking me…. Oh, oh!"

"Naturally!" said Sebastian Rodriguez y Ruiz, alias Morales, watching the young couple go back into their clinch. "Naturally," he said again, and for the first time that evening smiled his broad Latin smile.

THE ARGOSY LIBRARY ™

SERIES 2 INCLUDES:

* BRAND * BRENT * ADAMS *
* MacISAAC * ROSCOE *
* GIESY & SMITH *
* BECHDOLDT *
* MONTGOMERY *
* FARLEY *
* DAVIS *

THE BEST FICTION
FROM THE FRANK
A. MUNSEY LINE

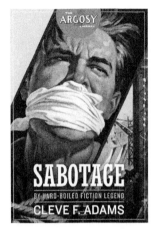

SABOTAGE

BY HARD-BOILED FICTION LEGEND

CLEVE F. ADAMS

CHAMPION OF LOST CAUSES

BY WILLIAM F. NOLAN

MAX BRAND

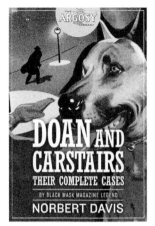

DOAN AND CARSTAIRS

THEIR COMPLETE CASES

BY BLACK MASK MAGAZINE LEGEND

NORBERT DAVIS

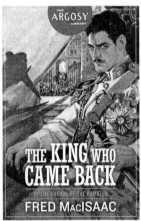

THE KING WHO CAME BACK

BY THE AUTHOR OF THE RAMBLER

FRED MacISAAC

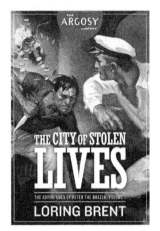

THE CITY OF STOLEN LIVES

THE ADVENTURES OF PETER THE BRAZEN, VOLUME 1

LORING BRENT

THE RADIO GUN-RUNNERS

BY SCIENCE FICTION LEGEND

RALPH MILNE FARLEY

BLOOD RITUAL

THE ADVENTURES OF SCARLET AND BRADSHAW, VOLUME 1

THEODORE ROSCOE

THE SCARLET BLADE

THE RAKEHELLY ADVENTURES OF CLEVE AND D'ENTREVILLE, VOLUME 1

MURRAY R. MONTGOMERY

SEMI DUAL

THE COMPLETE CABALISTIC CASES OF

THE OCCULT DETECTOR, VOLUME 2: 1912-13

J.U. GIESY AND JUNIUS B. SMITH

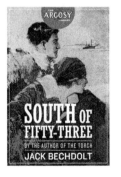

SOUTH OF FIFTY-THREE

BY THE AUTHOR OF THE TORCH

JACK BECHDOLT

SERIES 2 • AVAILABLE SPRING 2015

Printed in Great Britain
by Amazon